A QUEEN OF ICE

ELISE KOVA

Silver Wing Press

A Queen of Ice

ELISE KOVA

Published by Silver Wing Press

Cover Artwork by Polar Engine
Developmental Editing by Rebecca Faith Editorial
Line Editing by Melissa Frain
Proofreading by Kate Anderson

ISBN (paperback): 978-1-949694-66-6
ISBN (hardcover): 978-1-949694-65-9
eISBN: 978-1-949694-64-2

ALSO BY ELISE KOVA

A Trial of Sorcerers
A Trial of Sorcerers
A Hunt of Shadows
A Tournament of Crowns
An Heir of Frost
A Queen of Ice

Also set in the Air Awakens Universe
AIR AWAKENS SERIES
Air Awakens
Fire Falling
Earth's End
Water's Wrath
Crystal Crowned

GOLDEN GUARD TRILOGY
The Crown's Dog
The Prince's Rogue
The Farmer's War

VORTEX CHRONICLES
Vortex Visions
Chosen Champion
Failed Future
Sovereign Sacrifice
Crystal Caged

Married to Magic
A Deal with the Elf King
A Dance with the Fae Prince
A Duel with the Vampire Lord
A Duet with the Siren Duke
A Dawn with the Wolf Knight

Dragon Cursed
Dragon Cursed
more to come

Arcana Academy
Arcana Academy
more to come

See an up to date list of all books and learn more at:
http://www.EliseKova.com

for those who go where others
wouldn't dare

TABLE OF CONTENTS

THE
MAIN CONTINENT
VANGAR
GRAYSTON
SOLARIN
"THE CAPITAL"
RIVEND
MOSANT
THE GREAT IMPERIAL WAY
TIX
OPARIUM
THE
SOUTH
LYNDUM
PACA
CR
SHAN
LEOUL
THE FINSHAR
DELTA
HASTAN
THE
EAST
CYVEN

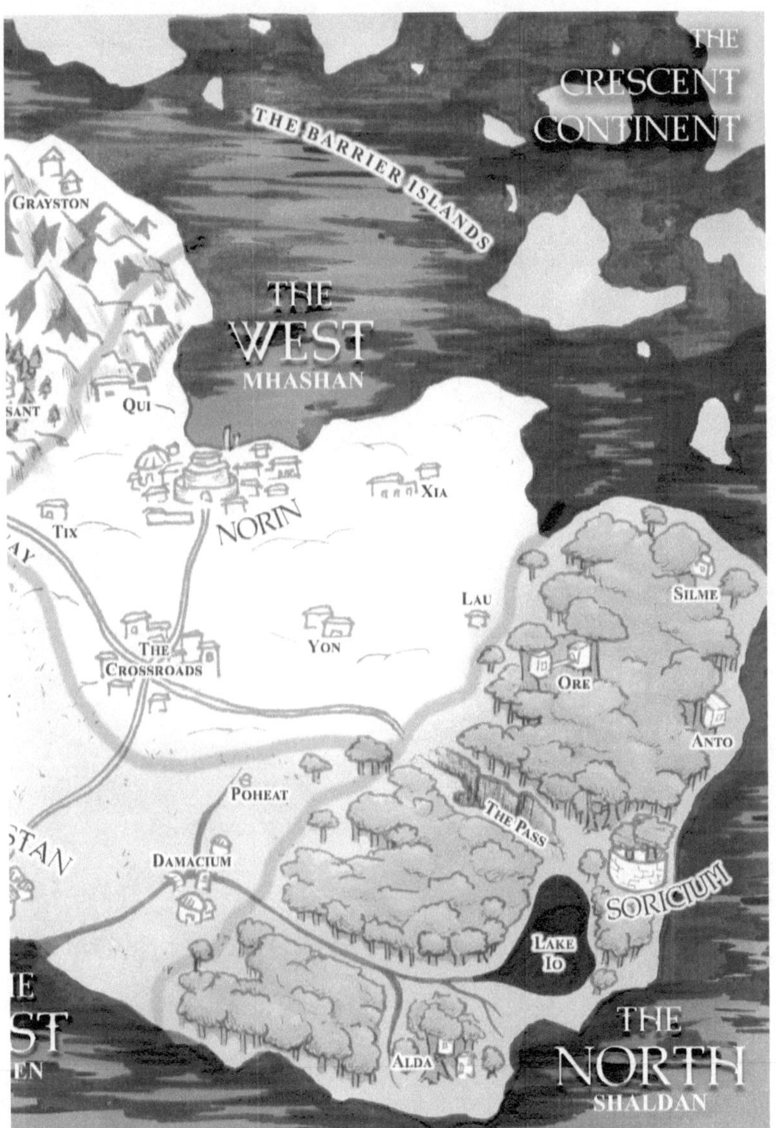

THE CRESCENT CONTINENT
THE BARRIER ISLANDS
THE WEST
MHASHAN
GRAYSTON
SANT
QUI
TIX
NORIN
XIA
LAU
SILME
YON
THE CROSSROADS
ORE
ANTO
POHEAT
THE PASS
STAN
DAMACIUM
SORICIUM
LAKE IO
ST
EN
ALDA
THE NORTH
SHALDAN

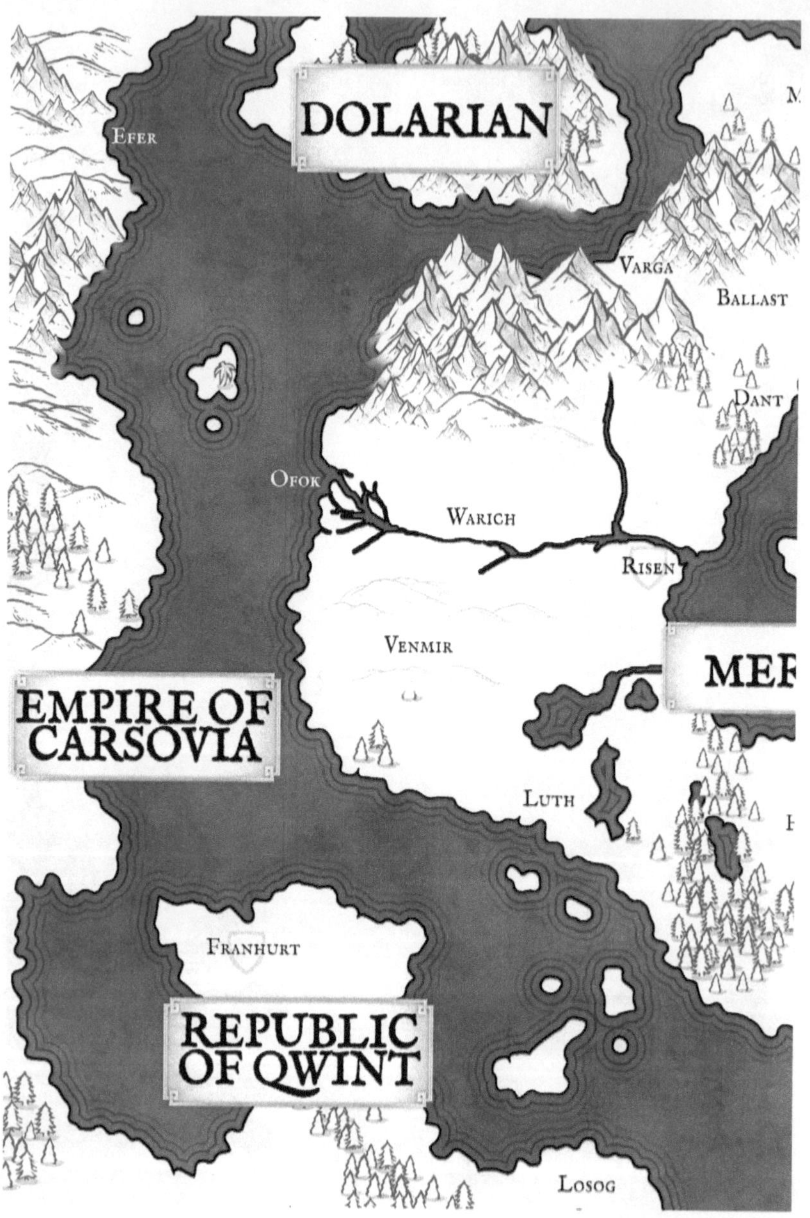

EFER
DOLARIAN
VARGA
BALLAST
DANT
OFOK
WARICH
RISEN
VENMIR
MER
EMPIRE OF CARSOVIA
LUTH
FRANHURT
REPUBLIC OF QWINT
LOSOG

MONLAN
TWILIGHT KINGDOM
LAST
TORIS
ANT
ERU
PARTH
HOKOH
SORICUM
NORIN
CROSSROADS
HASTAN
SOLARIN
OPARIUM
SOLARIS EMPIRE
ISLE OF FROST
THE ATERED ISLES
N

Need a refresher on what happened in the previous books?

Head over to this page of my website...

https://elisekova.com/a-trial-of-sorcerers-summaries/

... to read a full summary of what happened in the previous four books to make sure you're ready for the epic conclusion of Eira's story.

CHAPTER

ONE

E IRA DIDN'T HAVE to kill them. She *wanted to*.

Rain battered her face as her ship was propelled forward on currents of her own making. Magic swirled with the ocean tides. The canvas of the sails had been struck before the storm had come in, long before Crow had spotted the Carsovian vessel between flashes of lightning.

The vessel they had stolen to escape enemy shores after infiltrating and destroying the mines on Carsovia had been a trader's ship. It had a good hull designed for long hauls, but the structure was originally intended for cargo and not weaponry. It had taken some outfitting with Alyss working her magic on the wood, and Adela's generosity, to get the cannons into place that Yonlin was now preparing.

"Captain, we have four shots," Fen reported.

"We'll do this with one." Eira kept her focus on the ship that was running from them. It had picked up their pursuit minutes ago and made a hard turn. No doubt seeking out refuge somewhere in the cliffs that fringed the distant coast. If she tore her eyes away, she'd risk losing them. "Tell Yonlin I want him on starboard. The rest, prepare for boarding."

"Very good." Fen bowed his head and left. Neither he nor Crow had objected to joining Eira on her ship when Adela had ordered them to, defying Eira's expectations. Fen and Crow were both deeply loyal to the pirate queen and Eira would've expected them to fight to stay on the *Stormfrost* at all costs. But whatever Adela said behind the scenes must have been convincing, because they had boarded Eira's vessel without so much as a second look.

"Are you sure it's worth expending cannon fire on them?" Cullen asked from her side. "They haven't attacked."

"*Yet*," she finished pointedly. "The less of them, the better." Eira glanced his way, tilting her head back. She wore an almost bored expression, but it issued a silent challenge for him to question her further. "You know what they did to Noelle."

He nodded, a grim expression on his face.

"If the roles were reversed, she would burn down the world for us." Eira narrowed her focus on the distant ship, murderous intent chilling her blood.

Cullen folded his arms. She braced herself for his objection—to tell him to get belowdecks if he couldn't support her. But the Cullen who was standing next to her now wasn't the man she had once known.

Drenched to the bone, he had murder in his eyes. Raindrops danced in the air over his shoulders as raw power radiated off him. Cullen pushed his hair back; it stuck to his face, almost black in the night and soaked as it was.

"If we do this," he said, voice barely audible over the howling wind and pounding rain, "then no one survives."

"My vengeance is absolute."

"Captain, cannons ready," Fen shouted up.

Leaving the point of the bow, Eira crossed back to the edge of the quarterdeck. Unlike the *Stormfrost*, a massive tall ship with many decks at varying heights, this vessel was a flatter design. She was only a few steps above those on the main deck.

"We will swing starboard, on my mark, cannon fire. When they are crippled, unleash your full wrath," she commanded.

Her crew was ten strong, including her. Not many, but these were the people that she trusted above all else. The people who had just as many reasons as she did to seek out vengeance.

There were nods and looks of agreement. People moved into position. Olivin was at the edge of the railing, right by Ducot. Lavette was by Varren. Crow held back; she'd help manage the ship with Fen—no one knew the ropes better than they did. Yonlin was already belowdecks.

The only one who looked even remotely uncertain was Alyss. She held Eira's gaze silently, with a stare that was almost a challenge. Eira gave her one long look, before turning back to the bow.

*Alyss…sweet Alyss…*the only moral compass any of them had left. The only heart that could be so tender and, yet, stronger than the rest of them combined. Eira hoped she never lost it. Even if Eira would have to ask hardships she never wanted to and then some of her.

"Are you ready?" Eira asked Cullen. They were gaining on the other vessel with each passing second, Eira's magic superior to whatever the sailors for Carsovia were using.

He nodded. "Say the word."

Eira pushed her magic and the vessel surged forward. They gained on the other ship faster than the Carsovian militia could man their guns. With nothing more than a twitch of her fingers— *No tells*, Adela's voice echoed in her mind—the ship swung. Currents pushed and pulled, turning them. They were close enough now to hear the shouts on the opposite vessel. Close enough to see eyes wide with fear.

"Now!" At her command, several things happened at once.

Cullen thrust out his hands, lowering his palms toward the deck. A vortex of wind formed over the opposite ship—ripping rigging and tearing off masts with the groaning of a thousand planks of wood. The vessel was pinned, crew shattered.

Beneath their own decks, a *boom* resounded that challenged the thunder in the sky. There was a flash of light and a surge of magic that sizzled the air—evaporating raindrops as they fell. The side of the opposing vessel had a hole ripped in it.

The wood that was sheared from the side of the hull froze mid-air. Alyss shifted her hands and they heeded her will, forming a bridge between the two ships. Olivin was the first to charge, Ducot close behind, followed by the rest.

"Keep them in place," Eira shouted to Cullen.

As she moved to leave, he caught her hand. "Shouldn't you stay here?"

Eira frowned at him, a pointed enough expression that it was its own response.

"You are the captain of this vessel. What if something happens to you? What would the rest of us do?"

Eira looked to the opposite deck. Her friends had wasted no time engaging the soldiers. Magic sparked between flashes of lightning, twisted faces of pain and anger highlighted by Olivin's Lightspinning circles.

I should be there with them was her first thought.

Noelle died because of me. Because she hadn't been strong enough, fast enough, determined enough…a good enough leader.

That second thought was what prompted her to stay. To widen her stance and shift her focus to the currents around the opposite ship as well as her own. She had allowed them to be disorganized in the mines—had allowed everyone to make their own choices, and Eira had witnessed the consequences. She'd been working to learn and implement every day since the notion that it was possible to be the leader her friends needed and deserved while still giving their opinions and thoughts voices.

Eira squeezed Cullen's fingers and nodded, showing she understood. A brief expression of relief overtook his features. For a second, the rain seemed to slow. The chaos halted. It was so quiet she could hear him breathe. Quiet enough that Eira checked her magic to ensure she wasn't stopping the raindrops mid-fall.

Affording no more than a second of distraction, Eira's focus returned to the battle. With a flick of her eyes, the sailor engaging Olivin went rigid. Olivin's sword sliced through her chest effortlessly before his eyes darted Eira's way. She gave him a slight nod. One that was returned before he continued to the next. Eira shifted her attention to another.

Ice. Wind. Light. Runes. All magic combined to be a symphony of death. They made quick work of the ship, so quick that something important was overlooked. By the time Eira felt the flare of magic unique to flash beads, it was too late.

The Carsovian sailors had responded with artillery of their own. Her ship swung off-kilter. Eira lunged for the railing. At the same time, an upswell of wind pushed on the opposite side of the vessel, preventing them from keeling over. Her fingers closed around the railing.

Eira pushed her magic into the ship. Frost crackled out from her hand, spreading across the railing and onto the decks. It spilled over the side of the vessel, covering the fresh opening they'd ripped into her hull. She could feel every jagged edge of the ravaged wood. Every opening where water pushed through.

Enough of that, Eira thought. The ocean that had surged into their vessel was forced out like low tide. They righted themselves, frost covering the entire ship from bow to stern.

Eira straightened and looked back over to the decks of their enemies. Her eyes met a sailor's—a woman who she had no attachment to or affiliation with. A woman Eira was certain she had never seen before and would never see again. A cold realization crossed her features that had nothing to do with the frost curling the wind.

"Adela."

Eira smirked before her magic seized the woman's heart, squeezing until it stopped beating.

The other ship was sinking. The fight had been won well before the crew decided to return, retreating off the decks that were about to be consumed by the waves. Once the last of them—Olivin—had returned, Eira shifted her focus.

"Push us away," she asked of Cullen as her magic surrounded the other vessel.

The winds that had been pinning down their enemy shifted, pushing on the ice Eira had patched the side of their hull with. They drifted back and away. At the same time, she created a swirling vortex beneath the dark waves. It sucked the opposing vessel down. Wood and rigging crunched, chewed up by churning currents. Eira narrowed her eyes.

Down, down, and down farther still. She'd condemn them all to an oblivion from which there was no escape. The only things that would tell of what happened here were flotsam and frost-bitten carcasses.

The moment she was satisfied, Eira returned her magic to her own ship in full. The waters propelled them away as she descended to the main deck, where everyone was still catching their breath. Even Yonlin had emerged from belowdecks.

"The cannons?" Eira asked him.

"We lost one," Yonlin said gravely.

Eira made it a point to not look back to Cullen. She hoped he had the decency not to gloat. But she wasn't going to tempt him with an opportunity.

"Good thing we only needed one shot. We'll keep our focus from here on," she said. Cullen had been right. It wasn't worth it to chase down that little vessel. But it was hard to think clearly.

"Crow, can you navigate us back on course?"

"In the middle of a storm?" Crow had to raise her voice over the wind and rain. "I'm good, Captain, but I'm not that good."

"I think I can get us somewhat back on course," Cullen offered from behind her. Eira turned to face him with an arch of her brow. He elaborated, "We're close enough to land that I can feel how the wind sheers off beaches and rock. I can use that to navigate us."

"Do it." If they were close enough to land for him to feel that, then it meant they were close enough to land for another patrol to find them. Part of their hull was still open, her ice the only thing preventing the ocean from pouring in. As much as Eira wanted to drown all of Carsovia, she knew when a tactical retreat was best. Though, if any were to make the mistake of crossing their path…

With a nod, Cullen headed toward the helm, assuming command. His wind swirled around the vessel, guiding it as much as her currents would. Eira eased her magic, following his lead. Cullen's powers had grown so familiar to her that it was effortless to support as he needed. She could sense what he was about to do before it was done.

"Captain," Crow said, stepping closer so she didn't have to shout. Eira turned her attention to the woman. "Surviving our first battle means this vessel should have a name."

She hadn't named it yet. It had seemed so…unnecessary before. This small ship was purely to get them from one place to another—to be a means to an end. Eira hadn't been planning on getting attached enough to give it a name. But now that the question was presented, she felt more responsible for it than ever. As responsible as she felt for her crew. This collage of wood and ice was the only thing that kept them safe.

"*Winter's Bane*," Eira said with little thought. The name was the first thing to pop into her mind and it felt right.

"*Winter's Bane* it is," Crow repeated.

"Everyone but Cullen, head belowdecks," Eira ordered, gently enough that it was clear that the command wasn't firm—more of a suggestion. "Get some rest. Cullen and I will see us out of the storm." As she spoke, her magic searched for the edge of the rain.

Varren and Lavette wasted no time. Same with Crow and Fen. But Olivin and Alyss were on the opposite side of the deck. Crow's body had been concealing them.

Olivin was crouched by Alyss. A faint glow of magic illuminated Alyss's face from underneath Olivin's palm. Yonlin was at her opposite side, saying something Eira couldn't hear over the rain.

She approached. "Everything all right?"

"She—" Yonlin started.

"Got a scuff from the battle." Alyss's brave smile was painfully obvious to Eira. "Nothing that Olivin couldn't fix."

"Are you sure you're all right?" Eira asked as Yonlin helped Alyss to her feet.

"Absolutely." As she said the word, lightning cracked in the distance, followed by the roll of thunder, causing Alyss to jump.

"All right, get some rest." Eira knew better than to push the matter. If her friend had nothing to say, then they'd leave it at that.

Yonlin helped Alyss away, even though she had no visible wounds any longer.

Olivin lingered. Eira's eyes met his.

"How bad was it?" Eira knew he'd be honest with her.

"She was more shaken than injured. A scrap of wood her magic didn't catch in time clipped her ear and took out a chunk. Nothing major. But if she had been standing a step over…" Olivin didn't have to finish.

Eira noticed a narrow slab of wood on the deck, more like a stake than a piece from a ship. She kicked it into the sea. "If it had posed a genuine threat, Alyss's magic would've saved her."

"Eira…" Olivin shifted, taking a half step closer to her. The same concern that had been in his eyes for weeks now was still there. But now it was enough for him to cross the line he'd been minding and say something. "Alyss is powerful, but even the strongest of sorcerers aren't immortal."

"I know that." She wasn't sure if he was intentionally referring to Noelle or not. Either way, the mere idea of a suggestion stung.

Olivin touched her forearm lightly, fingers trailing down almost to grab hers. Hers twitched in response. She wanted to reach for him. But she couldn't… There wasn't warmth enough in her right now to offer him. Noelle's memory left nothing but anger and cold rain. He abandoned the motion.

"I know you'd be… If something happened to…" He sighed and abandoned the thought that couldn't coalesce into something he'd want to say. "I know you care about all of us, and you're doing your best. But maybe don't chase down enemies that haven't even seen us?"

She pursed her lips. Unable to object with the ship in its current state. Resignation escaped as a sigh.

"All right. Straight to Qwint from here on. Unless we're attacked first."

He nodded and stepped around her. As he moved past, the backs of his knuckles brushed against hers. Her fingers twitched. His were waiting. For a second, they brushed together. Not quite lacing. But not nothing, either.

There was a void in all of them that took the shape of the woman who should've been there with them. Noelle's ghost was a companion, and a void.

As Eira turned, she found one other remained. Instead of heading down, Ducot wandered to the front of the vessel, hand on the railing.

It was just three of them now on deck. Cullen back at the helm, Ducot at the bow, and her in the middle. Eira looked between the two men. Cullen caught her eyes and gave a nod, as if he knew what she was debating. But of course he did. He knew her heart in many ways better than she, even if Eira didn't always want to admit it.

She ascended the quarterdeck once more, crossing to the bow and stopping next to Ducot. He looked out to sea with unseeing eyes. Wind pushed the rain over his cheeks, forming rivulets that almost looked like tears. Almost.

But he had already mourned an ocean. They all had. There was nothing left in the echoes of their sobs and cries. It was a void as deep as the sea churning beneath them, a vast endlessness—as dark as the pit.

"Thank you," he said, finally.

"You've nothing to thank me for." Eira gripped the railing, ice crackling around her white knuckles. "If I had the resources and time, I would sail along their coast for the rest of my life and show them the meaning of fear."

"Perhaps once we have taken down Ulvarth."

"Perhaps," she echoed.

The future was a blank slate. As unknown as what lay past the horizon at the edge of the storm. But Eira was charging toward it, one way or another. First, they would go to Qwint. They would drop off Lavette and Varren and secure supplies and allies. Then, they would sail back to the large bay of Meru, rejoining with Adela where she darted between the Shattered Isles, wreaking havoc among the Pillar's ships.

Then, it was to Risen, facing and ending whatever chaos Ulvarth had wrought.

After that…who knew? Survival for all of them, Eira included, wasn't a foregone conclusion. So Eira kept her focus in the moment. One battle at a time. One enemy. One distant dawn.

T HE HORIZON HAD been beckoning them since the sun had first risen. For two long days and nights, they watched it grow closer, until today they could make out details on the distant peninsula. A morning mist had settled upon the sea, gulls wheeling and calling through it, giving Qwint the illusion of rising from the sky, rather than the sea.

Eira crossed the decks, eyes on the distant shore, a strange mixture of emotions swelling on the salty breeze. On one hand, there was relief that they had made it to relative safety, despite their skirmishes and close calls with Carsovia's navy, four weeks after saying goodbye to Adela and the *Stormfrost*. But on the other hand were all the unanswered questions that now lurked like the churning waves beneath the fog. Would they succeed in soliciting Qwint's aid? How would Qwint receive them?

As she gazed upon the distant cityscape, it occurred to her that she'd been imagining the coastal city she'd grown up in: Oparium. She'd had no idea what to expect from Qwint, and that had resulted in her filling in the blanks with what she knew best. That realization was tinged with a pang of longing for her former home. Oparium was never the place she had once dreamed it to be; yet, her heart ached for the home it had occupied in her mind. A longing that would always remain unfulfilled as the question of what home was to her—where her final port was—remained unanswered.

Perhaps part of her assumption that Qwint would be more like the quaint harbor of Oparium than, say, Norin, came from the knowledge that it was a relatively young nation. A place just finding its start. She certainly hadn't conceived it'd be the thriving metropolis that she now laid eyes on.

Great spires reached toward the sky with thin tendrils of smoke curling up between them, dancing with the pennons that fluttered in the breeze and suggesting a bustling populace. Every spot of land was dotted with towering structures and vibrant green inner gardens enclosed by high walls topped by wide stone balustrades. Windows caught the sunlight, winking like daytime stars. Massive breaker barriers stretched up from the sea, protecting against the battering waves and oppositional forces, enclosing the entire peninsula with a patchwork of stone that formed a fortress. So far as Eira could tell, there was only one entrance and exit—a break in the wall framed by two guard towers that were lined in cannons and archer's slits.

It was impressive, imposing, and nothing like Eira had ever seen before.

"Home." Lavette's whisper was barely audible over the sea breezes that were beginning to clear the fog and cries of gulls that swooped therein. Varren stood next to her at the bow, all-consuming relief crumpling his features. He looked as if he was about weep. Knowing his story, and given all they'd been through, she certainly wouldn't blame him if he did.

Eira cleared her throat as she approached, drawing their attention to her. "Should I know anything before docking?"

"Shortly, once it's clear enough that we do intend to enter the city, they'll send out a guardsman's vessel," Lavette explained calmly and methodically. Detailing the processes of her home seemed to grant her immense comfort. "It'll be small, but with the finest soldiers currently on duty. They'll seek to board and guide us into the harbor."

Eira bristled at the idea of giving over command of her ship. But she bit her tongue and kept her hesitations to herself.

"They'll take us to a section of dock for visitors and tie the vessel right up, since we're small enough. The wharf behind the walls is deep enough even for tall ships, but the docks can get cramped…" Lavette continued, detailing how they would be escorted to the high magistrate's office for questioning, but assured Eira that there was nothing to worry over. "One thing, though… Would it be possible to remove the ice on the side of the ship?"

"Not if you don't want us to sink." They had tried to have Alyss patch the hole in the side of the hull. While she was incredibly talented, Alyss wasn't a miracle worker. She couldn't conjure wood and earth from nothing, and they'd left the site of the skirmish too quickly for her to collect the pieces that had been blown apart. There wasn't enough extra material on the ship to properly patch it.

Luckily Adela had prepared Eira for just this type of occurrence by giving her control of the *Stormfrost* multiple times.

"Sinking wouldn't be ideal." Lavette clicked her tongue in thought.

"I'd say not."

"Can you make the ice less noticeable? I worry over Adela associations…"

"I'll do my best." Eira shifted the flow of her power, focusing on the ship for a moment. Frost trailed out from underneath her, giving her a clearer picture of the damage and where the ice needed to be and how it could be adjusted.

"I'd also remove the dagger." Lavette's eyes dropped to Eira's thigh, where the dagger Ulvarth had so kindly gifted to her after she killed Ferro was strapped. "Don't want them to be more on edge than they already will be."

"Fine." Though Eira hated the idea of parting with something that was so integral to her plans. She was going to end Ulvarth with that dagger—completely and utterly.

"One more thing," Lavette said as Eira's ice returned to her and the straps of the sheath on her thigh came undone. "When we're there…let me take the lead. I know this is your vessel but—"

"This is your home." Eira gave a respectful tilt of her head. "You know its ways and its people."

"And she's well respected," Varren said with a touch of admiration in his tone and his eyes. Eira had begun to wonder if Lavette's ignorance of his fondness was willful. It was rather obvious to the rest of them. But if Varren wasn't saying anything then Eira certainly wouldn't, either.

"Indeed," Eira agreed. If the stories Varren had told her of Lavette were true, then she certainly was.

Lavette's expression hardened at the praise. Her gaze pierced the city, staring at something Eira couldn't see with purpose. This certainly wasn't the homecoming they had imagined for themselves when the tournament started…but at least it was a homecoming, which was so much more than many of the competitors and spectators could say.

"There." Lavette raised a finger, pointing at a small ship that was making its way out of the inner wharf of Qwint. "That's the boat that's coming to greet us."

"I'll let the rest of them know. Take the time to gather your things." Eira stepped away, returning to the main deck where the others had gathered, and gave them a quick rundown of everything Lavette had said.

"So, we're not supposed to let them know that we're here on behalf of her supreme coldness?" Crow folded her arms.

"Treat Qwint as you did Meru." Eira remembered Adela's orders that they were not to interfere with Meru's politics and hoped it made things clear. "Now is not the time for piracy. We're here as guests."

"Can't say we pirates get to be guests often." Fen folded his hands and put them behind his head. "It's been some time since I've been on solid land for a few days, longer since I'd been anything that could remotely be called a guest. I think I will enjoy it."

"So long as 'enjoying it' has nothing to do with thieving, murdering, or any other unsavory acts, enjoy." Eira swept her gaze across them. "We'll see how things go, but I don't expect to be here longer than a day or two. Long enough to patch the ship, restock, and see what aid from Qwint we can secure."

In preparation for their arrival, Eira distributed some of the coin that Adela had generously given them for their journey. *I'm not a charity; I expect you to earn it*, she'd said in a firm tone, yet, with a hint of humor. *Don't waste it. You're not getting more from me*. Eira had assured her that they were more than capable of paying their own way.

After receiving their monetary rations, the crew quickly set to hiding anything that could be considered pirate paraphernalia alongside their valuables and packing light bags to venture into the city with. While Lavette had assured Eira that their ship would remain safe in the harbor, she had also said it would be searched, and it was all too easy for one bad actor to have sticky fingers.

Eira entrusted the dagger to Crow, telling the woman to guard it with her life while they were on Qwint. Then, she went about squaring away the rest of her things. As Eira was packing her own bag, a glint of red in the twilight caught her eyes, causing her to cease all movement.

Nested atop wads of clothing—what precious little items Eira still had left to her name—was an unassuming pouch of soft leather, its drawstrings loosely undone and contents barely visible. Eira's fingers glided over the scars of time that crossed the worn patches of material. She kept her magic tightly to her, unable to bear the thought of catching a rogue whisper of the thousand stories that must be contained among the jewelry within.

Every piece was more intricate than the last. Designs that hadn't been in style for years back on the Solaris Continent. Rings, pendants, and bracelets of breathtaking beauty twinkled in the beams of twilight that struck through the planks of the decks above. Their polished surfaces refracted Eira's face, illuminated by lamplight. Patina clung to their edges.

Her grip tightened around the bag as an invisible fist closed around her heart and Eira drew a shuddering breath.

Turning, she crossed to Ducot with purpose. Eira could feel the others glancing in her direction, no doubt curious as to what had caused the shift in demeanor. Even though she knew Ducot could sense her, Eira dared to rest a hand on his shoulder. He tensed and it reminded her just how little contact they'd had—physical or verbal—since Noelle's death. He blamed her for it. She blamed herself. There wasn't much to be shared between them as a result.

She spoke first. "You should have these."

Ducot held out his hand and Eira placed the bag in its center. "She would've wanted you to."

His lips pressed into a hard line as he realized what Eira was handing him. Ducot took the pouch and tugged at the drawstrings. Slowly, he explored its contents, eventually selecting a small, golden signet ring with three rubies dotting its surface.

Wordlessly, he set the pouch into his own trunk and slipped the ring onto his left little finger. It had been crafted for a hand much smaller than his. "Thank you. I'll bring the rest back to her family. That's what she would've wanted…and they deserve to know."

Eira felt as much obligation to notify Noelle's family as he did. She owed it to them to accept responsibility for what her choices had wrought and stand before their judgment. But she also didn't know if Ducot would want her there.

"If I can help you find them, I would be glad to," were the words she settled on.

He nodded and Eira stepped away, leaving it at that. There was an aching gap in her heart that Noelle had once occupied, made wider still by the distance Eira now felt with Ducot. She'd do anything to return to the place they'd once been. But, finding their way back, the trust, the openness… It might be too much for her to ask for.

She ascended back onto the main deck, taking over from Crow and Fen so they could gather their things and ready themselves. The small boat was almost upon them and they were now close enough to the city that Eira could see the men and women who lined the upper walls of the ramparts that overlooked the sea. Attention trained solely on them.

"Lavette," Eira called down belowdecks, "They're nearly here."

"Almost finished!" The reply was accompanied by the heavy *thud* of a bag hitting the floor.

Eira turned her attention back to the small boat. But no sooner had she than another set of footsteps approached. She knew who by the sound alone.

"Are you nervous?" Olivin asked, coming to her side.

"Not really." Eira shrugged. "Should I be?"

"It is a new place…but, given what you've already survived, I suppose very little would make you nervous."

"The same could be said for you." She glanced his way.

"Like you, I am not nervous, either. Merely eager."

"For?"

"To carry on." Olivin's tone was hard to read. "This is their homecoming. But I am ready for my own—ready to eliminate the Pillars once and for all and claim retribution for my family. There is no future until that is done." A sentiment Eira knew all too well. "The sooner we do what we must here, and move along, the better."

Olivin hadn't been the closest among them to Noelle, but the ordeal in the mines seemed to have impacted him, too. Perhaps it was the realization of just how far the Pillars' influence stretched. How they were maneuvering strong allies from all corners of the world. Or he saw how fragile they all were—even though it had been Noelle at the opposite end of a flashfire, it could've been any of them, his younger brother, Yonlin, included. If Eira were honest with herself, the skirmish on the sea didn't help, either.

"I don't plan on lingering," Eira assured him.

"A *tiny* bit of lingering might not be so bad."

"Oh?"

"Perhaps…" His focus dropped to her mouth. Eira gave him

a knowing smirk, one he returned. "We might find some time to ourselves once we are on the mainland."

"Perhaps," Eira agreed. She opened her mouth, ready to make a few suggestions on what they could do. But she was interrupted by a sudden burst of magic, a minor explosion rattled the side of the ship—a warning shot.

She jerked toward the origin. The small boat that had been meandering out toward them had come alongside. Eira had sensed them, but she didn't expect them to come swinging. Her mistake. A man held out his hand, runic bracelets locked into place. Another was spinning his runes, readying them for attack.

Eira gritted her teeth and shifted her feet, prepared to counter when the knight shouted,

"Take one more step, Pirate Queen, and we'll sink your vessel here and now."

THREE

"I'M NOT SURE if I should be flattered that you think I'm mighty enough to be Adela. Or perhaps I should be offended on her behalf that you'd think if I were, you'd be able to best me." Eira tilted her head, looking down at them both literally and in the metaphorical sense.

"Lies won't save you this time, Pirate Queen." With determined grimaces, the two soldiers locked their runes into place on their bracelets, ready to levy unknown magic.

This time? Eira noted with a touch of amusement. Just what had Adela been up to in Qwint?

"I am not your enemy. You have a case of mistaken identity." The calm coolness of her words cut through the blazing tension. She could almost see the men working to consider this. But they only held out their arms straighter. "I will submit peacefully. There is no need for the sinking of any vessels, or any other bloodshed, today."

The knights didn't move a bit. Their skepticism was understandable. If they truly thought she was Adela, they had no reason to believe she'd go peacefully.

"That's just what Adela would say." The man went to move, and Eira's magic surged.

Lavette's voice shouted over all of them. *"Enough!"* The woman rushed up from belowdecks.

Took your sweet time, Eira barely resisted saying.

"She's with me." Lavette held up a strip of green fabric. It looked like something the Qwint competitors had worn at the tournament. That must've been what she'd been searching for.

One soldier relaxed. "Lavette D'astre, daughter of Qwint."

Her reputation preceded her, and it was going to save their lives.

"This woman speaks the truth. She is not the Pirate Queen Adela," Lavette said firmly.

"But, the ship…"

"She's a Waterrunner, from the continent of Solaris, and a fellow champion in the Tournament of Five Kingdoms. We were attacked by a Carsovian scouting ship a few days ago. There were no other means to repair our vessel on the seas so we improvised with the skills available to us. We would've all been dead if not for her abilities." Lavette's explanation was even. Not hasty or desperate. But not lagging. She held herself with an air of authority greater than any Eira had seen from her to date. This was a woman in her element. "This woman has been working to bring us home."

Lavette motioned to the hatch and Varren emerged. The men recognized him as well. Though, since they didn't immediately attach a name, Eira suspected they only knew him because of the sendoff the champions had.

"I… We…" The leader seemed at a loss. His eyes darted between Eira and Lavette. "We were told, explicitly, to sink the ship."

"Under the presumption of Adela being on it, I would assume," Lavette countered. "Escort us in and we will speak to the Hall of Ministers and clear up this whole misunderstanding."

The soldier frowned, eyes settling back on Eira skeptically.

Eira sighed dramatically. "Fine, if it suits you, take me in chains."

"What?" Olivin hissed at her side.

"I assume you have some?" Eira arched a brow. Sure enough, the knights glanced back into their boat. "Good. Take me to your ministers in them."

"You're sure about this?" Olivin whispered.

"I never said anything about putting the rest of you in chains," she muttered with a slight smirk.

"I still don't like the idea of *you* in shackles," Olivin murmured under his breath.

Eira ignored his defensive tone and continued addressing the knights. "But you'll have to let us dock first, and my friend repair the ship. If you remove my connection to my channel now, then our vessel will sink."

"You want us to let you into the bay with your power?" The knight was aghast at the idea.

"Surely my word means something," Lavette chimed in again. "She is no risk to you and is being more than fair."

"Ride aboard the vessel, knife at my throat." Eira shrugged. "Between that and all the cannons you have lining the wall, you should feel well protected."

There was a brief discussion. Then, the knight whom they had been negotiating with called up, "Fine."

"Fen, please lower a ladder for our new friends."

The pirate glanced at Eira skeptically from the corners of his eyes, but complied as the soldiers maneuvered their boat close enough for the leader to board with the shackles thrown over his shoulder. But, before getting to Eira, he paused at Lavette.

"It is truly a relief to see you." Raw emotion was heavy in his words. "After the news of—"

"There will be time for reunions soon." Lavette rested a gentle hand on his elbow. "First, I want to step foot in the city of my forefathers and ensure my friends' safety."

"Yes." With a nod, the soldier moved to Eira. He was clearly still skeptical that she really wasn't Adela. Eira knew her appearance wasn't doing her any favors as his eyes roved over her face several times.

"I won't hurt you." She offered him an encouraging smile. But somehow that made him flinch, even more nervous. It was as if murder and piracy hovered in the air around her like frost, and this soldier could sense it.

                    Elise Kova

He bristled, offended by her platitudes. "Keep it moving."

She did as she was commanded and the ships lurched forward toward the glistening city.

The harbor within the walls of Qwint was packed tightly. Ships of all shapes and sizes bobbed in the waves. They slowly maneuvered through them and headed for a secluded section of dock, reserved for official business, just as Lavette had said.

Eira remained still as a statue as Alyss was allowed to use some basic supplies at the docks to patch up the side of the vessel. It was by no means seaworthy, but it'd float after Eira pulled back her magic. Then, she offered her wrists to the shackles.

The second they closed around her flesh, runes flared and her channel went quiet. The normal hum of power was gone. Everything from the sea to the ambient moisture in the air was… normal. Dull.

They wasted no time in escorting her off first, leading her away from the vessel as other soldiers closed in around her. She glanced over her shoulder. Her friends moved freely, unbound. *Good*, that meant the soldiers had believed her. There'd be no way they'd allow the true Adela's crew such leeway.

It also meant that, should the worst come to pass and they *had* to fight their way out, they could.

Her focus landed on Cullen and he held her attention. A slight, sly smile played on his lips, as if he was as amused as a part of her was with this whole charade. Something about the look filled her with confidence, a rush that went straight to her head. There wasn't a trace of doubt in his eyes.

Feeling significantly more confident, Eira turned her focus to the city ahead, and the gathered crowds. Word must've spread quickly among the populace of Qwint. Men and women were packed tightly on either side of the street, heeding the orders of soldiers and staying out of the main path, but eager to get a look at the alleged pirate queen.

Eira kept her chin high, an easy smile playing on her lips. She glanced at them from the corners of her eyes. Children shrank closer to their mother's skirts and clung to their father's necks. Sailors stared with a mixture of horror and awe. Noblemen and women had eyes gleaming with fascination, and hate.

The crowds, the attention…it vaguely reminded her of the first time they'd emerged from the champion's manor in Risen following the death of Ferro. Their prying eyes. Their misplaced hatred. It had bothered her so much, then. She'd tried to conceal her discomfort with anger and forced nonchalance.

This time, Eira's footsteps were lighter. Her smile was easier. She didn't walk in haste and her blasé attitude came naturally.

Think what you want of me. She welcomed it. *Your opinions make no difference and hold no bearing.*

The attention quickly shifted off her the moment Lavette came into view. Joy and relief at the sight of "Qwint's daughter" warred with confusion at her association with the woman they perceived to be Adela. Eira glanced over her shoulder at the sound of murmuring and jubilation—the soldiers hadn't stopped Lavette from darting over to people in the crowd, shaking hands, embracing loosely. Where Eira created worried looks and scowls, Lavette left smiles in their wake.

Qwint was a *democracy*, Eira reminded herself. A new concept still being tested that Eira could only wrap her head so far around. But based on how it had been explained to her, the will of the people was what mattered most. Those in power were chosen by free and open ballots cast by the average person. The same people Lavette was already winning over on their behalf.

Trusting Lavette to help them navigate the politics of the land, Eira took in the sights and smells of the city. Alleyways led to courtyard marketplaces. Windows opened overhead and people lounged on balconies, pipes hanging from lips and laundry hanging from lines. There was the perfume of incense, and the less savory notes of sewage that couldn't be escaped even in the finest of metropolises. It was a symphony for the senses boxed in by the towering buildings.

Walls of brilliant white stone, accented by glass of every shade imaginable, cast rainbows of glittering light. Murals were painted and tiled. Even the gutters that ran along the rooftops were works of art, crafted by a meticulous hand.

Eira had the sense that she could wander these streets for years and not uncover the depths of their secrets. Qwint was a city that had been built once, and then built again right on top of its previous iteration. Like children's blocks, the buildings rose, hiding secrets only Yargen knew.

Despite Lavette saying they would be taken to the magistrate's office at the docks, Eira got the sense they had long bypassed that location. Her insight proved correct when they crested the top of the hill they'd been plodding up along to emerge into a vast square lined with columns. At the opposite side was the largest of the buildings, domed at the top. It reminded Eira vaguely of the senate's halls in Solaris, but several times more grand.

They were escorted in without fanfare. The entry was as impressive as the outside. Sculptures stood in alcoves that lined the walls. A map of tiny mosaic tiles spread underneath their feet, allowing them to traverse entire oceans with a few steps to nations and continents Eira had never seen. A small part of her wondered if, someday, when Ulvarth was dead and her work was done, she'd venture to those distant shores.

Eira didn't have much time to take in the details, as they were already progressing through another series of antechambers—smaller, but all as finely appointed—until they came to a stop before two oversized wooden doors. Heated debate was muffled by them, but only briefly as they swung open and the words came into clarity.

The innermost room of the building was centered directly

under the gilded dome. Chairs were positioned along its circular walls on risers, giving everyone a view of two half-circle desks at the lowest center points, where three people stood, addressing the others.

An upper balcony circled the dome that was full of spectators. *The citizenry is an active participant of the government,* Lavette had said in one of her previous explanations to Eira. *The government is beneath them—in service to them. Without the will of the citizens, we have no power.* Certainly, from this vantage on the floor of the hall, it did look as though the citizens were above them all.

The attention of all those present in the chairs below the balcony—at least fifty people—was solely on them, the debate on the floor and murmuring of the crowd above falling to a sudden hush. The thrall of silence accented the focus of the ministers. Eira assumed they were ministers, given that they all wore the floppy green hats with wide, white bands around their brims, accented by a blue feather, that Eira had seen in the coliseum.

"I recall your orders having been to kill the pirate queen, not to bring her before us," one of the three people in the center said. Eira didn't recognize him. But he did wear a special green sash.

"I believe there has been a bit of confusion." Lavette stepped around the soldiers, coming to a stop at Eira's side.

The woman at the center practically threw the man out of the way to rush to Lavette. She swept her up in a crushing embrace. "Darling girl," she whispered tearfully.

"Hello, Auntie," Lavette responded with a warm embrace, but pulled away respectfully, not allowing the raw emotion to drag on.

"I thought you were lost with your father and the rest," she choked out, hands on Lavette's face, as though she couldn't believe Lavette was real.

Eira was reminded of her aunt Gwen. For a blink, she was back in the soldiers' bunks—Gwen telling her not to let the shames of her past hold her back any longer. Eira swallowed her own emotions before they could get the better of her.

"So Father is…" Lavette's question trailed off.

Her aunt nodded, unable to form words.

"I—" Lavette cleared her throat before her emotions choked her. They were all battling valiantly for their composure and, so far, winning. "I had assumed as much, but it is good to know."

"There was a vessel of refugees," the woman explained. "Not many made it."

"I will thank every rune for protecting those that did," Lavette said softly.

A heavy tapping of the gavel of the man still impatiently waiting in the center brought all their attention back to him. "As touching as these reunions might be, it is essential that we remain focused on dealing with the *allegedly* not pirate queen."

Lavette stepped away from her aunt to address the full assembly. With an open palm, she motioned to Eira. "This woman is not the infamous pirate queen. Her name is Eira Landan; she is—"

Lavette's speech was interrupted by a sharp shriek.

"Eira! *Eira!*"

Eira's attention was jolted to the balcony. Her heart skipped several beats. It raced as though she were back in Carsovia, fleeing the knights. Fighting their way out. In an instant, she was no larger than a girl—a small creature in a wide world. Desperate for the love and approval of two, above all others.

"That is not the pirate queen!" The words soared above the pounding of the gavel. Above the frantic beats of Eira's heart. "That is my daughter."

FIVE

*M*OTHER.

The word that no longer fit quite right. That didn't seem to describe the woman calling after her. And yet, Eira had no other label that would fit.

"We will have order!" the man boomed over his gavel. "The floor is not open for comment from the gallery."

There was a commotion above. Eira found the source of the voice. She squinted into the light that filtered through the dome. The figures above were cast in shadow.

It couldn't be…

Lavette cleared her throat and resumed her movement from before. "This woman is not the infamous pirate queen. Her name is Eira Landan. She is a Waterrunner from Solaris and a champion in the Tournament of Five Kingdoms. I knew her as a fellow competitor and can vouch for her identity. If not for her quick thinking and skill—and the skills and cleverness of her friends—my fellow champion from Qwint, Varren, and I would have died with the rest. It is because of her that we were able to return to you. So, I seek her immediate release from these shackles."

"Even if she is not the pirate queen herself, she could be in cahoots," a minister said from the stands that circled the room. Some agreements. Some contrary remarks that "Adela works alone."

"Perhaps not Adela, but the one to have brought Ulvarth that infernal armor," another said.

Armor? Eira had heard nothing of the sort. But there was no time to inquire further.

"I propose this motion on behalf of my niece." Lavette's aunt stepped back to the center of the room, equally eager to reclaim decorum and wrap the matter up as quickly as possible.

"I second the motion," the other man in the center, who had been silent until now, chimed in.

The first man who had spoken and who had been attempting to keep order—the eldest among them—continued to regard Eira warily. He begrudgingly said, "Then the motion is brought to a vote. All those in favor of releasing this *Eira Landan* and allowing her crew to be free within Qwint, raise your paddles."

Around the room, green paddles rose in vast majority.

"Those against."

Only a handful of blue paddles dotted the sea of hats.

"And those abstaining."

A couple of white paddles.

"Those in favor have it." The elder man picked up a small mallet, striking a tall, tubular bell that stood at the end of one of the two desks.

As soon as the chime echoed through the hall, the soldiers removed Eira's shackles. She massaged her wrists. The physical relief paled in comparison to the sensation of her magic surging back to her.

"With that, we shall adjourn our special session of the Hall of Ministers regarding the potential threat of the Pirate Queen Adela Lagmir," the elder man continued to speak in his authoritative tone. "Let the record show that it was not, as first assumed, Adela off our waters, and the matter is now closed."

All those in the circles of chairs that ringed the hall at varying levels banged their fists on the railings before them three times. With that, the air seemed to clear with an unheard sigh. People rose to their feet and began to chat. Eira noticed that, with the threat deemed no more, they seemed to hardly pay her any attention— save for the few who had voted against her. Those men and women still regarded her with wary glances and skeptical looks.

The immediate threat quelled, for now, her attention drifted up toward the balcony. The space where the woman had claimed Eira was her daughter was vacant now. Cleared out with the rest. Perhaps cleared out by force.

"Eira?" Alyss whispered from her side. She hadn't realized Alyss had worked her way to stand next to her.

"It couldn't have been…" She still searched the empty balcony for answers that weren't there. "How could she be here? She was in the coliseum…"

"You're here," Alyss pointed out.

Eira's wondering was cut short as Lavette and her aunt stole her attention by approaching.

"Everyone, this is my aunt, High Minister Morova D'astre," Lavette introduced with a motion.

"A pleasure." Morova introduced herself to each of them in turn. When she made it to Eira, she paused, mid-grip, staring. "The resemblance is uncanny."

"My reputation precedes me." Eira offered a slight smile.

"Only by way of the survivors who made it back from the tournament." A pause. "It seems you might know some of those from Solaris."

"Yet to be confirmed," Eira said cautiously. But who else would claim to be her mother? Who would lie about that? Was it more likely that this was someone trying to manipulate her into a dangerous position, or that her mother was actually here? Both seemed impossible. She worked to remain focused, even when a thousand unanswered questions ricocheted across her mind. "Regardless, I'd like to assure you that those rumors about me are greatly exaggerated." Eira released the woman's hand.

"Glad to hear it, otherwise I would end up looking quite foolish for defending you."

"We don't want that," Eira agreed with the unsaid. "Speaking of what happened at the tournament, there are a few matters I would like to discuss with your council."

"Regular session will not begin until tomorrow—today was

technically an off day, until you arrived. But I will gladly bring your matters before the hall then," Morova assured her.

Eira refrained from being more insistent. This was the way things were done here. And one night wasn't likely to make a significant difference.

"Who else made it back?" Varren interjected.

"Only a small group of spectators and Minister Gourdun." A heavy frown weighted Morova's words. The pain of the wound was still real. "There were a few survivors from Solaris, as well, who had been sitting among those with Qwint in the stands."

There it was, a plausible explanation. Yet, Eira still wasn't ready to believe it.

"So few survived…" The rest of what Lavette might have said was lost, no doubt to her crumpling into her own grief. The woman was doing an impressive job of holding herself together. But her brows were fighting a pained furrow. Her eyes reddening at their edges.

Her aunt seemed to notice, too. "Come, we should get you home where you can relax in comfort."

"Home?" Lavette blinked, returning to the present. "*Home,*" she repeated, softer, her voice filled with longing. Then, she turned to Eira. "Aunt, do you think you will be able to take Eira to meet the refugees from Solaris? I believe she might want to confirm the identities of a few?"

"If it isn't too much trouble?" Eira forced herself to say. Her voice remained level even as her insides trembled.

"It shouldn't be. I can have two of our soldiers lead you to the refugee house we have set up for them." Morova was motioning for a nearby soldier as she spoke, quickly repeating the instruction and ending with, "Then escort her to the D'astre residences."

"Understood." The soldier dipped his capped and plumed head.

"We can all go together?" Cullen offered. He looked more worried about her right now than he had when they'd been skirmishing with Carsovia's navy.

"Of course." Eira nodded, immediately assuming he wanted to ask after his father. Her hand moved of its own volition, touching his forearm gently. Cullen had as complicated a relationship with his family as she had with hers. But that didn't make this any easier. "Alyss, do you mind joining as well?"

"I doubt my family came to watch." She rubbed the back of her neck. Eira held her gaze. Like always, Alyss figured out the unsaid. "But I should check."

"Then we shall see you three at my home later." Lavette was still working on her composure. It seemed wildly unfair that Eira would have an opportunity to reunite with part of her family—the people with whom she had a deeply complicated relationship at best—and Lavette only received confirmation of her father's death. A father Lavette clearly loved deeply.

Fate rarely played fair.

They parted ways. Lavette went with her aunt, the rest of them in tow. Cullen, Eira, and Alyss were escorted by the soldier out a different exit and back onto the streets.

"It'll be all right," Alyss encouraged with a whisper, taking her hand. Eira hadn't realized she'd been balling her fingers into a fist that was so tight she'd nearly drawn crescents of blood into her palm.

"What will I say to them?" Eira breathed. Her parents were here, even if her heart still objected to the notion.

Cullen walked a step ahead. Eira couldn't tell if he was intentionally trying to avoid intruding, or if he was lost in his own world. Probably both.

"Start with hello, see where it goes from there," Alyss said.

"It's not that simple."

"It doesn't *have to* be more complicated."

Eira glanced at her friend from the corners of her eyes. Frustration simmering not at Alyss, but at the fact that she was right. Alyss seemed to understand the distinction and a sly smile arced her lips.

"Just…" Alyss trailed off as their feet slowed to a stop before a small building that bore the seal of Qwint over its door. Eira was vaguely reminded of the homes in the Champion Village—well made, but not overly appointed. Comfortable enough. Vaguely, she wondered if it was the same one that Varren had been taken to when he'd managed to escape Carsovia. "Be honest with yourself and with them."

"I don't know if I can be," Eira admitted.

"You're strong enough." Alyss knew just what she needed to hear. She'd been there every step when it came to matters of Eira's family.

"I…I know I am." The words tasted somewhat of a lie. But were more or less truth. Eira had the luxury of strength because she no longer needed them as the woman she'd become. But the girl who she had been still longed, just once in her life, for their approval. "But I'm not sure if my honesty will break them. If that will be worth it."

I don't have to break them to mend myself. The words stung. A petty, childish part of her wished they weren't true. But they were. Her being no longer depended on them. Wounding them was unlikely to heal her.

"That's a decision only you can make. But don't sacrifice your peace for their comfort. You aren't responsible for how they feel."

Eira heard Alyss's words. But hoped by the time they entered the building she'd fully believed them.

"Alyss is right." Cullen finally spoke, drawing Eira's attention solely to him. But he only stared ahead. Focused intensely on the door. "Say what you need to say. Speak like you'll never have another chance to—you never know if you will."

What would he have said to his father, if he'd known that there wouldn't be another chance? How would he have acted differently, all those weeks and months, if he'd known that his whole life would crumble? But from the rubble he could build something new, entirely on his own and for himself, after so many years of having the design of his life be dictated by those around him.

She didn't have the heart to ask him, at least not in this moment. Not even when Cullen shifted his weight to look back at her. Wordlessly, he reached forward and grabbed her face with a single hand. The touch was steady with need, but not overly demanding. It was the unhesitant ease that had her leaning in. "For luck," he murmured against her lips before kissing her as if it was the last time he ever could.

As abruptly as the kiss began, he pulled away, squaring off against the door. Without another word, he entered the building. Leaving Eira to feel a twinge of envy at his boldness.

"So, you and Cullen are still…" Alyss glanced between them.

"Yes."

"And Olivin?"

"Also yes." Though things with both had been in a sort of stasis following Noelle. It hadn't been the time, or place.

Alyss nudged and squeezed her hand. "Now that's something you could share with your parents."

Eira barked laughter at the absurdity of the suggestion. Alyss joined in. The effort to lighten the mood worked. But only for a moment. Tension settled back in with a sigh from Eira.

"All right, let's go." Eira stepped forward. Alyss's hand dropped from hers when she didn't move in step with Eira. The question never had a chance to leave her lips. Instead, Eira saw the answer written on Alyss's face. "No," she whispered.

"You need to do this on your own."

"But—"

"I will be right here when you're finished. And, if necessary, I'm sure there's somewhere in this city that sells sticky buns."

"You're the worst." It was already hard to speak.

"I know." Alyss jerked her head toward the door. "Now, go on."

The soldier that had escorted them had taken his position off to the side. Eira walked past him, debating whether she should assure him they'd only be a minute. But she ultimately decided against it. Who knew how long this would take?

Unlocked, the heavy door provided no resistance. A foyer connected to a long hall before her, stairs stretching up one side to a loft above with more doors. Eira paused, debating where to go next. Cullen was nowhere to be seen. The heavy shutting of the door behind her was ultimately what made the choice for her.

"Yes?" An unfamiliar woman emerged from an archway in the back, wiping her hands on a rag. It was strange to hear the tones of Solaris after becoming so accustomed to the accents of Meru and Qwint. "Are you with His Lordship?"

"Yes—but no," Eira quickly corrected herself. She was traveling with Cullen, but in this moment they had to go their own ways. "I'm looking for Reona and Herron Landan." Eira spoke the words, but they somehow felt like they came from someone else. *This couldn't be happening…*

"Reona, Herron," the woman called into the room attached by the archway. "You've a guest."

She'd barely had a chance to finish saying the words before a woman breezed past her in a blur. Eira's eyes widened a fraction as her father emerged behind her mother. It was the first time they had laid eyes on each other since Marcus's death. In a second, Eira was back in Solaris castle…alone…waiting on word. Fearing her family hated her once and for all—for good.

"Eira." Reona rushed forward. Eira didn't have a chance to react before her mother's arms enveloped her, crushing her. She was so startled that it wasn't until her mother drew a shuddering breath that Eira realized her cheek and shoulder were wet from tears. "We thought we'd lost you, too."

Those words had her arms closing around the woman who was both mother and stranger. Friend and foe. The woman who had raised her, and also managed to tear her down. But, for a second, none of that mattered. It all could wait as they, at long last, shared in a grief that only they truly knew.

HER PARENTS TOOK her to their room upstairs. It was basic and sparse, underscoring how they had only managed to escape with whatever was on their backs. Still, Eira couldn't resist sweeping the room with her magic, catching echoes that clung to each object. Neither of her parents were sorcerers, so she, somewhat expectedly, didn't find much. All the voices were unfamiliar and likely belonged to previous owners of the bedframe or chair.

"How did you end up in Qwint?" Eira asked as she settled on the lone chair. Her parents were opposite, side by side on the edge of the bed.

"When…it happened," Herron began. Reona's eyes were instantly vacant as they stared through the present and back to that fateful day. "We fled with the rest. It was chaos…so much fire and violence."

Eira barely resisted pointing out that she knew viscerally how chaotic and bloody that day had been. But, clearly, she'd had more success over the past few months working through the echoes of that night than they had. She let them explain it in their own way, and their own time.

"We were pushed along with the pack of people trying to escape. There were people who fell…barely recognizable."

Reona grimaced, staring at her feet as if she could still see the men and women who had been trampled beneath her.

"It wasn't your fault," Eira was compelled to say; she was familiar with how easily guilt wormed its way through every thought. Both of her parents seemed startled. "Those people, while incredibly unfortunate…it wasn't your fault they died. It wasn't anyone's. It was just how it happened." A crowd moving that quickly was more dangerous than a ravenous beast. "There was nothing you could've done to save them, either."

"It's hard to find peace with a cruel death like that…there's always something that could be done," Reona said softly.

The contradiction to her sentiment caused Eira to bite the insides of her cheeks. She resisted the urge to further emphasize her point. But doing so would only put her in a different bind. She'd be admitting to them just how many people she'd killed. A fact that they knew only the tip of, now. Something that was also underscored by her mother's statement—*hard to find peace with a cruel death like that…* Like the deaths by Eira's own hands? A peace that her parents would never have with someone like her? Even after all they'd seen, they still believed there was a simplicity to the world that indicated there would be justice, good and evil, righteousness. All lines that had blurred together in Eira's world into a flat, gray color.

"In any case"—Herron seemed to sense the tension and continued—"we followed the masses. One group had split away, talking of a boat along the river that could escape the carnage. They didn't object to anyone boarding. We got on with the intention of getting off at Risen but…"

"By the time we got there, they'd already burned all the Solaris ships," Reona finished.

"How did you escape?" Eira asked, veiling some of her curiosity for the state of Risen with her compassion for them. "Was Risen mostly normal other than the attack on the Solaris ships?"

"Far from it." Herron shuddered. "The city was burning, led by a man they claimed was anointed by the goddess."

Ulvarth.

"He certainly looked it," Reona added. "Neither magic nor weapons could touch him. They all seemed to reflect off."

"Reflect off?" Eira repeated, curious. Ulvarth didn't have

magic…unless he'd managed to open his channel once more? It was worth knowing what she'd be facing when she arrived. Though the likelihood of getting clear answers from her parents were slim with how little they knew about Lightspinning.

"We didn't get close enough to see." Reona shook her head.

"Nor would we have wanted to. We were focused on surviving." Something about the way Herron spoke made Eira think that he assumed she'd be upset at them for not investigating. Eira held her tongue. Any remark she'd make about how Ulvarth would annihilate them with a look would be offensive.

"There were those pillaging the river so we had to move quickly," Reona continued, "but somehow we made it out into the great bay of Meru. From there, we managed to stop at the port of Parth."

Eira knew the city: It was one of the last major ones on the southern half of Meru. A port that could collect resources like furs and timber from Hokoh—the largest city—and ferry it to Risen faster than the land routes.

"I take it the Pillars hadn't made it to Parth?" Eira asked.

"Not from what we saw," Herron said. Though Eira was instantly skeptical of that, after Ofok. Though, perhaps Ulvarth had exerted his force there because he knew if she were to escape by water, it was there or Risen.

"Those from Qwint took us in. There were no vessels going to Solaris and it didn't seem safe to stay on Meru any longer. We didn't want to wait and see what happened," Reona said. "They said Qwint had a long history of taking in refugees and allowed us to come. That it was also a seafaring city, for the most part, and they'd find a way to get a ship back to Solaris."

Eira resisted pointing out that if their goal was to keep themselves safe, they'd picked an odd location by going farther from Solaris, from Meru where Solaris would likely be sending forces to take vengeance, and to a city-state that was in constant peril from their larger neighbor. But, however unlikely, their choice had worked out. Because she was here, now.

"How did you escape?" Herron turned the story to her.

"And come to be associated with the dreaded pirate queen?" Reona whispered in horror. She moved faster than Eira could react, falling to her knees and scooping up Eira's hands. Between the contact and her mother's wide, glistening eyes, Eira was stunned to silence for a beat. "We tried so hard to save you from this slander. From the rumors and myths that we feared would haunt your every step. Forgive us that we failed."

Reona pressed her forehead into Eira's knuckles, drawing shuddering breaths. Eira was still too startled to react. Part of her felt like she should offer her mother comfort. The other part wanted to tell her parents that she was, indeed, "involved" with the pirate queen's slander and had loved every minute of it. That the "dreaded Adela" had become part mother, part teacher to her.

But Eira stayed her verbal blades. She wanted peace with them more than she had realized when she'd entered.

"It's all right," she encouraged. Hoping that if they walked away thinking one thing, it would be that. The more she said it, the more she realized it was all that she wanted, too. She wanted things to be all right enough that she could move on from this once and for all. "I went in the opposite direction as you—to Ofok. It's a town to the northwest of Meru and the other exit of the river. I had a ship I also escaped on, and then managed to find another vessel that was more seaworthy. We came here to deliver Lavette and Varren—the only two of Qwint's competitors that survived."

Eira made the choice to gloss over certain elements that pertained to Adela. Everything she said was more or less true… as true as they needed to know.

"What matters is that all of us are all right." There were those words again, said softly, as if she were speaking to a child. Eira shifted her grip and lifted her mother's face to give her an encouraging smile, feeling like the roles were reversed. "Did you find Uncle?"

Reona shook her head, withdrawing a hand to stifle a sob.

"We tried, but we didn't see him," Herron said.

"I'm sure he's all right," she offered, sounding more confident than she felt. There was nothing guaranteed, but… "If we all could manage to survive, then I'm sure he could, too."

"Yes, I'm sure." Reona smiled, brighter and more hopeful than she should be…but Eira wasn't about to diminish that flame. Instead, she smiled back and said nothing as her mother continued to speak. "It's such a relief to see you here—to know you're safe."

"Is it?" Eira couldn't stop the words from escaping. She'd been doing so well. But they slipped out.

"Of course it is." Reona's eyes went wide. "How could you ever think otherwise?"

"You weren't overly concerned with my safety after Marcus." Her words had more of a chill than she would've otherwise wanted. But there was no going back now. For all she wanted peace—and part of her did yearn for it—Alyss was right; this was better settled.

"Eira—" Herron began.

She cut him off with a look. "Don't take that tone with me." Her mother drew away, aghast. Her shock turned Eira's chill into a deep freeze. "Don't speak to me as if I am a child acting out."

"Isn't that what you're doing?" He frowned.

"No. I am trying to speak with you both about how you wounded me. I needed you then. I needed you after. And you weren't there."

"We were mourning." Reona stood. "Our only son had died."

"And your daughter was still alive." *Unless you never saw me that way?* She couldn't bring herself to ask the question. Even after all this time, all she'd been through and learned. It was too much. "*I needed you,*" she repeated, more desperate than the last. "I was alone, and scared. I blamed myself every second of every minute of every hour of every day for his death."

"We're sorry." Reona sat heavily back on the bed. Even though she said the words Eira had been hoping to hear, they didn't quite feel the way she'd been hoping they'd feel. It didn't alleviate the tension that had knotted between her shoulders from the moment she'd entered. "I could barely eat. Barely function… What could I have done for you?"

"Been there for me," Eira answered, even though she suspected the question was rhetorical. "I know I wasn't, in many ways, the daughter you wanted, but—" Herron opened his mouth to speak. Eira held up a hand to stop him. "Let's be honest with each other, shall we? I'm not a child any longer. I know the truth about everything."

"Everything?" Reona whispered softly. Eira wondered if her mind had gone to Adela. To the mysterious symbol that had been pinned to Eira's breast as a babe and had somehow, in a way her birth mother could've never imagined, set in motion Eira's destiny.

"Everything," Eira repeated, allowing them to think what they would about the context of the word. "I know the two of you did the best you could. But there were times where it wasn't enough. Times where all I wanted was the same support I saw you give to Marcus and yet I never got it. I was left to feel second, unworthy, and at times unloved."

The moment she said those words, Eira felt lighter. She could sit a little taller and breathe a little easier.

"Of course we loved you." Herron's face flushed with offense. "We took you in, raised you—we braved the seas to see you compete and to cheer you on."

"I'm grateful for those things," Eira said. "I am. But there were times that I needed so much more and I saw it was in your ability to give. I just wasn't worthy of the effort." Eira stood, sensing the conversation was reaching its end. She crossed over to her mother, who looked up in shock as Eira leaned forward and kissed her forehead gently. As if Reona were the child. "But, despite all that…I do love you both. I know you did the best you could with what you were handed—with who you are."

"Eira," her mother whispered, clutching for her hand as if

to hold her there. Clinging to what might be their last moment together. Maybe a part of her still clung to the girl Eira had once been. Back when they all still had a chance at being a real family.

Eira smiled faintly. "I'll make sure you get home all right."

"What about you?" Reona asked.

"I have work to do," Eira said solemnly. "I can't go back to Solaris…probably not for some time. But, when I'm able, I will. And I will make it a point to see you both."

She meant it, and perhaps they knew it too because their shocked stares shifted into what more closely resembled quiet resignation. Eira held out a hand to her father. He looked between it and her face, searching. For a second, she thought he'd refuse her peace offering. But ultimately he took it and they shared a firm shake.

"Thank you for all you did do for me," Eira said gently.

"We do love you," Reona said, and Eira truly believed that she meant it.

"I know. Be safe, and be happy." With that, Eira left them. She immediately heard another muffled sob, murmurs of her father. Hasty conversations. But they didn't follow her down the stairs. Eira paused on the last step, looking up, wondering if they'd chase after her to beg her to come home. To scold her one last time.

But they did neither.

It was over.

They would always be a part of her past. But they were no longer relevant to her present. Neither were the wounds they'd left. Those could finally scar over for good, the redness of the infection fading with every step.

Alyss was chatting with the soldier when Eira emerged. Cullen was at her side.

"Need a sticky bun?" she said without missing a beat. "Lou here says he knows a good spot that has some kind of sweet bun unique to Qwint but it seems close enough."

"I don't need one." Eira took in a breath of fresh air. "But I think I'd like one."

SEVEN

LAVETTE'S HOME ENCOMPASSED the entire top floor of one of the tall buildings in the center of Qwint. Composed of several rooms with towering ceilings and more curtains than doors, the whole place had an airy and open feel. Walls of honeyed plaster reflected the late afternoon light, casting every room in a warm, golden hue.

The building's height afforded panoramic views of the entire city-state by way of a wide veranda that wrapped around the entire exterior—from the breaker walls that shielded Qwint from the ocean and opposing naval forces, to the distant land wall, far to the west, that separated their land from Carsovia's.

Eira, Alyss, and Cullen had been escorted to the tall building, still licking sugar off their fingers the entire time they climbed the many staircases up to the D'astre apartments. As soon as they arrived, Lavette quickly got them up to speed on what little they'd missed and gave them a tour of her family's home that included explaining how the rooms had been divided among them.

Everyone was taking time on their own to rest and freshen up. After doing the same, Eira had made her way through the central common area and out to the widest part of the veranda, positioning herself at the farthest point of the arc and surveying the city as she would on the bow of a vessel.

Curls of magic teased her palm, as though an invisible hand was trying to lace its fingers with hers. Eira pushed off the railing with her elbows, shifting to face Cullen.

Trousers of deep navy clung low to his hips, a wide sash holding them in place. What looked like a checkered blanket, or oversized scarf, was wrapped around his shoulders. With no shirt underneath, swaths of the sides of his abdomen peeked out above the trousers and below the scarf. His arms also on display.

He huffed soft amusement, running a hand through his still-wet hair. Proper bathing in fresh water was a luxury not afforded on ships that they were all taking their turns indulging in. "Do you like what you see?"

"Life on a ship has been kind to you, Lord Drowel."

"Cullen, please." He grimaced at his family name, as if it were strange and unwelcome to hear. Eira could relate to that feeling all too well. "Or beloved. I'd accept that, too."

She laughed softly and shook her head. Her attention drifted out over the city once more. In her periphery she saw his do the same, gaze softening. They'd spoken about nothing of consequence during their sticky bun excursion—focusing more on the reprieve, the pretend normalcy.

"Speaking of your family name… Did you find him?" she asked as delicately as she could manage for a man she had never much liked.

"No word." He didn't elaborate, and Eira left it at that. Whatever the truth was, it wouldn't be found in Qwint. "Though, speaking of families…"

Eira hid a grimace. She'd opened this avenue of questioning; it was only fair of him to turn it back on her.

"Are you all right? You came right out here to be alone after the bath."

"We are all doing our own things." Eira gestured inside. Ducot was sitting with Crow on one of the wide sofas in the common area. Olivin and Yonlin were still sorting themselves. Alyss had promptly gone off to take a nap the moment she saw the bed. Lavette and Varren had secluded themselves as well.

"Probably because this is the first time we can be more than forty paces apart from each other," he mused.

"Probably."

"Would you like me to be forty paces from you?" He arched his eyebrows.

Eira shook her head. "You're welcome to join me. There's a lot of railing."

"Even railing that's roughly forty paces away."

"You know, I'm going to start thinking *you* want to be away from *me*."

"Well, let me prove the contrary." He stood next to her, sides almost touching, elbows brushing as he leaned forward. The touch somehow reminded her of the first time their knuckles had brushed back in Risen. The tingling happiness of that memory was weighted by all the times at the bow of the ship where he had been her silent companion in their mourning. "Seriously, Eira, how was it?"

"They were as they've always been." Eira sighed and let her walls come down. It was still all too easy—instinctive, even—around him. "As I never wanted to see them…"

"We're all blind to the faults of our parents." Cullen could speak from experience. "We never want to see them as who they are. It means admitting their shortcomings… Even for those who had the best of parents, that's still the moment you realize that they aren't the paragons we once imagined them to be, and accept that you can't depend on anyone but yourself."

Eira hummed, supposing it was true. Part of her had been holding out hope that her parents would prove her expectations wrong. Even though, at every turn over the years, they had shown her exactly who they were.

"But I honestly don't care about them. How are *you*?"

"I'm all right." She was grateful he didn't contradict her because she meant it. "It feels…done. They're not shut out of my life forever. But they're not a part of it either. They hold no power over me—I don't need them. But that also means I realized I don't need to shut them out entirely, either. It's…"

"Complicated," he finished for her.

"I imagine you must feel similarly about your father." Every word was spoken as though it were cradling fine, blown glass. Eira glanced at him from the corners of her eyes. His face was stony, but not grimacing or crumpling.

Cullen nodded. "Part of me hoped he'd be there. But another part of me…" He made a noise of something like disgust. "Thinks it's for the best he wasn't. I've begun to wonder what I might say to him if I'm ever presented with the opportunity. How he might see me now."

"And?" She was, admittedly, achingly curious.

"I've a lot of choice words." Cullen chuckled darkly, eyes shadowed and gaze intense toward the distant horizon. "But, at the end of it, I made my own choices. I should have been more of a man and stood up for myself. I can't blame him for everything."

"Look at you, accepting responsibility." She nudged him with her shoulder.

"I know, what a shock." Cullen hung his head and glanced her way through strands of hair that had fallen loose from its usual part.

"It was, once."

"Once," he repeated, and a disbelieving smile carved across his face. She wondered if he, too, was thinking about just how far they'd come.

The talk of family—of surviving and not—had Eira's thoughts wandering back to Noelle. The back of her throat was saltier still from all the tears she'd refused to shed today.

"It's unfair that we're both here—that my parents, of all people, managed to be here—and she's not."

"There are a great many things that are unfair about her death." Cullen straightened, looking back over the city. "She would've loved it." The words were barely more than a whisper on the wind, carried over the rooftops toward the distant horizon, where the watercolor sky blended with darkening sea.

"She would've told us how much better Norin was."

Cullen snorted, stifling a laugh. For a while, even smiling

had felt like a betrayal to her memory. Laughing was practically forbidden among them. But all ice thawed eventually, it seemed.

"She would've," Cullen agreed, looking out again once he'd managed to compose himself. "Totally convinced she was right to the point that we'd all agree."

"Absolutely."

A silence stretched on for what felt like eternity. Amid the sunset, she could almost hear his thoughts. It wasn't until lights from distant buildings began to flicker on, mirroring the early stars overhead in the twilight, that he spoke again.

"You know, it wasn't your fault," he whispered.

"Don't," Eira said firmly, straightening to look him in the eyes. "Don't," she repeated, gentler, but as unyielding as steel. "You keep her death and her memory in your way; let me keep it in mine."

Cullen seemed poised to object but thought better of it when a pointed look from her silenced any retort. He turned his face back toward the sprawling city with a sigh. His voice carried a surprising conviction when he said, "Let's go out."

Eira made a surprised noise and lifted her brows.

"We're in a new city, for the first time in weeks we don't have any kind of stink, and our pockets are still heavy with Adela's gold." He grinned. "Why not go out?"

"We need to stay focused."

"On what?"

Agitation tugged on the corners of her lips at the question. "We need to ensure our ship will be cleared to sail when next we want. That it's properly repaired and restocked so we have all we need. And anything else we can do to ally ourselves with Qwint so they return to Meru's aide."

Eira counted on her fingers as she spoke, listing off everything she wanted to accomplish.

Cullen grabbed her fingers with an encouraging squeeze. "None of that will be done tonight. Except maybe getting some supplies, which won't be done here. We'll have to go out anyway."

"You can be stubborn, you know that?"

"I think you like me stubborn." He smirked, the fading light highlighting every bit of confidence Cullen wore in new ways that Eira realized she might not have fully appreciated before, if ever.

· CHAPTER ·

EIGHT

THE EVENING AIR brought with it a chill from the sea that cut through the humidity that clung to the city walls like graffiti. Eira relished in the brisk breezes. For a city so cramped, Qwint benefited greatly from its proximity to the ocean.

The group had divided themselves. Ducot, Crow, and Fen had decided to go to the markets down by the docks and scope out materials they might need for their ship. Eira had given them leeway to procure whatever they thought was necessary. She was still learning the ins and outs of running a ship and trusted Crow far more than herself to know what needed to be acquired for the next stage of their journey.

Lavette and Varren had gone off on their own to reunite with the other survivors of the tournament. Eira had briefly considered joining them, in a display of solidarity. But she ultimately decided that was a meeting that her presence would do more harm than good with. Eira knew just how illogical survivor's guilt could make someone. It would be all too easy for one of them to ask why she, a random woman from Solaris, was there in Qwint when their loved ones were not.

That left her, Cullen, Yonlin, Olivin, and Alyss to explore together. Lavette had given them a general direction that she recommended they go in and the rest was up to them.

Their footfalls echoed on the cobblestone streets, a drumbeat that pulsed underneath the cacophony of the market that they emerged into. It was a massive square containing all manner of stalls. Wares were laid within wooden cabinets positioned underneath wide awnings that were affixed to the sides of the buildings. Tents were set up in the center, creating a hazy maze of fabric and heat. They moved through the opulence, senses heightened, taking note of all there was to see, smell, and hear.

"I'm going to see if I can find a new journal," Alyss announced.

"Another?" Eira asked. "Didn't you get one in Black Flag Bay?"

"I did, but it is already full." A sheepish grin curved Alyss's mouth. "Besides, I think I'm about ready to begin writing the story itself."

"Oh? Am I to believe that we will no longer be used for research, then?"

"You will *always* be research." Alyss's grin was not encouraging. Eira kept her cringe inward, not wanting to discourage her friend. But it seemed to have failed because she erupted with laughter. "You know, some would be flattered to be immortalized."

"I'm sure some would be," Eira said dryly. "I'll let you know if I find anyone."

Alyss snorted. "Just think of what book two will look like."

"I've yet to even formulate my thoughts on book one."

"It'll be published soon enough."

Published. The word stuck with Eira but she couldn't quite figure out why. Of course she wanted that for her friend—wanted Alyss to succeed at all she set her mind to. But the notion of Alyss publishing felt…off, somehow.

As Eira was struggling to figure out why, Yonlin chimed in, "You know, I actually think we have friends of friends who owned printers in Risen. They focused more on the paper pamphlets of news." His eyes darted to Olivin, who nodded.

"Assuming they still exist." Olivin's words were soft and somber. Barely audible even to Eira, who stood next to him. There was real hurt in his softened gaze.

Yonlin either did not hear, or ignored it, because he quickly turned back to Alyss, even more eager. "But I'm sure they have information on the printers for books—if they couldn't do it themselves. And I think we might know some bookbinders, also…"

Their discussion trailed off as Yonlin and Alyss walked in the opposite direction. Eira didn't miss how Yonlin's hand seemed to drift awkwardly, twitching at times. As if he wanted to maybe link elbows with Alyss, or grab her hand, perhaps even put his palm on her hip. But couldn't decide which one. And probably didn't know if the gesture would be welcomed.

"My brother's hopeless." Olivin wore an amused expression, coming to a stop next to her. "He's never taken an interest in someone before. He lacks experience."

"As long as he doesn't hurt her." Eira was sure her tone did away with any notion that what she had with Olivin would prevent her from choosing Alyss if it ever came to that.

"He never would, not on purpose."

She agreed. Her defensiveness aside, Yonlin was a good man. Better than Olivin or Cullen was, honestly, which made him *slightly* worthy of Alyss. She couldn't stop a huff of amusement and a little smile. Alyss deserved only the best.

"What is it?"

"Thinking of how well-connected your family seems," she lied, rather than admitting to her real thoughts.

"We were one of the premier noble families…before Ulvarth." His eyes were filled with longing. Voice steeped in hate. "If my sister hadn't betrayed us, our lives would've been vastly different. We probably would've grown up in the queen's inner circle."

"Perhaps for the best you weren't." Eira linked her arm with Olivin's, tugging him away from the spot, and hopefully the memories of Queen Lumeria's box exploding at the end of the tournament.

"And why is that?"

"I can't imagine it'd go over well for a member of the 'queen's inner circle' to be close with a pirate." *Or engaging in piracy, for that matter.*

Olivin's eyes shone with amusement. "That's the nice thing about power, Eira. When you have it, you get to make the rules."

"And what rules would you make?"

He paused, an emotion almost akin to longing crossing his features. The question suddenly became much more serious than she intended. "When I was younger, I had a lot of feelings on how to make Meru a better place. Perhaps because I had been so betrayed by the leader of the Swords of Light—the people sworn to protect the Faithful of Yargen, and then felt so wronged in the aftermath, I was consumed by righteous indignation and composed a list of what I'd change if I could. It's what drew me to the Court of Shadows in the first place."

"Really?" Eira was surprised to realize they'd never talked much about his motivations behind joining the Shadows. She'd always assumed it was solely because of his need for vengeance against his sister, Wynry. And that likely was the case also. But not the only reason.

Olivin nodded. "Deneya suggested that my hate could be used to make something good. Not that I suppose any of it matters now, with Meru as it is. I doubt I'll be rubbing elbows with any nobles or royals any time soon."

"Take it from me, you're probably not missing much. Being close to royalty isn't all it's made out to be," Cullen chimed in, doubly surprising her. The two men were friendly with each other. But going out of their way to offer comfort or encouragement wasn't usually their manner.

"I'll take your word for it. Can't say I've ever had the opportunity." There was a note of finality in Olivin's tone that had the conversation moving on. But a question lingered in Eira's mind as they browsed the stalls.

Would you want it?

She remained the default leader, guiding them from one stall to the next. There was a natural ebb and flow between them. When one got too close, the other would respectfully step away. Suddenly fascinated by something else. Then, as the other neared, the first would back off. Eira was mindful not to show either of them too much favor. Things were still in a state of unknowns between the three of them.

The last time they had addressed their feelings, it had been left in a place of "we'll see" with both of them. An opportunity for her to explore and learn the pathways of her heart. Them aware of, and content with, the other. Then, they had gone to Carsovia and the mines had happened. Since then everything had been…

Eira paused.

The thought of Noelle had been what had originally stilled her. But now Eira's eyes snagged on a dagger laid out among several on a table toward the very back edge of the market. It wasn't anything overly fancy. Unadorned, really. But there was a small serpent etched into the pommel, coiled around a ruby so tiny that it looked like a drop of blood. Eira had seen these weapons up close in the mines of Carsovia. The guards all had them strapped to their waists.

"See something you like?" an unfamiliar voice said, startling her back to the present. A man with a shaved head leaned in the doorway behind the table, Eira was certain he hadn't been there when they'd walked up. The shadows seemed longer. More ominous as they clung to him. He was dressed in a similar style to Cullen—loose trousers, shirtless, a knitted scarf draped over his shoulders and chest. Lines were tattooed across his pale body in dark blue ink. They seemed to move like ribbons in the oscillating light of the market.

"Perhaps," Eira said noncommittally, returning her focus to the dagger she'd just been looking at. Hoping she was wrong, she allowed her magic to sink into the blade. She barely managed to conceal a flinch, instantly regretting the decision when a barked order and a scream echoed from a time before. Her fingertips rested on the edge of the table, frost spiking around them. "More curious as to why you have a dagger from the mines of Carsovia."

The moment the words left her lips Cullen and Olivin were on edge. The shifts in their stances were doubtless only perceptible to her.

The man merely smiled. "Call it a trophy. A memento of personal triumph."

"Triumph how?" A lot hinged on what he said next.

"Of using it against my oppressors."

"And you would part with it?" Eira still wasn't sure if she could take him at his word and kept her magic at the ready.

"No…" He plucked the weapon from the table, sheathing it. "Was merely waiting for it to catch the attention of the right buyer. Which it seems like you are."

"And why is that?"

"You strike me as someone who would enjoy using Carsovia's weapons against them. Come"—he gestured inside—"my best wares are inside."

Eira tapped the table in thought.

His pale eyes darted around, as if looking for anyone who might be too close. His voice dropped. "I assure you, the heir of the pirate queen will find my stock worthwhile."

She wasn't sure if she was more unnerved or curious. "I've no idea what you're talking about."

"Of course you don't."

Eira assessed him. He wasn't calling her Adela's daughter, but *heir*. Was that a guess based on Eira being Adela's daughter? A colloquial terminology? Or…was this man a pirate? Did he have some information and his coy yet careful wording was intended to lure her within so he could impart some information?

Or was he one of the rare less savory types that Lavette had warned them of? It was possible that he had identified them as potential targets being new to the city and was guessing based on the rumors that swirled at her arrival. Eira had certainly made a show of herself.

Only one way to find out.

"Sure, show me what you got." Eira shrugged as if it mattered little to her.

"Are you sure this is a good idea?" Cullen whispered under his breath, taking a step closer to her.

"I've weighed the risks." She ducked her head to hide her words as she followed Olivin around one end of the wares counter and back toward the opening. Even if there were people waiting to ambush them, Eira was confident that the three of them could handle themselves with little issue.

Eira had been expecting a trap at worst, an extension of the shop at best, but she was met by neither; rather, a dimly lit, one-room home. A hearth smoldered underneath a pot on a hook. A single table, two chairs. A bed. Everything was…simple. Of decent quality and make. But nothing like the lavishness that sprawled across Lavette's home.

"This way." The man pulled on a shelf in the back of the room. It slid to the side, revealing another doorway that he pushed through. That was a bit more suspect, and a bit more in line with what she'd been cautious about.

Olivin looked back to Eira and she gave him a nod of approval. They pressed on. Cullen remained close to her, taking up the rear. She could feel the tiny currents of air that swirled as he searched for anyone who'd come up behind them.

"Do you have a name?" Eira asked around Olivin's broad shoulders as the man led them up a stairway wedged between buildings, so steep it might as well be a ladder.

"Drogol," he answered without looking back. Instinct told her the name was real. It flowed easily off his tongue, but not without a moment's hesitation—as if he wasn't sure if he wanted to tell them. Perhaps he was a very good actor.

"Eira." She extended the same courtesy in reply.

"I know." They stopped on a landing between buildings, only big enough for Drogol and Olivin to stand on. Eira and Cullen were still behind on the stairs. "Your reputation precedes you."

"Lovely," Eira muttered under her breath. But she was finding she minded it less and less. If she was going to inherit Adela's fleet someday, then she should get intimately familiar with infamy.

Drogol led the three of them into a dark room. With a snap of his fingers, a lantern *popped* to life, casting an orange glow on the walls lined with all manner of weapons. There were swords and daggers, of course. A particularly impressive-looking crossbow. But, in the back, there was an entire wall of flashfires.

In the shine of the firelight, she was leagues away. She was back on a field of blood and flash shale smoke. There was a rider approaching, a knight of Carsovia drawing her flashfire.

Eira's attention swung, following the barrel of the weapon to meet a familiar pair of dark eyes.

"Save me," the specter of Noelle whispered. Each word was a dagger to Eira's heart. Her whole body fell under cold more brutal than the longest winter. More unforgiving than frostbite. "Eira…"

"Eira?"

Eira blinked. A bloody hole had been carved in Noelle's chest. A dribble of crimson ran down her lips as she whispered, "Why?"

That was the question, wasn't it? Why hadn't she been stronger? Been smarter? Why hadn't she been able to protect the ones she loved most? It was the question that gnawed a hole in her chest as wide as Noelle's, but nowhere near as bad. Never as bad. She had paid the ultimate cost for them all.

The specter opened her mouth once more. "Why—"

"Eira?"

She blinked again and the real world came back into focus. Olivin stood before her, illuminated on one half of his face by the dim lantern light. She swallowed thickly. The dagger had brought her mind to places she hadn't allowed herself to wander for weeks.

"Sorry," Eira muttered, and turned her focus back to the wall of weapons.

"It is an impressive collection, I know." Drogol was either legitimately oblivious, or very polite. Either way, Eira was grateful. "But there is one I think you will find the most interesting."

Drogol retrieved a key from around his neck and unlocked a

thin, wide drawer that he proceeded to pull out. There, lying on a bed of silk the color of Noelle's blood, was a flashfire smaller than any other Eira had seen. She took a step closer, assessing the weapon at a silent invitation by way of a wave of Drogol's palm.

The entire flashfire was smaller than her forearm. It had all the makings of its larger cousin—the usual flashfire that she'd seen wielded with one strong arm, or two hands in most cases. There was a wooden handle at one end, a rune that mirrored the same one imprinted on a small, silver ring set off to the side. There was a space for a small flash bead. However, unlike the other flashfires she'd seen and the ones on the wall, this had dozens of runes engraved down its steel barrel. Each one shone with a glint of power left entirely to the imagination.

"What is it?" Olivin asked for them.

"My master calls it a *pistol*," Drogol said proudly.

The name wasn't what stuck out to Eira. "Your master?"

"Yes, the woman you are going to rescue for me."

NINE

"**P**RESUMPTUOUS.**" EIRA FOLDED her arms, easing away from the weapons. However curious she might be, she didn't want to come off too eager and lose any leverage. Even if a part of her recoiled at the idea of using Carsovia's weapons, she knew better than to rule out a potential advantage over personal scars.

"I know why you are here." Drogol mirrored her movements and leaned against the case behind him, looking rather confident with himself. "The leadership of Meru has been decimated. Solaris is scrambling with a lone heir on the throne, no doubt inclined to turtle back into the Dark Isle they spent so long hiding on."

Meru's status was something she had assumed. But the confirmation was a good thing to have. The news on Solaris was somewhat surprising. *So Vi, Vhalla, and Aldrik Solaris had all perished in the blast at the coliseum?* That's what Drogol clearly believed, which meant it was a prevailing rumor. She was skeptical of that but Eira kept silent and allowed him to keep talking, grateful her companions followed her lead.

"Qwint is too nervous about Carsovia to get involved with the other nations again. They're too small, and outgunned, to fight a war on two fronts."

It was another suspicion of Eira's coming to pass. Qwint had involved themselves in the Treaty of Five Kingdoms for the sake of having an alliance that would make them look strong to their aggressive neighbors. But now that the treaty had dissolved, they risked retaliation on Carsovia's part for their boldness. That, combined with the inability to fight a war on two fronts, meant that Qwint wouldn't support Meru against the Pillars out of fear of Carsovia seizing it as an opportunity to strike while their forces were stretched thin.

"You're saying that without assurances or improvements in Qwint's military might, they won't be of any help to us," Eira summed up the point she assumed him to be guiding them to.

"You pick things up quickly." Drogol smirked.

"And this master of yours is going to help tip the scales in Qwint's favor," Eira continued voicing her assumptions when he didn't proffer any other information.

"Her name is Allun. She's a master of the runic arts. Her theories led to the creation of the pistol. A smaller flashfire, able to be held in one hand. But one that is so powerful it could tear through any magic force, any shield, any wall—even those reinforced by runes."

A tool that was likely to be invaluable to get to Ulvarth, when the time came. A tool that, when combined with Eira's natural inclinations and Adela's teachings, could make her unstoppable… especially if the crew—or Yonlin—could disassemble it and learn the machinations behind the magic.

Runic magic was still largely a mystery to her. She'd gathered the broad strokes from Lavette and Varren. But Carsovia seemed to have their own approach to the power, tangling with forces beyond the spinning bracelets of Qwint.

"Where is Allun?" Eira asked.

"Carsovia."

A wave of nausea crashed against the back of her throat at the word. At the implication that she was going to have to go back there. Eira swallowed hard and ignored the whispers in the back of her mind that sounded once more like Noelle.

"She had been making her way here, but unfortunately was intercepted in a distant town. She's too valuable to be kept there, though. Now that they know what—*who* she is, they'll move her to the golden city—the capital. While she's being transported you'll have an opportunity to liberate her."

"Does she *want* to be liberated?" Eira asked, remembering the woman in the mines who had been ready to turn Eira in for the opportunity to return to her old life serving the empress.

"Above all else, Allun is a magical scholar. Carsovia throttles her ambitions with their unending attempts to dictate what she should, and should not, pursue and how. She is not their tool; she is a marvel." Given his almost glassy-eyed endorsement of the woman, Drogol's loyalties couldn't be questioned. If he was telling the truth, she was certainly a force worth having on their side. "If you bring her here, Qwint will respect her talents. She will become their secret weapon—unbridled."

Ambition unbridled wasn't always a good thing. But the long-term ramifications of this would fall on Qwint, not her. It'd be up to them how they'd want to manage this new ally. But having such an ally could be the key to Eira getting what she needed—beyond a fancy pistol.

"So, how do we get to her?"

Olivin glanced at her from the corners of his eyes when she said this. But continued holding his tongue.

"That'll be made clear tomorrow morning when you are brought to the Hall of Ministers once more." Drogol pushed away from the case and closed the drawer, locking it. "Do this for me, and you'll not only get the first ever pistol, but you will also gain an ally that will be able to outfit your ships and crews for years to come."

Eira gave a slight nod and followed behind him, leading the three of them, as they left the secret back room of weapons. With a simple goodbye, Drogol left them at the doorway of his home, retreating into the shadows as they were once more engulfed by the bustle of the market.

The night air wafted through the chiffon curtains of her room. Eira's quarters at one point had been an office, but a large sofa served as a suitable bed. Not that she seemed to be able to use it for such.

She'd spent the better portion of the night pacing with a book in her hands. She was skimming as many of the tomes that Lavette's father had kept as she could, keen to learn all she could about Qwint. But even as she scanned the pages eagerly, her mind wandered elsewhere, time and again.

Eira returned the latest book to the shelf with a sigh and rubbed her eyes. Come morning, she'd task Alyss with the reading. The woman could get through a book, cover to cover, faster than Eira could read a couple chapters.

Tonight, her mind was too occupied with other questions that all revolved around who, exactly, was Drogol? Just a refugee from Carsovia looking to be reunited with his master? Or someone more? He seemed to know a lot about Eira…

She bit the nail of her thumb in thought.

He had to have accomplices. He'd already let it be known that he had allies in the Hall of Ministers pulling strings. But there had to be more. How else could he have known she was going to stumble upon his stall? No… Drogol hadn't left that to chance. There had to have been people hiding in plain sight in the market, guiding them back toward that secluded corner. It's what she would do if she had the means and intention of meeting someone.

Did he have a network? Only here on Qwint? Or perhaps beyond?

It made Allun seem all the more important.

A soft knock interrupted her thoughts. Eira was already on her way to the door so it only took a second for her to open it, revealing Cullen.

"I saw the light through the crack." He glanced down at their feet and then back up, somewhat expectantly. "May I come in?"

"Always." Eira wondered if he had been kept up thinking about the events of the evening, too.

Cullen closed the door behind him. "Are you all right?"

"I still can't decide on the extent of his network." She launched right into her theories, feet and hands moving as quickly as her hushed words. "Is he a pirate? Is he a double agent? But that pistol, if it's genuine, it could be invaluable to get to Ulvarth—we already know he has people who have skills in the runic magics. There was that mention of something about armor at the Hall of Ministers, also? Whether that's important or not, we shouldn't face him unprepared, and fighting runes with runes might be our best bet. I know going into Carsovia would be a risk, but it's a calculated—"

"It's not our fight," Cullen interrupted with a small step forward. "Carsovia, Qwint, they're not our fight."

"But—"

"Either you are a citizen of Solaris or a pirate. Neither is responsible for what happens here." Cullen closed the gap between them and rested his hands on her shoulders, sliding them down to her hands, lacing his fingers with hers. "I came to see how *you* are."

"It is our fight," Eira objected, pointedly ignoring the second half. "Anything that can help us bring down Ulvarth is our fight."

"I want to take him down as much as you do—so let's go and get him and not waste any more time here. Qwint will do as it pleases. Your place is on the seas."

The thought had crossed Eira's mind. That any portion of their excursion here beyond dropping off Lavette and Varren and restocking was a waste of time. But…

"I want to use Qwint as a distraction on Meru, when the time comes," she admitted, barely more than a whisper. "If we can get them to stay aligned with Solaris and any remnants of Meru's leadership, then the three nations can make a focused attack on Ulvarth's forces, engaging them and drawing their focus. If we can coordinate it for when we arrive at Risen—"

"The chaos that ensues will give you time to maneuver into Ulvarth's inner circle," Cullen realized.

Eira nodded. "Ulvarth's eyes will be on them, while I'm focused on him."

Cullen squeezed her fingers, looking down at their interlocked hands. "Regardless, I don't think you should return to that place."

"I'll be all right," she assured him gently. "Qwint won't help Solaris without the additional support of Allun—assuming she's that good. They'll need some assurance to divide their forces."

"You are strong enough with just Solaris and Meru," Cullen encouraged.

"I appreciate your faith." She genuinely did. "But if I am to end this, I need to do all I can to stack the deck in my favor."

His eyes searched her face. She could see him chewing over his words with the tension in his jaw.

"Eira… I saw you in that back room, the moment you saw the flashfires." The instant he said those words, Eira wanted to withdraw her hands from his as if she could withdraw from her weaknesses. "If we are to use Qwint to achieve our goals, then let us. But I don't think it should be at the expense of your well-being."

"The only thing that matters for my well-being is seeing Ulvarth dead." She tried to pour every bit of spite into the words so he knew just how serious she was.

"That's not true."

"But it is." She locked eyes with his, not looking away. Unflinching. Unyielding. "All I care about is ending him."

"Eira, you are many, *many* things—don't sacrifice them all merely for the sake of bringing down Ulvarth." There was a hint of caution, and sorrow, to his words.

"I'm not backing away from this fight." If she did, how could she ever claim to be worthy of Adela's legacy?

"Nor should you," Cullen said hastily. "But…"

"But?" she encouraged when it was clear he was going to leave the notion hanging.

"You have so much around you. Be a pirate. Go sailing. Make the world yours. Why bother with these political schemes?" His words were gentle, almost timid, as if he were afraid he'd scare her from the conversation if he pushed too hard. He was right. Yet he persisted anyway.

"Rich of you to suggest ignoring political schemes."

"I changed." Cullen shrugged.

She couldn't argue that… "I'll have time to terrorize the seas under Adela's banner later. Ulvarth comes first."

"If you sacrifice all you are simply for the sake of ending him, then he still wins."

"Noelle sacrificed all she was."

"That wasn't because of Ulvarth—"

"If not for him, we wouldn't have been there." Eira pulled her hands from his, turning away from Cullen—from the truth she'd so readily ignored. *If not for him, I wouldn't have pushed us so hard. Noelle would still be alive*, were the words that burned her lips, ignited by the fire consuming her chest. Ulvarth had claimed her brother. Her friend. And countless others. "My mind is made up. I'm doing this, no matter what."

"Then…just know what you're willing to sacrifice."

"Everything," she said without hesitation.

"Everything?" he repeated in disbelief. "Your place with Adela, sailing freely? Your friends? Us?"

"Everything," she repeated. But this time she was slightly less confident, though she didn't let it show in her voice or posture. In the following silence, Eira slowly turned, looking over her shoulder.

There was that expression again, that wounded look. That heartbreak. What else could he expect? He had been there when Noelle died. He knew that the blame ultimately came to Eira, and Ulvarth, and the deadly web she'd ensnared them all in by getting roped in through Ferro now years ago.

"She wouldn't have wanted that," Cullen whispered. "She would've wanted you to go on and live freely."

The words stung. *He means well*, Eira reminded herself to keep from lashing out in reply. She gathered herself, allowing the conversation to wither on the vine in silence. Then, she calmly said, "As long as Ulvarth draws breath, I will never be free. Now, goodnight, Cullen."

"Eira—" He moved for her.

"Goodnight." She stood her ground.

Cullen froze, searched her face one last time, opened and shut his mouth, then left without another word.

She cursed under her breath and ran a hand through her hair. What he was asking of her—suggesting… She couldn't just leave this be. To not do everything in her power to bring down Ulvarth, no matter the cost, would be an insult to Noelle and Marcus. It would forever be a stain on her own legacy to allow her enemies to thrive. Adela certainly wouldn't. If it were Adela, she'd freeze Ulvarth and all who harbored his ilk and hold them as eternal statues as a warning to the world. Eira couldn't simply sail away like Cullen suggested. How could she inspire fear in anyone ever again if she did?

"He doesn't understand." Olivin stole the words directly from her mind. Eira whirled in place. He leaned against the doorway that Eira had opened to let in the cool night air. She hadn't even heard a whisper of his presence. Though, that shouldn't surprise her. Olivin was a better Shadow than she had ever been. "He can't. He hasn't lost like you and I have."

Eira gave a slight nod. Part of her agreed. But she'd seen Cullen's distant stare after finding no word of his father. Felt his pain, as palpable as her own, following Noelle. Before that, even, he'd lost the identity he'd built around himself like an impenetrable fortress.

He'd lost, hadn't he? It just looked different… Yet, she couldn't get the words out before Olivin spoke again.

"Sorry for listening in." Olivin pushed away from the door and took a step into the room. "I had been coming to visit you, seeing as every room is connected by way of the balcony and

Yonlin snores…and I promised you I'd find some time alone with you."

Eira huffed lightly in amusement at the implication of *that*.

"He was already here when I approached and, well…" Olivin shrugged, not looking guilty in the slightest.

Eira sighed. "It's fine. There wasn't anything particularly intimate about that conversation."

"Are you often intimate with him?" Olivin paused his movements. He was impossible to read.

"Is that jealousy?" Her tone was playful but she genuinely sought the answer. If it was, then her time to explore options was coming to an end.

"Hardly. Nothing more than curiosity." Olivin seemed genuine enough. Eira relaxed.

"I'm intimate with him when it pleases me," Eira answered somewhat coyly. Then her tone turned serious once more. "He knows me, parts of me from my past that are even hard for me to explain or understand now, as the woman I am."

Olivin shrugged and stepped forward. "I care little for who knows your past; what I want to know is your future." He took another step. Suddenly, the distance between them was compressed into almost nothing. His sharp blue eyes never left hers. Every movement was graceful, almost deadly. "A future that I still want to be a part of."

"Is that so?" Eira pointedly asked. "And what does this future look like?"

Olivin's palm landed on her face, firm. Demanding with only a touch. "Paradise. Revelries and power. A new world order beyond simply sailing wherever the wind blow us. We will be the headwind, the north star, the aspiration and the envy."

"I could grow accustomed to power." Eira tilted her head, looking up through her lashes.

"You should be well accustomed as it is, given your might." There was nothing but admiration in his eyes.

"It's not enough." To defeat Ulvarth, she still needed to become so much more.

"Then I look forward to seeing what you will become." Olivin's arm snaked around her waist, his scent and heat overwhelming. The way he looked at her now crashed upon her like the hottest day of summer, the temperature of her core rising. Nearly unbearable. "I will have you, if you'll let me."

"I am yours for the taking."

No sooner had she whispered the words, he spun her, pushing her up against a bookcase. One hand on her waist, his hips pressing against hers. The other on her face, thumb dragging across her lips before he claimed them and the rest of the world vanished, taking her former worries with it. It was like the first gasp after emerging from beneath the waves. It was a *crack* that ripped through her body, trembling through her. He kissed her deeply, passionately, as if trying to scare away all the panicked thoughts that had threatened to consume her for weeks.

Escape with me, every shift of his mouth seemed to whisper. *Let me take you far from here—far from your body.*

Eira's muscles relaxed and she eased farther into him. Without warning, he pulled away, looking right through her. A sly smirk slid across his lips. Perhaps…she had been the one to say those words—to think them, will them into existence.

"Eira—"

"I don't want to be able to walk straight, never mind speak or think," she whispered, words ragged.

"Good."

Hands frantic, clothing suddenly far too cumbersome for either of their liking, they grabbed and pulled until there was nothing left that would keep them apart. Olivin pushed her up, her rear sliding over the wide counter-shelf a third of the way up the bookcase. He traced her lips with his fingers, then the outlines of her curves.

Tremors rippled through her in anticipation. Her skin flushed. The space between them collapsed with a gasp that wrapped into a moan. This was it…what she'd been waiting for. That blissful mindlessness that smothered all other worries and fears.

For the rest of the night, Eira allowed herself to trade her worries for passion, escaping the thoughts that continued to gnaw a hole in her chest, unbidden.

WHEN MORNING BROKE, she was alone. Olivin's absence didn't sting and she spent her entire time dressing for the day wondering if it should. Wondering if it meant anything that it didn't.

Their evening activities had been good. She'd wanted— needed it. Satisfying like a well-earned meal. Now she was full, and could focus on the day.

Which led her back to Qwint's hall of government.

Eira followed Lavette down the hallway between the rings of chairs that led to the center of the Hall of Ministers. Her other friends had been relegated to the balcony mezzanine that circled the room. Fortunately, so far as she could tell, her parents weren't in attendance. Eira wasn't sure if she'd ever see them again and was oddly comfortable with the notion. She genuinely could wish them well while simultaneously not ever needing them again.

Lavette exuded confidence. Eira suspected that, unlike her own appearance, Lavette's was genuine. She had nothing to fear here.

Eira, on the other hand…her fate, and the fate of her friends, of Meru and possibly this whole swath of the world, was about to be decided.

The center of the room was bathed in dawn's muted glow. It cast everything in a gray, almost somber tone.

Dozens of eyes were fixated on her, above and below. Some had mild curiosity, others didn't even bother to expend effort to hide their disapproval. Eira took a breath as she moved into position on a steel ring that circled before the lowest rung of chairs, but outside the circular pedestal where the three head ministers stood—Morova among them. Lavette had given her a primer on what to expect, but that didn't stop her from feeling somewhat like she was on trial once more.

The bell behind her chimed.

"We call this meeting of the Hall of Ministers into session," High Minister Uhn said. Eira's snooping in Lavette's late father's office last night had served her well in offering the broad strokes of people and positions. "The first matter is brought before us by Morova."

As the last echoes of the elderly man's voice faded, Morova stepped forward.

"I bring forward a matter on behalf of my niece, Lavette D'astre. I yield my time to her to present her case."

Lavette stepped before Eira with confidence. Every movement seemed practiced and trained. When she spoke, it was without a second of hesitation.

"Eira Landan has come to us from distant shores. She went to Meru as a champion of Solaris. Then she survived the Pillar's bloody uprising. She has sailed from Meru to Carsovia, and now here, all to return myself and another of Qwint's champions. Her mission is to unite the peoples of the world's edge together once more in a common cause." Lavette's words were part factual and part inspirational, already trying to compel others to their cause. And judging from some of the faces, she was doing a good job of it. "Carsovia has backed the force on Meru that was behind the attack on the tournament. It is because of them that our friends, family—our brothers and sisters in democracy were lost. She sees our aid. A force to join Solaris, and the remnants of Meru to expunge those behind this coup and regain the treaty we fought so hard for."

"And tell me," a man interjected, standing, "why should we care about a coup on Meru?"

"If Meru should fall—or become a puppet to Carsovia—then we are surrounded on all sides by a hostile force. How long will it be, then, until they turn their eyes to us?" Lavette retorted without missing a beat.

After the matter is brought to the hall, there will be open debate. It's free-flowing, so long as it's kept orderly. During this time, you can walk along the steel ring that surrounds the center, but step nowhere else, Lavette had instructed her before they entered.

"Carsovia is already knocking on our door," a woman said. "Lavette is right. Do we want to risk having two fronts?"

"You always were courting the favor of the D'astres, Sahm. Tell us, who owns the land your manor is built on?" another jabbed.

Sahm bristled. "That is hardly relevant, Orloth."

"Oh, I think it is," he retorted.

The bell rang behind Eira and they silenced. "Let us focus on the matter at hand," Uhn said with a scolding note.

"I do not seek aid that you cannot give." Eira took the opportunity to interject her voice. "A single ship, a small but mighty force that can join with the remnants of Meru's army and Solaris's forces. I have seen firsthand the extent of Qwint's magics. It will not take many from among you to be formidable."

"As you have aptly taken note of, we are a small city-state. While, yes, we do possess our strengths, those strengths must be kept for ourselves and the benefit of our peoples. We have little and less to spare," Orloth countered.

"Which I assume is precisely the reason why you sought the aid of the treaty to begin with." Eira wasn't going to be thrown off, or dissuaded. "I spent the first half of the evening yesterday admiring your city." She began to walk along the lower circle slowly, addressing the entire room, everyone, all the way up to the balcony. As subtly and slowly as the incoming tide, she allowed her magic to flow across the room, lapping against jackets and shoes, listening in the back of her mind. "Your buildings are breathtaking. Artistry stunning. Your naval fortifications are—

and I assure you this is not empty flattery—the best I have witnessed in this world.

"But you know what I did not see?" She paused for emphasis. "Fertile farmlands. Mountains rich with resources to mine. Trees to fell for lumber to build your houses and warm them through the winter."

"Those magics you so praised can make a little in resources go a long way." Orloth was positioned behind her now.

"If you had enough, you wouldn't have joined the treaty in the first place." She barely spared him a glance over her shoulder.

A purse of his lips was his only retort. But there were other murmurs. She knew she was risking their offense with that remark. But it was worth it to strike at the heart of the matter.

"The Solaris Empire has been building its armada—a fleet that is still strong and free of the Pillars' influence. A fleet that will join our cause and could ferry all those resources you need from the lands of Solaris." Eira folded her hands before her, standing a little taller. She allowed an authoritative tone to creep into her voice, giving her words weight. "I am not asking for charity. I am proposing a deal."

"And how will we know Solaris will keep its side of the bargain?" someone else asked.

Eira lifted her eyes. *Don't hate me for this,* she half hoped, half silently begged. Her gaze landed on Cullen. His eyes widened a fraction.

"I sail with a noble lord of the Solaris Court, the first Windwalker returned, favored by the Empress Solaris herself. He will have the ear of the Solaris senate, the people, *and* the Imperial family, whatever remains of it."

Eira had been expecting Cullen to resent her. This whole time, he had been trying to escape the trappings and expectations of his nobility. And here she was, pulling him back to it. Demanding that he wear the mask and take on the mantle.

But, instead, an expression of raw determination overtook

him. There was fire in his eyes, contrasting with a slight but confident smile. His chin dipped. *I will*, the movement said.

She brought her eyes back to the hall, more determined than ever.

"And, if not Solaris, then Meru will be forever in your debt. There is no way Qwint doesn't succeed," Eira finished.

"Unless your attempt to overthrow the coup fails," Orloth said bitterly. Murmurs followed his response.

"Minister, if we fail in unseating Ulvarth, then Carsovia has won and you face not one but two fronts as you so feared," Eira said gravely, framing the circumstances in a way that would matter most to all of them. "Helping me—helping Meru and Solaris is the only way for Qwint to come out ahead."

Silence fell over the grand chamber. In the hush, Eira's magic snagged on a familiar voice.

She's going to do it, said the echo of Drogol. *Expect her tomorrow.*

Eira's attention landed on a woman. She gave the unfamiliar minister a pointed, knowing stare. There was expectation in it. Recognition flashed in the minister's eyes. Then, a brief, impressed rise of her brow. The woman slowly stood, as if she had been waiting for Eira to find her among the crowd—as though finding her had been some kind of lingering test for Eira to prove herself and her magic.

The subtle expression on the woman's face faded as if it were never there at all.

"I think what my fellow ministers are trying to say is…how do we know we can trust *you*?" Her voice was steady, a stark contrast to the murmurs and nods. "You want us to have our ship follow yours, into waters where Adela sails, to certain danger that awaits on Meru. *You*, a woman who has been rumored to be associated with Adela herself, want us to follow your orders blindly."

"I am not—" Eira wasn't given the opportunity to get in an objection. The murmurs had given way to outright whispers that carried all the way to the balcony. Skepticism was threatening to crumple the house of cards Eira had been building her hopes upon. Wasn't this woman supposed to be helping her? Unless hindering her was its own help. An invitation. "Then perhaps I could pass some sort of test?"

"A test?" another minister chimed in. The woman was silent, with an expectant stare.

"Surely there is some task I can perform that would prove both my trustworthiness and lend aid to Qwint?" Eira hoped she wasn't being too obvious.

"My fellow ministers, perhaps she is right. Is it not true that what we fear is weakness before Carsovia?" The woman gestured to the room and was met with nods of agreement. Though a fair amount of confusion at where her final point rested. "I would propose we send the young woman into Carsovia to weaken them. Let her be the one to compensate for the defenses we shall lose by sending forces to aid Meru."

"You mean to send a *child* into Carsovia?" Sahm bristled.

"Minister, I assure you that I am *not* a child," Eira couldn't stop herself from saying. Let them be skeptical of her alliances, but not her abilities. "I have infiltrated Carsovia once before and lived to tell the tale. I am more than capable of bringing back whatever it is you need."

"Good." Drogol's ally smiled thinly. "At the same time, we can send a small vessel to Solaris. We shall not follow Eira's commands to their letter, but make our own path. In this way, we can independently test Solaris's willingness to align with us— send back their citizens, too. It will earn goodwill and be less mouths for us to feed."

Nods and murmurs of agreement blanketed the assembly.

"This lord of hers can write us a letter. If she speaks true of him, then they can verify her claims—further proving that she can be trusted. Vote yes to my plan, my fellow ministers, and we shall know where Solaris stands, verify Eira's loyalty, and gain new weapons in the process. We will not send any more resources until we have confirmed Eira can be trusted. At the worst, we shall only lose a little bit of time and a fast ship."

"It is…a suitable proposal," another agreed after a long minute of contemplative silence.

"Worth considering."

"*If* she can be successful."

"But what do we lose if she's not? Not much."

"Is it worth risking at all? I've my doubts in the woman—look at her."

The gauntlet was thrown at her feet. The challenge made. All Eira had to do was rise to it.

"It was me and my crew that brought down the flash bead mines of Carsovia," Eira spoke above the rising murmurs and mumbles. "I am no stranger to trials; I outright welcome them. They were what started me on this journey, and they shall no doubt be the last that I conquer. Give me this opportunity to prove myself and my skill. If my loyalty is what you seek, then I will give it to you with abundance."

"Then let us call this matter to vote," Morova said. "All those abstaining?" A speckling of white paddles. Not many. "Those against?" Five, maybe seven of the fifty paddles. "And those for?"

A sea of green answered her last question.

Eira stood taller, shoulders squared. She was going back to Carsovia.

A SMALL GROUP STOOD before the wall at the western edge of Qwint. It was the same wall that wrapped around the entirety of the city in a protective embrace. From the ground, Eira realized once more just how imposing the structure was. It was twice as impressive as any of the towering buildings in the heart of Qwint. She hadn't fully appreciated just how fortified it was when she'd entered the city by sea, given the circumstances of her entry.

The group was an assembly of familiar faces, new acquaintances, and men and women whose names Eira hadn't bothered to learn. Lavette and Yonlin stood off to one side behind them with the contingent of ministers who had regarded them warmly—even who had gone out of their way to escort them from the front door of Lavette's building. Opposite them were a group of ministers who looked far more skeptical. They were here to see if Eira got cold feet, no doubt. Drogol's ally was among them. Knights that fanned before them.

Of all the people present, Eira, Cullen, Olivin, Alyss, Yonlin, and Ducot were the ones who were prepared to venture forth. They all had a pack of essentials weighing down their shoulders.

"Three days," Morova reminded them for what was the tenth, maybe fifteenth, time. "Based on our intelligence, Carsovia will be moving their prisoners now, which means they will cross through the main road just west of here in one to two days. That will be—"

"Our best chance," Eira finished with a determined nod. Drogol's ally had worked her magic on the Hall of Ministers after

Eira had left, securing their mission to focus on retrieving Allun. "Our supplies will last only three days," she echoed something else they had told her. Though, Eira suspected they could make a fourth day stretch, if they had to. "We'll be back in time."

"We will only open the door on the dawn of the fourth day, so do ensure that you are," Drogol's ally said curtly.

Eira gave a slight dip of her chin.

Their goodbyes were brief; most of the parting had happened the night before, along with their planning.

Fen would be taking the ministers to Solaris. He knew the Shattered Isles and Adela's routes within them—he could avoid her so there were no unfortunate crossing of paths. And if they did happen upon the pirate queen, Fen could ensure that they made it out alive.

Crow might be a better choice for coercing Adela, given how close she was with the pirate queen. But it was precisely because of that proximity that Eira wanted Crow watching over their ship in the harbor. It had been relinquished from Qwint's control, but Eira knew that it wouldn't take much for the ministers to decide to reclaim it. And, should that happen, Eira trusted Crow to do what was necessary to keep their vessel safe.

As for Lavette, she was going to stay as their eyes and ears with the ministers. Varren wasn't about to leave her side…especially not to return to Carsovia. And none of them were about to ask him to do anything otherwise.

The farewells were brief. When Eira shifted from giving Crow hasty reminders, Lavette took her hand. Without warning, she pulled Eira close, arms going around her shoulders, holding her tightly. Eira hadn't thought they were the sort to share tearful embraces, but—

"They're telling you three days, but you have two," she whispered hastily. "I heard rumors of it this morning. They'll move to deem you dead before full time is up. I'll stall as I'm able. Be early."

"Thank you." That was all the gratitude Eira could offer for the warning. If they clung to each other much longer it'd look suspicious.

"This way." The leader of the knights before them gestured with a nod of his head and guided them toward the wall.

The rest of them stayed back at the city's edge, watching as they ventured into the strip of barren earth between the vertical buildings and steep wall. No architect dared to venture too close. No citizen would consider living within a breath of Carsovia's border. It was as if the earth itself was poisoned.

An arm snaked through hers. Alyss took a step closer.

"We have to do this," Alyss whispered. Though, Eira didn't know if the solemn reminder was for her, or if Alyss spoke for herself. Eira tensed her bicep and Alyss's eyes swung her way.

Eira inhaled sharply. Somehow, in a breath, she saw Noelle standing there. Looking up at her, questioning that unending wondering.

Why?

"We're going to be fine," Eira whispered to Alyss. "*All* of us." *I'm not about to lose another friend.*

"I know," Alyss mouthed more than spoke. She dared a brave smile. But it didn't reach her eyes. "It's just another thing to get over with."

"And we'll be stronger for it."

"One of these days, I'll have enough strength and won't need it tested." Alyss laughed softly. "I'd be fine if that day came sooner over later."

Rather than guiding them through the formidable steel gates that dominated the sheer face of the wall, the knights led them to the side. The one in charge rotated his bracelets, glancing back at them, as if resenting them for making him share this secret. Pursing his lips, he snapped his fingers, and the stone rippled and redesigned itself, retreating like a curtain to reveal a narrow stair that led down beneath the wall.

"Carsovia always has knights trained on the gate," the knight explained as they descended into the darkness. Eira drew in a breath, about to ask Noelle for light. Instead, the air burned her lungs, the question unasked, as a glyph flickered into existence over Olivin's shoulder. "The moment it opens, they'll strike."

The stairs ended at a landing, barely large enough for all of them to cram into. Opposite the last stair was a dark hole, a single steel rung of a ladder glinting in the light of Olivin's glyph.

"Down that way. There's only one passage. You'll go down before up again. Be careful with your magic; you don't want them to sense you." The knight stepped back onto the stairs, paused, and glanced over his shoulder. "Good luck." With that minimal encouragement, the knight left them, starting back up the stairs, as if he were all too ready to leave them behind.

"Shall we?" Eira looked to the start of the ladder.

"I'll go first," Alyss offered. "That way if we're in a real pinch, I can sort the stone."

"You heard him about magic." Olivin glanced at his small, spinning glyph.

"I'm not going to let us—" Alyss stopped short. "I won't let us die. We'll be careful, but safe."

"I'll take up the rear, then," Ducot said. "My magic is more of a blunt tool than yours, but it'll work in a pinch."

They were more words than Eira had heard from him in weeks. Perhaps having a mission was what they all needed. Especially when that mission involved an opportunity to fight against Carsovia once more.

Had they taken on this task truly because they had to, or because they were all ready for any excuse to fight? The question followed her down into the depths. That was one of the many bright spots to her future with Adela. There would always be a distraction whenever she needed one so long as she kept pushing forward.

The deep tunnels started out narrow and condensed into suffocating. The air was thick and stale, a poignant blend of earth, the sweat that rolled off them, and lingering dread from whatever poor souls had slowly carved out this place with pickaxes. Each of the walls bore the scars of their labors: toiling in the dark, using physical effort over magical for fear of discovery.

"Brace yourselves," Alyss whispered, somehow sounding both near and far at the same time. Sound played oddly off the damp walls. "Narrow, here."

Even with the warning, the tunnel condensing around Eira threatened to squeeze out her breath. It was as if the earth had swallowed them whole, gulping them down past one jagged wall at a time. Yonlin's ragged breathing was the first sign of the panic that was beginning to thread through them.

"Yonlin."

Eira looked over her shoulder, the worry in the way Olivin said his brother's name sparking fear within her. *Something was wrong.*

"Yonlin," Olivin whispered, hastier than the last.

It was almost impossible to see Yonlin with how narrow the cave had become. He was on the other side of Olivin and the long shadows that the glyph cast almost completely obscured him.

"Yonlin, what is it? What's wrong?" Olivin's panic rose in time with his brother's ragged and hasty breaths.

"Dark… Small…" Yonlin rasped. "No way…out."

The words struck Eira at her core. In that second, she understood.

"Alyss, widen the cavern," Olivin demanded.

"But the magic…" Alyss was understandably uncertain.

"Alyss—" Olivin's tone was so harsh it was almost a growl.

"Yonlin," Eira interrupted him. She still couldn't quite see the young man. But his hasty breaths continued, every exhale filling the passage with hot panic. "Yonlin," Eira repeated, a little louder.

A sharp inhale, a pause. Eira slid her hand across the wall, wedging it between the rock and Olivin's stomach. He tried to move to give her space, but there was nowhere to go. Even her level head was threatened by the reminder of just how tight the passage was. How long they'd been still. The claustrophobic heat from just their bodies made her dizzy.

"Yonlin," she said again, her hand breaking through flesh and rock to make it to the other side. Stone pressed into her wrist, sending pins and numbness up the length of her arm. "Here."

He sucked in air and didn't immediately exhale. Eira held her breath, too, stretching as far as she could. Some shifting. Two fingers brushed against hers and Eira hooked them as though she were his only lifeline—afraid that if she let him go now, he would be lost to them.

The golden light of Olivin's glyph reflected off of two eyes that turned to her. Eira could only see one, but she focused on it with the same intensity with which she still hooked his fingers.

"You're not there." She emphasized every word and all the other unsaid meanings that were wedged between them. "They don't have you anymore. And they never will ever again."

His breathing leveled and his fingers squeezed hers in return.

"I have you—*we* have you. You're safe."

"Thank you." His words were barely audible.

"You can do this," she reassured him before withdrawing.

"Eira?" Alyss asked.

"We're fine. Press on." Eira confidently spoke for Yonlin. She could confidently surmise what he was feeling—a potent mix of misplaced shame and heady determination.

After what felt like an eternity, the tunnel opened up once more. The covert passage was long and tedious, but safe. So none of them were in any hurry to rush the process. The faint echoes of their footfalls were in chorus with the *plops* of water.

They reached the end. It was a curve of stone that the faintest glint of pale sunlight ran along the edge of. One last, narrow zigzag of passage and they'd be out. Back into enemy territory.

"ALYSS, THE SLIGHTEST bit of magic, just to see if someone is on the other side," Eira whispered, not daring to raise her voice louder than necessary.

With a nod, Alyss crept to the opening. She sidestepped halfway into it. A ripple of magic whispered across Eira's senses, barely there, and only perceivable because she knew to look for it.

Alyss disappeared around the bend. They collectively held their breath. Another flutter of magic. Alyss shuffled back.

"So far as I can tell, we're alone." Even though she sounded confident, she still kept her voice down. Probably because of what she said next. "I can only sense in the immediate area though without using more magic."

"I'll scout ahead," Olivin offered. "Being a Shadow gave me practice at keeping hidden without magic."

The tunnel had opened up enough that Olivin could squeeze by the rest of them. Even though it wasn't the time, or place, Eira didn't have complete control over her body's reaction to his being pressed against her once more. The smell of his skin alit memories of the night they shared. A flush burned between her collarbones, threatening to rise to her cheeks if she didn't keep it under control.

But Eira managed.

He was past her, and the rest, and out of the tunnel. By the time she firmly had control over her thoughts, he had returned.

"Everything seems clear," he whispered. "There's some behind us—watching the wall, just as the soldiers of Qwint told us—but none ahead that I can see. They must feel pretty confident their 'insignificant' neighbor wouldn't dare be sending anyone into their territory."

"Onward, then." Eira nodded to Alyss, who led them out. "Ducot, ride up on a shoulder." Without a word he pulsed into his mole form and scurried up Yonlin's leg, causing the other man to squirm. "Olivin, help me with an illusion."

"Trying to make this many invisible will use a good deal of magic," he cautioned.

"It's all right if it's not perfect, just enough that we won't be obvious."

He nodded and followed after Alyss, the rest of them behind.

The moment she stepped into the sunlight, Eira balled her hand into a fist with a sigh of frost. *No tells,* the Adela that lived in her mind scolded. Eira relaxed her fingers, but not her magic. She focused on keeping it wound tight to them—no sudden surges that could alert the knights behind them.

Their enemies were perched on top of the hill that they had just emerged from, none the wiser that the very people they were watching for were right behind them. Carsovia had entrenched themselves. A few small, earth-bermed shelters were constructed right into the hillside. An endless rotation of sleeping and keeping guard.

A thin copse of trees surrounded them. It was minimal coverage for prying eyes so Eira was grateful for their illusions, however slight they were.

She navigated to Alyss, resting a hand gently on her friend's shoulder and leaning in to whisper, "Keep a trail, we'll have to come back this way."

"Already ahead of you," Alyss murmured in reply.

"This is why I keep you around." Eira squeezed her shoulder.

"I can think of a few other reasons I make myself useful." It was nice to hear the confidence in her friend's tone. Eira knew Alyss's reservations. Her fears were reasonable. But there wasn't time to look back or question. Their only path was ahead.

They progressed through the thin woods. Much like the first time Eira had ventured into Carsovia, she was overwhelmed by the eerie sense of just how *empty* it all was. They walked for nearly three hours before seeing their first structure—a small farmhouse settled among the slowly flattening land that they had been descending through. The building itself wasn't anything special. But what it did have was people and a road that cut through the fields, tall with crops, leading toward no doubt more civilization.

Taking a moment to catch their breath, they studied the maps that Lavette and Varren had gone over with them, ultimately determining that this was the outer fringe of a town called Calsveil. There was some debate over the best next steps. Cullen suggested they swing wide. Eira disagreed, prompting them to continue. Alyss offered to cover their tracks through the fields, but that would be slow, and exhausting for her. The best path was the fastest, and least conspicuous…but also the most dangerous:

The road.

There wasn't any more discussion as they donned the cloaks and other clothing that had been given to them back in Qwint. The unique combination of colors had been chosen with care— mostly drab. *Don't stand out, don't seem too lowly. Just exist*, was hopefully what the clothing said.

Eira led them out of the woods and onto the dirt path that circled the farm. She almost paused at where it joined with the actual road. Would it look too obvious that they were emerging from the woods? What if this was another knight stronghold, only made to look like an unassuming farmhouse to lure anyone from Qwint into a false sense of security?

No… She kept her feet moving. *People were trying to get from Carsovia to Qwint, not the other way around.* The knights were watching Qwint's gates for signs of an attack, or other intelligence—signs of pathways like the one they took. They might seem a bit strange wandering from that direction, but Eira trusted that anyone who saw them would come up with some explanation that wasn't an infiltration group from Qwint.

Her theories, and hopes, were put to the test when they crossed paths with the owner of the small house, situated out front, sharpening a tool of his trade. He gave them a small but friendly greeting. Eira worked to return it, but she was sure their awkwardness was evident by how stiff their movements were. Yet whatever he thought of them wasn't enough to stop them or raise any other alarm. So they kept moving.

The hours passed them by like the fields around them. Monotony was their newest companion, keeping pace with nervousness and dread. Each house was much the same as the last. Every field grew one of the same three crops. And none of them seemed very keen on talking.

All the while, Cullen regarded everything with a far-off stare. Even though the crops were nothing like the rolling fields of wheat she'd heard described in the East, she had to imagine this was something like his homeland, a place he hadn't returned to since he'd Awoken and destroyed an entire town. She couldn't stop herself from slowing her pace and angling her steps, coming up to his side.

The backs of her knuckles brushed against his and Cullen's head snapped in her direction, wide-eyed. Eira didn't know if he thought there was some kind of threat she was alerting him to. Or, if he realized he'd been caught—that she'd seen that distant and haunted gaze.

Eira offered him a small smile. His expression relaxed some. With a twist of her fingers, her knuckles slid between his.

Cullen squeezed her hand in reply and released. Eira saw the appreciation, and understood the dismissal. He wanted to be left to his thoughts, and that was all right. For now, at least.

The motion brought back the sensation of Yonlin from earlier. Eira stared at her empty hand. A rough patch on her wrist, forever scarred from the shackles of the pit. There were the ghosts of burns from the fires of the coliseum when she hadn't had her magic to protect her. Tiny scars lined her fingertips from prying the flash shale out of the mines. Each one so minuscule that they'd be missed at a glance. But Eira could read them like a book.

They all carried the stories of their lives so far inked in scars both seen and unseen. Wounds that would never quite heal. Breaks that couldn't be mended by magic—only time.

Yet, these scarred hands could still be held on to. They could still pull someone back from the brink of succumbing to ghosts. But…they hadn't been enough to pull her friend from the arms of Death.

Balling her hand into a fist, Eira squeezed away the thoughts. When she relaxed, there was nothing left of them…save for a whisper on the wind that sounded like Noelle's voice asking, *Why?*

The sun was burning the edges of the horizon, illuminating the silhouette of a large town, or small city, in the distance—Calsveil, undoubtedly.

"That's where we're going, right?" Yonlin asked. He had one of the best senses of direction among them, save for Alyss. The two had been navigating in tandem all afternoon.

"Let's hope so, otherwise we've gone wildly off course," Eira said.

"Into the city tonight?" Alyss suggested.

Eira had been debating it ever since she saw the first trail of smoke winding into the sky from the town.

"No." She pointed toward a barn in a field, unattached to the farmhouse that it no doubt belonged to. "Let's make our way there tonight. We'll plan our approach to the city for the morning."

Two days, Lavette had warned her. It had taken the better part of a day just to get this far. That meant, tomorrow, they had to find Allun, free her, and get out all in the span of one day. They'd have to be strategic and well-rested.

Navigating the fields under the haze of sunset proved relatively simple. The family who was in the farmhouse had already tucked in for the night, oblivious to and undisturbed by their unexpected guests. Still, they made it a point to progress with deliberate and measured steps, keeping low to the ground. This time, Alyss covered their tracks, ensuring there was no trace of their passage in the soft earth and every blade of crop was mended.

By the time they reached the weathered barn, it was nothing more than a shadow against a plum sky. It wore its years with dignity, its front facade thick with patina and the doors heavy with smudges and streaks of regular use. The main doors were still open, the temperate night not necessitating a need to block out the elements from the animals within. The scent of the beasts permeated the air, hide and hay mingling with earthiness and life.

"Up to the loft," Eira suggested, climbing a rickety ladder to the hay loft that creaked threateningly under their weight, but held. Most of the space was claimed by an expansive amount of hay, already in preparation for the winter ahead.

It took little time and effort to settle into their temporary sanctuary. Not much more to do other than drop their packs. The hay made for suitable bedding and the roof must be well-kept because it only had the faintest trace of dampness brought on by the cooling night, rather than any previous rainstorm. The warmth of the day still clung to the rafters, mingling with the heat that rose from the menagerie below. As each of them sagged into the hay, glances were exchanged. Expectant gazes turned in Eira's direction.

"To start, there's something I should tell you all." Eira took a breath. "We only have one day to get in, get Allun, get out, and start our return."

"One day?" Alyss blinked.

"But I thought the council gave us three days?" Cullen said. "That means we should still have two."

"That's what they said. But before we left, Lavette told me that there was already a push to shorten it to two days. That she'd stall as best she could but—"

"There's little faith we'd actually do it." Olivin situated his pack by his feet, rummaging through it to distribute some rations to everyone. "To think, after all we've proved ourselves, they still doubt us."

Eira shrugged. "It'll make proving them wrong that much sweeter."

"What's the plan, then?" Alyss asked. "If we only have a day, we need to be strategic."

"We'll go before dawn," Eira said. "While it's still dark and our features will be harder to see clearly. That way we'll hopefully have more freedom to maneuver among the masses throughout the day."

"The streets will be emptier, though," Yonlin pointed out. "We'll stand out more."

Eira had already considered the prospect. "That's why we won't be moving as a group."

"You want us to split up?" A frown tugged on Cullen's lips.

"We'll cover more ground that way and it'll look less suspicious than six of us walking in at once," Eira explained her reasoning.

"Split up…" Ducot huffed in disbelief, the sound devolving into a dark chuckle. "Yes, we know how well *that* worked last time."

The words were a blow to her chest, an impact strong enough to nearly carve out the spaces between her ribs. Eira stared at him, searching for a response. But there was none to find. He was right.

A long stretch of silence dragged on where no one seemed to want to be the first to speak.

Finally, Eira broke the silence. "We'll talk more about the roles in the morning. For now, let's get rest while we can. But we should have someone keep watch in case the family comes out to check something in the night." Eira stood. The squeaking boards of the loft suddenly sounded like screaming. "I'll take first."

No one stopped her as she descended the ladder. Eira heard them settling. She thought she heard Alyss murmuring something to Ducot. But Eira intentionally didn't listen to the words. She didn't want to hear Alyss's defense, or agreement.

If she could, she would descend into the shadows of the barn and never emerge again.

But the ladder was only so long. And there was still a job to be done. Eira perched herself on the inside of the open barn doors, looking out toward the farmhouse and trying to allow her mind to go blank. The effort only lasted so long when a shifting in the air alerted her to the presence of another.

"Olivin," Eira whispered. No one else could move as silently as he.

"He didn't mean it." Olivin's voice was as hushed as hers, barely audible even from a few steps away.

"He did. And he was right to." Eira folded her arms, leaning against the large barn door. Moonlight danced in the breezes that rippled through the crops beyond. "I didn't make the right decisions then—I wasn't enough of a leader, enough of a decision-maker. I'm trying to do better now, but…"

"If there's one thing I've learned, it's that you can't control everything."

"I wish I could." Eira's hands balled into fists. "All I want is to protect those I love."

"I know that feeling all too well." In a couple steps, he was next to her. A breath away. "You're doing better than you give yourself credit for."

"Yet, it feels like it doesn't matter because nothing I do now will bring her back."

"Of course what you're doing matters." Olivin shifted to face her, brow furrowed in a way that spoke of his disbelief that she'd think differently. "If you succeed, Eira, you're setting all of Meru free. Noelle is gone, and I know—*I know* that pain. But what you, what *we* have the chance to do is prevent the pain of countless other Noelles from being suffered across Meru."

She sighed. It was a beautiful thought, but… "Anything beyond us, our group, my crew, hardly feels real." *Or like it matters*, if she was being honest. She wasn't killing Ulvarth for Meru. She was doing it for herself and the memories of Noelle and Marcus.

"What you're doing for all of us is a help, too."

"Risking your lives?" she asked dryly. Doubt was a spiral and farther down she spun.

"Yonlin would've been lost, earlier, if not for you." Olivin squeezed her shoulder gently. "How did you know?"

"After they took me…the darkness was different. Locked doors weren't the same; they might as well have been prison cells." Eira reached a hand out into the moonlight. "Sometimes, even hazy moments like this, there's a blur of reality—and the fabrication they made for me to believe was real. If I let my mind wander, I can begin to doubt I ever escaped that place, as if all of this is somehow still part of their game."

"It's not." As if to emphasize the point, he rested a palm on her hip.

"I know." Eira shifted to rest her hand over his, holding him to her. "The pain is too sharp." Sharper than the blade of the dagger she'd entrusted to Crow, waiting to be plunged into Ulvarth's chest.

"I wish…I could ease your pain." He leaned toward her, nose brushing her temple before his lips pressed gently against her flesh. "Yours, Yonlin's… I know you doubt, Eira. I understand that feeling. But you're doing better than you think. Thank you for being there for him in a way I couldn't."

"You've nothing to thank me for."

"My gratitude says otherwise." He sighed softly into her hair, his forehead pressing against the side of her head. "You're not the only one, Eira, who looks at the suffering around you and sees all the instances of the good you failed to do. But, I believe there could be a future ahead for us, once and for all. A future you and I can build together."

Eira shifted to look up at him, meeting his eyes. She'd seen intense expressions on him before. But this…it was nearly overwhelming.

Reaching up, Olivin cupped her cheek.

"You, and me, and all we can achieve will be glorious." He spoke the words like a vow, sealing them with a kiss.

THIRTEEN

THEY APPROACHED THE small city in groups of two before the sun was up, staggering. Eira and Cullen were first. After them would be Alyss and Yonlin. Olivin would be last, Ducot on his shoulder.

Eira's hand rested in the crook of Cullen's elbow as they passed underneath the entry that hung over the road at the edge of the town. Just like the hamlet they'd seen on their way to the mines months ago, it was two upright columns, a beam across the top. Unlike the town, this didn't have anyone strung up and gutted. Hopefully it still didn't by the time they left.

There were no knights guarding the entry, but Eira knew that didn't mean there weren't any already watching. She scanned the rooftops and windows, looking for any signs of someone who was paying a little too close attention. But most of the buildings had been shuttered for the night. Only a few had the flickering of an early riser's candlelight behind them.

The buildings were constructed from solid slabs of stone, tiny lichen speckling them like age spots on the cheeks of an old man. Weathered carvings at the corners bore witness to everything that happened on the streets beneath. The construction was mildly similar to the buildings in Qwint—magic playing an obvious hand with how some stones were set at angles impossible to achieve through traditional means of construction. But, unlike in Qwint, Eira noticed the copious amounts of runes carved into the walls and doors. Etched like protective talismans…or symbols of death.

Overhead, pennons of red and gold fluttered. Each one bore

the symbol of Carsovia upon them: a serpent coiled in on itself, almost like a figure eight, never-ending. Their shining threads glinted in the first traces of a pale dawn, like a thousand eyes winking down at them—watching them.

"It's…a lot," Cullen murmured, noting the oppressive atmosphere without having to outright say as much.

"Do you imagine Solaris would feel like this to others?" Eira whispered, shifting closer to him so her words would be as quiet as possible. "We have our share of pennons flying with the Blazing Sun of the Empire."

Cullen hummed. "Perhaps it would."

Eira wondered if it would feel like this to her when—*if* she returned. She'd been an outsider to begin with. The woman she was now was certain to fit in even less. She'd told her parents that she would go back when she was able, and would visit them when she did. But even only a few days after that conversation, it felt like a lie.

"But I think there is a different feeling to willing patriotism versus…whatever this is," Cullen murmured.

What was "willing" when it came to patriotism? Could you tell if it was engrained in you from your first breath? She wanted to ask, but didn't. This wasn't the time nor place for that debate. The line between pride and mindless following blurred so quickly, especially when the truth was kept under lock and key and sword-point.

Nestled at the heart of the city was a large, official-looking building. Rows of knights were positioned before it along the raised walkway that encircled it. A single stairway was the only entry or exit. Its towering walls were even more fortified than any of the other buildings.

A market had been set up in the square before it, offering Eira and Cullen the opportunity to covertly watch the comings and goings of the knights for nearly an hour as they milled about. Most of the knights looked on at the citizenry with dull, detached gazes.

"I don't see an opening," Eira whispered, fearing that they were now just wasting time. "We're going to have to find another way."

"I could create a distraction," he offered. "Lure the knights away. You illusion us, we slip through."

It was a bit of a haphazard plan, but better than the alternative of continuing to meander.

"This way." Eira guided them through the markets and into a sheltered alcove. Looking around, she made sure no one's attention was turned their way and drew an illusion over them. A thin layer of magic coated them like frost glistening on their shoulders. Eira wove the power tightly into place, keeping it close. "Ready."

Cullen closed his eyes and Eira could feel the surge in his power. In response, a gale swept across the city. It turned tents in the market into sailcloths, flipping them. Wares were sent scattering. Dust from the fields and streets was blown into people's eyes. Shouts and commotion rose as people scrambled to collect their things.

Another burst of power. One man was sent toppling into another. Cullen repeated the process, sending one, two more off-balance.

The third had the desired effect.

The man who'd been nearly fallen on rose with a shout. Things escalated quickly. Chaos broke free.

Eira took their chance, moving at the same time the knights did. Her hand clutched tight with Cullen's, they darted along the fronts of the buildings that lined the square. Glancing over her shoulder, Eira met Cullen's eyes. A shimmering haze surrounded the edges of his face, the only tell of the illusion that she wove around him.

"Wind under our feet," Eira said, not worrying too much for who might hear. There was enough noise in the market as it was. The likelihood of someone hearing and placing the sound was slim.

Cullen's reply was a nod, his attention shifting to the building before them. Eira had gone for the far corner instead of the main stair at the front. The knights in the middle were the first to respond to the fighting that had broken out, the others shifting down.

At the wall, Eira leapt and a surge of wind propelled her upward. Her stomach shot into her throat as weightlessness made her head spin. She inhaled sharply and the rogue thought of what it might be like to soar as free as a bird crossed her mind. A question for Cullen, someday in the future.

They landed gently on the stone walkway, the closest knight a few paces ahead.

Eira kept moving, slower now, ensuring their footfalls didn't give them away. Her lungs burned as she fought her hasty breaths, forcing them to be slow and shallow, even when it caused lightheadedness.

Open the doors, her heart begged, *open the doors*, she wanted to scream. There were no windows that they had seen. This was the only entrance in and out and they'd yet to catch a knight rotation. For all she knew, the knights didn't even come from this central building whenever they did change out.

Without warning, the doors burst open. Eira skidded to a halt, slamming herself, and Cullen, against the wall. A group of knights rushed out around a central figure that held a flashfire aloft.

An explosion rung out over the city as he flicked his finger over the triggering mechanism.

"We will have order," he boomed across the square.

Eira's heart thundered with the echo of the flashfire. A cold sweat drenched her from head to toe, every muscle in her body tense. With every blink, she was on the walkway one second, back at the mines the next. The sulfuric smell of the flash bead combining with the sizzle of magic across her flesh made her nauseous.

End him. Have your vengeance, a voice whispered. Eira didn't know who it belonged to. Ulvarth? Noelle? Herself?

A squeeze on her fingers ripped Eira back to the present. She turned to Cullen, who gave her a pointed stare. They shared a thousand unspoken words. He'd seen her struggle. He knew. Just as well as they both knew this wasn't the moment to give in to her ghosts, or her most murderous impulses.

Get in. Get out. Keep everyone safe. Accomplish your mission and be stronger for it. Eira reminded herself that those things were all that mattered.

Side-stepping around the group of knights that surrounded the man in charge, they slipped through the entry and emerged into a marble-clad, empty hall. Four doors were on either side of them, two in the back. At the center of the ostentatious room was a sculpture of the eternal serpent of Carsovia, cast entirely in gold, gleaming ominously in the sunlight that streamed through a skylight above.

The room was, otherwise, empty of all else—people included. But she doubted it would be for long. The commotion in the market was going to be quelled in only a few minutes.

"Where to?" Cullen breathed. He must be thinking the same thing she was.

"Can you feel anything in the currents of air? Dampness that might be from dungeons?" Eira replied hastily, pulling them along.

Cullen dug in his heels at the center of the room, eyes closing. Eira waited, her attention on the doors. She couldn't hear what was being said to the people in the market. But the noises had quieted.

"That way." Cullen pointed to one of the side doors in the back corner.

Wasting no time, she pulled him over and pressed her hand to the lock. As ice filled it, pushing against the interior tumblers, forming a key ring that extended out beneath her waiting palm. The door swung open and they slipped through, easing it closed behind them. Judging from the voices and footsteps they shut out, it wasn't a moment too soon.

A labyrinth of corridors awaited them, connecting various rooms that were packed so tightly together that the walls could hardly be more than a stone thick. Cullen shifted to lead. Without needing to communicate, or ask, he knew the direction in which she wanted to go. He knew what she needed from him.

Without warning, he pulled her into an alcove created by a door. Eira crashed into him from the momentum. It wasn't enough for her magic to waver, but it was enough to steal her focus, especially as his hands landed on her hips, clutching her closer—protective.

They inhaled and exhaled together, eyes locked, bodies flush.

A pair of knights walked through a cross hall, oblivious to the two of them. Thanks, in part, to Eira's illusion and Cullen's quick thinking. But all she was focused on was him. For a second that seemed to stretch on forever, they didn't move. They didn't pull apart. It was only them.

The slightest smirk tugged on the corner of his lips, as if he also couldn't believe the thought that was crossing his mind before he said it.

"Do you remember the trials?" Cullen whispered so softly that Eira could've sworn she had heard his thoughts. "When I pulled you aside like this? The first time I kissed you?"

"I'd never forget." She couldn't, even if she tried. No matter what, he was a part of her. He was etched onto her lips, her heart, her body. A stain—a gilding. Shame over all she should've done better and pride in what they had accomplished. "I..."

"You?" he breathed.

She was aware of the time that was being wasted. Of the precious seconds they didn't have to spare. Yet... Eira leaned forward.

"I enjoyed it," she confessed to herself more than him.

"I would've never said I did, if you'd asked then," he agreed. His thumb dragged across her lower lip. When had he started holding her face? "But when I kissed you...I knew I—"

Eira interrupted him by pressing her mouth firmly against his.

Cullen's hand was in her hair, nails scraping against her scalp. It was seconds long. Nothing much. Brief enough that it could've been forgotten in a breath.

Yet, if it was nothing more than a breath, it was the first breath of spring. The first breath of air after being under too long. When her eyes fluttered open, she met his gaze and a thousand questions ripped across her mind.

"I knew, from the first time I kissed you, it'd be easier to cut off a limb than cut the other from our lives," he finished his earlier statement, causing her heart to skip a beat. Then, Cullen was the one to say the obvious. "We need to keep on. I don't sense anyone else around."

Eira wondered if he had been stalling for that reason, or just to savor those moments as she had. Either way, their brief reprieve had ended. With a nod, they carried on. Their window of opportunity was fleeting, and every second counted. There wasn't time here and now to waste on kisses, as much as she might have otherwise wanted.

He came to a stop at the bottom of a stairwell. "I think this is the lowest point; the air is the most still here. But that means I can't find a path forward for us anymore."

"I'll take it from here." Eira closed her eyes and shifted her focus with her magic without releasing any of the other feats she was simultaneously performing. She strained her ears magically, sifting through the benign to the horrifying to find the mention of a single name: *Allun*. Eira opened her eyes and strode off with purpose. "This way."

After two other instances of narrowly avoiding confrontation with patrolling knights, they reached a row of cells. It wasn't hard to find Allun thanks to the echoes. She was positioned far in the back, the lock surrounded by an extra thick chain, covered in runes, as though they fully expected her to attempt escape even though her hands were bound.

The flickering torchlight danced upon the iron bars, barely reaching back to the woman hunched in the far corner of the cells.

She was little more than a faint outline. Long shadows clung to her.

Yet, despite their deft silence from their honed movements, despite Eira's skilled magic in crafting an illusion, and the shackles that surrounded Allun's wrists…her head rose. Hazel eyes pierced the darkness to meet Eira's and a familiar sensation of being watched overcame her. Eira knew this woman. She'd seen her before, but only for a moment that had been overshadowed by the flames of that day.

"Why, hello there," Allun whispered, low, slow, ominous. A serpentine smile sneaked across her lips. "It's been some time, incarnation of Adela."

E IRA DROPPED HER magic like a silken curtain, returning to the realm of perception. "It's you."

"You recognize me?" Allun seemed surprised, but genuinely pleased. "It was brief, and I was but one among the masses."

"You looked at me like you knew me, then." It had been a brief meeting, and Allun was merely one among the masses in the mines. It was when Mel had escorted her into the large cavern the prisoners of the mines were kept in. That night, Eira had seen Allun, though she hadn't known the significance of the woman then.

The explanation of her recapture and finishing the job from Drogol suddenly made a lot more sense.

"I know the visage of Adela, even years younger."

Eira allowed her parentage to remain somewhat ambiguous, neither confirming nor denying Allun's suspicion. "How did you end up there?"

"How anyone else does; I was careless and foolish at the wrong time." There was a bitterness to Allun's words despite her grin stretching wider until it looked almost crazed. "Once they realized what they had in me, they stopped wasting my talents and put me to work."

Eira wondered if the workshop she'd encountered on her entry to the mines had anything to do with Allun. Seemed likely.

"Then, thanks to you, they lost me, and tried desperately to reclaim me every second after that. Unfortunately they were successful." The woman stood, a bit shaky on her feet, but more confident than Eira would've expected from her emaciated frame. She moved over slowly—it was as if the very shadows were trying to claw her back and she was embroiled in a valiant struggle against them.

As light sharpened her edges, Eira noticed markings etched into her forearms that were somewhere between tattoos and scars. "I've seen these before." It had been on Adela's ship, the night they were attacked.

"Ah, yes… I heard rumors that you managed to thwart someone with my work on his flesh." Allun lifted a hand, studying her forearm as if for the first time. "Yet another reason I hoped our paths would cross again."

"You knew about the lutenz?" How could word have made it back to Carsovia? It had been the first night Eira had controlled the *Stormfrost*—when a Carsovian ship had attacked them. The man had markings all over his flesh that Varren had called forbidden magics.

"I do not give my work to many, so I know all those who bear it. Moreover…it is a rare thing for someone to be able to overcome it. And to do it again, you're going to need my help." Even the movement of lowering her arm was smug, as if she already knew Eira was eying the markings.

"How so?"

"A rune-reinforced suit of armor I made wasn't destined for Carsovia. The specifications were for a certain elfin man."

"Ulvarth." Eira breathed the name. It tasted like bile and hate. The mention of Ulvarth's armor during her first meeting with the Hall of Ministers, and what her parents had said, suddenly made a lot more sense. "It can reflect magic."

"That was what I designed it to do." There was a spark of fascination in Allun's eyes. "Did it work?"

"Allegedly."

"It's frustrating how good I am," Allun lamented, both sincere and coy at the same time. "If you let me out, I'll give you the power to destroy it."

"Gladly." She was going to let Allun out regardless, but this was even more of a reason to.

Eira placed her hand to the lock. The runes that stretched across the bars and chain were as hot as tiny branding irons sizzling her flesh. They fought against her, sparking with magic that melted her ice and reinforced the chain. The metal went white-hot from all the power coursing through it.

Despite the pain, and frustration, a grimace that was reminiscent of a smirk crossed Eira's lips. The challenge was almost…delightful. *More*, she internally commanded herself.

Eira vaguely heard the soft hum from behind the bars. Her eyes darted to Allun, who was raising a hand to her lips. The woman took the pad of her thumb between her teeth, biting through the paper-thin skin, worn down by years of imprisonment and neglect. She reached through the bars to sketch out a rune on the back of Eira's hand that was pressed against the lock.

The woman's movements were deft, the symbol only taking a second to make. As soon as she withdrew, a surge of power coursed through Eira. The rush made her head spin and halt all at once. Internal seas calmed where there was once a struggle.

With a burst of power, the ice snapped through the chain. The lock was twisted metal, shards imbedded into jagged ice. With wet plops, the ice collapsed as Eira withdrew her hand. She stared at the mark on the back. The drying blood was already smearing and flaking off.

"What was that?" she couldn't help but ask.

"An enhancement rune. I'll show you much more than that when we're out of here." Allun stepped out of the cell, taking a breath and holding out her hands. "I am so tired of being chained by them. The key, and my things, should be in their storerooms by the cells."

"Do you know the way?" Eira knew a request when she heard one and she wasn't about to waste precious time debating if it was a smart idea or not.

"I've a suspicion from when they took me in." Allun pointed in the direction opposite from where they came.

Eira let her lead. Cullen's eyes continued to dart around, his magic humming at the edge of Eira's senses. She relaxed her own magic, conserving her energy. A few of the other prisoners seemed to notice something was amiss, but the three of them were gone before any could raise a fuss or an alarm.

They reached an open doorway. The knights didn't even bother to keep their storeroom under lock and key when they had the people themselves sequestered. The spoils of Carsovia's misbegotten victories against their own people were strewn about carelessly. It wasn't a gleaming treasure room of a king, but a pile of loot, haphazardly stuffed into trunks and strewn about in a disjointed jumble.

"They take everything that seems remotely interesting," Allun said with disdain, grabbing some keys off a nearby hook and fitting them into her shackles. One popped off the cuffs and she began to rip open trunks and haphazardly throw things around the room. "Doesn't matter who it's from, what they did—or didn't do. If they come through your town and want it, it's theirs."

Her words illuminated the trophies in a new light. Eira's attention shifted from the precious metals and intricately dyed silks to rustic fur coats, well-worn satchels, keepsakes that were no doubt once treasured by their owners—lockets with dented fronts, stained letters, portraits in broken frames. She knelt and ran her fingers over the stitching of a doll. Her eyes were mother-of-pearl, and dress lace, but nothing about her could've been valuable. She was just another abandoned memory in this patchwork quilt of upended lives and harsh realities.

"Surprised they let you keep anything in the mines."

"They didn't. I stashed it all." Allun opened a trunk with a snap.

Cullen jumped at the sound. He looked back into the hall, then back at Eira. She held his gaze, question unspoken. He shook his head and she assumed it to mean, *No changes, still safe.*

"When I got out, I returned to my hiding spot and made preparations. First I got to Drogol—he was elsewhere—got him out of Carsovia first and then I was going to join him," Allun continued.

"But you got caught a second time," Eira finished.

"They didn't know who I was the first time I was captured, when they sent me to the mines." Allun held up a well-laden satchel triumphantly. Its stitching was nearly bursting. "But when they saw this on me…one look and this time they knew they had someone worthy of bringing to Her Supreme Highness." Even though she spoke a term of respect, nothing in Allun's tone betrayed it. She slipped the satchel over her shoulder.

"What's in it?" Cullen asked.

"My work." The answer was somewhat cryptic. But, given what they knew of Allun, it was more than enough. Especially having seen the pistol. Allun grabbed two more things—a scarf that she drew over her head, tying it under her chin, and a jacket that she threw over her shoulders. It wasn't much of a disguise, but it was better than nothing. "Let's get out of here."

"With pleasure." Eira held out her hand to Allun, grabbing Cullen's with her other. Linked together, her illusion slipped over them once more as they returned to the hallways, racing for the exit.

They were over halfway, by Eira's assumption, when a rumbling at their right had them skidding to a halt. Eira released them, readying her magic. The wall next to them crumbled as though it were little more than sand. A perfect archway had been carved into the side, revealing a staircase that led up to the main street.

"Told you I sensed them down here." Ducot had an air of smugness about him.

"I never doubted you, for the record," Olivin said.

"Neither did I." Alyss was defensive. "I just wasn't completely convinced at how exact we'd be able to be."

"With your magic, precision is never in doubt," Yonlin praised.

"Your friends, I assume?" Allun said with a glance toward Eira.

"Yes."

"What's the plan?" Olivin looked to her as Eira entered the narrow stair that led back to the street. Behind them, Alyss was weaving the stone back into its place.

"Did anyone see any of you?" Eira asked.

Olivin snorted. "Who do you think you're talking to?"

"They have guns along the outer wall," Yonlin reported dutifully. "If we make a run for it in broad daylight, they're going to pick us off."

"I could tunnel?" Alyss offered.

Eira considered it, but shook her head. "That's too strenuous, and too much of a risk of them sensing your magic."

"More of a risk than this?" Alyss finished the question with a flourish of her hand. The stone buttoned up behind them, the wall smoothing out.

"You have a point," Eira admitted. "But tunneling will take a lot longer so it'll be more time for them to sense your magic."

Alyss hummed in slight agreement.

"We leave like we entered," Eira decided. "In small groups. Heads down and unassuming."

"They'll realize I'm gone soon," Allun said with a note of severity. "Even bound as I was, they still checked on me often." A bitter smile graced her lips briefly. "They knew what they had."

"Then we go now." Eira glanced around at her friends; they all gave slight nods. "Nothing flashy, no heroes. Allun is with Cullen and me. Exit as we entered."

Alyss and Yonlin went ahead, quickly disappearing through the side alleyways and onto a major street. With a pulse of magic, Ducot scurried up Olivin's side to perch on his shoulder. The two of them went in the opposite direction, quickly turning to walk parallel to Yonlin and Alyss.

"Morphi," Allun hummed. "A rare people. Hunted nearly to

extinction." Her tone turned serious. "A fate too many in Carsovia can relate to."

"Oh?" Eira dared to ask. It might not be a particularly wise conversation. But walking too stiff and silent wasn't wise, either.

"We've an expression in Carsovia: The Empress sings, and the people are in harmony. Errant voices disrupt the chorus," she recited, pausing to blink up at the sun as it flashed briefly between buildings. "What no one says is that those 'errant voices' are silenced."

"Is that what you were? An 'errant voice?'" While this rescue was going to happen regardless of what Allun said, Eira was keen to know more about the woman she was risking her neck for.

"An errant scream is more apt." Even though the words were playful, there was a somber and almost sinister note beneath them. As if it were both a promise, and a threat.

As if summoned by the statement, a scream ripped through the otherwise dull hum of the city, the sound chilling them to the bone.

"What was that?" Cullen whispered.

"Nothing good. But nothing changes." Eira moved slowly from the side street they'd been walking on. A line of knights rushed past them, oblivious that the people they were looking for were right beside them.

A crowd had formed at the gates. The knights were pushing the people into a line along the buildings. Eira's eyes met a familiar cerulean pair that quickly turned stormy with worry. Olivin did little more than glance her way, but the look said a thousand words, few of them good. His attention returned to a woman who had been ripped from the group, hunched on the ground.

She wept over a man whose face was no longer there. A burst of magic had been ripped through it. Three knights loomed over her, the middle one brandishing a rifle.

"We will ask you one more time. Where did the strangers you saw in the market go?"

The woman couldn't formulate a response. It was all ragged breaths and sobs.

"Answer me." The knight extended the rifle. His words were calm, but the threat was obvious.

"I don't know. I hardly even know their faces! Please, please I know nothing. Let me bury him. My—"

The knight shifted his grip. Eira saw what was about to happen before it did. Just like she saw the silken strands of dark hair falling over the woman's shoulders, shorter than Noelle kept hers. Her skin a fairer shade than Noelle's. Her frame more waiflike.

But, for a horrible second, it was Noelle kneeling on the ground. Her chest exposed. The rifle pointed, primed, ready with a thumb on its trigger.

The knight almost sounded nonchalant when he spoke next. "If you don't know then—"

A pulse of magic. Ducot leaped from Olivin's shoulder with a roar of rage, magic swirling in waves off of him. Eira didn't have a chance to speak, to breathe, before he crashed against the knight and the rifle exploded.

FIFTEEN

Ducot snapped a chain off his wrist that whipped out and stiffened into a blade with a swirl of magic. He moved faster than the other knights could even get out yelps of surprise, skewering the knight with the rifle straight through.

Even though shouts and screams were rising. Despite the thundering feet of people running—some to the commotion, and some away. Eira could hear Ducot's whisper on the wind.

"For Noelle."

Cullen grabbed her elbow, jolting her back to the present. "We need to hide."

"We need to fight." Eira glared at him. Didn't he see what she just had?

"What happened to no heroes?"

"That bird has flown!" Eira gestured to the knights. Olivin had engaged one of the others, moving around Ducot's attacks deftly. "It looks like we're not getting out of here without a fight."

"Don't lose sight of the goal," he cautioned, releasing her.

"All right, then!" Allun shouted over the rising chaos, stuffing a hand into her bag. "I've been waiting for just the right chance to break these out." Throwing out her hand, Allun released small balls—no larger than flash beads—that exploded with pops and fizzles, more distracting than dangerous.

Eira launched forward, joining the fray. Ice crackled around her, ready to overtake the knights with a thought. They went as rigid as wooden training dummies, helpless before Ducot and Olivin's assault, each wielding their own blade forged from different magics.

The cobblestones vibrated under their deadly dance, pulsing with Alyss's powers. She kept the knights off-balance and swallowed one whole beneath the earth. Screams were stopped short as a group of knights were stopped mid run, their open mouths eerily silent, gasping soundlessly as their existence was ended by Cullen drawing the air away from them before it could fill their lungs.

Each of them was lethal. Yet, it was unexpectedly difficult to gain ground. With every minute that ticked on, there were more knights. An endless stream of them. Olivin conjured shields of spinning gold light to block their attacks—though they flickered as the explosions from the rifles crashed into them. With pulses of magic, Ducot changed swords into silver ribbons that fell helplessly, or glass that shattered as it slipped through their hands.

"For Noelle," Eira echoed his words, lost in the thrall of battle.

"For Noelle," Ducot repeated like a vow.

There wasn't enough savagery between them—not enough in all the world to satisfy them. The fight was intoxicating. It was liberating. It felt so good that Eira wanted to scream, to weep. Her magic raged unchecked as Eira swung her gaze to a new horde of knights rushing toward them from the central square.

Eira lifted a hand. There was enough power for this. She could stop them all in their tracks and—

Movement distracted her.

The rooftops.

A man had positioned himself at the roof's edge, rifle trained on her. Time seemed to slow as her focus narrowed on his hand, thumb gliding over the trigger. In a blink, the roles were reversed. Noelle was holding the rifle, and it was Eira's chest that was blown through. Vengeance for the way in which Eira had utterly failed her.

Eira's fingers quivered. Magic didn't come fast enough as she was distracted by the phantom pain that arced between her ribs.

Why? The inevitable question echoed over the explosion that followed.

A gale tore through the town. It rattled windows, tore off shutters, and slammed doors. Glass shattered, flying through the air like deadly confetti. The man was thrown from the roof before he could take the shot. Eira looked over her shoulder to the entrance of town—the epicenter of the swirling storm conjured out of nowhere on a clear spring day.

There, Cullen stood, radiating power. In the eye of the storm, he was perfectly still, immune to the howling winds that ripped at her hair. Behind him were clear blue skies, an exit out of the array of brutal winds.

In his eyes was a promise: He'd tear down the town, if that's what it took to save her.

Screams began to rise, louder than the woman's, than Noelle's. These people had suffered enough. Eira began to run toward Cullen and the entrance of the town.

On her way, she shouted, "Fall back!"

"We have them!" Ducot snarled.

She grabbed Ducot's elbow, pulling him with her. "They'll have more reinforcements before we know it."

"I'm going to kill them all!"

Eira yanked him to face her, putting both her hands on his cheeks so he knew she was looking right at him when she said, "She's gone, Ducot. All the blood and vengeance and death in the world won't be enough of a payment to bring her back."

Ducot's face twisted. He opened and shut his mouth, as if he wanted to object but didn't know how to. A guttural gulp escaped, like a sob cut short.

"I am not losing you to them, too." The words faded into the wind. Eira's thumbs stroked his cheeks, wet with tears. Her own might have been wet, too.

Wordlessly, Ducot stepped back. For a breath, Eira thought that he was about to run back to the knights held at bay on the other side of Cullen's wind. That nothing would satiate his bloodlust until he killed them all—or joined Noelle by their hand.

His lips moved. Eira couldn't hear the word. But it looked like *Goodbye*.

Ducot outstretched his hand in Eira's direction. She took it firmly and turned to run toward Cullen and the rest of their team. Ducot stayed at her side, trusting her to lead him from the swirling magic and chaotic city.

She didn't make it more than ten paces before a shot rang out. A shout of both surprise and pain ripped through her as her leg gave out. Ducot's hand fell from hers and Eira tumbled to the ground.

· CHAPTER ·

Sixteen

"E IRA!" Cullen's voice was the only thing she heard above the roar of the wind.

"Eira!" Olivin, more distant.

"Eira! Eira!" Alyss and the others.

Ducot was crouched at her side, hand gliding over her back, arm linking with hers. He yanked her upward as though she were little more than a sack of grain. Eira hissed, leg threatening to give out again.

She dared to look down.

The thing was mangled. Chunks of muscle were held together by strips of flesh. Bile rose in the back of her throat as her head spun.

Get yourself together, girl! Even though Adela was nowhere near, her voice still lived in Eira. The pirate queen was forever a part of her. Guiding her when she needed it most.

Another shot rang out, *whizzing* past and exploding against the dirt road, leaving a deep pockmark. They were trying to shoot through the wind. Cullen's magic was deflecting it, but not outright stopping it.

She looked to him, instantly finding his magic. She'd know it anywhere, his powers as familiar as her own. With a thought, she deepened his access to his power.

Another flash drew her attention. Eira braced herself but this time it never made it to them. Cullen unleashed a primal roar and with it a staggering—nearly frightening—amount of power. The winds roared, picking up not just dust and loose debris, but ripping through entire buildings. They turned into a dusty gray wall of stormy violence.

"Go." Eira barely managed the word through gritted teeth. Ducot did as she commanded. She wrapped ice around her thigh, holding flesh and bone together in a clumsy splint. With every step, she adjusted the amount and placement, trying to find the right combination to allow them to break into an all-out run.

Together, they ran into the fields, Cullen's magic still howling in the city. Alyss's hands shifted and spun magic to hide their tracks. Eira's own powers arced above them, lacing with Olivin's as their fingers and breaths had two nights ago, casting a cloak of invisibility over them.

They ran away from the town, away from the road that had knights in the distance racing toward the commotion, and away from the grief that was being left behind.

They stopped by a stream. The sun was low in the sky. Blessedly, between the chaos and their magic, they'd managed to give the knights the slip. But the going was slow through the fields and it wasn't until they came across a canal made to water the crops that they stopped to catch their breath and recover their strength.

Eira immediately collapsed.

Alyss was at her side in an instant. "Let me see."

No sooner had Eira's magic withdrawn from her leg than Alyss's appeared. The woman moved her hands over Eira's mutilated flesh, fingers twitching as if tugging on invisible threads. Her flesh knitted and Eira let out a sigh as the pain began to fade.

"How is it?" Alyss asked.

Eira bent and straightened her leg. "Good as new."

Her friend gave a heavy sigh and shook her head. "That was too much…too close."

"I'm fine." Eira rested her hand on Alyss's.

"This time. But what about next time? Or the time after?" Alyss's emerald eyes searched Eira's.

"Alyss—"

"I can't watch another friend die!" The words nearly choked her. They had Eira by the throat as well.

"I won't, Alyss. I'm not going anywhere."

"What if it wasn't you?"

The question was truly one of Eira's worst nightmares.

"I won't let anything happen to any of you. Not after…" Eira couldn't bring herself to say Noelle's name.

"We'll look after each other," Cullen chimed in.

Alyss's face jerked in his direction, brow furrowing. "Look after each other? Is that what you called that?" Her tone was harsher than Eira had ever heard it.

"What're you talking about?" Cullen wiped sweat from his brow.

"You practically destroyed that town."

"But I did not." To his credit, Cullen didn't flinch, even despite his history. "Only a few homes by the gate were damaged. There were no casualties other than those in the immediate area—which were almost all knights."

Alyss stood and took a step toward him. "It was an unnecessary risk."

"We had to get out alive, I tried as best I could to minimize the impact, but sometimes there will be collateral damage," he said calmly.

"You could've hurt innocent people," Alyss said. Cullen merely looked away, perhaps in guilt, perhaps because he was done with the conversation. Alyss stilled, leaning back slowly as horror widened her eyes. "You knew it and didn't even care."

"Sometimes, what must be done is uglier than we'd like." Cullen still didn't look at her. His eyes were fixed back on the town. Eira wondered if he saw the last town he'd decimated with his winds.

"This isn't you, Cullen," Alyss whispered.

"You don't know me or what I'm capable of." The words were plain. Simple. And somehow more fearsome for it.

"Maybe I don't…because I thought you were better than that." Alyss's tone was disappointed, wounded even. Just as Eira was about to move for her, Yonlin crossed over.

"Alyss, it's all right." Yonlin said, tugging her away. "Allun needs your help, if you're able…"

Cullen sighed and knelt beside Eira. "Are you all right?"

"I'm fine." She nodded, both for him, and for Olivin who cast a concerned look her way. "I am, Cullen. I'm just going to consult the map."

He nodded, hearing the dismissal in her tone. They all needed a moment.

She took the rudimentary map that had been given to her, trying to assess where they were. *Two days…* She needed to get them back into the tunnel before dawn came. Eira massaged her leg in thought.

If her guess was correct, they could follow this canal back to the woods, then cut at a diagonal to the entrance of the cave. It would take them late into the night, but the darkness would be a good cover. No doubt the knights had already sent word of the commotion and prison break to those at the wall. They were probably expecting that Allun would be making a run for Qwint…

"Eira?" Ducot crouched alongside her.

"Ducot?"

After a long stretch of silence, he said, "Thank you."

With a sigh, she folded up the map and returned it to her pocket. Eira stared down the long trough of water that stretched toward a hazy, sunset horizon. "You've nothing to thank me for."

"If you hadn't pulled me out, I would've died there—I would've got myself killed," he corrected gravely.

"You probably would have," she agreed softly. "I might have too."

Eira's attention swung over her shoulder and back to Cullen. Yonlin and Olivin were off to the side talking with Allun. Alyss had flopped on the ground, looking as if she was allowing the agitation to evaporate off her body. But Cullen was dutifully filling everyone's waterskins and repacking their rations after handing out portions. Perhaps trying to make amends for the awkwardness he'd just created.

There had been a time when she had resented him for his endless pursuit of duty and obligation. How tirelessly he upheld what was expected of him. She'd never stopped to appreciate how that same trait meant that she didn't have to think about her cup being full and her bed being warm. That when she was busy worrying about everyone else…she had someone worrying about her. As annoying as it could be, sometimes, he was right to do it. And a part of her would always be grateful. Especially when it was a man who was ready to destroy the world for her, if that's what it took.

"Don't throw it away," Ducot said softly.

"What?"

"Your love, your affection, this crew you've built. Don't throw it away."

"I know." She sighed and ran a hand through her hair, teasing out the tangles. Eira began weaving it together so it wouldn't snag on branches or get worse during their final trek. "I've… tried not to."

He nodded. Another stretch of silence crossed their path.

"If it'd bring her back, if it wouldn't risk any of us, I'd burn it all to the ground for her," Eira whispered. The last thing she wanted was for him to think she no longer cared. That she was content with letting Noelle's murderers roam the world when their friend burned eternal in the fires of the flash bead mines. "I'd dismantle every brick and stone of their order. I'd end every person responsible for that place."

"I know. And maybe we can work toward that." Ducot had a tired smirk cross his face briefly. It was the closest thing to happiness she'd seen on him in ages. "You'll get practice utterly destroying something with the Pillars. After that, perhaps we turn our sails to Carsovia? Wreak havoc along their shores?"

"I'll be at the whims of Adela."

"As will I. But in my experience the pirate queen rarely says no to brutal piracy, especially against those she has a grudge with." He chuckled.

Brutal piracy…as good as it sounded to her, Eira's eyes darted to Alyss. Her friend was so concerned over innocents. *How would she ever settle into such a life?* The unsettled sensation from when she and Alyss were in Qwint's market returned, now coalesced around a question. It'd be best if Alyss didn't go ashore, when the times came. She was excellent support on the ship, anyway.

Ducot continued, oblivious, drawing Eira from her momentary panicked musings, "Adela had been doing a fairly good job at striking fear into them before your existence sidetracked her, so I doubt she'll resist encouragement to do it again."

"And you'll stay with me through it?" The question had been looming over her for weeks now.

"Adela still has the core of my loyalty." That didn't surprise Eira to hear. She was practically a surrogate mother figure to him. "But you seem to have her faith, and are her declared heir. If she's put that trust in you, then you have mine as well."

"Even if—" Her throat closed involuntarily, forcing Eira to choke on the words. "Even if it was my fault Noelle died?"

"It wasn't, though." Ducot frowned. "Not any more than it was mine, or Cullen's, or the Empress of Carsovia's. We all made choices that led her there. But at the end, it was her choice to go, and to stay." The words were somewhat forced, practiced even, as though he had said them countless times over and over to himself to believe them. Not that Eira hadn't been attempting to do any different. Perhaps…what they had both been waiting for was to hear it from someone else.

"You're right," Eira forced herself to say as well. "But that hasn't stopped me from hating them."

"I hope it never does." Ducot twisted the ring he'd taken from Noelle's collection around his finger. A part of her he'd always carry with him, no matter what his future held.

But, perhaps, there was more that ring could offer him…

Emboldened by the success of freeing Allun, Eira outstretched her hand. "May I see it, just for a moment?"

Even though Ducot surely knew she wouldn't take it from him, he still hesitated. But only for a breath.

"Yes," he said.

Balling her hand into a fist, Eira turned all her focus—and her power—to the ring. She had been practicing with Adela now for months. The time where this skill would be put to the test was near…if it even worked at all.

No. It would work. It had to.

Sure enough, as she suspected, there was an echo in the ring. Noelle was too strong of a sorceress not to create unintentional echoes, especially in things she'd be wearing all day long. The words were inconsequential but they still had Eira's eyes prickling and a lump forming in her throat at merely hearing them.

Yes, almost ready, Noelle's voice echoed from a different time and place. Was she preparing for the games? The ball before their start? Or was this from earlier? Noelle continued, clearly speaking to herself given the murmured words. *Too much with the necklace? Maybe? No. Ugh, I hate these ribbons. There. Better. All right, I'm ready!*

The voice faded away with the sound of footsteps Eira's own imagination fulfilled. She could see her friend with such clarity, sprinting off, ready for whatever event awaited her, looking fabulous as always. Eira had kept tight control of her magic for so long to avoid hearing anything she didn't intend to, in part because she was afraid of this moment. Afraid of hearing her friend once more.

It hurt as sharply as she'd expected it to. But there was also a sweetness to the pain of hearing Noelle's voice again. Their friend lived on and this was tangible proof. That was the reassurance Eira wanted to share.

Taking Ducot's hand in hers, she placed his palm over her fist. Confusion furrowed the glowing dots along his brow, but he didn't ask questions. Eira allowed her magic to swell once more.

The echo repeated in her mind, but Ducot didn't react.

More power. Adjusted in a different way. He had to be involved with the magic, perhaps?

Frost coated her wrist and began to creep over his fingers.

"Eira?"

The echo repeated once more. No reaction. She pressed her lips into a hard line of focus. The frost was beginning to harden to ice.

"Eira!" Ducot yanked his hand away. "What're you doing?"

The rest of the group looked her way. She quickly dismissed her magic, placing the ring back in Ducot's palm. He seemed grateful to have it, but his confusion understandably didn't abate.

She didn't offer an explanation or answer his question, instead saying, "We should get going."

"We just stopped," Alyss groaned.

"She's right." Allun stood, dusting off dirt and dried grasses. "The longer we stay in one place, the more dangerous it'll be. If they find me a third time, I doubt they'll take me alive again."

"Moreover, we only have until dawn," Eira added, reminding them of their time limit. That the three days they should've had were actually two.

"Eira—" Cullen grabbed her wrist before she could start walking. "Your eyes… Are you all right?"

"What's wrong with my eyes?" Eira blinked in confusion.

"They're, they almost seemed…" He trailed off.

"What?"

"Almost like they glowed? Or that the color was draining from them?" Cullen shook his head. "Never mind. I must've imagined it."

With a nod, Eira started onward and the rest of them fell in tow. Ducot was half a step behind her, suddenly feeling like a protective guard. Even though he couldn't see it, Eira couldn't stop herself from casting a warm smile his way. It was good to feel like they were on the same side, with the same understanding, once more. She caught him sliding on the ring again. To Eira's surprise, he didn't ask again about what she'd been attempting. Perhaps he didn't want to know. Or he already suspected and couldn't handle the heartbreak of her failure.

Cullen slid in tightly at her left. "Thank you, by the way, for your help back there with my magic."

"Of course." She nodded. "You're lucky you're the first person I started working on that skill with. I don't think I could've been as fast with anyone else."

"Generally, I like it when you take your time."

She snorted with amusement. Cullen grinned as well. But the expression quickly vanished.

His tone turned somber. "You must be careful."

"Something tells me that you're not still worried about my eyes, or warning me against the obvious dangers ahead with making it through whatever patrols Carsovia's knights might have set up by the wall." She had tried to look at everything from every angle. Consider all options. But she knew from his tone alone that there was something she'd missed.

Cullen's voice dropped to a hush. "Qwint is setting you up for failure." Olivin wasn't the only one who maintained his noble instincts.

"How so?" She had suspicions, but she wanted to hear his interpretation.

"They have given you what they are clearly thinking is an impossible task," Cullen explained. "Either you will fail, and they are proved right. Or you succeed, and they are likely to use it to bring calls again that you are, without doubt, Adela's spawn. Should that belief take hold…" He couldn't seem to bring himself to reach the logical conclusion.

So Eira did it for him. "They will likely hold me hostage or use me as leverage."

"Or worse," he finished gravely.

"They can certainly try." Eira chuckled. "But I don't think they realize the fight they're in for if they do."

"Once more, running headfirst into danger." Cullen didn't sound upset in the slightest.

"I feel more confident doing it when you're at my side." She looked up at him and his attention swung to her. Cullen's lips parted, brow furrowing just a little. Could he really be in that much disbelief? Her expression eased into a tired, but genuine smile. "It's true, especially after that display in town."

"I will always be there to try and get you out of trouble," he vowed. "And to help you avoid it, when the need arises."

"Even if it might frustrate me sometimes, I do appreciate your counsel," she said sincerely.

"Well, you frustrate me sometimes, too, if it's any consolation. Because if I'm being honest, I want to help you make that trouble." He chuckled softly. Eira echoed the sound.

"Lord Cullen, what a scandal to admit," she said, jokingly aghast.

"If only the Solaris Court could see me now," he mused. Her eyes darted up and down him. *Indeed,* she agreed silently, because from where she stood he was a sight to behold. "But even when you drive me mad, I couldn't imagine being anywhere else but your side. The idea of you being in danger when I'm not there to help you…that's more gutting than anything else. If it—" He stopped himself short and finished with, "If standing by you is something you'll let me do."

That wasn't what he'd been about to say. *If it had been you that day.* Eira had heard those unsaid words with perfect clarity. She had felt them hitting her heart like a mallet, one by one. Stinging the backs of her eyes.

Ducot carried his ring with its echo…but they all carried scars on their hearts. Noelle had been the one to die that day, she had been the one to pay the ultimate price. Yet, something inside each of them had been burned away by those flames. And now, new growth was beginning to bud from the ashes. But what would eventually bloom in its place was still a mystery.

T HE REST OF the trek back was exactly as Eira had been expecting. Carsovia's knights had upped their patrols. But, with some patience and a thick layer of illusions, they managed.

"Do you want me to seal it behind us?" Alyss whispered from the inside of the cave.

Eira considered it. Qwint's runic magic would be enough to open it up again. Though it would depend on the individual having the right runes for the job…

"Leave it," Eira decided. "If they knew it existed, they would've already been monitoring it. If they come behind us, it'll be easy enough to pick them off, or seal the tunnel, then. It's not worth risking any more magic."

There wasn't any debate. They plunged back into the quiet darkness. This time, Yonlin positioned himself behind her and left little doubt to it being intentional when they arrived at the tight squeeze. He stayed close. Once, his fingertips brushed against Eira's, as if looking for reassurance that she was actually there—that the moment was real.

She glanced over her shoulder the instant his hand fell away. Whatever words of encouragement she'd been about to offer him vanished when she saw he was looking back at Alyss behind him. It was impossible to make out their expressions in the dim light of Olivin's tiny glyph, but Eira could've sworn she saw Alyss mouth something to Yonlin. So Eira said nothing, leaving them be. Yonlin was in good hands.

They emerged up the ladder without incident, settling on the landing by the sealed door in the wall to wait.

"How much longer do you think until they'll come and open it?" Alyss asked, heaving a sigh of relief.

"Not sure, but it also doesn't matter." Eira pressed her hand onto the door, coating it completely in a thick frost. Her brow furrowed with focus as ice cracked and ground against metal. When she withdrew her palm, the ice vanished with it and the door swung open.

They emerged into the night and it didn't take long before the soldiers of Qwint were surrounding them, spun bracelets substituted for shocked looks and wide eyes.

The meeting with the Hall of Ministers went just as Lavette and Cullen had foretold. There had been a growing call to claim they were lost. Just as there had been murmurings that, if Eira had succeeded, then it meant beyond doubt that she was Adela's offspring. Lavette and Varren had been doing their best to sway the discussions in their favor, but were fighting an uphill battle.

Luckily, thanks to Lavette's warnings, she'd made it back fast enough that they didn't have time to reach a consensus on what to do about it if she was as they suspected. For Eira's sake, a benefit of governance by many voices was that it took some time to make decisions. So Eira proffered that it would be for the best, for all parties, if she simply excused herself from Qwint within the coming days—as soon as her ship finished being properly mended and restocked.

In the absence of a better plan, the ministers agreed. Most seemed ready to be done with her. Eira barely refrained from pointing out that if she *was* the daughter of Adela, it was far more foolish to provoke the pirate queen's ire by capturing or harming her than to just work with her. Offering them a peaceful departure was more than a fair deal.

Negotiations and voting took half of a day—a short span of time, Lavette assured her, even if it felt needlessly tedious—and Eira walked free.

The hour had grown late and Eira walked with Olivin as her only companion through the tangle of wooden stalls and canvas tents of the market. The rest of their crew were attending to matters regarding their restocking, and generally recovering from the ordeals in Carsovia. Be it from exhaustion, or the hardships they'd faced, none of them had been particularly talkative since returning to Qwint.

Wordlessly, Olivin slipped his hand into hers, fingers lacing. Eira guided her steps closer to him, their sides brushing. He released her hand, shifted his arm around her, and settled his palm on her hip. For a moment, they felt normal. A sentiment he obviously shared with what he said next.

"Someday," he started, a slight smile teasing his expression and softening his brow, "I'd like to think we might walk like this through a market without having to look over our shoulders. Once Ulvarth is dead and gone and we can move on from him, we can live a normal life in a world of our making."

"A normal life," Eira repeated with a wistful sigh, imagining what her new normal might look like. There were ship battles and leisurely days adrift, swimming in the middle of the ocean away from any other souls but their crew.

"For so long, the idea of killing Ulvarth and avenging my family was nothing more than a dream. I never thought it'd be so close." Olivin's fingers gently caressed her side in little circles. "And it's all thanks to you."

"I will end him." There was no doubt in her mind. Even if it cost her everything, she'd be the one to finish him.

"I believe you. And it's opened a whole new world of possibility I'd long written off."

"Oh? Tell me of your world." She looked up at him with a

smile, thinking of what he might accomplish when he no longer had to lurk in the shadows. All his skills without holding himself back or operating in secret.

"I see you in it." He glanced her way, nothing but admiration in his eyes.

"Well, that's good to hear."

"Is it?" Olivin arched a brow.

"You seem surprised?" She leaned a bit closer.

"Merely pleased." His expression eased into a genuine smile. "I think, when we are no longer pressed beneath the weight of Ulvarth looming larger over our lives—when our vengeance is secured—there will be nothing we can't do."

"In that, we are in alignment," she said contentedly. Eira could see it now. Her legacy secured with Ulvarth's death, she could be a worthy heir to Adela. There would be nothing stopping them.

"I've begun thinking about what I would like to do for you, when the time comes."

"Oh?"

He nodded. "So much of my life has been consumed with the end—with breaking things. Burning them down. Destruction. Either what was reaped upon me, or extracting it from others as vengeance. I think I'd like to build something."

"Like what?" she asked delicately. Her heart sputtered despite herself for reasons she only wanted to admit to seeing the outlines of. *What if what he wanted to build didn't involve her? Would that be okay?*

Yet, Olivin continued to surprise her. "Whatever a pirate queen might desire. Perhaps I could be some sort of fleet master for you?"

A smile broke from one ear to the next, spreading wide across her face. "I think I could use someone like that."

In the back corner of the market, barely perceptible, was the familiar entrance to what Eira was fairly certain was a mostly illegal shop. She'd been guiding them there. But apparently she wasn't the only one with this idea.

"We've been expecting you." Drogol emerged from the doorway as they approached with such impeccable timing that Eira wondered if they had some kind of runes that alerted them to her presence. Or if he'd truly been waiting for her to arrive.

"Have you?" Eira asked to conceal her surprise.

With a nod, Drogol led them in and through the concealed back door, up the staircase, and into what had been his showroom of illegal goods. But he'd wasted no time in converting it into a workshop for Allun. The shelves still had weapons, but they were now stacked between jars and boxes. The scent of flash shale nearly had her staggering, tripping back into her memories of the mines. But if Allun could still handle the stuff after all she had endured there, then Eira certainly wouldn't waver.

"Drogol said you've been expecting me." Eira approached the table in the center of the room that was positioned between her and Allun.

"I assumed you'd come for this." Allun turned, holding the pistol in a bed of silken fabric nestled within a box. Her eyes drifted to Olivin's. "Your brother should be able to suss out the finer points. He's a clever one, certainly."

Yonlin had been talking Allun's ear off nonstop during their journey back to Qwint.

"No doubt." Olivin stepped forward as Allun rested the box on the table, shutting and clasping it before sliding it to him.

Allun's attention drifted to Eira. "I made the modifications needed. It will be able to break through the strongest armor—even the runic-enforced plate I was forced to make." She shifted, both seeming uncomfortable and smug at the same time. "Do destroy that forsaken set of armor. I dislike my work being on the shoulder or in the hands of those I do not choose myself."

"Certainly." Ending Ulvarth would be no problem. But Eira didn't want to leave the matter to one weapon alone. She had gone into the mines with no plans. She'd approach Ulvarth with several. And there was a second way that Allun would be able to help her achieve her ends. Her attempt with the ring had only cemented further the necessity for Eira to become stronger. Stronger than she ever could by traditional methods of training.

"What are you going to do with your freedom?" Olivin tucked the box under his arm. "It must be a relief to make it out of Carsovia at long last."

"I've yet to ascertain if I have traded one tyrant for another, as is so often the case. I admit to knowing little about Qwint, though they speak quite poetically about their government." Allun leaned back. Her eyes drifted to meet Eira's. "Though, I would hope that should I ever need another escape, I might have the favor of the pirate queen and her heir?"

"There's only so far that I will risk my crew for another."

"Am I not worth it?" Allun smirked.

"That remains to be seen," Eira said, mostly as a challenge. She'd goad the woman into doing what she wanted, if that was the requirement.

"Is my pistol not enough?"

"I've no concrete proof your work is as good as you say."

"Watch your tongue," Drogol growled protectively.

Allun raised her hand with a slight smirk. "She has a fair point. And she's risked enough as it is for me."

As if intentionally, Allun practically invited Eira to ask what had been brewing in the back of her mind. She balled her fingers into a fist, remembering the surge of magic that came from just a small marking on the back of her hand, sketched in blood, through bars. If that much could be accomplished by so little…

I'm not enough as I am.

Eira hadn't been enough to save Noelle. Her powers, though great, still weren't enough to manage more than three or four feats of magic at a time, even small ones. Meanwhile, Adela could freeze a whole island with an errant thought and hold that frost for decades as she terrorized the seas.

The pistol would help, but it wasn't the final solution to defeating Ulvarth and claiming her destiny. It was a good alternative—a backup. But to bring him down *she* needed more.

Not things, or people…her power, her magic, the far-fetched plans she'd been working on with Adela for months and secretly continuing to develop on her own.

"The rune you put on my hand…I want it permanently," Eira demanded. Allun didn't look surprised in the slightest, as though she had been waiting for Eira to ask.

Drogol had enough shock for the both of them. "You want a rune…embedded into your flesh? You aren't a piece of metal or stone—you're a person."

"Thank you, I am aware," Eira said without taking her eyes off Allun. She still didn't see a trace of hesitation or doubt.

"This comes with risks," Drogol clarified, as if somehow that was necessary. "You carry your own magic…adding a rune could conflict with your power."

"I'll take your weapons, gladly." Eira still spoke only to Allun. "But a pistol, any weapon, however powerful it might be, can be stolen—can be broken."

"A person can break, too."

"I will not break." There wasn't a trace of doubt or hesitation in her voice. "Merely killing Ulvarth won't be enough. I must destroy the very idea of him, and to do that I need a power that I can't yet reach."

Allun rested her palms on the table, leaning forward. She kept her eyes locked with Eira's, gaze level. Eira could almost feel her trying to root out any doubt or fear.

"I will not break," she repeated.

"You should think about this and consider the risks. Come back tomorrow, or better, two or three days from now, and make sure this is what you want." Allun eased away from the table and returned to her shelves along the back wall of the room. She began rummaging through the various boxes as if Eira and Olivin weren't even there. Eira knew an act when she saw one.

"I leave with the dawn."

"All the more reason not to." Allun shook her head. "We

wouldn't want to disrupt your channel or magic before you continue along on your *important work*, whatever that might be."

Eira refrained from allowing herself to be offended. Allun no doubt saw her as nothing more than a pirate, out for her own. Perhaps that's all Eira was. To herself, quietly, she could admit that she wasn't killing Ulvarth to get revenge for his actions against Solaris or Meru. Liberating the peoples was a fringe benefit, but not even remotely the driving force of her motivation…

She wanted to kill him for herself. To end him because he had crossed her—taken from her. And that, she could not abide.

She didn't work for all this strength to sit idly by as the people she loved most were hurt.

"It is because of my 'important work' that I will do this."

"Eira, are you sure about this?" Olivin whispered, taking a half step closer. "You've only just been healed."

"Alyss's magic is impeccable. I was completely healed back in Carsovia." She tilted her head, speaking only to him. "I've thought it through."

"You are strong enough without any rune." Even though she knew he meant well, his encouragement felt hollow.

Eira knew better. "I'm not strong enough to take on Ulvarth. Not yet. But with this I will be."

Olivin shifted, positioning himself fully between her and Allun, consuming her vision. "This might impact you forever."

"I hope so."

"It could have implications you don't intend down the road."

"I'll cross that bridge when—*if* it comes." Eira rested her fingertips lightly on his forearm. "Olivin, thinking of the future is all well and good, but it's daydreams until we've killed him."

He took her hand in both of his. "Don't risk everything to gain only a little." His caution had shades of Cullen from the other evening. Strange how they could be so different at times and yet so similar.

"I'm risking everything so that I have the power to kill any who would stand in my way, defend those I love, and take what is mine."

Olivin's eyes darted over her face, searching. "I can't talk you out of this, can I?"

"No."

With a sigh that betrayed a breaking point, he rested his forehead on hers. "Please, be safe. I can't lose you."

"I will be fine," she reassured him one last time and then stepped around him. Her mind made up, she strode to the table, resting her palms on it.

"You *will* do this for me." Eira locked eyes with Allun. "Because you owe me a life debt, twice over."

A long pause. Finally, a soft "That I do." When Allun turned, she didn't look upset in the slightest. In fact, if anything, she looked excited. Her hands were already laden with various supplies—knives, jars, chisels, ink. "Get on the table."

Olivin's hand closed around her own. "I'm here." Those two words were all the reassurance she needed.

"Good, because I suspect you'll need to carry her back." Allun began to set out her supplies. Despite his initial reservations, Drogol fell into line, sorting various implements for Allun so they'd be in their places before she even needed them.

"Carry her?" A worried note crept into Olivin's question.

"A suspicion. But we'll see how she takes to it." Allun looked to Eira as she settled herself on the table. "Where do you want it?"

Eira stared at the back of her hand where Allun had drawn the rune in her blood. It'd be a fitting location for it, symbolic. And the marking would likely become a calling card that could strike fear into the hearts of her enemies and inspire her allies alike.

But…it was also likely to inspire others to try and imitate her. An inevitability, likely. The progression of magic's endless evolution was impossible to stop. More were likely to be seen emerging from Qwint with runes upon them, just as the lutenz had on the ship all those months ago. But Eira wanted to keep her edge as long as possible.

More practically, a hand was easy enough to cut off, as Adela had so unintentionally demonstrated. Eira didn't want to make it easy for someone to cleave this mark from her. She wanted them to work for it—to kill her for it.

"My chest." Eira reached the natural conclusion aloud. "Low in the center, between my breasts." Somewhere that even the most revealing clothes would likely hide.

"Sounds painful, but it's your body." Allun shrugged. "Take off your shirt and lie back."

Eira did as she was told. The moment the table hit her bare back, her skin puckered into gooseflesh. *This was happening.* Allun paraded all manner of sharp instruments as she finished sorting herself. Olivin continued to stand at her side. Clearly, he still held his reservations. But his expression was as determined as Eira felt.

"Once I start, I will not stop until I'm finished," Allun cautioned. "It is too much risk to both of our magics for me to stop halfway."

Eira looked up at the woman, feeling somewhere between a patient awaiting a doctor's skilled hand, and a slab of meat before the carver. Her chest being completely exposed to two strangers hardly struck her as odd, given the circumstances. Eira realized she couldn't care less who saw her body. She had nothing to hide and was proud of every line and scar that had been carved into it. Perhaps this would be the one she was most proud of, of them all.

"I won't ask you to stop." Enhancing her magic would be worth any pain.

Though, perhaps Olivin's comments wormed their way into her mind. Though likely not in the way he'd intended. *What would Adela think?* The rogue question was instantly answered with a gut instinct that was too sudden to be wrong:

She would be proud.

The notion emboldened her. This was what Adela would do.

The pirate queen wouldn't be afraid. She wouldn't hesitate to claim power. And she certainly wouldn't let anyone else have her second-guessing.

"Let's do this," Eira emphasized.

"Very well. Let's begin." Allun selected a thin knife, as delicate as a fountain pen. Liquid swirled in a chamber behind it. "As much magic as you can muster, please. Flood yourself with it."

Eira concentrated, her vision softening as she eased her focus on the room before her and brought it internally. She had reached for her own channel most of her life. Had been perfecting widening others. And yet, trying to do so on her own remained slippery and elusive. Still, she tried.

Frost coated her skin, pouring off her in waves of white and flecks of snow. Within, Eira imagined the ocean to be filling her. Blood replaced entirely with cold seawater. Nothing but the endless tempest of storm and waves.

Yet, the first strike against her breastbone felt like an earthquake. Her focus threatened to crumble. She exhaled, as though punched in the gut.

"Come now, you're stronger than that," Allun chided lightly, and sank the blade in farther.

Eira gritted her teeth, focusing on her magic. Focusing on the ancient magics that were fusing with her own. She would weave magic into herself like Lightspinning, like the runic arts.

Wave after wave of white-hot pain ripped through her. In the ebb between each, her power surged. Frost numbing the pain. Knives and needles punctured her skin, ink blooming between scars into an intricate pattern that she couldn't see but could feel so sharply that she could almost draw the design.

Magic etched its way into her flesh, her blood, her channel. It felt as if she were a lidded tank, filling with water. Too full. Too much. And yet more came. The pressure building.

She would not break.

Her joints popped and bones creaked. Eira's jaw squeaked

from how hard she was clenching it. Hours dissolved into mere seconds. Each exhale more horrible than the last. Each inhale strength she had only ever imagined.

She would not break. It was a mantra. Over, and over, and over again. Words that perhaps were spilled from chapped and whispering lips like too many tears that had been shed.

The pain was a price and it was her turn to pay. There was no other choice, no other way to become the person she had to be to end Ulvarth. No one else could afford this cost—nor did she want them to. She would endure. She would take the blood on her hands and the hatred that would follow. She would be their nightmare.

The infamy and the power. It would all become hers.

All at once, it was over. Allun came back into focus as she took a step back, examining her work. For a second, it almost looked as if she were going to lean back in and start anew. But, to Eira's delight, she didn't.

"You're an impressive material, Eira," Allun said tiredly.

Eira sat, the excruciating pain forgotten the moment she looked down at her chest and saw the rune that had been carved into her flesh, raised slightly with scars, a constellation of dots and lines surrounding it as if it had been physically woven into her. Her fingers lightly pressed against the symbol. It was icy to the touch.

As she rose to her feet, she felt different, stronger.

Unstoppable.

THE PAIN WAS almost sweet. The dull ache, though incredibly uncomfortable, especially when she moved, was tempered by the surges of magic that rushed through her—filling her to the brim. It made her strong enough to walk back to Lavette's home. It also made her powers more volatile than they had been in years. Water dripped from her fingertips without warning. Her footsteps left frost behind. She was left to shake snow from her hair as they ascended the stairs.

Olivin asked her twice how she was. The second time, Eira emphasized that she'd never been better, despite what her erratic displays of magic might suggest. She felt like she could make the world hers. Any drains on her magic were little more than murmurs in the back of her mind.

She felt confident enough that upon arriving she summoned everyone to the common room. Despite it being the middle of the night, they all obliged, albeit somewhat confused.

"Ducot, may I see Noelle's ring again?" It was going to work this time; she was certain of it.

He didn't hesitate before sliding it off his pinky finger and handing it to her. His willingness to indulge her didn't stop him from quipping, "Does the frost polish it?"

"Something like that…" Eira balled it in her fist once more, allowing her magic to swell around it.

But, this time, she didn't merely apply a brute force of power. Adela had been training her to focus on the currents of power. The way they ebbed and flowed. *There is a way in which you sense these echoes*, she had said. *You pick up on the innate magic that has been imprinted on the unintentional vessel. Find it. Use it.*

Eira did just that. She allowed her magic to swirl around the ring and pick up on the power within it. Power that now rode the waves of her own. A haze of frost began to cloud the air around her fist.

The echo reverberated in her ears. But none of her friends reacted. *Not quite right,* Eira chided herself and adjusted. The power needed to be shared with them. She had to use the tide of her magic to guide the echo to them.

A chill swept through the room, dragging shivers up the spines of her friends. The moment it reached them, Eira could sense their raw essence. For a frozen second, they were adrift in the same ocean she perpetually existed within.

Eira brought the echo to the fore once more.

Yes, almost ready. Too much with the necklace? Maybe? No. Ugh, I hate these ribbons. There. Better. All right, I'm ready!

The power vanished with the last of Noelle's words, taking the chill with it. Eira met the wide, shocked stares of her friends. The parted lips and soft gasps. But none were louder in their silence than Ducot. Tears shone where they collected in the corners of his eyes.

"That…that was her," he whispered.

Eira returned the ring to his palm, curling his fingers around it. "It was."

"You— How?"

"It's something Adela and I have been working on." She smiled. Exhaustion was hitting her all at once. Perhaps she hadn't been feeling as good as she'd thought and had merely been running on enthusiasm. Or the effort had taken more from her than she'd realized. Either way, Eira felt about ready to keel over. Not that she wanted to show it, though. The last thing she'd display would be some kind of weakness that would give her friends a reason to worry. "I thought I could share the little bit of her that we still had with you all."

Ducot clutched her hands tightly and whispered, "Thank you."

"It is my pleasure." Eira eased away. "Now, if you'll all excuse me, the day has been long." She didn't miss their murmurs as realization settled in of what she'd just done. An echo had never been played aloud before and Eira wanted to lie down before they could trap her with questions.

Eira shut the door to her room and heaved a sigh, nearly collapsing. She barely had the strength to stagger over to her makeshift bed before falling into a deep and dreamless sleep.

The next morning was a complete about-face from the evening prior. One good night's rest and her strength was back and better than ever. As Eira dressed for the day, her clothes were suddenly soaking wet, then frozen, then completely dry as a mist filled the room, water releasing with a particularly aggressive shake.

Eira stopped to take a breath when she'd finished stuffing her pack. Her exhale was part snow. The room whispered to her with little more than an errant thought. The oscillation of power was something she'd need to temper. But time and practice would sort that. A bit of additional focus on her control was nothing compared to all the benefits the rune had offered her.

Ulvarth wouldn't recognize her when she stepped foot on Meru again. He didn't have any idea what was coming for him.

Massaging the center of her chest one last time, Eira slung her pack over her shoulder and strode from the study that had been her bedroom while in Qwint. But her reflection in the polished silver of a decorative crest on the wall gave her pause. Eira leaned in and plucked a strand of hair that curved around the side of her face.

It was stark white.

Not platinum blonde. White. Eira turned her head, trying to get a better look, but her eyes didn't lie.

Odd.

Eira tucked the strand behind her ear, trying to pull the rest over it. She didn't want to answer questions. Or give Olivin more fodder to worry for her. There was no space for her to project anything but strength.

With nothing but confidence in her mind, Eira entered the main room.

"Are you all ready?" she asked, seeing her friends loading up their own shoulders in the main room.

"More than," Ducot said, speaking for the entire crew.

Eira shifted, facing Lavette and Varren. Their shoulders were bare, arms free of supplies. "I'd ask if you're sure you want to stay, but I've no doubt you are."

A tired smile crossed Varren's lips. "If I ever leave Qwint again, I think it will be too soon."

"What will you do now?" Alyss asked, sounding genuinely curious.

"I actually enjoyed helping Lavette in the Hall of Ministers." Varren looked fondly in the other woman's direction. "I think, if I'm lucky, she'll take me on as her aide when she becomes a minister herself."

"That is far off," Lavette said, though Eira expected she didn't actually believe as much.

Her suspicions seemed further confirmed when Varren added, "Elections will be held again in a year and I am sure if you ran, you would win."

"There is never such certainty."

"Spoken like a true politician." Varrien's tone was nothing but admiration. Lavette rolled her eyes, which was contrasted by the affectionate nudge she gave him. "Well, whenever you decide to run, I will be here."

Eira had no doubt he was going to make good on that claim. She could already imagine him living out his days in the comfort and safety of the impressive walls that surrounded the city.

Probably on the balcony that she'd first admired Qwint from, if his future with Lavette unfolded as she suspected it might.

"And I would be honored." Lavette adjusted the sleeves on her checkered coat. Even though she wasn't yet a minister, she was already dressing for the job, practically a walking flag. On just about anyone else, it would come off as insincere. Pandering to the masses whose support she needed to consolidate power. But on Lavette, after all Eira had learned about the woman, the garb looked natural. *That* was who she was meant to be, what she was meant to do. "We should get you down to the docks before any of the ministers change their mind about what to do with you."

"Lead the way." Eira nodded.

Lavette escorted them down the many flights of stairs. They were much easier descending this morning than ascending last night following her inking. Eira was immediately behind Lavette, then Varren, then the rest trailing behind. When they emerged onto the street, everyone had a little more breathing room and fanned out a bit.

But Lavette stayed at Eira's side. It didn't take long for her to speak again. "I trust you will not forget the kindness Qwint has showed you."

"Threatening to kill me or use me as leverage, sending me into hostile territory to do their dirty work for them, plotting to maneuver me into a situation where I cannot win… The kindness will linger." Even though the words were a bit harsh, Eira flashed Lavette a smug grin.

Lavette shook her head and muttered under her breath, "Bloody pirates."

Eira couldn't stop a laugh. "Listen, I know why your people did as they did. Honestly, I can't much blame them for it. And they're letting me leave without further issue, so I think I'll let it slide this time."

"You're going to be unbearable, aren't you?"

"Going to be?" Eira thought she was already fairly unbearable.

"When you inherit her ship." Even though there was no one

immediately around them, they were on an occupied street, and Lavette knew better than to say Adela's name, or *Stormfrost*, outright.

"Probably," Eira agreed. "Though we've some time until that happens."

"But it will come." Lavette's focus dropped to the box tucked under Eira's arm. Eira took it as a good sign that there wasn't any shift to her chest, assuming it to mean that the rune couldn't be sensed. "I think we all have gotten what we want out of this arrangement."

"This wasn't exactly a gift from Qwint."

"Not confiscating it was."

"Does anyone know but you?" Eira arched her brows and phrased her question carefully. She wasn't entirely certain whether Lavette knew what she was carrying or just could make a good guess, given what Allun's skills were and Eira's absence the night before.

"Not as of yet." Lavette's smile bordered on smug. "And they won't so long as you keep goodwill toward us."

"Seems like a steep price for such a small thing." Eira kept her tone light, but allowed a weight to sneak into her words. The life ahead of her was hopefully still long. And, if it was anything like her life so far, would be filled with unexpected twists. The last thing Eira wanted to do was narrow down her options. She saw how well that was working out with Adela promising to leave Meru alone.

"Well, perhaps there could be more 'small things' in the future to keep garnering your favor." Lavette shrugged. "I hear Qwint recently became the residence of an exceptionally talented runesmith. I'd imagine we soon will have many things that could assist you on your…*adventures*."

So this was how it was going to be… Lavette was ready to provide weapons to the Pirate Queen Adela for the sake of sparing her people from having another enemy on the seas. Well knowing that those same weapons would be turned against the people that she'd claim to have alliances with. If there was one thing Eira could say she had confidently learned during her time in Qwint, it was that they were so worried about Carsovia they would do whatever it took to avoid having enemies on two fronts. Useful knowledge to tuck away.

"Then I think we should see how this friendship of ours continues to unfold, wouldn't you say?" Lavette said with a slight smile.

"I say I look forward to it." Somehow, she sounded sincere. Despite the uncomfortable introduction they'd first had, the unfortunate circumstances they'd originally got to know each other under…they'd formed something that resembled a friendship. No…perhaps that word was too familiar. An understanding, at the very least.

They were both women of action, charting their own courses. And while Lavette's choice in path of navigating politics appealed to Eira about as much as returning to the Pillars' pit, she could understand it. She, too, had a destiny she sought to forge and—Eira glanced over her shoulder, back at her friends—people she wanted to protect.

With a few quick steps, Olivin came up. Just as Eira had been about to say that she hadn't been intending to summon him, his focus fell solely on Lavette.

"So, what will you do now?" Olivin asked her.

"Help my people, as I'm able. Try to piece together the remnants of my life with the new pieces fate has handed me." The remarks were made lightly, but Eira suspected they were anything but.

"Is it daunting?" Olivin seemed genuinely curious.

"In some ways…exciting in others."

The two conversed for the entire length of their walk. Eira was content to be a silent observer. Olivin seemed particularly keen to learn the future of Qwint, and Eira took a moment to be grateful to have someone at her side who was so willing to learn about the political landscapes of ports she would likely have to navigate around in the future. *A future fleet master, indeed,* she mused.

Crow was waiting for them at the docks, the dagger Eira had entrusted to her when they arrived in hand. Eira was all too grateful to have the blade strapped to her thigh once more. Crow had been sleeping on the boat, guarding it. Eira suspected it was more that the woman found being on dry land for more than a day or two utterly unpalatable. The prospect of getting out of port must've had her bursting with excitement as the entire vessel had been scrubbed from top to bottom.

There were a few ministers who had come to the docks to see them off, but it wasn't a grand affair. Intentionally so, Eira suspected. The last thing they wanted was to invite questions about what Adela's rumored bastard daughter had been doing in Qwint, and why they were just letting her leave.

"I'd say keep safe," Lavette said as she and Varren followed them alone down the docks to the ship, the other ministers electing to hang back. "But I know you all won't."

"You're right about that." Eira held out her hand.

"Don't forget all we've spoken of." Lavette clasped it firmly.

"I won't. We both have obligations to uphold," Eira said, earning a curious glance from Varren. Neither she nor Lavette bothered to explain. He had the sense not to ask.

"Good luck with the Pillars."

"Good luck with the next election." Given all that Lavette had said about the systems in Qwint, Eira suspected she needed luck more. At least killing a man was straightforward.

The gangplank beckoned. As Eira ascended, frost coated her fingertips in anticipation. She could already feel the currents shifting beneath the hull as though her control was upon it.

The others said their goodbyes to Lavette and Varren, one by one. Eira noticed Alyss slip something into Varren's pocket when she hugged him.

"What was that?" Eira kept her voice hushed as she continued to review the rigging. It gave her a good vantage to see most of the goodbyes.

"A bit of encouragement." Alyss winked. "I don't think he'll ever do it on his own."

"Do what?"

"Come now, you're not that dense." Alyss grinned. "You know he pines for her."

"*Ah*," Eira huffed softly. "That he does."

"I told him to take it from me and just tell her. Love stories don't start until you let them." Alyss shrugged and went belowdecks, no doubt to unload her things.

The sentiment brought Eira back to the goodbyes, the last person who lingered—Cullen. *Love stories don't start until you let them*, Eira repeated to herself. Was that what she had been doing with him and Olivin? Initially, she'd like to think not… but now?

Her chest ached again, and Eira suspected that this time it had little to do with the still healing wound.

"I wish things had been different between us," Cullen said softly to Lavette. Eira kept her head down, but didn't stop herself from straining her ears to listen.

"I don't," Lavette said with a bright and airy laugh. Eira dared an outright look at Cullen to see how he took that. He couldn't hide the flash of hurt from his eyes. Lavette rested a hand on his shoulder and said reassuringly, "We weren't made for each other. Maybe, in a different place, or time. But you didn't know what you wanted, then. And when you had the space to decide, well… it was never going to be me." And Lavette didn't sound wounded about it in the slightest.

"You're probably right."

Eira shamelessly looked at Cullen outright. She'd never heard him sound like that. She'd never seen that easy smile or tilt to his shoulders as he shifted his weight. It had been weeks, months. She had held him, kissed him, but had she really stopped to *look* at him? Hear him?

I want to see if the man I become is someone worthy of you. If I can make you fall in love with me all over again. That was what he'd said, wasn't it? More or less? The words felt like a lifetime ago now.

Who was the man he was now, and had she been paying attention?

Her thoughts had muffled the rest of the conversation. So Eira blinked with surprise as everything returned to focus solely on Cullen. Lavette and Varren were halfway down the docks, returning to their new, old life. And he just stood there, smiling up at her. In that little curl of his lips she saw shades of the man who had taken her to Court, who had shined so brightly. And the outline of the man who had shattered her heart.

A thousand questions swelled in her like the tide and Eira didn't know if the answers circled like sharks or shone like a clear sky.

"Permission to come aboard, Captain?" Cullen arched his brows, as if, somehow, he saw the swirling uncertainty.

For a second, she nearly told him no. How much simpler would it be if she had just cut him out of her life, then and there?

"Permission granted," Eira said.

Cullen ascended the gangplank and halted right as he had been about to step around her. Without a word, he reached up. Eira's brows furrowed, trying to make sense of what he was reaching for. His fingers hooked on the strand of hair she'd tucked behind her ear that morning and promptly forgotten about. Tugging lightly, he freed the streak of white.

"What's this?" The question was unreadable. There wasn't worry, anger, confusion, or any other strong emotion. A mild inquiry at what was certainly a notable oddity.

Eira plastered on a bold smile and shrugged. "Getting old, I guess."

Cullen laughed and shook his head. "It suits you."

"Being old?" She tilted her head.

"If that's what you want to call it, then certainly." He released the strand of hair, knuckles brushing against her cheek as he did. "You shouldn't hide it."

With that, he stepped around her, setting out to put his pack down belowdecks and then help prepare the ship. Eira hovered, her cheeks unexpectedly warm. No questions, no worries. Just… admiration.

She turned out to sea, gathering herself and running a hand through her hair. Then, she commanded, "Pull gangplank. Cast off!"

The crew set to work. As those thick ropes unraveled, it was Eira who felt their departure—not the wood of the vessel. She was the one who turned toward the unbound freedom that beckoned from the open sea.

Their movements were instinctual, a rhythm that was almost like a song of calls and callbacks. Of clacking rigging and the quick rumbling of hasty steps across the deck. With little more than a beat of her heart, the ship eased away from the docks. The vessel was alive with her magic, moving through water without need of sail or oar.

She paid little attention to the larger vessels that anchored in the wharf of Qwint, save for avoiding their lines. There was a sense of isolation that swept over the ship like a cloud over the sun. They were on their own once more. But rather than being unnerving, Eira found peace in the solitude. They had all they needed.

A sigh of contentment escaped her lips as they glided between the watchtowers of Qwint. The stoic soldiers continued to regard them with uncertain stares. But none moved to stop them.

Her heart echoed the thrum of the waves against the hull. Her spirit soared as free as the wind in their sails. Her magic propelling them toward beckoning blue.

"Where to, Captain?" Crow asked, coming up alongside her.

"To Adela," Eira announced, certain others would hear.

"Then I would suggest we head—"

Eira held up a hand, stopping Crow. "I know where she is."

"You do?" Crow arched her dark brows in surprise.

The ocean beneath them was a map unraveled. Beyond the walls of Qwint, laden with their runes, there was nothing to impede Eira's senses. She swam through the vastness and raced along the surf. It expanded her awareness and, in the far, far distance, brushed against the familiar hull of a much larger vessel.

"I can feel her," Eira said with an enigmatic grin, and offered no other explanation to Crow's questioning gaze.

NINETEEN

THE TEMPEST-TOSSED SEA posed a unique challenge, one Eira was eager to throw herself and her ship headfirst into. She didn't know if Adela had willingly run into the storm, or perhaps conjured it herself, but the pirate queen was most definitely using it as a tactical advantage against the three Pillars vessels that were desperately trying to sink the *Stormfrost*. Ulvarth's hubris was a poisonous mix with the zeal of his followers.

Roars of gunfire echoed between thunderous cracks of magic over the seas. Eira and her *Winter's Bane* bore down on the chaotic melee. Even if Adela had the matter in hand, she wasn't about to sit idly by and leave it to chance.

"Yonlin!" she shouted down to the main deck, drawing his attention. "Bring me the pistol."

"The *pistol*?" he repeated in a way that showed he'd heard her, but didn't quite believe his ears.

"Now." She made it clear that this wasn't the time to question, though made every effort not to sound agitated. The confusion wasn't unreasonable, given the size of the weapon. Yonlin moved belowdecks and Eira shifted her attention. "Cullen, offensive actions. Olivin, defensive. Alyss and Ducot, guard the ship."

Everyone jumped into action at her commands. Eira turned back to the bow, assessing the landscape of the battle and trying to determine her best entry point. Adela had to know of her presence by now. But the Pillars might still be oblivious to her little ship darting through the darkness.

"Captain!" Yonlin rushed up to her side, holding out the pistol.

"It's ready?"

"Yes, one shot loaded."

"Good." Eira turned the weapon over in her hands, feeling the power it contained. The might was almost as great as the sea beneath her and raging sky above. The rune on her chest had opened her to the world in a way Eira had never experienced. She could feel *everything*. Every drop of mist in the air, every current of magic. "Go and ready the port guns, wait for my signal."

"Understood."

As Yonlin ran off, she turned back to the warring ships before her. Eira slipped the triggering ring onto her thumb. The pistol seemed to hum in response.

"Be ready!" she called behind to the crew. That was the extent of the warning she could offer. She had moved them into position and had given them clear goals. From there on, she had to trust them to take the right actions based on what was thrown at them.

Winter's Bane was smaller than the rest of the vessels, but made up for lack of size in speed. The Pillars had more impressive vessels than Eira had first suspected. Small wonder that they were able to put up a reasonable fight against the *Stormfrost*. The very sight of them confirmed her worst fears—Ulvarth had infiltrated the highest ranks of Meru. He had access to their navy, which meant their other weaponries as well.

He was in total control of Meru.

For now.

Eira gathered her power and the ship danced over the waves, gliding and weaving between the worst of them. With little more than a glance, she halted a massive swell from breaking upon them. She knew her ship—down to every scuff and scratch in every plank—just as well as she knew the ocean beneath it. With only a fraction of her focus, she carried the vessel in currents of her own making, not flinching as another deadly cascade of cannon fire was volleyed against the *Stormfrost*.

"Ready now!" Eira called over her shoulder. They were close—almost close enough for a Pillar ship to notice them. She called to Crow who was across the deck, "You're in charge in my absence."

"Wh—" Crow didn't have a chance to act.

With a thought, Eira coated a section of the wall belowdecks in frost. It was her signal to Yonlin, an easy way for her to tell him when to fire without having to rely on him hearing some sort of relay. The cannon beneath the ship erupted, ripping into the hull of the nearby vessel.

At the same time, Eira launched herself from the bow. The water rose to meet her, supporting her. Eira glided across its surface toward the second of the three ships. She was nothing more than a streak in the night. But when those on the ship decided to try and launch weapons and magic toward her, the water beneath her collapsed and sucked her beneath the waves.

The ocean might once have terrified her—an abyss as dark as the pit, water as icy as the night of Marcus's death. But now it felt like home. She knew every current and could sense the presence of every creature.

Propelling herself directly underneath the ship, Eira slowed to a drift. She'd managed a good breath and the water had formed a bubble around her head. It took a lot for a Waterrunner to drown. She had time.

Like a monster rearing from the depths, Eira slowly lifted the pistol. She adjusted her grip and assessed the best place for her shot. Rip through the hull, not port to starboard, but bow to stern. They'd take on water too quickly. And with Lightspinning alone, they wouldn't be able to mend it fast enough.

Cannon fire lit up the water above her, casting eerie beams that accompanied their rumble—low and ominous beneath the waves. She timed her shot immediately to follow, right when they would be scrambling, focusing on reloading.

Let's see if you were worth it, Allun, Eira thought as her thumb grazed over the trigger with a *pop* that was more felt than heard.

Magic exploded. It was a force unlike any she'd ever felt before. A column not of flame or ice, but of woven light. However, unlike the magic of Lightspinners, this wasn't gold, but a silvery, shapeless mass that frayed into a cone the farther out it spread from the muzzle of the pistol.

Eira was propelled back through the water as it shot forward, ripping away the vessel—completely dissolving the wood. She blinked at the fading, silvery trail, silhouetted in ghostly blue from the blinding light. The shattered hull that now gaped open like the final gasp of a mighty beast brought to heel.

For a second, the world was completely still. Sounds were muffled by the sea. The weightlessness of her body made her feel untethered from the entire world. It was just her, alone, in a vast nothingness, holding the future itself in her hand and staring at the consequences it was likely to reap.

This weapon could be put into the hands of anyone—sorcerer, Commons, it did not matter. With the right hand to craft it, and the right material to fuel it, it could unleash destruction with little more than a flick of a finger. Eira stared at the pistol, barely visible in the haze of battle above, glinting from flashes of cannon fire. It would be a new era, the likes of which the world would never be able to turn away from. And she would be right at its spearhead.

The pitching of the ship brought Eira back to reality. She slipped the pistol into a holster that Alyss had fashioned for her, securing it tightly before drawing her magic. A waterspout enveloped her, bringing her back upward to the surface. At the same time, the sea rose around the Pillar's ship, ready to finish the job she'd started.

Dark ocean came to life like a hand wrapping around the ship, dragging it down. Eira turned her attention to the other two vessels. The *Stormfrost* had focused on the ship on their far side, which was collapsing under a final volley of cannon fire. But that didn't mean they had neglected the vessel on their port, the one that they'd managed to get close to sinking as well with the support of Eira's small crew.

Eira shifted her focus and her waterspout over the vessel.

This, combined with the continued attacks, was too much. The mast was ripped from deck, and the hull torn in two.

Rather than descending on her own deck, Eira touched down onto the *Stormfrost*. The crew actually paused what they were doing to stare at her, as though they were…impressed. The water splashed around her, retreating into the ocean or freezing against the permafrost of the vessel, thickening Adela's fortifications.

"I'm not sure what you're all gawking at." Adela's voice cut through the momentary silence. "You have treasure to collect for me."

The crew launched into action—some throwing themselves overboard. Adela had raised up the ships anew, flotsam now littering the frothy waves. The Pillars who were still moving were the ones the pirates targeted first, ending them with ruthless precision.

"I see you became more showy while you were gone." Adela sounded a mix of impressed and annoyed.

"Stretching my magic a bit."

"A bit?" The pirate queen arched her brows. "I think you've much to tell me."

Adela turned and Eira went to follow, but immediately wavered. She hadn't realized just how much magic she'd used until it hit her all at once. She was going to fall. Eira tried to lean back for the railing, but she couldn't reach it. Instead, her hand met a pillar of ice not unlike Adela's cane. The frost hardened around her boots, keeping her feet from slipping out from underneath her.

At a glance, it'd look like she'd done nothing more than stumble, her bone-deep exhaustion hidden. But it hadn't been Eira who'd stabilized herself.

"Come along now," Adela said softly, pointedly. It almost sounded like a warning.

Eira collected herself and scraped up enough magic to free her boots from their place in the frost and the cane of ice. She leveraged it to get to Adela's cabin, not trusting herself to be stable enough. *What a sight the two of them must be, a mirror of each other…*

"Sit." Adela pointed to one of the usual chairs along the back wall the moment they entered.

As Eira crossed, she caught her reflection in a polished piece of silver. *Mirror, indeed.* Another streak of her hair had turned white and, like Cullen had pointed out in Carsovia, her eyes seemed to glow. But Adela said nothing of it, so Eira focused on getting herself to the chair and collapsing into it. The moment she did, the cane she'd been using disappeared with a hiss of mist. She could let the cushions swallow her whole.

"I don't know if I should be impressed that you were able to come up with such power on your own, insulted that you did not flourish so underneath my tutelage, or murderous that you'd hide it from me."

"None," Eira assured her. Adela poured amber liquid into a glass and delivered it to Eira, who took it readily. The familiar spice burned satisfyingly all the way down, warming her from the core.

Adela took her seat opposite. "Start from last I saw you."

Eira obliged. She told Adela everything from when they had last been on the *Stormfrost*. Of fighting against the navy of Carsovia, continuing to work on the magical theories they'd begun together, their arrival on Qwint, the prison break, and, ultimately, all the details of Allun.

"Show me," Adela demanded as soon as Eira finished.

Once more, Eira didn't question or hesitate. She unfastened the clasps holding the pistol in place and rested it on the table between them. Adela wasted no time taking it, turning the weapon over in her hands. But her eyes continued to flick to Eira expectantly. She knew what the pirate queen was asking for without words. Eira straightened and undid the buttons of her shirt, opening it and then working on the lacings of her bustier, loosening it just enough to expose the still-healing mark.

Adela shifted forward, inspecting it closely. She looked

between it and the pistol. Eventually, she leaned back in her chair and settled the pistol on the table. Eira took it as a sign that it was fine to redo her clothes.

"I've only one critique."

"Please," Eira invited, even though Adela was certain to tell her anyway.

"You should have taken this Allun character for us. The work is truly that of a mastermind. She'll be wasted in Qwint."

"And risk my standing with the government?"

"Since when do I care about standing?" Adela had a note of disapproval to her tone.

Eira chuckled. "You might not, but that is the benefit of having me. I can broker these deals. If I took Allun, then Qwint would've been after us—and, moreover, weakened for the fight against the Pillars. By leaving her there, *for now*, I've enough goodwill to return quietly and get weapons like this whenever it pleases us, with one less mouth to feed in our crews." Eira took a long swig of the burning liquor. She was still exhausted, and it offered her a sweet haze that hid the aches of her body—notably the shoulder of the arm that had been holding the pistol. The weapon might have been designed to be able to be used by a Commons, but it seemed when a sorcerer wielded it, their own power enhanced the shot. "And whenever it suits Your Frostiness, I can go and collect her for you, because Qwint's doors are still open to me."

Adela pursed her lips and steepled her fingers against them, looking at Eira through narrowed eyes. "You do know that pirates don't usually negotiate this much, don't you? We take what we want."

"I'm merely prioritizing the taking," Eira assured her. "Unlike nobles, royals, or politicians, I care little about going back on my word, at least when it comes to those beyond my crew. For now, it benefits us most to play their games and let them think we're all on the same side."

"Good. Ensure that never changes." Adela stood. "Now,

you look practically dead by exhaustion and it's an insult to my presence to bring that weakness into my room."

Eira laughed and stood. The world tilted again, but she was ready for it this time and kept herself stable. "If you'll excuse me, then, I've a hammock to get to."

"No, you don't."

"Pardon?" That gave her pause.

"You have a cabin."

TWENTY

"Cabin?" Surprise raised the word slightly at the end.

"Yes." Adela paused, her gaze as sharp and piercing as the icicles that hung outside of her windows. "You didn't honestly think I would have my chosen heir to the *Stormfrost* sleeping with the rest of the crew, did you?"

There was a *lot* to that statement and Eira didn't know where to start. "What about my ship, *Winter's Bane*?"

Adela hummed. "Not a bad name. I appreciate the homage. Worry not, Crow and Ducot will see she stays afloat."

"I should be on my vessel."

"*This* is the only vessel you should truly care about." Adela tapped her cane for emphasis. "You will have many ships under your command, Eira. They will come and go. Sometimes, you will even *choose* to sacrifice them. But this ship is the one that your loyalty, focus, and heart must return to. Everything else is little more than pretty bits of wood. They will come and go, but the *Stormfrost* is the flagship—the symbol of all I have built and all you will inherit. As long as she sails, the terror of the seas lives on."

The way Adela spoke was like a teacher to a pupil. Or, perhaps…a mother to a daughter. Her tone was still as biting as the wind over the deck of the ship. Her gaze was harsh. But somewhere between the cold warnings, Eira saw compassion and understanding. Just the same as she could hear between those words that Adela wasn't simply warning her about ships. She was talking about people. Those that would come, and go, and sometimes require sacrifice.

"Do you understand?"

"Yes," Eira said, on every level. At least, her mind understood. But her heart was still raw from Noelle. Or was that what Adela was speaking to? *It wasn't your fault*, was the softest whisper to those words, a balm in the only way the pirate queen knew how to give.

"Good. This way." Adela led her out onto the deck and immediately off to the side, where there was now a small door.

Eira struggled to remember what this space had been previously. Storage? Part of Adela's cabin? It was an impossible addition to the vessel, but the ship was occupied by some of the strongest sorcerers Eira had ever known and their leader was one of the greatest of them all. If there was any way to siphon off a little bit of space from here and there, perhaps bump out the side of the vessel a tiny bit more, Adela would find it.

A slight curl of Adela's lips broke her usually stoic demeanor as she opened the door. "It's not much, but it's yours. Just don't go expecting your own door guard."

Eira sucked in a breath as slowly as possible in an attempt to cover her surprise. She stared at the small room. "Thank you."

"Don't disappoint me, or I'll have to kill you." Adela's usually cold mask snapped back into place at the sound of Eira's gratitude. The pirate queen who feared nothing seemed to be willing to do anything to hide the slightest bit of affection. But, at the same time, would make a gesture as grand as this.

"I know." Eira gave her a slight smile.

With a huff and a mutter of having more important things to do, Adela walked off.

Eira knew she should go find her friends. Adela had immediately called on her following the fight and there hadn't been time for her to do much other than verify by sight that *Winter's Bane* was still afloat, her crew seemingly intact on its decks. Surely, if they weren't fine, someone would've come and told her by now, wouldn't they?

Stepping over the threshold, Eira found herself enveloped in the quiet embrace of her very own haven. Much like the inside of Adela's cabin, or the lower decks, the frost hadn't crept beyond the doorjamb. Eira closed the door behind her so the rain didn't pour in and leaned against it, her eyes tracing every detail of the narrow room.

Wooden panels lined every wall, warm in comparison to the ice outside. A medley of soft blankets and furs was piled at the foot of a narrow bed, against the back wall, as though the individual who helped Adela set up the cabin couldn't have been bothered to actually make the bed. Shelves were tucked into the wall at Eira's left, opposite a porthole on the right—the only source of light, save for a dark lantern.

Her hands trembled and a lump grew in her throat. It wasn't fancy. It wasn't particularly special in any way…but it was *hers*. Adela had taken time, and energy, and space from the very thing she loved most—the *Stormfrost*—to give to *her*. This wasn't just a cabin, it was a public declaration of acceptance. Of all Adela had promised her in private and hadn't said in so many words.

It was…home.

A knock on the door had her jolting, spinning, and pulling it open.

"I was told I could find you here." Alyss smiled tiredly. "Mind if I come in?"

"Please do." Eira stepped back. There wasn't much room to step aside in the narrow space. To pass each other would require the two of them being pressed against opposite walls and still having to squeeze.

Alyss entered, pulling the door shut behind, no doubt having the same idea about the rain as Eira did. She held out a familiar pack. "I brought your things."

"Thank you," Eira said as Alyss did her own visual sweep of the room.

"Not bad," Alyss murmured softly. "Adela can be nice. Who knew?" There was the barest touch of a sarcastic edge, but Alyss did sound genuinely surprised by the revelation.

"When she wants to be." Eira settled her pack on the floor underneath the bed. One benefit of the bed touching three walls was that it had been suspended, so there was some additional storage in the room. "Though she didn't give it to me without threatening me within an inch of my life in the process."

"Well, it is still Adela." Alyss went to the lone lantern in the room, affixed to the wall. There was a striker next to it and she sparked flame to life, bathing the room in a soft, golden glow.

"You're right about that. I assume everyone's all right?" Eira wasn't particularly worried since Alyss didn't seem frantic.

"They are now."

"Now?" The guilt at enjoying her new room while someone was wounded was instant. "Who?"

"Yonlin." Alyss didn't look back at her, so she missed Eira's flinch. "He was down on the gun deck when we took a shot. I got to him in time." The words were hollow, void of details that Eira could imagine weren't pretty.

"I'm glad you were there," Eira said softly. "I'm sure he was, too."

Alyss continued to stare into the flame of the lantern. "When this is all over…are you going to stay?"

The way the question was asked twisted in Eira's gut like a dagger. It made her want to say, *No, of course not, Alyss. I'm not a pirate, not really. I'm not cut out for this life. We'll go back to Solaris together when this is all over…* But those hasty thoughts were lies and they both knew it. She respected Alyss and their friendship too much to try and say otherwise.

"This place, these people, they're the first time I've felt like home." Eira sank onto the bed with the weight of the realization. "I don't have to be anyone else. I don't have to pretend to fit into a mold that's 'accepted' by the average individual. My past…" She laughed bitterly. "No one cares that I killed a peer. In fact, I think half of them would praise me for it." Adela wouldn't, not because of some inclinations toward any kind of morality but because it had shown Eira losing control of her powers. And that was something Adela didn't tolerate.

Alyss shifted to look at Eira, who had, until then, been staring at her knees. Even though Eira knew her choices were her own, and she wasn't wrong for them, something about this whole interaction had her feeling like a child in trouble. Shame, guilt, sorrow, some combination thereof and more was raining down on her harder than the storm out on the deck. She felt worse in this moment than she had telling her uncles she was going to disobey their direct wishes and compete in the tournament nearly two years ago.

It was because Alyss mattered more to her than her uncles, or even parents, ever had. They weren't the family Eira, in every corner of her heart, had chosen. They weren't the ones who had stood by her through thick and thin.

Don't leave me, Eira wanted to beg. But when she lifted her gaze, the words vanished.

Alyss had leaned against the wall, the lantern illuminating a warm smile. There wasn't a trace of anger, or disappointment. Perhaps, at worse, resignation.

"I know." Those two words, said another way, would be: *It's all right.* Somehow, the resignation and acceptance hurt more.

Eira bit back an apology. Instead she said, "Pirate ships would be great fodder for stories. Always someone on board falling in love. Distant cities to inspire you. New people to meet all the time."

"Deadly naval battles and pillaging innocent towns." Her tone was similar to how it had been when she'd dug into Cullen following the incident in the Carsovian town.

"Carsovia is hardly innocent." The words were instantly seething. A fire hotter than the mines burned in her whenever the thought of that place even crossed her mind. "They're the ones I'm going to target."

"At first, but a life is long, Eira." The calmer Alyss was, the more wounded and agitated Eira felt. Her friend wasn't wrong,

Eira knew it. Yet, the truth was bitter. "And, even attacking Carsovia, you won't always be striking against the people at the root of Noelle's death. There will be innocent people in those towns."

Eira glanced out the window. "Kingdoms and empires rise and fall. Innocent people get hurt in the process. We've seen as much already."

"Just make sure you're all right with being the one doing the hurting."

There was no way they were ever going to see eye to eye when it came to this. Alyss's nature was too good, too pure, especially when it came to Eira's. And for all Eira wanted to keep her friend close, she didn't want it to be at the cost of everything that Eira loved most about her.

"I suppose there aren't a lot of printing presses on pirate ships," Eira whispered. "So, when are you leaving?"

"We'll see." Alyss shrugged. "Maybe never."

"But—"

"You're not the only one who's on a journey, Eira. Who's changing. I don't know what I want and what I can stomach. The only thing I know is that…I can't watch more people I love die." The words grew soft, barely audible to the end. Eira could see on Alyss's face that it was Yonlin on her mind. Whatever the injury had been, it must've been severe.

The cabin's warmth had vanished, turning as cold as the rest of the *Stormfrost*. The raw wound of Noelle throbbed in the silence. Even as they moved past it, it still ached with a pain Eira wished she could physically rip from her body. It returned, picked open again every time one of them stared down death.

She should have known how to handle grief following Marcus's death. But, because of mourning Marcus, Eira knew these wounds were ones that would never close. They just hurt, and hurt, and hurt…until you became familiar with the pain enough that it could be ignored. More or less.

"That's one thing I can promise you…" Eira massaged the

center of her chest. The only people who knew about the rune were still Olivin and Adela. It wasn't something she was going to make public knowledge. "I am going to keep the people I love safe. I've lost too many as it is. From now on, I will stop at nothing until I have the power to destroy any who would dare threaten my crew."

"You might not be powerful enough."

"I will be," Eira vowed. She thought of what Olivin had said—that he would carve a world with his own hands that'd be safe for him, and Yonlin, and her. "I'm making myself powerful enough. I will be the monster that guards your door."

"Perhaps." The smile that Alyss wore didn't quite reach her eyes.

Eira could only return the slight, tired expression. But when she opened her mouth to speak next, she was interrupted by the abrupt opening of the cabin door. Jolted to her feet by how it slammed against the cabin wall.

"Eira," Cullen panted, wide-eyed and pale-faced.

"What is it? What's wrong?"

"You—on deck—"

Eira was already moving as he struggled to speak. In her mind, a thousand possibilities swirled. They were under attack again. The Pillars had brought the entire force of Meru's navy. Ulvarth himself had come.

Cullen grabbed her wrist just before she pushed past him into the rain, halting her. Their sides were flush. Faces forced within a breath by the narrow opening of her cabin.

"It's your uncle."

· CHAPTER ·

TWENTY-ONE

FOR A SECOND, Eira was too stunned to move. To even speak. She stood there, replaying the words over and over in her head.

"He's…here," Cullen managed, realizing how impossible it sounded.

Eira gave a slight nod, not trusting herself to speak as she emerged back onto the deck of the *Stormfrost*. The rain was beginning to lessen. The fat drops that had plopped heavily on the deck had now thinned to little more than a mist. The clouds broke into patches, giving more opportunities for moonlight to stream down.

The deck of the *Stormfrost* was still mostly dark. Adela only kept a few magical lanterns that glowed with a pale blue, bioluminescent moss—taken from the Twilight Kingdom, Eira had heard. Running a dark ship helped them slip by undetected and gave them the element of surprise.

So Eira couldn't make out the features of the crowd of sailors. But she did see Adela standing among them. Her clothing, a pale white and gray, reflected the light as though her body were entirely made of snow and ice, not just one arm and leg. The pirate queen shifted, no doubt sensing Eira's approach rather than hearing or seeing her, given the commotion that surrounded Adela.

"Cullen seems to think you know this man, and he claims the same." Despite having two people vouch for it, one whom Adela knew personally, she still sounded skeptical.

The crew that had encircled the man parted, allowing her through. Eira halted the second her eyes landed on the hunched figure. He was waterlogged—soaked to the bone and bound. A gag had been stuffed into his mouth, though he wasn't even attempting to speak, at least not at this point.

But the hair that was slicked against his head was undeniably golden, highlighted by the light of a lonely lantern that one of the crew held. His eyes, as they rose to her, widened to the point that there was no mistaking their shade of blue. They immediately welled with tears, brow furrowing in relief.

Eira stepped forward and knelt. She reached around and grabbed one of the ties of the knot on his gag and pulled, freeing it from his face. She'd never seen her uncle with stubble before, or shadows quite so dark underneath his eyes.

"Eira." Her name was little more than a shocked exhale.

"Hello, Uncle," she said loudly enough for all of the crew—Adela included—to hear. She didn't want any of them getting any ideas that he was going to be thrown overboard. "You keep surprising me by showing up in the place I least expect."

"This time, I can say the same for you." He choked on his emotions a moment, struggling to quickly collect himself. "And here I thought having the ship sunk and being captured by pirates would be the death of me. Never before have I been so relieved to find out Adela and the *Stormfrost* is not a myth."

"Neither is my cruelty," Adela added with all the bitterness of winter.

"Captain." Eira gave the pirate queen deference, especially when she was about to ask her for yet another favor so soon after receiving such a significant gift. "I'd like to ask for some fresh clothes from the supply, and a hot meal for my uncle. He's a talented Waterrunner and can lend his aid to the vessel in any way befitting of his skills before we send him on his way." Eira covered the other oppositions Adela might have—that there were no handouts on the *Stormfrost* and that Eira wasn't about to ask for yet another member to be added to the crew. She needed time to figure out what to do with him, though.

Adela narrowed her eyes slightly. She raised her cane, bringing it to Fritz's chin and lifting it to look him in the eyes. Disapproval radiated off of her.

"If you so much as blink in a way I do not like, I will kill you and her for it."

Fritz opened and closed his mouth, unable to formulate a response.

In the wake of his stunned silence, Adela lowered her cane and turned, starting back for her cabin. "You all have work to do, I believe."

The crew collectively gave Eira wary and uncertain looks. Even as Adela's declared heir, they became so skeptical of her so quickly. Not that she blamed them when she continued pushing her luck at every turn.

"All right, Uncle, let's get you warm." Eira made quick work of the knots that bound him.

"You seem skilled at undoing a captive person's bindings," he observed thoughtfully, but his tone was ambiguous as to whether he thought it a good or bad trait.

"I've had a few months to get familiar with various knots." Eira left it at that. She stood and held out a hand, helping him to his feet.

As the crew dispersed, her friends remained, and approached.

"Thank you," Fritz said over her shoulder, directed at Cullen.

"Of course, Minister." Cullen bowed his head. "I wasn't going to let them drown you when you were putting up such a fight."

"It really is you." Alyss stepped forward and didn't even hesitate to wrap Fritz into a brief but tight embrace. The gesture surprised Eira a bit—while Alyss was a longtime friend, she'd never been so warm with Eira's uncles. Though what she said next gave Eira some clarity. "It's good to see a friendly face. I thought there would be no one left following the coliseum."

"I'd like to hear how you survived," Olivin added with a skeptical tone.

Eira noted that Yonlin was nowhere around, and hoped his

wounds were truly mended. But there was only time for one thing at a time.

"Let's discuss this in my cabin." The crew was already obviously displeased with this turn of events; Eira didn't want to put it in their faces. Plus, she had the benefit of privacy in a cabin now, so she might as well use it.

"Your…cabin," Fritz repeated softly as she led them over.

"Olivin, can you find something warm, whatever they have simmering in the galley? Cullen, can you find dry clothes?" Eira directed and the two men headed belowdecks. "In here." She ushered her uncle into the narrow cabin, Alyss still following.

"This is yours?" He still spoke slowly, words laden with disbelief, as if he thought everything before him was some strange fever dream.

"Only as of recently."

"And you're…friends with Adela?" Fritz looked her way.

"It's complicated," Eira was unsure of how to phrase things. Friends didn't feel quite right—her relationship with Adela was more than that, yet also not nearly as warm as "friends" implied. A knock on the door saved her.

Cullen was the first back. "I guessed on the sizes."

"We'll step outside and let you change." Eira took full advantage of an excuse to escape, practically throwing the clothes at her uncle and pulling Alyss out to snap the door shut behind them.

Hands on her hips, she crossed the deck and stared up at the silvery moon above. The rain had stopped and the remaining clouds were a thin lattice, nearly transparent. Eira cursed under her breath.

"What's wrong?" Alyss asked, catching up with her and no doubt hearing the language. "Aren't you happy to see him?"

"Of course I am," Eira said hastily, the question making her aware of just how her actions could be read, not just by Alyss and Cullen, but her uncle. She needed to be more mindful. "But I have no idea how I'll explain all this." Eira gestured around her.

"Well, you would've eventually, right?"

Eira made a noncommittal noise. "If I could've glossed over the finer points, I would've."

"Forever?" Alyss blinked.

"Ideally."

Alyss laughed and it had the echoes of their time in the Tower—it was the same tone as all the other times she'd gently and lovingly told Eira she was being ridiculous. "It's better to get it out."

"Easy to say when you're not the one 'getting it out,'" Eira muttered.

"You don't think I hadn't already thought about what I'd tell my parents, did you?"

"I'd assumed we'd all keep this one massive secret. No one needs to know from our past lives." It sounded utterly unreasonable now that she said it aloud.

"Eira…" Alyss's fingertips landed lightly on her elbow, drawing Eira's attention to her. Somehow, she seemed to glow in the moonlight. As if everything that was ever and *would* ever be good was encapsulated within her. "How you handle your past and its meeting of your present is up to you. None of us will judge you for it."

"I doubt that," Eira murmured under her breath. Alyss heard.

"None of us will and you know it," she said firmly. "You're just being difficult." Eira looked at Alyss from the corners of her eyes. Somehow that only made Alyss even more amused. "I understand why you might want to—have to, even—let go of your past to move forward. But that doesn't mean the rest of us will want to. Some of us might want to carry it with us."

Eira sighed. The notion that not everyone was running seemed…impossible. But she knew it was true, logically. Her emotions just twisted in her gut and got the better of her logic.

"Now, you should go back and talk to him. I'm sure that he's ready and he'll want to hear from you, just like I'm sure he'll have information you want to know." As Alyss finished, Olivin emerged with Ducot in tow. The former held a large mug that Eira could see steaming from where she stood.

"You're right." Resigned, Eira crossed with a few quick steps to where Cullen was waiting beside the door. Alyss was behind her. "I doubt we'll all fit," Eira said skeptically when she realized none of them were leaving.

"I want to hear what he has to say." Olivin's tone was so firm it startled her. It left little room for debate.

"As do I," Ducot added in much the same manner. The men were ready to fight if she resisted.

"Fine, but it's going to be tight." Eira took the mug from Olivin and knocked on the door. "Uncle?"

"I'm decent," he called from within.

Eira allowed herself a single, bracing breath. She steadied herself on the inhale. She was Adela's chosen heir. She had braved Carsovia, twice. She'd survived Ulvarth even more times than that. She'd learned magic that Fritz could only dream of, had dined with nobles, and had operated in the shadows on behalf of royals. Half of her sordid story he'd already learned about.

But would this be the breaking point, and, if it was, did she still care?

That was the question Eira didn't know the answer to. Was her heart in her throat because she still cared what he thought about her, because she loved him and sought his approval? Or was this feeling leftover conditioning of a young girl who had been told, time and again, to respect and revere her uncles?

Only one way to find out…

Eira opened the door and braced herself.

· CHAPTER ·

TWENTY-TWO

"I WASN'T SURE WHAT to do with my old clothes." Fritz pointed at the pile on the floor. "Thank you for the fresh ones, by the way. Those were the last things I wanted to keep wearing."

Eira knew all too well how ridding one's self of the clothing from an ordeal could feel like shedding the whole ordeal itself.

"We'll put them out on deck, for now." Eira decided. Cullen took the indirect order and passed them to Ducot, who unceremoniously *plopped* them outside the door. Some crew member would collect them and put them in the pile for someone to use who didn't have so many memories tied to them. She held out the mug to him. "Here. This should help warm you up."

"I'll take just about anything; it's been ages since I last had more than scraps."

Eira remembered her time in the pit…and her initial days with the pirates. She knew how poorly someone in captivity ate. With that in mind, she saw how loosely the clothes hung off his frame. How gaunt his cheeks were. It'd been months since the fall of the coliseum and it looked like he'd been given just enough to stay alive during that time. How he'd managed to have the strength to survive at all was a testament to his will. A curl of searing anger flashed in her gut as her hand fell on the dagger's hilt at her thigh. There would never be peace for her until Ulvarth was dead.

"What happened after the coliseum?" Eira asked, positioning herself beside him on the bed. Alyss wedged herself behind Eira in the back corner, shifting the blankets to fit. The men crammed in—Ducot and Olivin against opposite walls, barely enough space to not be flush against each other. Cullen shut the door behind him and leaned against it.

"There was the explosion…" Fritz shifted his hands on the mug. It was then that she noticed raised and gnarled scars that completely covered one. The heat of her anger at the Pillars would be an inferno soon enough. "Then, chaos."

"How did you survive?" Olivin asked.

"Barely." Fritz took a long drink of the thick stew in the mug, chewing it for a stretch of silence. "I made it out of the coliseum, but I couldn't find anyone." His eyes drifted to her. "Not your parents."

"They were in Qwint," Eira said.

Fritz's eyes widened. "Reona…"

"Your sister is alive." Her smile, however slight, was genuine. Eira knew the pain of losing a sibling and wouldn't wish it on anyone in the world. "As is Herron."

"I'm so relieved they're all right…and that you had a chance to speak with them." Fritz covered his mouth as though he was exerting physical effort to contain his emotions.

Eira didn't ruin the moment by elaborating on just how briskly their conversation had ended. She was certain they'd tell him when he returned anyway. "They went on a vessel back to Solaris. I'm sure they made it all right."

"I'm sure." Fritz lowered his hand to reveal that he was beaming from ear to ear.

"What about the royals?" Eira asked, shifting the topic from their family.

"Lumeria is gone," Fritz said gravely. "Ulvarth has seated himself as king and defender of the faith."

"As we heard," Ducot murmured, mostly to himself.

"Qwint, well, you know that some survived, but not many. And not the majority of the ministers they'd sent." Fritz shook his head. "I don't know about those from the Twilight Kingdom. The draconi seemed to have survived."

"Are they in league with the Pillars?" Olivin was the one

to give voice to what all of them were likely wondering, since they'd all seen the draconi competitors defending the Pillars as they'd emerged into the coliseum.

"I suspected as much. But I don't think so. At least not beyond a moment…" Fritz frowned and took another long sip, chewing over his words. "My impression from all that I could overhear during my time with the Pillars was that Ulvarth had struck a deal with the draconi, so they would be spared. But their alliance didn't go much farther than that."

"Anyone who works with the Pillars, even once, is always a threat." Olivin's hands balled into fists.

"They returned to their island. I haven't seen one since," Fritz said tiredly. Eira wouldn't have expected him to be defending the draconi…but he had always been the sort to stand against injustice.

"And just how much did you see, and hear, of the Pillars while you were with them?" Olivin asked. The tone that Eira had heard before was back in his voice: mistrust. A frown tugged on the corners of her lips.

"Not as much as I would've liked, or tried to," Fritz admitted. Eira couldn't tell if he was genuinely oblivious or not to Olivin's skepticism.

"Why didn't they kill you?"

"I was useful and promised I could make myself more useful…" Fritz described his time with the Pillars, but Eira could tell he was glossing over some finer details. When he spoke of being captured by them on the road and begging for his life, Eira could feel the blows that he omitted, as though they were on her own skin, blows that persisted until darkness consumed him.

He said he woke in a room of total darkness. A pit, in another name. Locked, forgotten, starved until finally someone came to him. She felt the desperation in her own stomach, tempered with rage-filled resistance at the idea of giving in to them for a few meager bites of whatever stale or mold-crusted scraps they were presenting.

She could envision the dance of words and actions that followed. The careful navigation of telling them what they wanted to hear, showing them genuine vulnerability…but keeping true strength for herself. The core of her mind, and heart, locked away.

"…Eventually, I convinced them to put me on a ship. That I could help them not only as a Waterrunner, but to navigate to Solaris," Fritz continued, nearing his conclusion. "They eventually agreed. Though they didn't have much of a choice."

"Why not?" Alyss mused.

"Lightspinning isn't particularly useful for moving ships around. It can be done, but…Waterrunners and Windwalkers are far more useful on the seas," Eira answered for her uncle. "Did they have others from Solaris captive?"

"I always assumed they did, but I never saw any," he said solemnly. "I would've freed them, were I able."

"And what of the Solaris royal family?" Cullen had been completely silent until now. But his expression was nearly murderous. Eira wondered if, as her uncle spoke, he, too, was playing the scenes in his mind based on what she had told him—had been seeing *her* in every situation Fritz had described. "You didn't mention them earlier. I take it they're not captive?"

"Are they…" Alyss couldn't bring herself to finish the question, even as little more than a whisper.

"I tried to get to them, but I couldn't before the explosion. I don't know what happened." Fritz finished the last of his stew and stared into the empty mug, as though the answer had been hidden on the bottom all along. "Ulvarth doesn't have them, that much I'm certain of based on what they asked me about the royals time and again. Once I had a bit more leeway with the Pillars, I picked up that they had been searching through the wreckage of the coliseum for them. Their bodies still weren't found."

"They're alive." Even though the words were soft, they were sure. Eira's confidence resounded in them now more than ever.

"How do you know?" Cullen directed the question her way.

"Vi." One name summarized all her conviction and then some.

She had known it in her bones and, all along, Adela had been unshakably confident in the idea that Vi carried on. All eyes were on Eira, but the only one who looked like he fully understood was Olivin. So Eira explained for the rest of them, her uncle included. "She was a leader of the Court of Shadows."

"Vi Solaris? The Court of Shadows on Meru?" Surprise was as evident in her uncle's tone as it was on his face.

"That was only the edge of her quilt of influence, I suspect," Eira said, mostly to herself. Then, louder, "She is a Lightspinner, in addition to a Firebearer."

"Impossible," Olivin blurted.

"She is," Eira insisted. "And I always suspected that was just the tip of her power. If anyone could've survived the coliseum—even with the might of flash beads—it'd be her."

"I hope so." Fritz's words were as wavering as his hope no doubt was.

Eira remembered what he had told her right before everything went sideways about Vhalla being his Alyss. She rested a hand on his knee and met his fearful eyes with confidence. "I'm sure she kept the Emperor and Empress safe, too. With all three of their powers together, how could they not survive?"

"I'm sure you're right." But he didn't sound like he believed it. Not that it mattered, because Eira had no doubts she'd eventually be proven correct.

"What can you tell us about the Pillars' operations?" Olivin's focus wasn't anywhere near Solaris. Though silently Eira admitted his persistence was the right call. Whatever was the true fate of the Solaris family would be revealed in time. And if Vi was an ally in hiding, that would be seen when the moment was right, Eira was certain. For now, their focus needed to remain on the Pillars and getting to Meru.

"I'm not sure how much will be useful, but I'll tell you all I know…" Fritz braced himself, gripping the edge of the bed.

He told them of the Pillars' infiltration of Risen—their swift and overwhelming rise to power. How there were only three choices for those in the city: death, captivity (which usually led to death), or joining the Pillars' crazed faith. And he spoke of the armor Allun had mentioned. Fritz didn't know the truth of it, but he did describe a "golden haze" that the armor surrounded Ulvarth in—from hidden runes, Eira suspected—and how the armor made him basically invincible. Combined with what her parents had said about it, Eira was glad she had the pistol.

The moment Fritz finished telling them all he'd seen and overheard, Olivin began peppering him with questions. They were shot faster than flashfires. Repetitive. Each faster than the last. Fritz worked to keep up, but eventually his answers began circling themselves.

"You honestly expect us to believe that's all you know?" Olivin finally snapped.

"I'm telling you it is." Fritz hung his head with a sigh. "Believe me or don't. That's up to you."

"You were with them for weeks."

"Rotting in a cell!" The exclamation came out of nowhere. Eira had never seen her uncle's brow furrowed so deeply, eyes so rife with pain. "If you want those answers so badly, why don't you go and get captured by them?"

"My brother was." Olivin's tone became harder and more dangerous.

"Which means you know nothing then." Fritz narrowed his eyes, Eira had never seen her uncle have this much rage before.

"How dare you," Olivin snarled.

"How dare you ask me about my time as their captive so callously."

"If you were captured to begin with and didn't go willingly." Olivin's words were as sharp as a dagger's edge.

"That's enough." Eira might not be the captain of the vessel they were on, but she was *their* captain. Their leader. And her tone ensured that would not be questioned. "He's told us all he knows."

She locked eyes with Olivin. He made a noise of disgust

in the back of his throat, shook his head, and practically threw Cullen aside to storm out the door. Ducot took advantage of the opening and followed behind. Eira glared after them, but her gaze instantly softened when it was drawn to her uncle's as he looked to her with pain.

"I swear it, Eira. I'm telling you all I know. I would never have gone with them willingly."

In that moment, he had become the child. He appeared scared and broken. A younger man who had endured the worst of the world's horrors and then some. Who had watched a mad king rise to power once before and was now forced to watch that ascension happen all over again.

"I know you are; just as I know that you never would be one of them." She reached over and wrapped her arms around his shoulders, pulling him in for a tight embrace. The mug clattered to the floor, forgotten. Eira could feel him trembling in her embrace. "You're safe now." She told him what she'd needed to hear so desperately the moment she'd escaped the Pillars and silently chided herself that it had taken this long for that phrase to be uttered.

Fritz drew a shaky breath as Eira felt Alyss moving behind her, sliding off the bed. "Thank you." A bitter chuckle. "Though, I'm not sure how…given that I'm on the *Stormfrost* and a captive of Adela."

"About that…" Eira rubbed the back of her neck as they pulled apart, searching for the words.

"We'll leave you both to it." Alyss pulled Cullen out the door, closing it quickly behind them. Eira heard the message loud and clear: it was time for her and her uncle to talk.

"You're not the only one who was taken captive following the coliseum, though it worked out much better for me." Eira folded and unfolded her hands as though she could repeat the motion until it undid the knot in her throat.

His hand entered her sight, resting lightly over her thumbs. The movement drew her attention to him.

 Elise Kova

"I'm glad it did." Sincerity shone in his eyes. Out of everything that he had endured, why did her being all right make him look like he wanted to weep? And how did it make tears threaten her own eyes? "Don't look so guilty." He laughed, as if he could read her mind. "Just because I suffered doesn't mean I would've wanted you too as well."

"I know. I simply…wish you didn't have to. I wish I'd been strong enough to defeat Ulvarth before he ever became this much of a problem." Eira's fingers balled into fists underneath his.

"You don't have to shoulder the weight of the world. It's not your responsibility," he tried to reassure her.

Eira slowly shook her head, bringing her eyes to his. The burning behind her lids was gone, and with it the tears she hadn't let fall. The knot in her throat hadn't yet unraveled. "Whether it is or isn't—should or shouldn't be—it doesn't matter, Uncle. I *want* it to be my responsibility."

"Eira…" he whispered sadly, losing the words briefly before finding them once more. "You don't have to do this. You can come home."

Home. There was that word again. The same word her parents had used. The word that had only just begun to reclaim meaning for her.

"Uncle, this"—Eira gestured around them—"is my home now."

"What?" He leaned back. "No, no no. Eira, you merely think that because you've been Adela's captive for so long. But we'll be able to free you. I'm here now and—"

She shifted her hands to grip his fingers. "Uncle, I don't need saving. This is what I've chosen."

"Is she really…" He couldn't bring himself to finish.

"My mother? No." Eira chuckled and briefly mused on if she'd ever say yes to that question purely because it was easier. But "mother" didn't quite fit Adela. The woman was mentor and something *like* a mother…but also not. And Eira didn't want to force her to be. The first time Eira had a mother, it hadn't worked out as ideally as she might have hoped. She wasn't keen on pressing the label upon someone else. "She's training me though. She's chosen me as her heir."

"You?" Fritz's brow furrowed and relaxed. He squinted then stopped. As if he couldn't quite see her. Perhaps he was seeing her truly for the first time. "If you're not her daughter, why would she want you?"

The fact that he couldn't understand it was all she needed to know. Without trying to, he showed her so beautifully and succinctly what Eira had felt all her life. *You doubt me, even still.*

Eira kept the thought to herself. It would get them nowhere, and Alyss had been right: she wasn't going to bring Fritz with her into this next stage of her life. Their time had passed. But she'd still keep him in her heart, as she would her parents. Enough to make good on her word from time to time that she'd visit them whenever the winds carried her into port, as she was able.

"After the coliseum, we fled onto a vessel moored in the river by Warich that I thought belonged to the Court of Shadows. But I'd misunderstood. It was Adela's…"

Eira told him all that had transpired at length. She spared him little—only the more intimate details of her interactions with Cullen and Olivin. There was her initial work with Adela, the revelations, getting her magic back, and Noelle's death. His fingers tightened and his eyes widened, shoulders slouching as his jaw relaxed and lips parted in shock. By the time she finished, he looked as if he had lived through half of it.

"…Now I'm going to go back to Meru. I will find Ulvarth and end this," Eira finished. "And when it's over, I'll see where the wind carries me."

Without warning, Fritz yanked her to him, throwing his arms around her shoulders once more and drawing a shuddering breath. "I cannot believe all you have endured."

"I'm fine." She gave him a firm squeeze.

"I can see that now."

Eira released him, wondering if it was true. Could he truly see her? Or would she forever be the girl living in Marcus's shadow? The untamed magic that threatened to bring shame as easily as pride to their family name?

"You should rest." Eira decided that for now there was little sense in digging deeper into those questions. Maybe they never needed to be explored. There were some things that were all right left unsaid. "I can only imagine how long it's been since you had a proper sleep. Take my cabin for the night."

"Are you sure?" He was already in the process of making the bed as he asked.

"Very much so." She stood to get out of his way. "I'll bring food in the morning." Her mind was already debating what she was going to do next with him. Though ideas were forming. "For now, rest easily knowing you're safe."

Eira excused herself and emerged from the cabin into the brisk night. She inhaled deeply the smell of salt and cold. No sooner had she taken a few steps than the feeling of being watched overwhelmed her. Halting, her attention swung, meeting a pair of familiar eyes that shone in the darkness.

"We should talk." Olivin's voice had a bit of gravel to it, as though the words were weighted by severity.

Eira had remembered the tone he'd taken with her uncle and gave a slight nod. "I think we should."

THEY MADE THEIR way in silence to the bow of the *Stormfrost*. It was one of the few spots on board that everyone seemed to respect as the place to go when you wanted to be alone. Privacy was a bit of an illusion on a ship, but it was a farce they all kept up. On the way, Eira stretched her senses through the waters beneath the vessel. Without having to turn her head, she knew *Winter's Bane* was nearby. Sailing right alongside the *Stormfrost* as Adela had promised.

But that ship is only temporary, Eira thought, reminding herself of what Adela had said.

As soon as they reached the bow of the vessel, Eira demanded, "Out with it."

Olivin didn't even pretend not to know what she was referring to. "I don't trust him."

"Clearly." Eira gave him a dull look. The fact that he needed to say it was almost an insult to her intelligence. "I'm asking why."

He pursed his lips and turned, hands on the railing with white knuckles. His biceps bulged as he gripped and relaxed. "They don't let people go."

"They didn't 'let him go.' We sank their ship and he survived."

"Quite conveniently."

"He's a Waterrunner. And one of the best in Solaris, second to me." Eira wasn't sure if the remark crossed the line from confidence to arrogance, but she said it matter-of-factly and was ready to be proven wrong, should the time ever come…though she doubted it ever would. "The ship went down on the open sea and they weren't limiting his magic so he could help them sail. It stands to reason he'd survive."

"*Exactly*, they weren't limiting his magic. Does that sound like the Pillars to you?" Olivin continued to keep his back to her. Eira doubted this was a good thing. "They don't let people go free, Eira."

"They let me go free." She walked slowly to his side, keeping every movement measured and her voice level.

"Because they thought you were working for them."

"A ruse he performed as well." Eira could see through to the root of Olivin's uncertainty. She knew where this questioning came from and it had a name: Wynry. So Eria tried to keep her tone gentle. This situation was scratching at several of his old wounds. "He was *surviving*, Olivin. He told them what they needed to hear—just as I did. He wasn't one of them."

"How can you be so sure?"

"I know him."

"You *think* you do." Olivin glanced at her from the corners of his eyes and, for the first time since meeting him, Eira didn't recognize the man. There was an edge to him that Eira realized he'd only ever hinted at. "You think your family is everything— that you can trust them, until the Pillars take it all from you."

"He is not your sister," she tried to say as delicately as she was able.

"Not that you know of." Olivin gave her another challenging look, but Eira didn't dignify the remark with a response. Her silence prompted him to continue. "Wynry wasn't someone I would've ever thought would turn on our family. She loved me and Yonlin up until the very day that she drove a dagger through my father's back. All it takes is Ulvarth in your ear and—"

"Do you think I submitted to Ulvarth because he was 'in my ear?'" Eira interrupted. "That I'm secretly one of them?"

"What? Of course not." Olivin looked startled every time she pointed out the contradiction in his logic.

"Then extend the same grace to my uncle." Eira dared to

approach him, settling a hand on his bicep. Unfortunately, it didn't have the calming effect she might have hoped.

"If he betrays us, it's on you," Olivin said coolly.

"I know." Eira's hand dropped from his person. Disappointment weighed heavy. "No matter what happens, Olivin, it's on me— because I am your captain."

"Then act like one. Look after the people you claim to care about." He was lashing out with the speed of a whip and Eira felt the sting. But she didn't flinch.

"What is this really about?" She kept the question calm as she continued to keep her head level. Eira still hadn't seen Yonlin, but if Alyss and Olivin weren't at his side, then his condition surely wasn't *that* bad. Yes, Wynry was a wound that might never quite close. But this felt like so much more than fear of another betrayal.

Olivin looked away. "I can't lose him, Eira. He's all I have left of my family. I swore I'd keep him safe." *So it was Yonlin, after all.*

"I know," she said gently. If there was one thing she could relate to, it was feeling like you couldn't protect those you loved. Ever since Noelle's death, they all seemed to be far more aware at just how mortal they all were, and the dangers the Pillars presented.

"I… We… We lost everything when Wynry betrayed us. Our home. Our standing in society. Our means. There was only Yonlin and me. I want to end Ulvarth, but not if the risks mean it might cost me my brother."

There was the line. It seemed everyone had a point at which they would back down from their pursuit of Ulvarth. Which meant she had to be even more unflinching. She had to be the one to do it for them all…and for herself. Everyone else had a weakness or a limit Ulvarth could exploit. She had to make sure she was the only one without.

"It won't."

He wasn't taking her reassurances. "You say that, but you

can't keep yourself safe—keep any of us safe. And now you would let a traitor—"

"Enough." Eira stopped Olivin before he'd say something he didn't mean. Something they might not be able to come back from. "You are heard, Olivin." She grabbed both his hands as if she could be the one to take hold of his fears. "Your concerns are valid; I know why you have them. But I'm telling you, as your captain, that this is my decision. We are going to care for my uncle until he's mended enough that he can be put on *Winter's Bane*, and then he will sail back home to Solaris, where he can be a voice for us on the inside of Solaris's government. That way, when we do move against Ulvarth, it goes off without a hitch— we will have Qwint and whatever is left of the Solaris armada."

Eyes locked with hers, Olivin looked as though he were about to object again. But he didn't beyond another shake of his head. Withdrawing, he said, "I really hope you know what you're doing."

He was gone before Eira could formulate a response, leaving a chill colder than the deck of the *Stormfrost* in his wake. She stared at where he had just stood. Not angry. Not wounded beyond repair. But still hurt. Taking a breath, Eira calmed herself and gave him space. She could only hope that same chill he exuded would lead to a cooler head prevailing by morning.

The next morning, Eira was one of the first up in the entire crew. Not *the first*—there was always someone who wasn't sleeping, because there were always duties to be attended to on a vessel as large as the *Stormfrost*. But she was among the few to greet the dawn.

She wanted to find a moment with Olivin to talk—apologize for the firm note she'd left things on the previous evening. But he was still fast asleep and she didn't want to wake him. Tensions had run high last night; they'd be okay again soon enough though.

She went to Adela's cabin bearing the gift of a hot meal. It was odd to see a pirate other than Crow stationed outside her door. But Eira was grateful to have the woman, whom she'd begun to look to as her first mate, on *Winter's Bane*. It hadn't occurred to her until that moment that perhaps such had been Adela's plan all along. If Crow could grow accustomed to Eira, and Eira to her, it was one less transition.

The pirate stationed didn't stop her, and Eira wasn't surprised to see Adela up as well.

They talked plans over breakfast, aligning on the next steps. The pirate queen didn't fight Eira's intentions with her uncle— save for Crow being the one to captain *Winter's Bane*. Even though the woman was one of the few Eira would trust to take the little vessel, she couldn't argue too intensely when her focus needed to be solely on the *Stormfrost*. And, to that end, it made more sense for them to keep someone as trusted as Crow near. Then their conversation shifted to Ulvarth, and reclaiming Meru.

The sun was above the horizon, though still golden with gentle early light, when Eira emerged. Adela was a step behind and they parted ways. Eira started for belowdecks, stopping short when she saw Cullen coming up, hands laden with his pack.

"Where do you think you're going?" Eira tilted her head. Had Olivin mentioned her plans about sending Fritz back to Solaris when he'd returned before her last night? Had Cullen heard?

Was he leaving her?

The thought hit her with a force stronger than her magic being ripped from her, leaving her just as breathless. Of course he would leave. He might not have taken the opportunity when they were in Qwint, too much was left unsettled then. This would be the perfect time for him to return to the lands he knew—his home.

Frankly, he would do more for them back in Solaris. His note had gone ahead of him, so they knew he was alive. But the man himself? He could turn the Court in their favor. The protégé of the Empress triumphantly returned. Eira could already see the gold and white pennons of the Solaris troops, Cullen at their head by Romulin's side, coming to reclaim Solaris's glory.

She swallowed thickly, hating how perfect it all seemed. And how, all at once, they were leaving her. One by one. Olivin no longer trusted her. Cullen would leave her because of course he would, and—

"I thought Fritz could use some supplies for the road."

"Right." Eira nodded, trying to keep the panic she was warring with concealed and seemingly succeeding. "Olivin told you?"

"What?"

"That I'd be sending Fritz off… Olivin must've told you when he returned," Eira reasoned. Yet Cullen continued to blink, looking as confused as ever.

"Eira…" He took two more steps up, standing just below her. Though, with his height, he could nearly meet her eyes even being one step down. "Don't mistake this arrangement. I am respectful of Olivin because I am respectful of *you*. If someone is dear to you, then they will be dear to me. But it is merely respect; I wouldn't call us 'friends' by any measure." The corners of his lips curled up ever so slightly. Smugly. "So don't think for even a second that the moment he might not be dear to you that I won't be done with him."

"Then…you're not leaving?" The question was as fragile as the hope which fluttered along over her heart. As desires she was just now realizing she'd been ignoring.

"Not unless you wish for me to." The way he held her gaze felt like an embrace and her entire body tingled with a warmth that not even the cold of the *Stormfrost* could puncture. "By your side, on this ship, with this crew, is where I want to be—where I am meant to be."

"You love the *Stormfrost*?" She searched his expression for the hint of a lie. He had made it clear he would be loyal to her. But to separate the *Stormfrost* from her as somewhere he wanted to be in its own right was new. "Because it is dear to me?"

"In part," he didn't deny it. But his eyes drifted across the deck, out to sea. "I find that this life suits me better than I might have ever thought. Granted, if you left it, I doubt I'd stay. But, there's something to this whole piracy thing." His attention returned to her with the smallest quirk of his lips. As if to agree with him, the salt-spray filled wind tousled his hair.

"I doubt I'll be leaving ever." In that, she was confident.

"Then, I will be with you through every storm and gale. Over the edge of the horizon and beyond where the seas run out. I will follow you until the ink runs dry on every map and we are well beyond the edge into the vast unknown."

Eira simply stared at him, vaguely aware that her lips had parted with surprise. That she was struggling to formulate words. Cullen merely held her gaze and his smile. There was something between the words, yet unsaid, but felt so sharply that he might as well have shouted:

I love you, Eira.

"Now, I should bring this to your uncle so he can finish getting himself ready to depart." Cullen brushed past her, as if he was somehow oblivious to what he'd just done to her.

"Wait." Eira turned and met his eyes once more. "How did you know I was sending him off if Olivin didn't tell you?"

"Because it makes the most sense. You're too clever not to do what's best." Cullen shrugged. "Which is why I figured you would want him readied to leave."

"So you took it upon yourself?"

"I thought it was faster than you making the order. One less thing for you to worry about. So focus on saying goodbye this morning and planning whatever we're off to next." Cullen smiled as if he somehow hadn't predicted her every movement. As if he didn't already know what Eira had in mind for their next several movements.

She watched him leave, the sea breezes caressing him like a lover, picking up his hair—dark brown, nothing special. Everything about him had always been *so conventional*. Almost to the point of being boring. But somehow the man that had once seemed "boring" now looked reliable. Dependable, even. Someone she could turn to.

Eira rubbed the center of her chest and started belowdecks. There was pain still there from a night shared before a ball. A heartache that warned her against falling back into the arms of a man who didn't deserve her.

But he had been changing…and perhaps she was starting to meet the man he was always meant to be. For now, she needed to smooth things over with the other man in her life.

It was late afternoon when *Winter's Bane* was ready to make the trip to Solaris. Eira stood at the edge of the starboard side of the *Stormfrost*, staring down at the vessel she thought she'd take to Meru to claim her vengeance against Ulvarth. But it wasn't meant for her in the end. It was meant for the man next to her.

Fritz's hands were empty. He had passed everything along to the pirates that were readying the vessel to go out to sea. Now all that was left was for him to join them.

"It'll be all right," Eira reassured him. She saw the tension in his jaw and the hard line of his lips. "I trust these men and women with my life, and they know you're part of my crew, in a way. They won't allow harm to befall you."

Fritz nodded, though that hard line had yet to ease.

"When you get back to Solaris, please—"

"You don't have anything to worry about," he interrupted. "I won't be sending the armada after you or Adela."

A chuckle she couldn't quite contain escaped as a snort of amusement.

"What?"

"I'm laughing because the thought of you sending the armada

after me hadn't even crossed my mind," Eira admitted. "Should it have?"

"You have aligned yourself with the most infamous pirate ever to exist," Fritz pointed out. *If only he knew the half of Adela's crimes…* "There will be those who come after you."

"Deals can be brokered," Eira said nonchalantly.

"Not with those in power whom she directly attacks." The words were a bit lower in volume, a bit harsher. She couldn't tell if it came from a place of genuine worry for her well-being…or disapproval. Eira chose not to read into it.

"Uncle, if there's one thing I've learned, it's that there is a shadow version of this world. An underside where the mirror reflects everything back not *quite* the same. That other place is just as influential to what happens in the daylight as anything else." Eira leaned against the railing, half sitting, and looked out to sea. Vi had made a deal with Adela for something. Eira had managed it with Qwint. "Sometimes, those in power need those of us who are untethered to be the shadowy hand that guides the destiny they want to see manifested around them."

He sighed heavily. Eira could almost see the hunch to his shoulders that whispered of just how much all this was weighing on him. She placed a palm on one, clasping it firmly.

"Don't worry about me. Send the armada if you like, even. But they'll be cutting off their nose to spite their face." Eira smirked. "Solaris, Qwint, Meru, Twilight, they all might loathe me, call out for my death. But under their breath, they'll confess that they *need* me."

"And when that need is met?"

"I have a fast ship and a lot of power." It vaguely occurred to her just how confidently she could refer to the *Stormfrost* as *her ship*. She made an internal note to be wary that the confidence didn't cross into arrogance. Adela was still the captain and pirate queen, not her. And the generosity she'd shown Eira could wither on the vine or blossom into the future she was dreaming of.

"They've tried to kill Adela for decades and look where it got them. I'm not afraid."

Yet another sigh. That was all her uncle could seem to do around her—his only response to all she was saying. Eira chuckled again.

"You know, you are fretting over me more than my parents did." Eira shifted her attention back to him. Fritz's expression was pinched still. His eyes glistening.

"Because I watched you grow up," he whispered. "As much—*more* than they did. Because I watched you, at every step of life, be willing to throw yourself headlong into danger and there was nothing I could do to stop you even when, every time, my heart seized and threatened to drop from my chest."

Eira shifted, the leg she'd half propped on the railing falling back to the deck so she could stand fully. His every word had her on tenterhooks.

"I…we…went through so much to make Solaris what it is today. I wanted to see you enjoy a good and quiet life in the peace and prosperity we had worked so hard for." He stared past the horizon, at a time long gone.

"Uncle—" Eira took his hand in both of hers, drawing his attention to her. "Maybe I am not meant for that peace. But that doesn't mean others aren't. That your struggle wasn't for naught."

"But *you* are the one I wanted to enjoy it."

Guilt ripped through her like an arrow to the heart. Eira tried to snap and pull it through, ignoring the pain. "My life is my own to live. You can't do it for me."

"How I wish that weren't true…" He squeezed her fingers.

"I know." Eira smiled faintly. He'd never understand her. But, in his way, he loved her. That love wasn't enough to have them seeing eye to eye…just enough to have him always tucked into a fond place in the corner of her heart. Eira slipped her arms around his shoulders and inhaled deeply the scent of her childhood. The warmth that was once both safety and suffocation, and was now little more than an air of nostalgia. "No matter what, I do love you. And I thank you for trying the best you knew how."

"I'm sorry if it wasn't enough for you." He squeezed her back so tightly that the words trembled in time with his hands.

"It wasn't about being enough, or not enough." They pulled apart and Eira gently wiped a stray tear from his cheek. "I was meant for something different, is all. Not better or worse." Though she knew he might disagree. "Simply different."

"It's hard when what you envisioned for someone who's like a child to you isn't the life they wanted."

"But there's also joy in them finding the life they were meant to have," she reminded him gently. "Now, you need to go back where you belong. Give Grahm my love as well. I'll come by whenever I have the chance." Though Eira didn't know when that would be, she was sincere in saying so. If she had the chance, she would return to them as Eira, not Adela's heir. Not to pillage, but to spend a quiet evening in a place that was once what she thought of as home.

"Please do." Despite everything, he sounded like he meant it. "I—we all love you."

"I know." As best they knew how.

She wore a slight smile the entire time they finished preparing Fritz for his departure. Alyss gave him the largest hug and a letter to send to her parents when he returned to Solaris. She'd been working on it, apparently, since they were in Qwint and Cullen had sent one of his own.

Cullen shared a sturdy handshake with the Minister of Sorcery and a few words that Eira couldn't make out. Though, she didn't try. Some things weren't meant for her ears, even if they burned with curiosity. What she did hear, though, was Cullen politely refusing Fritz's offer to take another letter for him.

"I've already said all I have to say. There's nothing more to send back from me." Cullen had an easy confidence to the polite refusal, one that had her gaze turning to his for a breath. Holding his stare. *I'm done with that place*, the wind that passed between them seemed to emphasize on his behalf.

Eira brought her focus back to Fritz, squeezing him a final time.

"Good luck," he whispered.

"Same to you," she replied.

And then, they parted. She watched as he descended the side of *Stormfrost* and boarded *Winter's Bane*. Even after the other pirates went about their work, she remained at the railing, Alyss and Cullen flanking her. All three watched the little ship melt into the eastern horizon until its flags could no longer be seen.

All the while, Eira's cheeks remained dry. So when she turned and put her back to the waters of the Shattered Isles that bordered Solaris, she didn't have to compose herself. There was no hesitation and no looking back.

All that was out there for her was ahead. To Meru. To beyond, where the ink bled off the edges of the maps.

It took two days and one other battle with the Pillars for them to successfully sail to the Isle of Frost. All the while, Eira continued to explore her new powers with Adela, testing if their long-thought-over plan would finally be viable thanks to Eira's rune. Fortunately, early work suggested it would be.

The old pirate mainstay was somewhat out of the way. But it was one of the few places on the eastern side of Meru that could be trusted to be safe to rest and restock. Even if the island had been deserted for years.

Eira had asked Adela why she had ever abandoned the legendary mainstay, but their conversation didn't go well…

"It was my decision."

"Obviously," Eira had said. "But what prompted that decision?"

"Nothing that is for you to concern yourself with."

"If I am to one day captain the *Stormfrost*—"

"*One day*," Adela repeated, tone harsher than winter. Colder than the ice that coated the island they spoke of. "But you are not her captain yet. And you are nowhere near ready."

Nowhere near ready… The words echoed within her even now, days later. Eira massaged the center of her chest, feeling the raised and gnarled scar underneath her shirt and small clothes.

"Eira." Adela jolted Eira from her thoughts. Eira glanced over her shoulder. The pirate queen approached and Eira stepped to the side so Adela could assume her position at the very tip of the bow.

"Can you sense when I'm thinking of you now?" Eira asked dryly.

"No. Thank goodness. I think we can both agree that's for the best." Adela gave her a sidelong glance. "Though you have my curiosity."

"I was thinking about how I might have been overstepping of late."

"*Ah…*" Adela hummed. "Our conversation still lingers with you."

"Only because I'm confronted with its original subject." Eira gestured to the island that was slowly growing on the horizon. "I was reflecting on everything I still had yet to do."

"Good." Adela rested both hands on her cane, keeping her focus to sea. "Complacency will be the death of you."

Eira gave a small nod and allowed the conversation to be drowned out by the waves that broke against the sturdy hull of the *Stormfrost*. The sun continued to ascend, its rays parting the chill gloom that settled on the island, turning it from little more than a shadowy gem to a sparkling jewel of the seas. It was held fast in a glacial embrace so cold that it almost glowed a brilliant blue in the morning light. So cold that time itself seemed to be captured in the grip of its eternal winter.

Adela narrowed her eyes and lifted her cane as her magic swelled in tandem. It was so rare to see or feel any kind of tell from the woman that Eira's gaze was drawn instantly to her. When she lowered her cane with a soft *tap*, magic exploded outward. It rushed across the surface of the ocean as if fired from the *Stormfrost* herself. The magic condensed on the seas, merging with every breaking wave. The swell rose to epic proportions, casting a long shadow, as it drew near to the Isle of Frost.

As the tidal wave broke against the frozen land, a low rumbling could be heard, not just felt, deep within the earth. Adela's magic had somehow crashed against the very foundation of the earth and even the air shivered with fear. The island came alive to her will. A thunderous *crack* echoed over the seas, drawing a cryptic smile into the corners of Adela's lips.

The central glacier, nestled into the curve of the island's mountainous arc, fractured and split. Walls of ice the size of ships carved off its faces, crashing into the ocean and generating waves so monstrous their offspring could kiss the *Stormfrost*. Waves of immense power continued to radiate out from Adela in reply.

As the ice splintered and melted into the sea, the frosty armor of the island gave way to a hidden world underneath. Wooden and stone structures began to emerge like the first determined blossoms of spring. They dripped with frost as they thawed. Masts of ships long hidden rose like skeletal fingers from the harbor, waterlogged banners struggling to catch the morning's breeze.

The island returned to life, still sparkling with snow and frost, and the crew became restless with excitement. Adela tapped her cane and shifted her weight, as if she were about to walk away, but then something crossed her mind, prompting her to stop. She met Eira's questioning gaze.

"See to it that everything is thawed and dry by the time we arrive." She smirked. "I'd hate for someone to slip and fall."

"Can't have that." Eira saw right through the pirate queen. This was a test, as much as everything else was.

"No, we can't." Adela left Eira to the task.

Eira faced off with the island once more, but this time stretched out her magic alongside her focus as she narrowed in on the spot of land. If Adela wanted all the water gone, she'd see to it that not even a single tattered flag on the ships in the bay was dripping by the time they arrived.

The town, in some ways, reminded Eira of a cross between

Risen and the port they'd escaped Carsovia from. There was a river that ran through the heart of the pirate city, splitting it in two, much like Risen was. But it was understandably smaller than the capital of Meru. Countless bridges crossed the river up and down its length adding to the overall mazelike quality of the island. The Isle of Frost was clearly prepared to house hundreds, if not thousands of pirates. Which made it all the more eerie that they were the only ones occupying it.

Though it did mean that their small crew was able to each claim their own home for the night, making their own little block nestled among the other pirates setting up their houses in ways that suggested much more permanence than staying merely to restock. Adela was opening the Isle of Frost once more, even though she didn't outright say so. Of course, Eira was wildly curious about this, and what it meant for her to do so after she'd spent years avoiding Solaris and Meru at all costs. But she knew better than to probe too deeply on the matter.

A banging on the door of her small, one-room home had Eira heading out.

Alyss didn't miss a beat, grabbing her arm. "We're going out tonight."

"I'm sorry, what?" The words practically blurred together into one.

"Food. Drink. Dancing. Down by the docks."

"Since when did you become one who wants to be in the thick of it?" Eira laughed, glancing around the square all their houses circled. There was no one else around.

"Since we have been cooped up on a ship doing nothing but working and fighting and having difficult conversations for weeks on end."

"Weren't we just in Qwint? We had an evening out there." Eira took two steps to keep up with Alyss. Even with her longer strides, she had to make an effort to maintain her pace with the smaller woman. Alyss was on a mission. She was going to have a good time, or else.

"We were *working*." That was certainly a way to phrase it. "There was hardly any time to enjoy ourselves. When we weren't in Carsovia, we were bartering for our lives or mending and restocking the ship. Here, we can relax."

The notion of relaxing was…odd. Eira couldn't recall the last time she'd allowed herself to embrace the idea. Even when she'd strolled in the market with Cullen and Olivin, there was always something in the back of her mind. Alyss was right, it'd been one thing after another, after another. Everything blurring together following Noelle's death.

She lost her footing and quickly recovered, missing a step. Alyss noticed, head swiveling back to look at her with a questioning stare.

"Do you…" The question sounded ridiculous, even to Eira, but she had to ask anyway. "Do you think that it's an insult to Noelle to let loose while her killers run free?"

Alyss slowed, but still made it a point to make forward progress. In the distance was a glowing point of light by the docks. Music and the muddled sounds of chattering could already be heard.

"Noelle lived better than most. She burned brightly." The phrasing somehow managed to sound like an homage to her memory, and not a bad expression. "She would've absolutely scolded us for sitting around all glum when we could be engaging in revelry with pirates."

"You're not wrong." Eira could hear Noelle in the back of her mind, encouraging her to go out—to do more. *Stop moping around.*

"I rarely am." Alyss gave a slight smile, as if she could even recognize that those words echoed Noelle's.

At the end of the river, down where it met the harbor, was a large square. Eira could imagine how, at one point, this area was used for commerce. Or practicalities of the docks. But, tonight, it was a large buffet. It was music and dancing and the burning liquor that she'd sipped on in Adela's cabin countless times.

Tonight, everyone danced and sang as though it would be their last night alive.

Alyss wasted no time in pulling Eira right into the thick of the dancing. Fingers hooking, skirts swirling, they spun and jumped with each other to the raucous music. A smile cracked Eira's lips for the first time in what felt like months. One that wasn't weighed down by calculations, plotting, scheming, or other concerns. The whole world melted away like the ice of the island had earlier.

Breathless, they stepped off to the side, hands still clasped.

"You know, pirates do have a fun side to them," Alyss admitted.

Eira gasped. "Perhaps we're growing on you?"

Her friend laughed. "You grew on me long ago, like ivy on the walls of the Tower."

"Are you calling me clingy?" Eira grabbed drinks for them both and they wasted no time.

"You'd be lost without me."

"I would be." Eira took a long sip of her drink. Whatever they'd tapped into was cold and strong. Citrus flavored—tart and sweet at the same time. "You could stay here." The moment Eira softly said the sentiment, she wished she hadn't. Pushing Alyss was the worst idea and she knew it.

Partly because she already knew the answer, and making Alyss say it was worse.

"I could," Alyss said softly, noncommittally. Even though the words were mild agreement, the tone said, *No*.

"I suppose it'd be hard to sell any books from an island of pirates. We don't exactly have a lot of printing presses here for Yonlin to connect you with," Eira agreed, offering Alyss an easy out. Then, in an effort to lighten the mood, "Though, I suppose I could kidnap some for you."

That got a laugh from Alyss. "We'll see." It was a nice sentiment for Alyss to give, though, in her heart, Eira knew better.

She wanted to beg her to stay. To reconsider. And for all Alyss sounded noncommittal, Eira knew in her heart that it'd likely be best for her friend not to live the life of a pirate. That what they were doing now, for Alyss, was a "necessary evil." And, if she put her selfishness aside, she didn't want her friend to change. She wanted Alyss to retain her innocence and good nature. Eira just wished that to do that didn't involve being around her less.

Yonlin approached, his focus solely on Alyss. "May I have a dance?"

Alyss made a show of considering the question. "I suppose one couldn't hurt." She took his offered hand and went back into the fray.

Eira lingered on the edge, situated among the ring of people that framed the dancers. The fiddler was still burning the strings of his instrument with wild fingers while a woman went red in the cheeks working a pan flute. Eira could recognize them, even if she drew blanks on their names. She knew who among the dancers were friends, family, couples, and who yearned to be more.

Everyone here was from the *Stormfrost*. Familiar faces. Which made those absent stand out even more. Olivin was nowhere to be seen. Given their last interaction…she worried what it might mean for him not to be around. She'd need to find time to talk to him again and make sure everything was smoothed over. Eira hated the idea of being at odds with him over what felt like little more than a misunderstanding.

"Want another?" A warm-cheeked Cullen jolted her from her thoughts. He gestured toward her empty cup with his own.

"Oh, no. Thank you." Eira stepped back and placed the cup on one of the long tables behind her. She had no doubt that these cups might be sitting for days or weeks, collecting rainwater as a washing. Doubtless, none of the pirates would care in the slightest. "I think I've had too much as it is."

"You're standing pretty tall and your words are even. I don't think it was too much." Cullen smirked. Barely perceptible was the faintest slur to his words. "Would you like to dance?"

"I just got off the floor."

"Since when do you stop while you're ahead?"

She laughed. Why did saying yes feel like a bad idea? But looking back, some of the worst decisions she'd made had led her to the best outcomes. Everything she shouldn't do became everything she'd wanted.

"Sure."

Cullen downed his drink in one gulp, wincing. The spiced rum was not intended for quick consumption but more ideal for sipping, so she had little doubt it burned the entire way down. He placed his mug next to hers behind them and held out his hand.

"Shall we?"

Her fingers slid against his, curling to a firm clasp. He led her out among the pulsing movement and twirling bodies and they fell into step. She spun. His palm glided over her hip, pulling her close before pushing her away again for another spin.

A smile cracked her lips and her chest heaved. Their feet pounded in time with the rest like distant, rumbling thunder. It wasn't slow, careful steps that would be found at a ball but barely controlled chaos. Eira nearly bumped into others several times… but the near collisions only widened her smile. Cullen beamed from ear to ear.

The next time he spun her, he pulled her close and a slight yelp of surprise escaped her.

"I should never have let you go that night," he whispered into her ear, breathless.

"You shouldn't have," she agreed easily. "You should have taken me as your bride then and there." Eira took advantage of his surprise to take a half step away. She appreciated how the shock slightly parted his lips and raised his brows. "I was young, and naive, and thought I was in love. I would've done it."

"Thought?" Out of everything, that was what he focused on, his hazel eyes burning in the torchlight.

"I was in love," she corrected. Denial was foolish when they both knew better. "As much as I could love, for what I knew and who I was."

"Was?" One-word questions continued to be the assassins of the coy facade she wore.

Eira's steps slowed, but her heartbeat and breathing didn't catch the message. Heart still racing, breaths still ragged to the point that her chest nearly brushed against his as he held her, she stared up at him. His head tilted, not enough for him to kiss her, but enough to narrow the world only to him. The night fell upon his face like a curtain, narrowing everything down to every breath he drew. To the glistening of his gaze.

"*Was?*" he repeated, demanding an answer. Everything around the question that was left unspoken was so loud it nearly screamed.

She opened and shut her mouth, unsure of what to say—of what was real. Did she still love him? After all this time?

"I didn't love you," she said carefully, throat thick. There was that same, burning feeling, racing from her core, all the way up. *I love you*, the words she dared not say, but part of her wanted to more by the day.

"For how long?"

"What?"

"How long did you fall out of love with me?" The opposite corner of his mouth drew up into a coy smirk. "And when did you fall again?"

A flush raced over her body. She wanted to punch him as much as she wanted to kiss him for his boldness. She whispered, "Let me go, forever. Or take me now." She would give him her body— her pleasure. But not her heart. Not just yet. There was still a fearful, broken part of her that had yet to mend. But maybe… with the right touch, and the right words, that part could finally heal.

He blinked, brows darting up. But then they settled into a relaxed smugness. "Then we should leave, because I want you all to myself."

A BASKET OF STARS had been overturned and scattered across the pitch canvas of a moonless sky. The moment they stepped beyond the warm glow of the torches that lined the docks, the music fell away. Brisk wind tumbled down from still-frozen mountaintops and ran through the town like the central river. It pinched at her cheeks, bringing a flush to them that Eira couldn't, and didn't want to, fight.

Cullen glanced over his shoulder, leading her by the hand back to their collection of houses. Or so she thought. He turned in the opposite direction, crossing the river on a rickety bridge before guiding her into a narrow alleyway.

"Where are you taking me?" There were the edges of laughter between the words. She didn't feel unsafe in the slightest. In fact, her feet bounced off the cobblestone streets as though Cullen was sneaking bursts of wind underneath her heels.

"Somewhere no one will find you." He threw a smirk over his shoulder.

"Oh? Sounds dangerous. Should I scream for help?"

Cullen unexpectedly stopped short, the crunch of pebbles on cobblestones under the balls of his feet the only thing that alerted her. Eira nearly ran into him from the momentum. The hand that was holding hers was quick to lace its fingers, moving her right where he wanted—pulling her in close. His other hand tangled itself with her hair, guiding her face to tip up to his and give him full access to her lips.

Her back hit the wall with a soft thud, but Cullen lessened the impact with the positioning of his hands and by easing his body against hers. For a second, he held her. Mouth so close that with a quiver their lips would meet. As if he were savoring every shallow breath.

Then, he kissed her with an urgent need that rendered her breathless. His tongue explored every inch of her mouth in a way that promised to do the same beyond. Eira willingly gave him full access, responding in kind. How long had it been since she'd kissed him like this? Since she'd given herself to reckless passion? Not since the first time they'd been together.

His knee worked its way between hers and his thigh pressed up hard against her center, their bodies completely flush. She could feel every tensing of the strong muscles as she explored every inch of his broad shoulders and back, him pulling her even tighter still. Eira grabbed a fistful of his shirt. There were suddenly far too many clothes. It was suffocating—every hasty kiss more breathless than the last, as if their need was squeezing out room for the air itself around them.

"I need you. Now." She rasped the desperate plea against his mouth. Half kissing. Half speaking.

A low rumble rose up the back of his throat as an amused hum, suggesting he knew exactly what he was doing to her—as if this was all going according to his plans. "Good. Wait."

The moment hung for a heartbeat as he pulled away enough to lock eyes with her, his hair mussed from the earlier winds and tickling her forehead. Just when she was about to lean in and kiss him again, he pulled away. A whine of frustration became a yelp of surprise as he tugged her forward.

They were moving again through the darkness. The buildings condensed further around them, as if they, too, were physically trying to squeeze their bodies together. Right when she was about at the point to tell him to take her against the wall if it meant he'd stop stalling, Cullen paused and opened a door, revealing a small, one-room abode that wasn't unlike the one Eira had selected for herself.

However, unlike the one that Eira had picked, there was a

lantern already burning in this room. Cozy blankets had been piled thick on a bed. Everything looked…tidied.

Eira blinked, processing what was before her. Cullen took a taper and lit one end on the lantern, proceeding to move throughout the room to light a dozen candles across the few shelves, the mantle of the hearth, the table that held a pitcher of water and a small bowl of food.

"You…prepared this?" It was the only thing that made sense. Yet her tone was disbelieving of what her eyes showed her.

"Yes." He didn't dance around it. "I knew that it was unlikely I would find time with you, *alone*, for a while. Perhaps as long a stretch as this past time has been." Cullen paused, snuffing the taper and waving it until the thin curl of smoke disappeared. The room was cast in a rosy light. Bright enough to see by. Dim enough that the harsher details were softened. "If I managed to steal you away, I wanted to make it worth your while. Something you would be…deserving of."

"Deserving of?" she repeated softly. "What do you think that is for a pirate queen in training?"

He chuckled at her questions. She drank in the sound, as thirsty as a woman lost at sea.

"Yes, a pirate *queen*," he emphasized. Cullen set down the taper, shifting to face her. As he spoke, he closed the distance between them and his nearing proximity emphasized each word more than the last. "You, Eira, are deserving of the entire world. Any morsels I can offer you, I do so gladly."

She tilted her head, looking at him through heavy lids. He was close enough for her fingertips to skim down the plane of his chest, landing lightly on his belt buckle. "And if I ask you to offer yourself to me?"

"I was yours long ago. All I am, all I will be, I offer to you." His palms slid around her waist.

"I will take your offering." Her arms circled his shoulders, nails scratching lightly against his scalp as her fingers ran through his hair.

"Good." His voice was husky and deep.

One hand ran up the side of her body, tracing every curve. It sent shots of lightning through her that set fires in their wake. The heat threatened to consume her. By the time his fingers curled around the side of her face, she was already tilting her head to offer her lips to him once more.

This time, when he kissed her, it was slow. Languid. He kissed her as though he would have forever to do it. He savored her like a man at the beginning of an epic journey, course charted, yet final destination unknown. A man still getting his bearings and soaking in every last detail so he would never lose sight of where he'd been, or where he was going.

Eira pushed forward. Control ebbed and flowed between them. He took, she gave, and it made her want more and more.

Cullen stepped back, and with her fists curled in his shirt over his biceps, she pulled him to the bed. When the backs of her legs hit the side, she stopped. Their eyes locked and a thousand words went unsaid. A lifetime of yearning, of sweetness and sorrow. Regret and triumph.

They simultaneously drew a shaky breath.

She tugged at his shirt. Cullen raised his arms and allowed her to pull it over his head. She mirrored the motion with her own and unlaced her bustier.

It was the first time he'd seen the mark she'd been hiding. Cullen's eyes widened a fraction. His fingers brushed along the raised scars, darkened with Allun's ink. He'd been around Lavette and the others from Qwint long enough to know what their runes looked like.

"What does it do?"

"Makes me stronger."

His hand fell to the waist of her trousers. "Then you must truly be unstoppable now."

"That's the plan." A smile worked its way onto her face. One that had more relief carved in it than expected. Ultimately, it didn't matter what he thought. What was done was done, and she wasn't ashamed. But not having him be repulsed by it was more of a relief than she expected.

The rune was quickly forgotten. There were other new things to appreciate. What difference almost a year made. Their bodies were leaner, harder. The soft glow of the candlelight nearly smoothed out the discoloration of their scars, but Eira could feel them as her hands glided over him. She explored him through touch, and he did the same to her. They mapped out each other's bodies, relearning every curve. She felt like a general, plotting out every place she would lay waste to before the night was done.

Wordlessly, she sat on the bed, then lay back. Her knees bent, feet pulling up. His chest rose and fell with slow, heavy breaths as he stared at her, completely exposed before him. The man nearly trembled from the tight control he was exerting over his urges.

"That thing you did at Black Flag Bay…" Eira lightly ran her fingertips down her thigh to her knee and back.

"Yes?" The word was nearly a growl.

"Do it again," she commanded.

He descended on her ravenously.

The moment his mouth closed around her, she let out a delighted sigh that nearly bordered on a squeal. All rational thoughts left her mind. Every urge that wasn't centered around him—around savoring these glorious feelings that only he had given her—vanished. The currents within her gathered speed, moving deeply. Churning, swelling. Powerful hands slid up her body as he lavished his affections upon every sensitive part of her. Every touch was scorching.

Heavy breaths turned to low moans that rose in pitch until they felt as though they were nearly ripping from her throat as he worked her into a frenzy. He seemed to know every movement to make—as though her body was as much his as it was her own. He pushed her further and further beyond every limit she'd ever relaxed against. The only thing that remained in her mind was to succumb.

All at once, she broke with a cry as it all became too much.

Her back arched. But he didn't stop. He kept going until she physically pushed him away. Cullen kissed up her thigh with the same satisfied grin of a predator that had claimed its prey.

"Don't you look smug?" Eira panted softly.

"I feel smug."

"You'll feel more than that." She snorted softly and sat. Her quick movement had his eyes widening briefly. Eyebrows rising with an unspoken question.

"Oh?"

"It's my turn." She swapped their positions.

It was as satisfying to give as it was to receive. The initial uncertainty in his eyes vanished the moment she claimed him. His head tipped back, exposing his neck. A hand buried itself in her hair, pushing. Demanding more.

She was eager to give.

But, all at once, he was pulling her face away from him. Drawing her up. Kissing her dozens of times over.

"Was it not—"

He didn't let her finish. "It was amazing. But I want to savor tonight. I want to feel you in every way you will let me have you."

She knew his meaning instantly.

Eira positioned herself over him and halted. For a breath, they simply stared into each other's eyes. Thousands of words whispered against her mind, as though he were trying to tell her something without so much as a sigh. But Cullen didn't utter anything aloud. His lips parted, but not a sound escaped.

Which left her to fill in the blanks. To question everything she felt and had felt for this confusing and frustrating man who, at times, she wanted nothing more than to be rid of. But…at other times—right now, she wanted to erase all distance between them until nothing was left.

"When morning comes, will you still be here?" she whispered. The words were fragile, still bleeding from the now ancient wound he had inflicted on her heart.

Cullen's hands massaged her thighs. One released, coming up to her face, thumb stroking her cheek. "I told you, I will be here as long as you want me. Not a second more, or less," he vowed. "I know I don't deserve you. But I want you all the same."

"It's up to me to decide who does and does not deserve me," she reminded him. "And tonight, you are all I want."

"Then all I must do is ensure that remains true every night from now to forever."

EIRA WAS MILDLY sore the next morning. She woke loosely framed by Cullen's arms. His body was halfway curled behind hers, warm breath tickling the nape of her neck. The candles had burned out in the night, puddles of wax spilling over into ivory stalactites.

Closing her eyes, she savored the moment. It spun out a fantasy, rebuilding the room around her. No longer were they in some abandoned home on the Isle of Frost, but the captain's quarters of the *Stormfrost*. He was her paramour and there were days where the only order she gave him was to remain in bed and be ready for her whenever the urge should strike her fancy. Other days, they would wake and emerge together, ready to strike fear into the hearts of all those ashore.

A soft, songlike noise of delight escaped her. It was followed by a gentle press of his lips into the back of her neck. She shifted, feeling the weight of his body behind her, the way their skin stuck together.

"Good morning." His voice was thick with sleep and rather delightful sounding.

"It's nice to have you here," she admitted.

"That's reassuring."

"You had doubts?" Eira rolled onto her back as he sat up, wiggling down to the foot of the bed and standing—giving her a delicious view in the process that she shamelessly admired.

"You've never woken up next to me. The last time…" He trailed off, pausing as he slid on his trousers, buckle in hand.

Cullen stared at nothing. "I don't deserve you. I didn't then and I certainly don't now."

Eira sat, swinging her feet off the bed. There wasn't the slightest urge toward modesty around him, so it took a minute before she gathered her clothes and joined him, dressing in silence. There were a thousand thoughts that weighed on her. Yet, none of them seemed to be cohesive enough to be worth saying.

"Maybe, maybe not." She finally spoke when her pants were on, as if each article of clothing restored her better senses. "I know my faults, Cullen. Over the past two years, they've been brought sharply into focus. I've been reactive and brash. I've acted without consideration for those around me—the people who matter most to me. I've made mistakes that have hurt people. That have gotten people killed."

"Noelle wasn't—"

She stopped him with a pointed look, tugging her shirt into place. "Noelle was and wasn't my fault. There was more I could've done and simultaneously things I blame myself for that were beyond my control. I recognize all of it."

His objection relaxed into a tiny smile. One that had a gleam of pride in his eyes. Eira sighed heavily at him to convey that she knew he was thinking about how far she'd come. That prompted a laugh from him, which caused her stony expression to crack into a smile of her own.

"In any case...I don't know if you deserved me or not as a general statement."

"Fine," he relented. "But at the least you deserved so much better than how I treated you that night."

"On that, we can agree, as did Lavette." She turned to face him, finding him fully dressed as well.

The air suddenly became thick. There was a weight on her chest that made it harder to breathe. Time went sideways and she wasn't sure if they stood there for a second, or five minutes.

There's no more running from this, a voice in the back of her mind nudged gently. *Not anymore*. There was only so long they would wait. Only so long until her own heart began tangling itself in ways that would become truly irresponsible to ignore.

"Do you think you'll ever forgive me?" The question was delicate and fearful.

There was a brief and deeply petty urge to tell him *no*. To take this opportunity to twist the knife in him. Hurt him like he had her when he was so vulnerable.

"I already have," she admitted. "That doesn't mean I've forgotten the pain. That there aren't parts of me that are still cautious of giving you that vulnerability again." To think, falling into bed had been so easy compared to entertaining the notion of giving him her heart once more. "But…I'm not that woman any longer. There's no point in me carrying her grudges. And you—"

"I'm not that man," he finished for her.

"So you've shown me." She looked him up and down, appreciating fully how different he was now, from then. "We should get back to the others."

His chin dipped, but he didn't move. She brushed past him, starting for the door, keenly aware that there was still something weighing on him. Eira chose to ignore it. Probing felt far too dangerous right now. And he proved her instinct right.

Fingers closed around her wrist, catching her. Grasping her gently but firmly. Eira slowed in a step, gaze swinging back to his. Cullen held her stare intently, lips parting, but no words came. She opened her mouth to say they needed to leave. This had the opposite effect than she was intending and prompted him to action.

"I love you."

There it was. The point of no return. The line in the sand that she, Cullen, and Olivin had been narrowly avoiding for weeks. Three words and he had made his stance...and now waited on hers.

Could she say it? Was she ready for that? And what did it mean if she did? She loved him. But did she also love Olivin? What did it mean if her heart wanted both men? They incapsulated different aspects of her, filled different roles that she wanted and needed.

Eira swallowed thickly. "Cullen, I—"

He shook his head. "You don't have to say it back. Not yet. Not ever, if it's not the design of your heart. If I ever hear those words from you again I want you to mean them."

"It's not that— It's only— You see—" She floundered, wanting to offer him reassurance yet at the same time having no idea what to say.

"Eira, you don't have to say anything," he repeated with a small smile. As if he knew exactly the source of her tumult and almost found it…amusing. "One benefit of being a lord is I have long since learned how to play the long game. I am a patient man when it comes to the things I want. My stance is unchanged— take your time, explore your heart, and, when you're ready, when your decision is made, tell me then."

"I love you," she blurted. Cullen's eyes went wide. "I do. I love you," she repeated. This time, the words were as fragile as the hopes and fears that they were built upon. "I didn't want to for a long, long time. But I can't expunge you, nor do I want to. Maybe you're good for me, maybe you're the worst choice I'll ever make. Either way, it seems my heart has made that decision for me and there is no going back." She drew a shuddering breath. For the first time feeling wayward, lost, and adrift. She had everything she wanted. Why was she afraid of taking it? Perhaps because wanting it and losing it, again, would be too much to bear. "But…I might also love him? I don't know. And it seems unfair to—"

He silenced her with a finger on her lips. "That's enough."

Is it? Her eyes asked the question without words.

"You are enough, more than. I'm sorry it took me so long to act like it. But here I am now. There's nothing else in this world that I fight for—live for—but for you and your goals. As long as I have you, I am content."

Eira gave a slight nod of understanding and he released her.

Still, neither of them moved. She continued to stare at him, working through what he said. The implications of it.

How was it that he was reassuring her that nothing needed to change while, at the same time, seemingly changing everything?

"Thank you." Her voice dropped to a whisper.

"You've nothing to thank me for. If anything, the reverse is true."

They shared a smile, fingers lacing.

"Let's return," she declared. "There's much to do."

She'd been keenly aware of his presence in the days that followed. When he stayed off to the side as Eira and Adela announced the next stages of their plans. How he dutifully followed orders and helped with packing their new vessel—one that had been previously frozen in the ice covering the Isle of Frost. The way his muscles strained as he tended the sails on their departure from the island.

He had admittedly become a distraction. But a pleasant one, and one that she had under full control. When her attention wasn't needed entirely on something else, Eira studied him like she had one of Adela's journals ages ago—learning as much as she was able about the man he was evolving into.

During the three days that it took them to sail to Meru on their new, smaller vessel, Eira dared to muse over what *after* might look like. Fantasies danced through her mind as she fell asleep in her hammock. Of the *Stormfrost*. Of a life of doing whatever she wanted, whenever she wanted. Living free of judgment because she would allow none to touch her. Of who she wanted by her side...

But, come each dawn, Eira put the daydreams aside. She couldn't get lost in the fantasy. The battle was ahead and nothing was real until she claimed her victory.

"We'll spend one last night here," Eira declared as the sails were struck. The sun hung low in the sky. Only Ducot, Olivin, Yonlin, Cullen, and Alyss had joined her on the mission to infiltrate Meru. When it was just the six of them, Noelle's absence remained striking. Her ghost still hovered between Ducot and Alyss, a reminder of their purpose. "Pack up and then sleep while you can; we'll rise before the dawn to get ashore while we still have the benefit of darkness."

She'd let the ship drift tonight, keeping note of the currents in the back of her mind. It didn't matter where they went ashore. Instead, Eira kept her magic focused on maintaining an illusion on and around the ship—a dense fog to conceal them. Not perfectly invisible so she didn't exhaust herself too much; just enough that, at a glance, no one would notice them from the shore. They were far from any settlements, but a thick forest went right to the edge of the rocky coast so Eira wasn't taking any chances.

They went about their business, packing their things. The vessel was small and they intentionally hadn't brought very much. By the time Eira had fastened the last strap of her pack, Ducot and Cullen had already tucked themselves into their cots.

She was about to do the same for herself when Olivin caught her eye. He'd been talking with Yonlin, who was in the process of studying the pistol Eira had given to him a week ago on the Isle of Frost. She'd made the decision that, when the time came, he'd be the one to take the shot. If anyone was going to be confident with the weapon, it'd be him. And she needed to preserve her strength in the battle with Ulvarth—she couldn't allow the weapon to sap her powers.

Olivin held her stare with purpose and Eira gave a slight nod. She ascended back to the main deck and he followed closely behind. Eira drew in a breath as she crossed to the railing.

"I'd been wanting to talk to you." Eira broke the silence.

"The feeling is mutual."

She gripped the railing and relaxed. "I didn't like where we ended things the last time." She sighed. "I was too harsh with you. I'm sorry."

Olivin shook his head. "No, you weren't. I was an ass. Yonlin being as injured as he was had put me on edge."

"I can understand." After what had happened to Marcus, then Noelle, she really could.

"I know you can. It's one of the many things I adore about you. You know what it's like…" Olivin drew a slow breath, abandoning the initial thought. When he spoke again, it felt as if he was starting from the beginning. "When Wynry betrayed us, we lost everything. Yonlin was all I had, and all the purpose I needed. Every day was survival, navigating as best we could, fighting for what little we had. All I needed was to take care of him."

"But?" She could sense there was more.

"Eventually, surviving alone isn't enough, you know? Eventually you begin to want more. To be comfortable. To thrive." Olivin continued to stare out toward the dark horizon. She shifted to face him, listening intently. "I keep thinking about Lavette and Varren."

"In what way?" Eira couldn't see how they were suddenly relevant.

"Everything had crumbled for them. But, even after all had seemed lost, they made it back home. They reclaimed a future that should've been lost. They found a way to thrive again."

Eira hadn't considered any parallels. But, framed like that, she could see it. At least see how it had struck Olivin as potentially similar to his and Yonlin's circumstances.

"Thanks to you." He turned to face her. "You did that for them."

"I only helped them because it was advantageous to me." She pointedly looked away.

His hand landed over hers on the railing. "I know you want the world to think you're this ruthless pirate. But I know you. You love so, *so* fiercely. You treat others well."

"I am also ruthless," she countered.

"Only in service to those you love."

Eira bit the insides of her cheeks, not wanting to argue. It seemed strange to be trying to tell him she was a worse person than what he wanted to make her out to be. But she wanted to make sure he saw her for who she was. All the good, and the bad. Looking in the mirror and truly seeing herself was something Eira had become comfortable with over the past year.

"I think…I want to stop surviving," he continued. "When this is all over, and we've won, I want to thrive."

"And what does thriving look like? Do you still have desires to be my fleet master?" Eira worked to keep her questions emotionless. Part of her was afraid of the answer.

He smiled, and nodded. But something about it seemed…less committed than before. The explanation presented itself when he said, "First, though, I'll need to see Yonlin settled. I don't think the pirate life is for him."

"Neither is it for Alyss."

"And I suspect they'll not be separating anytime soon." He had a note of sadness that mirrored her own. A bittersweet taste to the joy that two people they cared for had clearly found each other, even if it meant they were leaving their sides. "I can't abandon him—either of them—to the rubble of Meru. There will be a great deal to sort through in the aftermath to ensure another Ulvarth doesn't rise and take advantage of the power vacancy that will exist. I will not see Meru under another tyrant. And, I want to make sure my brother is safe and settled."

"So you'll be staying, then?" She didn't want to assume or mince words.

"Likely, for a time." He shifted to face her outright. Eira mirrored the motion and his hand lifted to cup her cheek. "Do you hate me for it?"

"Tempting, but no." As she spoke he leaned forward, resting his forehead against hers, noses almost brushing. "Not so long as you also look after Alyss."

"Always. Someone who is dear to you, is dear to me." So much was wrapped up in that declaration. Enough that it filled her with a pleasant pain. She was going to let this man break her, only to put her back together again.

"It's a deal."

"Then, I think I could give you leave for that," she said and leaned forward to kiss him. Olivin's other hand moved to her face and he held her delicately, as if afraid she could somehow break, despite how life had hammered her flesh to steel. Perhaps he held her with such tenderness because he knew, without her saying, that he held her heart.

The sun had yet to crest the horizon and they were all up on the deck. With a wave of her hands and the crunching and splintering of wood, Alyss tore into their ship. She broke off chunks from the bow and stern. The masts folded like paper. The strip of deck the six of them were clustered on began to groan under their weight as its supports were compromised.

Eira focused on activating her own magic to continue concealing the vessel. Fortunately the moon was still thin and the clouds tonight were thick. Between that and her shifting fogs, Eira was certain no one on the shore would see them. Which was good, because crafting an illusion over every piece of wood that swirled around them would've been impossible.

The bits and pieces pulled together, reassembling in the water in front of the ship into a small rowboat. With a thought, the sea rose, connecting the edge of the larger vessel with the smaller one and condensing into a bridge of ice.

"Everyone off," Eira instructed. They all did as told and she was the last to slide down, behind Alyss. "All right, Alyss, no remnants."

"You got it." Extending both her palms, fingers outstretched,

Alyss balled her hands and the vessel before them crunched in on itself. She twisted her fists in opposite directions, as though she were wringing a towel. Wood splintered and groaned, turning to dust.

"Cullen, if you please." Eira was already focusing on the shifts in her own magic, lowering the water that had been their ice bridge without getting so much as a drop in their boat. As the wind picked up, thanks to Cullen, blowing the parts of the ship far out into the massive bay of Meru, they were speeding toward the coastline. Part of her focus remained on maintaining the fog, and, somewhere in the back of her mind, she had the currents fold the remnants of the ship beneath the waves, scattering them to assist Cullen's efforts.

It reminded her of the first vessel they'd taken to the *Stormfrost*, crushed to keep their presence hidden. Like Adela, like Eira.

If anyone found pieces of the ship, they wouldn't have any idea who it belonged to. And it would be far, far away from where the hull of their rowboat crunched up along the shore. Eira leaped out and the rest followed without need of command. The only sounds were five pairs of boots on the gravel, seeing as Ducot had shifted into his mole form and scurried up onto Olivin's shoulder.

Eira caught Alyss's eyes and gave a slight nod. Alyss repeated the process as she had with the ship, crunching the rowboat. However, this time, there was no need of Cullen scattering the pieces. The sand and stones around the larger planks vibrated and the scraps of wood sank into the earth, consumed.

No footprints, Eira mouthed to Cullen. The beach was mostly rocky, but small breezes helped blow over their tracks.

Olivin knelt and reached out. Ducot ran off his arm, scurrying ahead of them, nimble in his tiny form. He would be their eyes in the darkness, scanning for possible threats.

Together, the six of them ventured into the dark woods, a force that left no tracks in their wake and marched toward death.

THERE WAS NO one in the woods, or the open fields beyond. Eira led them down to the road, keeping the hood of her cloak up. Ducot was still in mole form, but now rode on Olivin's shoulder. The rest of them had opted for clothing that mostly concealed their faces. Alyss wore a headscarf that also served to keep the sun off of her. Cullen's shirt had a high collar. Olivin looked the most normal of them all but, like Eira, whenever they passed another traveler an illusion sank over his face, aging him slightly, shifting his hair color. But there were few people on the road.

They moved much like they had in Carsovia, sleeping off to the side in grasses, trees, and, when available, barns or sheds. There was little conversation each day and night.

Which made the first real conversation they all had with each other feel odd as they slowed upon seeing a town in the distance.

"That should be Hokoh." Olivin stole Eira's words.

She'd intentionally guided them past the larger port in Parth. While her parents had said the Pillars had yet to infiltrate the city when they'd stopped in, Eira didn't trust that would still be the case. But she didn't dare venture past Hokoh, knowing Ulvarth would have regular patrols in the bay of Meru.

"It looks large." Alyss adjusted her headscarf one too many times to not be nervous. "Should we go around it? It looks like the forests arc behind."

"The long way would add on another week." Olivin shook his head and spoke with an air of authority that grated on Eira. "We should go straight through. The road is the easiest path and we might even be able to find a merchant cart making their way to Risen."

"I'd be keen to not have to walk all the way to Risen," Yonlin murmured. Eira disliked the idea of trusting someone else to cart them to Risen. But it was a pointless argument when it remained only a hypothetical.

"Eira?" Cullen looked to her, noting her silence.

"The forest would be the safer route…but I think we should go through," Eira reluctantly said. "It will give us an opportunity to see if we can learn something about the state of Risen."

"And perhaps get caught." Alyss was still unconvinced.

"If we're sloppy enough that they catch us here, then going to Risen is pointless as we're already doomed," Olivin said with a note of severity.

"Optimistic." Alyss gave him a sidelong glance.

"Realistic. At some point, we'll have to face the Pillars. We should be ready for it."

"Olivin is right, if we can't navigate here then we're not ready for Risen," Eira said. Just as Alyss looked like she was about to object, Eira added, "But we should still be careful and make sure we don't rush into anything."

Unease had her every footstep falling heavier than the last as they neared the city. Meru was dotted with settlements and towns, but Hokoh was an ancient city that had been here for hundreds of years. Over time, its occupants had invested in its defense, likely from the long-ago warring duchies period. The one that Lumeria's lineage ended.

She scanned the gates ahead of them. There was someone sitting up on the wall, seemingly casual, as if he was nothing more than an occupant of the town taking a moment to breathe in the fresh air. But he watched them like a hawk from his perch. She worked not to pay him too close attention, keeping her head down.

The hair on her neck and arms was on end the moment they passed through the gates. It was several times worse than when they had been infiltrating the town in Carsovia. There, Eira didn't have to worry much about being recognized. Somehow, the stakes seemed…lower. Perhaps because she was more removed from Carsovia's struggles. It wasn't personal like this was.

Or perhaps this was the first time she was seeing the mark of the Pillars in months, a reminder that Ulvarth's end was within reach.

The Pillars had slithered into Hokoh like vipers and had made it their den. Their mark was emblazoned on almost every door in golden paint—three vertical lines centered overtop three interlocking circles, stacked vertically. The doors that lacked the symbol had a black X streaked across them, windows shattered, insides dark and smelling of rot.

The message was clear: align or die.

Yet, despite the brutality, people went about their business. They walked in the streets, conversed on stoops. Commerce bustled in small squares down side alleys.

The Pillars' presence was as bad a stink as what originated from some of the houses. But, like all wretched things, one could acclimate to it. And acclimate people had. There were smiles and laughter. Children running around their parents' hems.

"Why does it feel so…normal?" Alyss whispered.

"The towns in Carsovia felt normal, too." Cullen's thoughts were aligned with Eira's.

"That—they—" Alyss could only sigh, abandoning her objection.

"Let's get somewhere with more people," Eira said. "See what we can overhear."

They followed her down toward a small square where tables had been placed opposite a handful of shops. Men and women sat outside, drinking from tall glasses. People roamed from shop to shop, full baskets on their hips.

"Eira," Cullen whispered, catching her hand. She shifted, turning toward what he was trying to get her attention on.

In an alcove, with mortar so fresh it was a bright, stark contrast to the old stone of the buildings around it, was a statue. The visage of the Goddess Yargen was a familiar one: an ethereal and timeless beauty, her long, flowing hair framing her outstretched arms. Behind her were the three circles and one singular line that was her usual symbol—but of course two extra lines had been added. That wasn't the only change. Kneeling in front of the goddess on one knee, holding a sword aloft, was a man whose face Eira would recognize anywhere. Even in a hastily made sculpture.

Ulvarth.

In time with the bitter echo of his name across her mind, the resonance of a low bell chimed across the city. All conversation stopped. People halted their movements.

As if in a trance, everyone rose from their tables, moving toward the statue and sinking to their knees. Not wanting to stand out, Eira did the same, her friends following. All those in the square circled the statue, heads bowed. With one voice, the entirety of Hokoh intoned:

"Goddess Yargen, holder of our past, present, and future, guide us through these dark times. Bless your chosen champion so that he might be strong and just. So that his sword might strike down the evils that still plague these lands, banishing them with the might of your light.

"Praise to Champion Ulvarth, to the Pillars of Truth, Justice, and Light—the foundation of Meru—to which we pledge our unending fealty and praise forevermore.

"From this day, until the last day of oblivion, we swear these words."

Eira kept her head down the entire time, trusting her hood to conceal the fact that she wasn't speaking along. Trusting it to hide her wide eyes and furrowed brow. Her jaw that was clenched so tightly it might pop. Her knuckles dug into the cobblestones, leaving behind red smears.

Ulvarth had continued doing what he'd always done—positioning himself as a goddess's chosen. But now he was doing it with all of Meru and forcing them to acknowledge him as such. Repeated enough times, anything could become truth. Especially when, as soon as the words were said, everyone could stand and return to their business as though nothing had happened.

Eira shared wary looks with her group. They were all thinking the same things, though none of them dared vocalize it.

"We should keep going," she said for them all. Even though the words gave nothing away, and weren't inherently suspicious, she still kept her voice down. "The sooner we get through town, the better."

They continued along the streets and narrow alleyways, heading in the general north, northwest direction that would lead them to Risen. Eira kept them intentionally on back alleys. More than once, she saw Pillars patrolling the streets, their white and gold-trimmed robes unmistakable.

Just when she was thinking that, overall, their luck couldn't have been better, it ran out.

She took one wrong turn and found herself face-to-face with a Pillar. The woman's shaved head shone in the afternoon sun. Eira's gaze dropped instinctively to her right hand, where the symbol of the Pillars had been carved, over and over, to permanently entrench itself as a pale and raised scar.

Turning around would be too suspicious, especially with five of them. Eira continued walking, trusting the illusion she'd crafted to alter her appearance to be sufficient—that if it wasn't, they'd all be dead already. The alleyway was small and it was impossible to pass by without twisting slightly. Eira's eyes met the Pillar's. She wondered if the woman could feel the chill sweeping off her body from the illusion over her face.

But the woman didn't stop. She turned forward. Eira kept her attention forward as well. It was so quiet that she could hear every shift of the woman's robes. All their breaths were shallow, or held.

Just when Eira was about to turn the far corner, and the woman would've emerged onto the larger street she was headed for, she spoke. "For the glory of His Holiness."

Eira froze. She shifted, half turning, eyes meeting the Pillar's. The woman wore a somewhat skeptical, probing expression. She was suspicious of them. What had given them away? Was it their clothes? Had she seen that they hadn't spoken the prayers?

Or was this simply something that was said whenever a Pillar was passed? And the longer Eira remained silent, the more suspicion she drew to herself, and to them?

Her mind moved faster than a light ship in a gale. She was back in that forsaken throne room deep beneath Risen. Pillars surrounded her. The first time she had seen Ulvarth. *What had they said then?*

"Respect, revere, fear," Eira said as soon as it popped into her mind. It had to have only been a second that had passed.

The woman's eyes widened. "May you be worthy," she whispered, as if correcting. Eira saw realization dawn on the woman's face that something was out of place about them. The Pillar took a step forward, a sinister smile curling her lips. In another moment of time, Eira saw Ferro approaching her.

Her stomach curdled but Eira remained calm. "May I be worthy," Eira repeated and lowered her eyes. "Forgive me."

"Are you new to Hokoh?" The Pillar shifted and then slowly approached. "If so, you should come with me. I will take you to our Temple. Once you say the rites, you will be part of our glorious family of Meru. One, holy, triumphant kinship in Yargen's name and for her Champion."

"Apologies, we have somewhere to be. Perhaps tomorrow."

"Once you are part of the fold, you will never know hardship again." She continued forward, even as Eira took a step back. There was a coaxing coo to her words. Not an outright order, but the threat of danger was present should Eira refuse. "Under his loving gaze, no one on Meru shall go hungry. There will be no crime, no suffering. Come, let us feed you and give you warmth and shelter. We shall show you his way."

"Perhaps later." Eira instinctively positioned herself between the woman and her friends. Yonlin had shifted his stance, hand on his hip by the pistol. Olivin and Cullen were at the ready. Ducot was still in his mole form, perched on Olivin's shoulder. But he could be back to his normal self in an instant. Alyss already had her palm braced against a wall. "We would be most enthusiastic to worship at his temple once our matters are handled."

The woman lifted her hand, resting it on Eira's shoulder in a friendly gesture. But her eyes were all sinister. Eira could see nothing but a Pillar looking to drag her back to their forsaken houses of worship.

"If you are not one of our holy family, then you are a scourge on these lands that must be removed. Are you a scourge, my sister of Yargen?"

There was only so much a woman could abide. Eira never broke her stare with the Pillar. She hardly moved most of her body. But her arm was faster than the woman had been expecting, Eira's movements sure, confident. With one thrust, she plunged a dagger of ice through the woman's gut.

She barely had time to crack her lips. Eira doubted the first wave of pain had crashed against her awareness when she moved with her other arm, the Pillar's hand falling from her shoulder. Before the woman could scream—before she could even gulp for air—Eira gouged out her throat without so much as flinching.

The Pillar collapsed to the ground, dead, instantly.

Eira stepped back, dismissing the daggers of ice. They fell as bloody rain from her hands, collecting in the cobblestones. Turning, she faced her friends and said calmly, and simply, "We should move."

· CHAPTER ·

TWENTY-EIGHT

HE OTHERS STARED down at the Pillar even as Eira walked away. Wordlessly, they fell into step.

Alyss caught up with Eira. "What happened to caution and not rushing into things?" she murmured, glancing around. They were moving faster now through the back alleyways.

Eira kept skimming over the streets, debating whether it'd be less suspicious to walk out in the open where they could move among the crowd. "She gave me no choice."

"We could've knocked her out," Alyss said under her breath, soft enough that she might not have been intending for Eira to hear.

"So she could wake up all the more suspicious *and* knowing our faces?" Eira couldn't fathom her friend's logic.

"We're concealing ourselves; she didn't get that good of a look."

"Why are you defending one of them?" Her question was harsher than she might have otherwise intended. But Eira couldn't fathom what would ever make Alyss argue for a Pillar's life. "You know what they did to me, to Olivin and Yonlin, all of us."

"Of course I know." Offense was written in the deep lines of her furrowed brow. "But *that* woman didn't do any of those things. She didn't deserve to die."

"Alyss, you've seen me kill. You've killed, too."

"Maybe she wasn't one of them." Alyss's musing was even more faint.

"What do you mean?" Eira wasn't letting the doubt be swept away. She wouldn't tolerate mutiny.

"You remember what your uncle said, don't you? That people didn't have a choice when the Pillars rose to power. They were forced to join or die." Alyss shook her head. "She might have been innocent."

Protecting the innocents… Eira knew that was what Alyss would cling to.

"I saw her eyes. I know she was one of them down to the core of her soul. Even if she hadn't yet directly crossed or potentially brought harm to us, she would've," Eira said without doubt. She slipped her hand into her friend's and gave it a gentle squeeze, trying to assuage some of her guilt. "Ulvarth's words are a corruption that, after a point, can't be cut out or cured. There is only one end for it. Whatever innocence she had was long gone."

Alyss squeezed her hand back and said nothing. Still, it served as reassurance that she understood what Eira was saying, and that she felt heard by Eira. After another second, Eira released her fingers, glanced around a corner, and continued on.

The truth was…she had thought little about that woman's history. Whether she was a devout believer of Ulvarth, or had been taken in, forced, twisted over time to their beliefs until the contortion felt natural. Eira didn't care. Everyone who bore the mark of the Pillars, who gave them safety or sympathy, were her enemy and she would be their end.

She rounded another corner and rethought her path, avoiding another close encounter with a few individuals in the alleyway. Fortunately not Pillars this time. Just some more maroon-cloaked men.

Wait. Eira's heart was instantly pounding. She trusted her instincts too much to think she was imagining things. Which meant only one thing:

They were being followed.

No, more than that. They were being herded. She'd been choosing the paths of least resistance—streets that were small and empty. Every fork in the road had some maroon-cloaked men and women milling about on one side.

Eira slowed her pace as she passed a window. The building was narrow and the windows aligned in just the right way that she could see through to the other side of the street. She grabbed for the door with a black X upon it. Unlocked, *thank Yargen*. She stretched out her magic and picked up on the echoes in the space.

We have to leave. Now. Before they find us. Get your things. We're going to the countryside… A brief conversation played in her mind of a family making their flight. For their sakes, Eira genuinely hoped they'd made it out of Hokoh before that X was painted on their door.

Without instruction, her friends followed her into the dark home. Another gift of the goddess was that it didn't smell like rot. Their escape must've been successful.

Eira crossed over to the far window and put her back beneath it. Her friends crouched down. Ducot scurried off Olivin's shoulder, darting into the shadows.

"What is it?" Olivin asked, sliding up to her side.

Eira slowly pushed herself up, glancing over the window. The maroon cloaks were nowhere to be seen. She sat back down, sinking into the gloom of the unlit home, and stared intently at the opposite window.

"We're being followed."

"What?" Olivin breathed. "By who?"

"I don't know yet." They didn't seem like Pillars. Of course, it could be some new sect under Ulvarth's powers. But the Pillars weren't known for subtlety…especially not since they had gained the upper hand. "Watch."

Sure enough, just as Olivin's eyes swung to the opposite window, the two cloaked men passed by. Though they now wore expressions of confusion. They glanced around before quickly backtracking.

"I don't know them," Olivin said cautiously.

"*Eira,*" Alyss rasped in alarm.

Eira's head jerked to her, but there was no need for Alyss to explain. She saw what Alyss had been about to warn her of emerging from the shadows in the back of the room. The glowing dots of Ducot's brow cut through the darkness first. Then the man emerged, a shadowed figure looming over his back.

She slowly rose to her feet. Her hand balled into a fist, frost coating it. She dipped her chin and stared up through her lashes. The figure's maroon hood became visible in the lowlight, though his face was still obscured. Her friends moved in tandem with her, readying themselves.

"What do you want with us?" Eira asked, trying to keep the question as neutral as possible—not afraid, so there would be no interpretation of guilt. Not demanding, so it couldn't be perceived as overly aggressive. Despite what Alyss might think, she genuinely wasn't looking to pick fights. But if the fight came to her…

"Such a tone… You always were quite the spitfire, though. Never could take an order to save your life. Or the lives of others." The man chuckled. His voice was deep and gravelly, raspy. As if it had suffered from overuse.

"What do you know about me?" Her tone had gone frigid at the mention of her friends' lives.

"Is that any way to greet an old friend?"

Ducot stepped aside. The man rose his head. Eira stared at a familiar face. A ring of scars lined his neck beneath his chin.

"Mother above. Lorn?"

*L*ORN. DENEYA'S LEFT hand. The counterpart to Rebec. He was the secret master for what had been the Court of Shadows.

The last time Eira had seen him had been in the chamber of the Specters, deep beneath Risen, the night it had been attacked by the Pillars. While that night had been hard, whatever Lorn had faced since had clearly been harder. His face was gaunt, eyes sunken and haunted. There was a perpetual furrow to his brow, giving his face the appearance of a hardened soldier in place of the somewhat secretarial image Eira had always had of him.

And the scars… It looked as though someone had tried to cut his windpipe from his throat. Given their severity, it was a wonder they hadn't succeeded.

"This is the last place I expected to see you," he said. "Granted, I *never* expected to see you again."

"I can say the same."

"Lorn." Olivin's illusion had dropped and he wasted no time crossing to the other elfin, clasping forearms with a friendly shake. "It is a relief to see you alive and in one piece."

"Alive, yes. In one piece…" Lorn released Olivin and massaged his throat. The savagery had impacted his voice.

"What happened to you?"

"Risen fell." He lowered his eyes and stared off into the corner.

"Lorn." Eira shifted her stance, folding her arms. She tried to summon the image of Adela. "I realize you have been through a great deal. But right now, we need information and you're the only one who can give it to us."

His eyes turned back to her. She saw the unspoken question in them.

"We are going to Risen to kill Ulvarth," Eira said plainly. If her worst fears that he had been indoctrinated by the Pillars were true, it didn't matter that she was telling him as much. They were already going to have to kill him for simply seeing them. "Any information you have, however out of date it might be, will be of use. So I need to know everything you know."

He assessed her for several steady heartbeats. Eira didn't move. Flinching, showing doubt in any way, would have him questioning her capabilities—her authority in the situation.

"Lumeria's castle is dust and every noble or commonfolk who was considered even remotely loyal died with her." He stepped back and leaned against the wall as if he could no longer support himself under the weight of her stare—more likely the weight of his memories. "The Pillars had infiltrated it, or tunneled beneath it, perhaps like they did to attack the Court of Shadows, and lined the bedrock with flash beads. The castle sank into the hilltop with a rumble and a gasp, collapsing as if it were never there in the first place."

"He had all the information he needed," Eira figured.

"What?" Olivin looked to her.

"He was the head of the Swords of Light. He'd had unfettered access to the Archives for years and knew them better than anyone. There were records in there about the architecture of Risen going back to its founding."

"I remember reading them," Alyss realized in quiet horror. "All about the architecture of the castle and Archives—the building of Risen itself."

"The Archives are his seat of power now. One ruler, ordained by Yargen, a merger of faith and law." Lorn's words turned so bitter that Eira's own mouth soured. "He returned from the coliseum and made a show of carrying a flame through the streets—a holy fire from where he had expunged Raspian's evil from our lands. A fire he merged with the smoking remnants of the castle."

"To make a new Flame of Yargen," Eira murmured. Unequivocally real this time. Sourced from godly acts, as Ulvarth spun it.

"It burns now not just in the brazier of the Archives, but all around it."

"Was there any resistance?" Yonlin asked. The words were filled with a childlike hope, fragile and pointless. "Surely not all of Risen submitted to him."

"Well, that's why I'm here." Lorn gave Yonlin a weak smile, not nearly as reassuring as he seemed to be making the effort for. "Not all of us gave in."

"Just most." Ducot read between the lines of Lorn's words in the same way Eira did.

"What were people to do?" Lorn gestured to the windows. "You've seen Hokoh, how they've gutted any dissonance—literally." Ulvarth was taking a page out of Carsovia's books. The image of the man being strung from the entry arch of the town was forever seared onto Eira's eyes. "And here is even without his displays of holy fire."

"Elaborate," Eira demanded.

"He summons flames and explosions without so much as a single glyph."

She suggested the obvious. "Flash beads?"

"We all think so…but it's seamless. Impossible to figure out how, in many cases." Lorn shook his head. Eira wondered if there was some kind of trigger on his runic armor, akin to the ring that fired the pistol. "Many have truly begun to believe he was ordained by the goddess—that he wields her divine power."

"Since most don't know about flash beads…what else would they think?" Cullen said gravely, folding his own arms in thought.

It didn't matter to Eira what others thought. Ulvarth could be the best thing that happened to Meru. She was still going to kill him.

"You said 'we all,'" she pointed out. "There's more in your maroon-cloaked resistance."

Lorn chuckled. "So you noticed we were following you… You're not the single-minded young woman I first met, blindly charging headfirst, are you?"

"Oh, I can still be quite single-minded." Eira's arms relaxed to her sides. "But I try not to rush in, especially when my friends' lives are on the line."

He gave an approving nod following a brief assessment, as if somehow deciding she was telling the truth. "Rebec is back in Risen, trying to hold the Court of Shadows together as best she's able. They're being a pain in Ulvarth's side, but unfortunately not a real threat."

Ducot let out an audible sigh of relief, so palpable that Eira felt guilty for ever doubting that he had genuinely cared for the woman to first find him and offer him shelter following Ulvarth's brutality. Even if he was a pirate and had Adela…Rebec's gesture meant something. Of course he cared.

"Deneya?" Olivin asked, almost timidly. Her name was a notable absence.

Lorn shook his head sadly. "We…We searched for her in the rubble. But came up empty-handed. She hasn't been heard from since."

A heavy moment of silence was shared by them all for the former leader of the Court of Shadows. She could still be alive, missing didn't mean dead. But Eira couldn't imagine a world in which Deneya wouldn't do everything in her power to aid the resistance. Her gut twisted with grief. She had a complicated relationship with the woman, but Deneya had been the first one to offer her vengeance. To offer her a way out of the life she would've been trapped in had she remained on Solaris.

The woman had deserved much better and, even if it looked bleak, a part of her would hold hope that Deneya would one day be found.

"I'm sorry," Eira spoke for them all, and meant it. Lorn's

eyes shone in the lowlight with tears he clearly did not let fall. Probably tears he'd already cried to the point that there was no more that he could bear to shed.

"It's been hard," Lorn admitted. The words seemed like a grave understatement. "There's only a handful of us left. Though our numbers grow by the day—lords and ladies who are resistant to this new regime change. What few remain after the tournament. Admittedly, in a self-serving way, since they were people who didn't stand up for Ulvarth when he was first tried and whom he now holds a vendetta against. But we aren't in a position to turn allies away.

"Our ranks grew enough that I could come here, to Hokoh. Thinking that perhaps if we could stop his influence from spreading—keep it to Risen alone—we could raise a resistance from the outside." Lorn dipped his chin and sank further against the wall. "It's proven challenging."

Eira opened her mouth to speak, but he moved before she could get a word out. Lorn practically lunged from the wall, hands out, appealing to all of them.

"But, with you all here…powerful, capable, fresh-eyed and full-bellied…we can launch our countermeasure and drive them out of Hokoh once and for all."

"What's this countermeasure?" Olivin asked.

Eira was already skeptical of the idea, but she didn't let it show.

"We're going to hit them where it hurts—their temple. If we can bring that down, then better sense is more likely to prevail and we can teach the people of Hokoh to fight back. The people whose hearts haven't been corrupted by the Pillars—which is still the majority—will know they no longer have to live in fear. That resistance is possible. By the time the Pillars back in Risen know of Hokoh having fallen at all, we'll have an army."

It was optimistic at best. Foolish, more realistically. She'd seen the people of Hokoh readily bow before the statue of Ulvarth and swear their fealty. There hadn't been rage simmering behind their eyes. There wasn't reluctance to their movements. Begrudging acceptance—resignation, at worst.

The people were hungry and desperate, tired of the upheaval. Eira had heard the woman: the Pillars were offering stability and reassurance. Why would they consign themselves to the fires of uncertainty once more? And even *if* Lorn got them to agree… there was no army to be had here. Hoping they could defend their city from being reclaimed was optimistic, even.

But it didn't matter. Hokoh's fate didn't concern her. Not really. Eira had other plans.

"Will you help us?" Lorn looked to Olivin, rather than Eira.

Olivin shifted. His eyes were filled with uncertainty.

"We will, won't we?" The words were said somewhat timidly, but there was expectation there. Eira lifted her brows. Olivin continued to hold his stare.

We don't have time for this, she wanted to say. But, clearly, Lorn was still important to Olivin.

"Of course," Eira said to him, and then shifted her attention back to Lorn. "When will this attack happen?"

"Sooner the better, less time for them to suspect things. Tomorrow?"

"Perfect." That meant they could quickly be on their way.

"I can show you to the headquarters, if you'd like?"

Eira looked around the abandoned home they'd stumbled upon. The shelves were thick with dust. It was evident that the glow of candles hadn't coated the insides of the lanterns in some time, given that cobwebs now were what clouded the glass, rather than soot.

"I think we'll stay here," she decided.

"Here?" Lorn sounded surprised.

"It seems as good of a place as any, and for the best that we don't have too many people going to your hideaway—or else it might raise suspicions. Given that we've already killed one Pillar, I suspect they will be on high alert."

"Very true." His surprise evaporated. Meaning, he knew they

had killed the Pillar. Eira had suspected that was what had tipped him off in the first place that they were potential allies. Or he had identified her with her ice daggers alone.

"I would like to see Hokoh's headquarters." Olivin stepped forward. "If I may join you?" he asked Lorn, then looked back to Eira. "One of us should know the way."

"Good thinking," she said. He was right. Yet, something about it felt unsettling. If someone was going to go, shouldn't it be her as their captain? Or should she stay with the majority like a captain stayed with the ship? There was something shifting beneath her ever since arriving back to Meru that kept Eira continually feeling like she couldn't find her footing.

"I'll be back later." Oblivious to Eira's struggles, Olivin readily followed Lorn back into the shadows.

THIRTY

THE REST OF them spent the remaining part of the afternoon settling into the abode. It was easy to get comfortable in the space, since it was actually designed to be a home, and the weather was fortunately mild.

The hardest part was not making any fires—Eira wasn't sure how closely the Pillars watched houses that were driven out or abandoned…but she didn't want to risk someone seeing flames where there shouldn't be any. An illusion had been considered, but they didn't want to take even the slight risk of someone passing by and sensing the magic—or Eira's power wavering when she inevitably slept.

As the twilight filtered through the grime and dust that caked the windows, Alyss closed her journal with a soft sigh. This was her third, or fourth one? The one that the actual story was going into, according to her.

"Is it fighting with you today?" Eira asked as she watched the back stairwell where Lorn had emerged from earlier for signs of Olivin…or of any enemies, passing her dagger from hand to hand while she waited. Every time the grip moved from one palm to the other, Eira thoughtfully made sure no magic was sticking to the blade.

"A bit." Alyss rolled onto her back. She'd been propped on her elbows for hours, writing away while there was enough light for it in a position that Eira was certain couldn't have been comfortable. "I've put my heroine into a tough situation and I'm not sure how she's going to get out of it."

"I'm always happy to bounce ideas, if you'd find it helpful,"

Yonlin said over the soft clanking of metal. He'd been tinkering and writing in his own notebook. Though a very different subject matter from Alyss. As he spoke, his eyes darted her way, almost sheepishly.

"Thank you." Alyss gave him a warm smile that was returned, and the expressions lingered long enough that Eira shifted to make sure her face couldn't be seen by Yonlin.

When he went back to tinkering, Eira whispered, "So…when is this *whatever-it-is* between you two going to materialize?"

"There's no whatever-it-is going on." Alyss rolled back onto her stomach, grabbing her notebook and flipping it open again. She was only pretending to write, but Eira wasn't sure for whose benefit. Hers? Or Yonlin's?

"It's not nothing." Eira kept her voice as low as possible.

As if realizing what she was trying to do, Cullen struck up a conversation with Yonlin, distracting him. Eira silently thanked him for the assistance. But she didn't risk looking back.

"I'm sure it is." The cap of Alyss's pen was still on, and she drew endless circles of invisible ink in the corner of her page.

"Sounds like you and he haven't talked."

Alyss sighed and sunk her chin into her palm. "He's…nice. Thoughtful. His obsession with machinations—especially of the weapons variety—is a bit strange, I admit."

"You adore me, and I'm pretty strange."

"You're right about that." Alyss grinned up at her, briefly. "I think if he loved those things because he loved the destruction they wrought, it might be harder for me. But he's very academic about it. I deeply admire his mind."

A small twinge of sorrow twisted in Eira's heart. *Obsessed with the destruction they could reap*…like she was. Eira couldn't stop herself from resting her hand on Alyss's. In her periphery, she could see her friend's look of confusion. But Eira didn't move.

For right now…she wanted a breath, two, ten, where she knew her best friend was still at her side and things were almost like they'd always been…if she pretended. She didn't want to acknowledge that fate and time were pulling them apart, even if it was only slightly. Even if the paths were parallel. She didn't want to lose the woman she cared about most in the whole world.

"You should tell him how you feel," Eira said. She tapped Alyss's notebook. "Your heroine would."

"I don't know, my heroine sometimes makes *dumb* choices."

"Wonder who you modeled that after," Eira said dryly. Alyss snorted. "Seriously, though."

"I know, it's just that…I don't know if he'd want someone like me." Alyss's voice had gone tiny with the weight of her insecurity.

"'Someone like you?' Someone profoundly kind? Thoughtful? Smart? Immeasurably patient? An incredibly talented artist? Not to mention absolutely gorgeous." Eira had just been getting started when Alyss interrupted.

"Someone who doesn't want the carnal acts of passion at all." Fear of how others would feel about Alyss's desires—or complete lack thereof—had always held her back. Ever since they were back in the Tower and Alyss realized she was "different" from most in lacking those urges.

"You were the person who taught me that there are many ways love can look, Alyss." Eira gave her hand one more squeeze. Her friend's eyes rose to meet hers and she tried to give the most encouraging smile she could muster. "You can't speak for him and what he wants. You must ask."

"I know." Alyss ducked her chin.

"You should do it before we get to Risen. Who knows what's going to happen…and you don't want to leave anything unsaid." Eira's words went soft.

"Sounds like that's advice you need to take, too." Alyss lifted her hand and held out her pinky. "Make me a pact, and we both will be brave about our hearts. After that fighting Ulvarth will be nothing."

"Absolutely." Eira hooked her finger with Alyss's and they

looked into one another's eyes with a nod of conviction. She wasn't entirely sure what she was swearing herself to, but Eira swore it with her whole heart. Perhaps…what she swore was to figure out that promise to herself. She scanned the windows and made sure the side streets were still empty before standing. "You should all get some sleep."

"What about you?" Cullen asked.

"I'm going to wait up for Olivin—make sure he gets back all right." She could feel Cullen studying her, deciphering how to read into the declaration. But his silent inquiry didn't last very long.

"If you need us, please wake us." He started for his bedroll. Very little seemed to bother Cullen these days, and she was immensely grateful for it.

"What he said." Alyss rolled onto her back with a yawn.

Eira left them to settle, descending the staircase in the back of the room where Lorn and Olivin had disappeared earlier. It led to a small cellar. The ceiling was so low that she had to duck. Eira placed her hand on the wall and frost extended out from her fingers, coating the room. She felt the void it sank into behind a large plank of wood. Not a very elegant cover to their tracks. But the operation was no doubt less sophisticated than the Court had once been.

Her magic retreated and she sat on the last step to wait.

It had been about an hour when the wood in the back shifted with a soft grunt. Eira sheathed the dagger she'd been passing from hand to hand as she had been plotting their next steps. She'd slipped it back into its holster on her thigh as Olivin emerged.

"Perfect, you're here," he said as soon as his eyes landed on her.

"How did it go?"

"Very well. Lorn has done wonders setting up a real network here. I think tomorrow will go well…" He wasted no time filling Eira in on the state of Risen, which led to comparisons with Hokoh. Then, the plan of attack for tomorrow, how Lorn would rally his allies and they would hit the Pillars where it hurt—the temple.

"He's sending us into the most dangerous place in the city." Eira stroked her chin.

"We're in much better shape than the rest of them. It makes sense."

"Or Lorn isn't as loyal as we hope and he's leading us into a trap."

Olivin seemed aghast she'd suggest it. "Lorn is loyal and true. He'd *never* work with the Pillars."

"He's been under the influence of Pillars for a long time." She paused, narrowing her eyes. "Much like my uncle was."

"Eira." His tone softened. "I told you I was sorry for how I acted. I was—and am. You're not going to let bitterness over it impact your judgment here and now, are you?"

"I'm not bitter." She sighed. Maybe she was, a *little*. But she quickly let it go on having it pointed out. "It is a valid concern is all."

"As was mine when I brought it up."

"You're right." Eira relented so they could move on.

Olivin sighed, deflating some. "I know Lorn better than most. He was there when Yonlin and I were figuring out what our lives were going to look like. He helped me join the Court of Shadows. He's worked at every turn to thwart the Pillars. He hates them for what they've done to his city and his people."

"I believe you." She tried to make it clear she wasn't picking a fight with her tone. "But I'm still unsure if we should spearhead this attack. Hokoh doesn't matter, not when it comes to killing Ulvarth. I do not want any of us getting injured before Risen."

"I completely agree. And I know you want to—*need to* be the one to kill Ulvarth. Which is why I've ensured there will be no harm that comes to you," he reassured her, missing the point. "You'll hang back and keep a perimeter around the temple with your ice to prevent more Pillars from joining as we destroy them from within."

"What?"

"You overseeing things will help keep the rest of us safe with your power—and you safe most of all." Olivin's hands fell on her shoulders, caressing her gently. "We are nothing without our leader. I wouldn't want to see anything happen to you."

"You didn't think to consult me before deciding what I would or wouldn't do?" The words weren't harsh, or cold, but matter-of-fact.

Still, they seemed to surprise him. "You had agreed we would help them."

"I hadn't agreed to what help looked like yet." The first lesson Adela had taught her—be careful negotiating and only ever say *exactly* what you mean. And the idea of her staying back from the front lines was utterly unappealing.

"You're a smart woman. I trusted you to see logic."

"Do not compliment me in the same breath that you are using to set aside my worries," Eira cautioned him.

"I didn't mean to, just that…I truly thought it for the best. We could help Lorn, free Hokoh, and have a base of resistance—maybe even distract Ulvarth in the process. And you would stay safe and ready to attack him when the time came."

She sighed and shook her head, at a loss of what to say. There were so many things that she *wanted* to. Yet, she didn't know where to start. It wasn't that what he was saying was *wrong*… But none of it felt right. Like they were singing the same song but at two different parts.

"You've said it yourself, we're going to need all the help we can get when it comes to defeating Ulvarth."

"I know." Eira shifted, looking up at him. Not harsh, not cold, but also showing no hesitation when she said, "In the future, I want to be consulted on these plans before they're decided, all right?"

He nodded. "Of course."

Even though that's what he said, Eira was left wondering just how the man who had once seemed to understand her more than anyone, now seemed to be making such lapses in judgment. Part of her wanted to ask, but she was afraid of what the answer might be.

· CHAPTER ·

THIRTY-ONE

T HEY WERE IN their places by dawn. Eira was perched in the window of a nearby building, ice under her skin so thick that it bloomed on the surface as spots of white frost. It was the only way to keep her agitation at bay.

She was going along with this plan solely for the sake of getting them out of Hokoh and on to Risen faster. Arguing would've chewed up more time and only seeded tension among the group. Neither of which she wanted. But she was far from happy biting her tongue and biding her time.

Who was Lorn to command her to be off to the side? Why did Olivin think it was even the slightest bit of a good idea to put her—arguably their strongest at this point and among their most skilled—where she'd do the least good? She'd heard his argument last night—that he wanted to make sure she wasn't injured before facing Ulvarth. But the fact was, if a random Pillar could wound her then she had little hope of facing Ulvarth.

It would've been better if she was down there. Why hadn't she argued more? Olivin seemed so convinced it was for the best…

Eira massaged the scar of the rune permanently carved into the center of her chest as she watched her friends get into their positions. The only reason she was going along with this, for now, was for them. At this point, it was best if they had the backing of the Court of Shadows. But her compliance was as fragile as spider's silk. It was going to snap sooner rather than later.

The bell tolled across the city. Pillars made their way through the early streets like ghosts in the thin morning fog. Eira stretched out her fingers as wide as they would go. She didn't need the motion to command her power, but it felt good. It was better than stillness, and she was alone, so there was no need to worry about others seeing the tell.

Like low storm clouds, the fog continued to roll over Hokoh, chasing the Pillars inside. With the last toll of the bell, the doors to their temple closed. Eira continued to thicken the fog. Her friends emerged from their hiding places.

In time with the wriggling of the fingers of her left hand, streaks of frost cracked across the roads. The windows were already hazy with white. A wicked notion echoed in Adela's words: *I'll freeze the whole city if I have to.* She'd said it before they'd left Ofok. That'd be one way to accomplish her goals…

Her friends had encircled the temple. They drew a collective breath. The bell tolled again.

With a pump of Alyss's fist, the wooden doors slammed open. Olivin and Cullen rushed in. Ducot's magic rippled through the air, changing things that Eira couldn't even see from her vantage. Alyss was the last to charge inside as the windows illuminated with Lightspinning.

Yonlin remained perched, like she was, but in a building opposite. One hand was on the pistol, the other ready to magically summon a rain of arrows.

Unlike her, Yonlin was content to be off to the side. It was the positioning Eira would've given him because it *suited him*. But an errant notion wouldn't abate that there were deeper motivations behind Olivin's decisions for his placement *and* hers.

Yonlin was everything to Olivin. His brother had been his mission to protect. Any future that Olivin built would be as much for Yonlin as it would be for himself, or Eira. He'd said as much— he was willing to give up journeying with her, at least for a time, to ensure his brother was safe and settled. She had seen what the mere notion of Yonlin being injured did to Olivin's composure.

He can't handle another loss, she realized. It was as bleak and obvious as the dawn. Olivin would do anything to avoid that pain, or the risk, and that drive was already leading him to push her to the side, consciously or not.

Anger streaked through her with a sharp, sorrowful ache. Did he even realize what he was doing? Maybe, maybe not. But her frustration was present either way.

Eira's hand closed into a fist. The streaks of frost across the ground rose as jagged walls—walls that she was only supposed to make in the unlikely case of reinforcements because it would make her presence obvious. She turned from the window and stormed down the stairs of the empty house. In a breath, she was out the front door.

The ambient temperature had dropped from the ice and chill mist. But Eira's breath didn't even cloud the air. Her feet made no noise as she crossed the frost. The window Yonlin had been perched in was thrown open. Eira met his eyes as he leaned out. He hadn't called to her and they shared a long, purposeful look.

She lifted a single finger, curled it, then pointed it down to her feet. *Come*, the motion said. A commotion was rising behind her, muffled by the wall of ice. It competed with the shouting and explosions from within the temple.

Ice rippled out from her, smothering the doors. The wood groaned and buckled as the ice continued growing around it. There was nowhere for it to go, and, with a mighty *crack*, the wooden doors of the temple splintered like the small boat she had used to get to Meru.

For a second, those within were too surprised to do anything other than stand there. A second was far too long for their own good. Ice and frost coated the room. It shot underneath her friends' boots and into the hearts of the Pillars.

This time, Eira didn't keep their hearts beating. They were as still and as cold as the grave.

"Eira?" Alyss whispered, staring at her with a mix of horror and awe. As if she didn't recognize her.

"What are you doing?" Olivin moved for her, recovering faster than the rest. "This isn't what we—"

"I thought you wanted to annihilate all Pillars." Eira gestured to the frozen room. "That is what I did."

"According to plan."

"Plans change."

His eyes shifted and he saw the buildings covered in frost and her walls of ice. Panic widened his eyes and his lips parted. "Now everyone will know you're here."

"Good." Eira glanced to the rest of them. "We're leaving."

"Good? *Good?*" Olivin grabbed her wrist, as if he had been about to jerk her toward him, but his fingers unraveled with a hiss. The flesh was pink, burned from the cold. He ignored what must still be stinging. "How is Ulvarth now knowing you're coming 'good?'"

"Ulvarth might think it's Adela coming…which she also is." Eira stood a little straighter. "Let him prepare for her arrival. If anything, this could distract from me."

"You're risking too much."

Am I actually? Or do you not like seeing any *risk?* She wanted to ask, but couldn't. This wasn't the time or place.

"What's done is done. What's next?" Cullen interjected himself into the conversation. Olivin shot him a glare.

"We're leaving. Now. We'll find the stables and take the best horses. On the way take whatever you think we might need—any supplies you see. We're riding straight to Risen." As Eira finished speaking, she was already walking out, Yonlin meeting them.

"What about Lorn?" Olivin asked, partly chasing after her now.

"What about him?" Eira parted the wall of ice like a curtain with a wave of her hand, unveiling chaos beyond. Men and women ran through the streets. Most of them didn't seem to be Pillars or Shadows. Many seemed to be citizens taking advantage of the chaos the ice had created. "He looks like he'll be fine. We cleared the majority, if not all, of the Pillars."

One looter ran from a shop, hands laden with goods that

tumbled to the ground as he skidded to a stop. A finger rose to point at her.

"Ah—A—Adel—" With a scream, he was gone, scampering away. Eira didn't mind how his terror felt in the slightest.

"Well, I think Ulvarth will be preparing for someone else now." Eira glanced back to Olivin. He sighed, a forlorn softness clouding his gaze. She stepped closer and tilted her head, looking up at him. "It will be fine. *I* will be fine."

"Sometimes I question if that's true."

"Then stick with me and let me show you."

Some resolve returned to his expression at that. Eira smiled slightly. Olivin did the same. And, with that, she moved on.

They did as she commanded and took what they needed. Ducot had no qualms over smashing windows to reach around and unlock doors. Alyss focused mostly on the houses that were already empty, picking like a hesitant bird. Cullen was a surprise; he was right beside Ducot, loading a pack with all manner of goods.

Olivin and Yonlin took up the rear. It surprised her. The questions associated with it lingered as they rode out of the town, simmering until they slowed to a trot among rolling plains and grasslands.

Eira tugged on her reins, falling back to Olivin's side. She wasn't going to let this be. Not when there was so much still ahead of them that they needed to work together through.

"If you do not wish to come with me then—"

"We're with you," Olivin said. Though he sounded more conflicted than ever before. Yonlin wouldn't even look at her.

"Truly," Eira insisted. "We can find a safe place for you both and—"

"We didn't come to pillage and steal," Yonlin interrupted. He sounded more wounded than outright angry. "We came to protect our home, to make Meru right again, do good by and help her people. Not to freeze their towns and pilfer their resources."

"What must be done to accomplish our goal might not always be pretty," Eira answered calmly.

"That was downright piracy."

"I am a pirate."

Yonlin opened and closed his mouth, as if the fact was sinking in for the first time. His attention swung to Olivin. "Are we just going to sit idly by and let this happen?"

"For the greater good, sometimes ugly things must happen," Olivin said begrudgingly. Hardly the endorsement of piracy she would've hoped for from her future fleet master.

Her eyes darted between the two men. Did Yonlin know what Olivin intended? When the time came, would Olivin be able to leave his brother's side?

"Eira… You are a good woman. You don't hurt innocents." It sounded like Yonlin was trying to convince himself.

"I don't delight in it. Nor do I go out of my way to do it." That much was true. She was more than content to let innocents live so long as they didn't force her hand.

"Then what do you call that back there?" Alyss had overheard and spoke up. Eira glanced over her shoulder. Alyss's stare might as well have stabbed daggers straight through Eira.

"I told you." She slowed her mount and spoke loud enough for them all to hear. "I will give Pillars no quarter. I am here to destroy Ulvarth and the rest of his ilk. The people I killed in there were Pillars through and through. They bore the markings and gladly praised Ulvarth. They were not innocent." She swept her eyes over them. "But, while my ice covered the town, I did not kill the rest of the townsfolk." At least not intentionally…if someone slipped on some ice and cracked their head, that was on them.

When she finished, she swept her gaze across them, searching for any signs of objection. There was none, and she turned her attention back to Yonlin.

"Am I clear?"

He nodded mutely.

"Good. Let's focus on riding; we've a lot of ground to cover before nightfall." Eira tried to soften her tone but she wasn't sure if she succeeded. It was hard at times to figure out where the lines were when it came to them. When she was their friend, lover, or confidant, and when she was their pirate captain.

Olivin came up beside her this time. "He means well."

"I know." She spoke as softly as he did. "But does he understand what this is going to cost? Will he be able to take the shot?"

"Against Ulvarth? Unequivocally." Olivin's lack of hesitation reassured her some. "The rest of the costs…I'm not sure about. But I will shield him."

She studied Olivin from the corners of her eyes. In her periphery, Eira could see a newer streak of white. It seemed every time she drew from the rune on her chest in a significant way, it took a toll on her physical form. But if he noticed, he said nothing.

"Like you shielded him from what you did in the Court of Shadows?" She remembered him saying as much, long ago.

"Something like that," he murmured. "But know that I am with you."

Eira nodded. His presence would always be reassuring to her. But if the cards fell, Eira was certain Olivin would do what benefitted Yonlin best, every time. What made the realization all the more painful was that she could understand it. There was a time with Marcus where she wanted them to be everything to each other. Siblings against the world.

But what if she was the thing Olivin wanted to protect his brother from? Where did that leave them?

They had barely made it into the woods to the west of Hokoh when a burst of flame had her horse rearing. She barely managed to avoid being thrown. Frost thickened under the palm that once held the reins as she twisted in her saddle. Cullen's magic spiked. The earth fractured around Alyss.

"I thought I told you not to come to Meru again, Pirate—" Vi

Solaris, Crown Princess of the Solaris Empire, emerged from the shade of the trees, stopping short at the road's edge. And she was not alone. Her eyes widened. "Eira Landan?"

I KNEW IT. T HE immediate vindication of seeing Vi emerge from the shadows into the light of the still-smoldering grasses had Eira sitting straighter. The princess wore loose-fitting and filthy clothes. Her hair, usually immaculately plaited, was drawn into a single, thick cord that ran down her back.

But despite the muck and grime, her eyes still shone bright with all the cleverness, determination, and cut-throat nature Eira had always seen in her.

"Your Highness." Cullen's initial term of respect became a hasty blurt as two other figures emerged. "Your Majesties."

Aldrik and Vhalla Solaris looked equally worse for wear. Their wounds, overall, seemed superficial. But Eira didn't think she was imagining that Emperor Aldrik seemed to favor one side a bit more than the other when he walked.

"Solaris competitors." Aldrik ran a hand through his dark hair, but it fell messily around his face. A far cry from the usual slicked-back and set style he preferred. "What a stroke of luck."

"Possibly." Vi's eyes had never left Eira. "If they're still on our side."

"Vi," Vhalla said with a scolding tone, stepping forward.

Vi stopped her mother with a straight arm. "We can't be too cautious."

"Darling girl, that is Lord Cullen Drowel." Vhalla's smile could've lit up the night sky. "He would never betray me."

Cullen had dismounted. He staggered toward the Empress and collapsed to a knee. Even in his profile, Eira could see how relief crumpled his features, folding his brow.

"Your Majesty, it is a relief to see you well."

Eira fought a smile and lost. Cullen had been more worried about the Empress than his own father. She had been better to him, more consistently, than his own father ever had been.

"We have not acted against the interest of Solaris. In fact, the contrary." Cullen's voice had shifted back into the lordly tone Eira could recognize from their days at Court. From when she knew him as nothing more than the lofty "Prince of the Tower." Her smile fell as an invisible knife twisted in her gut.

Olivin already had talked about the life of etiquette and nobility that had been taken from him. There had been enough longing in his voice that part of her yet worried he could lose him to it. Would Cullen fall prey to its siren call as well?

"Is that so?" Vi seemed to pose the question directly to Eira.

So she answered, "We have secured aid from Qwint, sent a ship back to Solaris with word to bring fresh aid, and have worked to clear the seas of the Pillars' stolen armada. This way, there is a path for help to arrive."

"Truly?" Vhalla asked, looking between Cullen and Eira.

"She speaks true." Cullen stood his ground. "Eira has organized it all."

"And how have *you* managed to clear the seas?" Vi knew. She was too smart and too connected not to.

"Oh, before I forget," Eira said hastily, shifting focus to Vhalla. "Fritznangle is on his way to Solaris as we speak as well. If not already there."

"Fritz?" Vhalla clutched her hands over her heart, face lighting up. A smile cracked even the Emperor's usually stoic facade as he wrapped an arm around Vhalla's waist. "I knew he'd make it. The Charem blood is strong, as evidenced by you."

"The seas." Vi wasn't about to be dissuaded.

Eira shifted in her saddle and adjusted the grip on her reins, ready to bolt if need be. "Adela has graciously agreed to lend her aid to the cause."

Vi barked laughter. "That old bitch."

"Vi, that is no way for a princess to speak." Vhalla's mothering tone had returned, aghast.

"Or a future Empress." Aldrik joined in.

Vi seemed unbothered by them both, her focus solely on Eira still. "What does she want in return?"

"She told me to tell you that she is only here to lend a hand. Nothing more or less." Eira did as Adela had asked of her months ago—*put in a good word with Vi Solaris.* The arrogant smirk that Vi's face fell into, eyes alight with pride, affirmed all of Eira's suspicions. Vi was, in fact, the one that had somehow sent Adela away from Solaris and Meru. But how? The question burned Eira to the point that she almost demanded answers. *Almost.* "Though…I also imagine she'll keep any ships she can salvage, or loot she can find."

"Of course."

"We can't be working with pirates." Aldrik scowled. "Adela least of all." Considering Adela had admitted to Eira that she'd murdered the Emperor's grandfather, she didn't blame Aldrik for his tone or feelings on the matter.

"Right now, we can't be too picky." There was a begrudging tone to Vi's words, but, for some reason, Eira suspected it to be inauthentic. Her eyes shone like laughter. She was deeply amused with this turn of events. "We can deal with the Pirate Queen, as is necessary, when the dust settles. But for now, the enemy of our enemy is our friend."

Eira heard the subtext loud and clear—this fragile alliance would be over the second the Pillars were dealt with. Eira included among it.

"Why would Adela be the enemy of the Pillars?" Vhalla still wasn't convinced.

"Adela has a personal grudge against Ulvarth," Eira answered simply. There was too much wrapped up in Adela's motivations to explain more than that. But fortunately, judging by Vhalla's expression, it seemed that was enough of an explanation.

"For what it's worth, I have found Adela to be surprisingly trustworthy," Cullen encouraged Vhalla.

"Oh no…don't tell me she captured you, too?" Vhalla rested a hand underneath his jaw. The movement was familial. It put a twinge of sorrow between Eira's ribs.

This would be what brought Cullen back… He would find his path with the nobles in Solaris once more. He'd see the good of it—all the good he could do when he wasn't solely at the behest of his father. And she…

She wouldn't stop him.

How could she? If that was the life he was meant for, then she'd be happy he'd found it.

"I am all right," Cullen assured the Empress.

"We should go help bring order to Hokoh. They look like they could use warming up." Vi turned toward the city in the distance, still glistening with frost. Eira made more of a conscious effort to relax her magic.

"Lorn is there," Olivin dutifully reported to Vi.

"Is he?" Vi sounded pleased. "Rebec had said he was going to see if he could solicit help."

"Rebec is alive, even still?" Even though Lorn had said as much, Ducot still looked for further confirmation.

"She is, last we left Risen. She was the one to help us get out." A frown tugged on Vi's lips. "I've no idea how long she could last there. The Pillars were relentless."

"It's amazing you could escape at all—that you even survived." Eira allowed the sentiment to carry a bit of weight. Judging by the lift of Vi's eyebrows, she heard it. "Not that I'm not grateful for it, of course."

"Never doubt the might of two of the strongest Firebearers to ever walk the earth." Aldrik placed a hand on his daughter's shoulder proudly. Vi's eyes just shone and she allowed her silence to be her agreement. But there was more to it. The woman had Lightspinning powers as well…and could frighten off Adela.

"What are your plans now?" Eira looked in the general

direction of Risen. "That magic could be of use overthrowing the Pillars."

"I know that Meru underneath the Pillars is bad for Solaris. And…" Vi's words dropped off and her fierce stance relaxed. She followed Eira's gaze, looking to Risen. "This is personal for me."

"Taavin." Eira scolded herself for being so dense. If he wasn't here with them, then it didn't bode well.

"They have him." Vi's hands balled into fists, white-hot flame licking around them. "They took him when we were trying to get out. He…"

"He stayed behind so we could escape," Vhalla finished for her daughter, lowering her gaze.

"Since Hokoh is liberated from the Pillars and already has operations thanks to Lorn, we'll use it as a southern base to collect our forces." Vi turned back to the city before them. Her resolve was ironclad once more. The trace of emotion and doubt completely evaporated. But Eira had seen it. And she could sympathize. "Then we'll move farther on to Parth. We'll have enough momentum to take it, and we can use their wharf to collect the armada from Solaris and move for Risen in a few days' time." Her focus returned to Eira. "Can you get word to Adela?"

"I can."

"What?" Ducot's surprise was across his face.

"How?" Yonlin asked.

"I have my ways," Eira said enigmatically. She and Adela had discussed a system before leaving. Though it had yet to truly be put to the test. "Shorter messages will be better than longer ones."

Vi nodded. Her lack of surprise continued to reinforce for Eira that her magical abilities extended far beyond what most considered possible. "Can you ask her, now, if she's seen the Solaris ship?"

Eira exhaled and released the last of her magic on Hokoh. She shifted her focus to the moisture in the air, the breezes that whispered of the distant sea. Her mind's eye plunged into those cold waters and swam in their currents underneath. Through white-capped swells and out of the bay into the ocean beyond.

Brow furrowing, it took her a minute to locate Adela's magic. And then two more to find the *Stormfrost*. A tether of power, thrown like a lifeline, raced up the side of the hull, skittered across the deck, and looped up Adela's cane, coming to a stop on the back of her hand as a pool of dew.

Adela lifted and lowered her cane and Eira could almost imagine her saying, *Out with it, girl.*

With an invisible hand, Eira wrote across the deck of the *Stormfrost* at Adela's feet in icy letters, raised from the permafrost on the deck: *Solaris ships?*

One tap of her cane reverberated through the magical connection. One tap meant *yes.*

Eira opened her eyes, but kept the connection with Adela alive. "She's seen the Solaris armada."

"Are they close?" Vi asked.

Eira closed her eyes again, forming the word on the deck: *Close?*

Another tap.

"Yes, they are," Eira reported.

"Good. It will take you two days, likely three to get to Risen from here. I presume you'll need an extra day to get into the city…" Vi stroked her chin in thought. "In five days' time, we launch our attack on Risen. The Solaris armada will join Qwint's, and whatever forces Adela might be willing to spare."

Before relaxing her connection, Eira wrote one more message: *Three days. Parth. Vi. Five days. Risen.*

There was a much longer pause, then, a single tap.

"I can't speak for Adela's assistance, but I can say that she'll aid the Solaris armada in getting to Parth in three days." Eira relaxed her connection, for now.

"Are you some kind of new sorcerer?" Alyss whispered in awe.

"I feel like it some days," Eira admitted.

"Then that's it. In five days, we will retake Risen," Vi proclaimed.

THIRTY-THREE

I T TOOK THEM nearly four full days to cross the distance from Hokoh to Risen. The city first came into view as they crested a ridge. The valley of the main river of Meru had completely changed from when they had last seen it.

"They…destroyed it." Yonlin's words quivered from horror or rage, likely both.

"Not all of it." Alyss tried to be optimistic, but the sentiment rang hollow, given what lay before them.

"Someone want to explain?" Ducot asked.

Eira described the sight for his benefit—the blackened husks of entire swaths of the city left like carcasses to rot. The vacant patches that were the outlines of buildings. Every scar on the once glorious city that led to the vast pit of rubble where the castle once stood.

"That castle had been there for thousands of years." Olivin gripped the reins of his mount with white knuckles and a quivering fist. "It was a testament to Meru's history, and our future."

"The castle is gone, but the Archives are more glorious than ever," Eira said, somewhat still for Ducot's benefit. The houses and districts that led to the Archives were the most intact. Walls had been erected up the hill that the Archives stood atop, glowing in the new "Flame of Yargen" that ringed them. She had no doubt there was some kind of checkpoint at each wall and only the most trusted were allowed to reside closest to Ulvarth and his unholy seat.

"City gates?" Ducot murmured.

"Closed and guarded," Olivin reported. He'd scouted ahead.

"So, Frostiness-in-Training, are we going in like Hokoh and freezing the whole damn place?" Ducot directed the question to Eira.

"As much as I wish…no." *Not right away at least.* "Olivin, Ducot, do either of you know of a second way in?" They'd treat this like Hokoh and go in quietly, getting as much information as they needed to make an informed strike. The only difference here was Eira's patience. She wasn't going to waste the one shot she had.

"I know of tunnels," Ducot said. "But they're likely monitored or collapsed. The Pillars knew the central operations for the Shadows."

"Given what Lorn said, I'm sure Ducot is right," Olivin chimed in. "But I think I know another way that the Pillars wouldn't be aware of."

"You do?"

"Follow me." Olivin led them off the main road and down to a rocky bluff. There, they abandoned their horses and continued on foot around the side of the city, toward where Risen met the great bay of Meru.

Down along the stony shoreline, they came to a halt before a flat slab of rock. It didn't seem any more significant than the others. But Olivin stopped directly in front of it.

"Alyss, can you move this?" Olivin pointed.

"Sure." She seemed as confused as Eira felt, but did so anyway. The slab revealed a cobbled tunnel, so small they'd have to crawl through. It was thick with algae and muck.

"What is this?" Eira demanded to know.

"An entry to our home." Olivin looked to Yonlin, whose lips parted with shock.

"You never told me—"

"I didn't want you exploring," Olivin interrupted him. "I didn't know where Wynry might lurk—she knew about this, too—and I didn't want you going off without me. So I sealed it and never spoke of it."

"I had a right to know…" Even Yonlin sounded uncertain.

"You were a boy," Olivin countered and turned back to the tunnel. "And I was doing my best to protect you."

How had she never seen it with such clarity? Olivin might have suffered grave injustices, but he didn't truly see himself as a Shadow. Even when he was giving the organization his all, that wasn't where his heart had ever been. It finally all slotted together. The contradictions Eira had been grappling with smoothed. In Olivin's mind, he was a noble knight. A fallen lord struggling to reclaim all the control that had been stolen from him. First, he'd wanted revenge, but at the first glimpse of being able to attain something more, he jumped at it.

He was nothing more than a boy who was afraid of losing the few people that were important to him after he'd already lost so much.

It was noble. But smothering and misguided at the same time. Rather than causing her heart to ache, the pain in her chest continued to knot further.

He loved her.

Never had it been more clear than in that moment. Never was something more sad…because if he didn't love her, he wouldn't be so bent on protecting her. He wouldn't be happy with relegating her to the sidelines—he would've seen the problems with even trying.

Eira kept the thoughts to herself and dutifully followed behind him into the tunnel on her hands and knees. They were at Risen now. Having this conversation would have to wait. Right before they took down Ulvarth wasn't the time.

The tunnel pitched down, then leveled, and sloped up again. Olivin and Yonlin's glyphs glinted off the slick walls. As her knees were screaming from the endless digging into jagged rock, Olivin stopped.

"Alyss, once more, in front of me," Olivin instructed.

With a pulse of magic that rippled through the stone around them, Alyss folded the ceiling of the tunnel above Olivin's head like a sheet of paper. Stone and mortar ground against each other. The cracking and creaking ended with a few pebbles that bounced down and skittered across the floor.

Now able to stand, Olivin pulled himself through the hole in what must be a floor. He turned and reached back for Eira. She took his hand, praying that something in her grasp didn't give away her realizations.

The room she now found herself in was a cellar, though it had been ages since anything was last kept in here, judging from the thick blanket of cobwebs and the piles of dust that had collected where various long-collapsed and rotted objects had been. Eira could almost see their silhouettes on the walls. An after-image remnant of bygone days.

"Where is this?" Yonlin asked as Olivin ascended the stairs tucked against one side of the room. At the top was a hatch.

"Just under the kitchens." Olivin put his shoulder into the hatch. It hardly budged.

"Would you like me to?" Alyss readily offered.

"If you don't mind," Olivin said.

"Under the kitchens? How did I never notice?" Yonlin spoke partially through their conversation.

"I closed it off before you ever entered the house again."

"And sealed the other passage shut. A bit much, don't you think?" Yonlin looked from where they'd come through the opening Alyss had made.

"You're clever, brother. Always have been. If anyone could find this place, it was you." With a pat on his brother's shoulder, Olivin marched up the stairs.

Yonlin lingered, strife furrowed across his brows. Sharpness in his gaze. Eira wanted to tell him she knew how he felt—especially after her latest realizations. And, as a younger sibling, she'd gouged that piercing look into Marcus's back countless times. But she held her tongue, for now, and ascended into what had once been a well-appointed kitchen.

"Had once been" could describe the entire manor.

Doors hung askew, limp on their hinges, rotted from the rain that pelted the inner courtyard of the square, three-story home. Windows were smashed. Furniture had long since been eaten by moths.

"Where were you staying after…you know?" Alyss asked Yonlin. It was clear that they hadn't been making this their home for some time.

"Deneya helped me set up an apartment," Olivin answered before Yonlin could.

"Deneya was behind our place?" This was news to Yonlin, it seemed.

"It took a long time for our estate to be returned to us. During which we had no money that we could access. No clout our name would give." Olivin led them through the overgrown courtyard. Eira couldn't stop herself from scanning the mezzanine that circled it on the upper levels. The building was as quiet as a grave. "We were wards of the crown, so it made sense for Deneya to assist with our arrangements."

"And then you started working for her." Yonlin sounded mildly wounded by it, even still. He'd only learned the extent of his brother's secrecy over the past few months and had—in Eira's opinion—taken it amazingly well in his stride. But those types of wounds could fester.

"I did what I had to do to keep you safe, and I always will."

"Always my safety." Yonlin took a few steps forward, breaking away from Alyss. "Never yours."

Eira was stilled to silence, seeing similar conversations replay in her memories. She'd said something similar to Marcus a number of times. The words and circumstances were different, but the sentiment was the same: *See me for who I am—I'm so much more than just your little sibling.*

Olivin, however, was oblivious. "I'm fine."

Yonlin rounded on his older brother. Even though he was slightly shorter, he managed to stare up at him with a piercing gaze. "Why do you get to decide how you are for yourself, but you don't extend that to the rest of us?"

"You're being a child," Olivin scolded.

"That's all you've ever seen me as. A *child*." Yonlin pressed his palm to his chest. "I'm eighteen, nearly nineteen. I'm a man."

"A man doesn't need to say he is such." Olivin shifted away from his brother, looking back to them. "I think we'll find somewhere salvageable enough to stay in the forward part of the building. From there we can make our plans for our strike, the other nations should be leading their attack tomorrow."

"Will you even let me be a part of the Court of Shadows after all of this?" Yonlin continued to step in Olivin's way.

"You shouldn't need to be. After Ulvarth is gone, our lives will look very different." At least Olivin was consistent in what he was envisioning for the future.

"Then will you let me be in the fray to fight him?" Yonlin seemed almost desperate.

"You know your role," Olivin said simply. "Eira gave you the pistol because you're the best shot among us. You'll need to find a good vantage—"

"Convenient that my role is away from the thickest part of the fighting." Yonlin's eyes darted to Eira.

She opened her mouth to speak, to reassure him that she didn't care where he was, as long as he could take the shot to remove Ulvarth's armor, but Olivin spoke over her.

"It's just how it happened."

Yonlin snorted softly and shook his head. "You can't keep things safe by locking them away, brother."

"I watched you die. I saw you and thought you were dead. I thought I had lost *everything* all over again." Olivin grabbed his brother's shoulders, staring straight through Yonlin. "If locking you away is what it takes to keep you safe from them, I will. I will do anything to protect you because they…they have already taken so much from me—from us. I refuse to let them have more. I will not lose anyone else I love. Not when we're so close to reclaiming a future that they tried to steal from us." Olivin's fingers were pressing dents into Yonlin's clothes.

Yonlin yanked his shoulders away from his brother's grip and stepped back. "I don't want to lose the chance to live my life because I'm forced to be nothing more than a piece of yours."

"Yonlin—"

"Include me, let me have a say, or I'm gone." Yonlin glared for one more breath. Right when Olivin opened his mouth to speak, he spun and ran down the hall and dashed up a side stair.

"Yonlin!" Olivin shouted. He lunged. "Yonlin—"

Eira caught his wrist. Olivin spun back but all the hot rage vanished from his cheeks when he laid eyes on her.

"Give him space," she told him firmly. "You're not doing yourself any favors by chasing after him."

"You don't know at all what it's—"

"Like?" she finished for him with a lift of a brow and a cock of her head. "You mean to tell me I don't know what it's like to fear losing a sibling? Maybe I don't know that fear, because I watched it happen right in front of me when I was too helpless to stop it."

"Eira…" His stance relaxed. But her grip remained.

"I know what it's like to have people 'protecting' you to the point that it holds you back—it stints you." She looked him dead in the eyes. "You're going to crush him under the weight of your fears if you don't relent."

Eira knew there were two ways he could react to this— with more anger, committing to his rage. Or with some kind of acceptance.

Fortunately, he chose the latter. Olivin exhaled the last of his frustration, for now, at least. And shook his head. Eira released his wrist and it fell limply at his side.

"I'll show you all to the rooms I was thinking of while he cools off." Olivin guided them past the staircase Yonlin ran up.

Alyss paused, staring up the stairs. Eira stilled as well. Alyss's eyes darted between her and the second floor. Yonlin was nowhere to be seen.

"You're right," Alyss mouthed more than murmured. Eira assumed her to be referencing the need to give Yonlin space, as Alyss followed the rest of them through to an entry hall and into a side parlor.

This was connected to another sitting room, and a study beyond that. The doors had been locked, and windows shuttered. Tarps were thrown over the furniture that were weighted down by dust.

But because of the care that these rooms had been given when they were closed up, they weren't in nearly as rough shape as the rest of the home.

"These were my mother's chambers," Olivin explained, even though no one asked. He ran his fingers along one of the side tables by the leather sofa. "She'd be aghast if she saw it now. She'd always kept it just so."

"We'll be grateful to stay here," Alyss said gently.

"Would you like me to fix it up for you?" Ducot offered. Olivin spun, shock on his face. "I'm guessing by your movements, this offer…surprised you?"

"The Shift," Olivin whispered.

"What is, and what could be." Ducot nodded. "If you'd like, I could do the whole house."

"Let's start with here," Olivin decided after brief thought. "There are some reminders of what I'm fighting for—what I've lost—that I still wish to keep."

Ducot set about to repairing the room. It was like watching a looking glass turn to water. Its surface shifting in the breeze, what Eira saw was different between every ripple. Time itself bent before the might of Ducot's magic.

"It's just like I remember." Olivin breathed deeply, as though he were trying to inhale remnants of his mother's perfume.

The notion gave Eira an idea. "Olivin, would you like to hear an echo?" She presented the question like a peace offering. The rest of them distracted themselves elsewhere, immediately figuring out that what was about to happen would be personal.

"An echo? Here?"

"You're a family of sorcerers." She gestured generally to the room. "Something would be caught up, I'd venture."

"I… Yes."

Eira let her power sweep across the room. Sure enough, there were multiple echoes, but she picked a weaker one in a mirror. Leading him by the hand, Eira ran her fingers along the gilded frame. Frost trailed in their wake. The magic was faint, and a bit harder to get a hold of. But she managed after only a moment of focus.

Olivin, Yonlin, we're going to be late, a woman—their mother, she presumed—called out.

It'll be fine. A man chuckled. *There are worse things than being late to court.*

We are always late to court.

And yet, everyone longs to be us.

She laughed. *You are so arrogant.*

And you love me all the more for it.

Eira stopped the echo there. Wynry entered immediately thereafter. But sharing just that much was more than enough. Tears welled in the corners of Olivin's eyes. For a moment, he did nothing but stare at himself in the mirror, almost longingly. As if he could see the boy who had once been called to go by his mother.

It sounded like they'd truly had a happy home. Her stomach knotted. Maybe…maybe it wasn't so bad for him to want that back. Or want it, at least, for Yonlin.

"Yonlin should hear this." Olivin inhaled deeply, gathering his composure.

"I'll go find him." Alyss was on her feet.

"I'll go with you." Olivin stepped forward.

Eira grabbed his hand, holding tight. This was perhaps the most perfect time for her to catch him on his own, and before they went to fight Ulvarth, she wanted to speak with Olivin alone. Hopefully her display had shown him she meant well.

"Or…why don't you go, Alyss?" Olivin said, somewhat begrudgingly. "I bet he's gone to his room. I'm sure he remembered the way. It's the second door once you reach the third floor."

"I'll be back." Alyss smiled and stepped away.

"We'll trail behind," Eira suggested to Olivin, by way of compromise. "Give them a moment alone first."

"Sure."

He followed her into the entry hall, leaving Ducot and Cullen behind. Alyss's footsteps were already fading on the stairs. Though Eira wondered if she was intentionally slowing them. If Alyss was looking for more "inspiration" for her book by eavesdropping on Eira and Olivin.

"What is it?"

Eira jumped right to the point. "I know what you're doing and I'd rather discuss it outright. You must know I'm going to keep running toward danger. You're not going to be able to stop me."

"What?"

"I swore to kill Ulvarth, and I will."

"Of course. We all will. With your help—"

"By *my* hand," Eira clarified, looking him in the eyes once more. His expression hardened some. "It will be me who does it. It must be me. No one else can bring down the very idea of him like I can."

"I know you think you're powerful but Ulvarth isn't one to be underestimated." Olivin seemed genuinely concerned that she hadn't fully considered the dangers.

"Do you think I got this solely out of hubris?" Eira pointed to the center of her chest. "For some kind of ability to gloat? Olivin, I know he's dangerous, I've faced him before multiple times and failed. So I know what it takes. I've been working on a plan for months now, I have power no one else does"—she gestured vaguely in the direction of the mirror in the other room,

her display was both a kindness and a reminder of her power—
"so I must be the one to do it when the time comes."

His eyes widened a fraction, as though he hadn't fully
considered this. "Then let me be your sword and shield."

"You can't protect me if your focus is your brother," she said
as gently as possible.

He took a step back in shock. "You don't want me to protect
Yonlin?"

"I want you to," she insisted. "That's why I'm trying to say,
don't worry about me. I need to kill Ulvarth because it was by his
hand that my brother died. I want to kill him because he tore apart
a land I dreamed of for years. A land with flaws and ugliness, but
also beauty and goodness. A land that wasn't my own and might
never be, but that I loved anyway. Because as long as he lives, I
and those I love will never know true safety. And…yes. Before
you even say it, you're right. I want to kill him out of my own
pride. Who would ever take a pirate seriously if she ran from her
first real enemy?"

Olivin listened in silence, his expression hard to read. But
something got through to him. At least she thought so…

"Why are you saying all this?" he finally asked. He was going
to make her spell it out.

"I know what you did—tried to do in Hokoh. I know your
heart was in the right place. But don't try it again." Her hand
slipped in his. Panic flashed through his eyes but she couldn't
tell if it was a result of what she was asking, or that she had
discovered him.

"I will not endure what he did." Olivin's words dropped to a
hushed whisper as he glanced toward Ducot in the other room. "I
will not watch you die."

"I will do everything I can to keep myself safe, along with
everyone else. But my life is not yours to live, or to keep."

Olivin tightened his grasp. "Why do you resist help?"

"I want your help." She wanted to plead with him to understand.
"I want you by my side, helping me, protecting me, but as an

equal. Just as I will do the same for you. Please, Olivin…" She had a thousand things she wanted to say. *Please don't make this complicated.*

Olivin searched her face, as if he could hear all those sentiments. Hear her fears and the dreams she hadn't even realized until that moment. Until she realized she might lose them.

"I love you, Eira."

"I know." She nodded, heart squeezing to the point of pain. "I know you do. You wouldn't have done it if you didn't."

"Do you…" He almost couldn't finish the question. "…love me?"

"I—" She didn't have a chance to finish.

Alyss's bloodcurdling scream echoed through the empty house.

Eira ripped herself away from Olivin's grasp and took the stairs two at a time. Noelle's soundless scream rang in her ears. Frost exploded from underneath her feet. She wouldn't let it happen again. She wasn't going to send off another of her friends to the worlds beyond.

The men were close behind as she rounded the stairs and continued up to the third floor. Just as Olivin had instructed. The third door was open. Pushed aside.

Snow drifted through the air around her as she turned the corner. Eira was ready to unleash all manner of frozen death upon whatever awaited her. But Alyss stood alone in the center of the room.

Her quivering hands covered her mouth. Eira slowed to a stop, chest heaving. The footsteps of the men slowed behind her…all save for Olivin.

He staggered forward, eyes fixated on the singular point none of them could look away from. Olivin reached up and touched the wall. His fingers came away bright red. Sticky, like the sick horror and rage that was coursing through Eira's veins.

"Blood," Cullen whispered.

"Damn her!" Olivin screamed. His knuckles cracked the

plaster of the wall, strips of wood jutting out like freshly cut teeth. It made a morbid period to the end of the statement that had been written in dripping streaks of fresh blood:

Hello, brother.

· CHAPTER ·

THIRTY-FOUR

"SHE HAS HIM," Olivin rasped between ragged breaths, head hung, shoulders quivering. "She. Has. Him." He withdrew his hand and pointed it, bloody knuckles and splintered flesh and all, at each of them. "Let him go. *Let him go*, you told me. And this"—he thrust a finger toward the wall—"this is what happens."

"Olivin—"

"If he had stayed, she wouldn't have him. She was probably waiting here for—" He stopped short and the danger they were in dawned on all of them.

"Go," Eira whispered.

They all scrambled toward the windows. Alyss threw out a hand and the wall around them crumbled, shutters clattering to the street below.

Eira shifted her steps, falling back to Ducot. He had moved with the rest of them. Even if he couldn't read the writing on the wall, he heard the panic in their voices, Alyss's magic, their sprint.

Her hand closed around his. "When I say, jump."

Ducot's mouth was pressed into a hard line but he nodded anyway, putting his trust into her. They closed the distance to the wall and, "Jump!"

Olivin landed on a disk of glowing light. Cullen floated down, feet pumping through the air. Alyss raced on stairs formed from rubble. Each appeared under her toes and crumbled away as her magic and feet moved from one to the next.

After Eira's stomach shot into her throat from the initial

weightlessness, she landed on a pillar of ice, Ducot wobbly. She shifted her magic and the ice became a chute, Eira guiding his fall onto the makeshift ramp. He slid on his back and she rode behind him, staying on her heels.

They were all about halfway down the second story when a zing of magic rippled the air.

Eira spun. Part of her magic continued to focus on easing Ducot to the ground. She skidded to a stop on what was now a pillar of ice where she stood and shifted all the rest of her focus. A thick wall of ice rose against the house.

Simultaneously, it exploded.

The sudden, magical force of the explosion only compared to one other that Eira had felt—the end of the flash bead mines. Eira held up both her hands, rising to the balls of her feet as she leaned forward. As though she were trying to smother the fire with her own body rather than magic.

Ice cracked like thunder. Popped like her jaw as she gritted her teeth. Her breastbone burned around the rune etched into it.

But her ice held. It blocked the shrapnel and rubble and contained the worst of the explosion. As the last of the shockwaves rippled through the ground, she eased her magic and descended to meet the rest of them.

"That was easily half a dozen flash beads you just blocked," Ducot murmured with awe. Out of everyone, Eira trusted he'd have the keenest senses when it came to the magic.

"I've been working on my magic." Eira tried to brush off the feat. She hadn't done it for praise. They had all seen the destruction just one flash bead could wreak before. "We have to move."

"This way." Olivin took the lead.

Eira fell into step and the others followed as they quickly dashed down the streets.

"Where to?" she asked.

"To get my brother back." That was the answer she'd been fearing he'd give her.

"Olivin—"

"They want to make this a fight, we'll make this a fight," he growled, turning onto a street that connected with a main road. The man wasn't thinking. He was literally going to march to the Archives right now. Eira took two quick steps forward and wrapped an arm across his upper chest and shoulders.

"Wh—"

"We cannot fall right into their hands." Eira shoved him up against the wall, holding him there. Olivin tried to break free, but she braced herself against him. She was stronger than he remembered, or gave her credit for.

He seethed. "They have my brother."

"I know. And I know you'll risk anything to get him back. But, for a second, *think about this*: they'll kill him once they can't use him as leverage to get to us. So if you hand yourself over to them, what do you think is the first thing they're going to do?" Eira shifted her grip, making sure she had a firm hold on him. Olivin looked away, but didn't answer. She took it as a victory. "Ducot, know of any Court of Shadows tunnels in this section of the city?"

"There's an entrance closer to the docks," he said. "I'm not totally sure where we are, but it shouldn't be far. I'm confident I'll pick up my bearings on the way."

"You want us to go down into the tunnels that Lorn said are now controlled by the Pillars? Yes, that's so much smarter than tackling this problem head-on." Olivin tried to break free again.

A dagger of ice pressed into his throat underneath his chin. Eira locked eyes with his as they widened, shocked by the threat.

"You would threaten me?" Hurt flashed through his eyes.

"Only until your better sense takes over. If we go to the Archives right now, they will kill us all. You are playing right into her hand. Anything you do now, she's planning for. She already has. We're finding a place to hole up and recalculate—doing the last thing she expects you to do: approach this logically and calmly."

"I don't—"

"Olivin, please," she said softly. *Don't make me do this.* "I swear to you, we will get him back. If not because we care about him—which we do, *I do*—because he has the pistol and without it, no one is defeating Ulvarth. So if you can't believe I'm going to prioritize getting him back because he's one of this crew and I care, then believe it's in my self-interest to do so." Eira tilted her head to look Olivin in the eyes, seeing all his fear and worry. "You're not going to help him if you're dead. Don't die on him. Don't put him through that."

Perhaps it was just how recently she'd brought up the pain of Marcus's death, but Olivin's shoulders sagged. He shook his head and made a noise of disgust—of pain she could empathize with all too well.

Ultimately, he resigned himself to her plan. "Fine."

"This way." Eira led them once more.

It wasn't hard to find their way to the docks. She remembered the pathways from the books she'd read on Risen and from their arrival. It also didn't take long until Ducot caught his bearings and led them down a side alleyway and into a door that Alyss helped open for them.

Eira was reminded of the storeroom by the Archives—the place where Alyss and Noelle had first been wrapped into the insanity of the Court of Shadows—and instantly wondered if this somehow connected. Even if the Pillars had brought down the Court, their underground labyrinth was extensive and there was no way they could monitor every tunnel. Even with the risk of the Pillars, she was betting it'd be a safer way to travel than aboveground…

"Through here." Ducot shifted a back wall into an opening that held a ladder.

"I'll go first," Cullen offered. "See if I sense anyone." He descended into the darkness. After a long stretch of silence, he called up softly, "I think we're clear."

Ducot was the next down the ladder. He paused and pulses

of magic radiated from him. He shook his head. "I don't feel anything either."

The rest of them followed.

"Good, so we're alone. What next?" Olivin was understandably eager.

"Let's find a place where we can spread out a bit and organize ourselves in safety," Eira suggested. The tunnel was rather cramped.

"There should be a supply cache not far from here." Ducot led the way.

They all followed him around a few bends and ultimately to a door. Inside was a basement. But another ladder going down farther made it feel like the attic of a completely buried home.

The room wasn't large, but there was enough space for them to spread out among empty crates and cracked barrels. The room had been picked clean, everything of use pulled from it. Still, Cullen and Alyss began searching anyway.

"It goes on forever down here," Alyss murmured, running her hand along the wall.

"Risen is an ancient city," Eira said. "Built and rebuilt upon its old footings for thousands of years." Who knew what could be found down here if they went looking? Perhaps there would be room for pirate stowaways in the future, or a good route to infiltrate the city, should she ever need to... For now, she'd keep her focus on what was happening on the surface.

"I can't believe she took him...that I let him go..." Olivin paced in the farthest corner of the room, berating himself under his breath. Just when he was feeling as if he might reclaim everything that was lost, this happened. Even if Eira didn't share his goals for the future...she still felt for him.

"This is what they do," Ducot said gravely. "You know it as well as the rest of us. It's what they did with Eira, with Taavin, with Yonlin."

"Twice," Olivin added unnecessarily.

"Once the dust settles, I want to move quickly." Eira set a

definitive tone in trying to shift the conversation away from the cycle of rage and annoyance to something productive. All eyes went to her. "I have a plan, but it's open for discussion."

"Tell us," Ducot demanded, keeping the focus.

For the next two hours, they debated the best steps for them to take to save Yonlin while not risking the attack on Ulvarth too early. Lamenting that their element of surprise was gone. But there were still things Ulvarth wasn't expecting—the attack from the other nations, hopefully, and with any luck Yonlin had kept the pistol secret.

They drew lines in the dirt on the floor, overexplained, and looked at everything in every possible way. The most important thing was to get Yonlin back, and Eira suspected she knew where Wynry and Ulvarth would put him. If it were her hiding Yonlin, she'd put him somewhere that she'd expect none of them to know about while lining the way to the dungeons with knights and other traps. So the plan was to get to the Archives—clearing a path when possible for the larger attack on the city—and then get to Yonlin.

By the time they all seemed more or less in agreement, Eira was confident the initial hunt for them on the surface had ended. Which meant that the Pillars were likely to turn their attention below.

"Take us on the least common paths to get as close to the Archives as possible," Eira commanded Ducot. "Alyss, connect passages when you sense another close by for us to move on different tracks."

They descended the ladder, farther underneath the streets of Risen.

She wasn't trusting Olivin to guide them, not when it was clear that Wynry was already anticipating his every move. Twice, they heard movement in the distance. Both times, Alyss pulled them onto a side path and they waited. It was impossible to know if the noises were from the Pillars, from Rebec's Shadows, or rogues and vagabonds. But Eira wasn't going to risk an encounter.

They began to ascend, eventually coming up to a cellar. Hunched and with breaths held, they listened and reached out with magic. There were no noises or signs of life above them.

Ducot moved for the door, pushing on it. Fortunately, it hadn't been locked or barricaded from the other side and they emerged from underneath the corner of an intricate rug in a house long abandoned.

"Thank goodness this is still here," Ducot breathed. "It should be all right to stay for the night."

"We're not staying the night here." Eira moved to a nearby window, lurking in the shade of the heavy curtains and trying not to sneeze from the clouds of dust her movements created.

"It's a Shadow safe house. No one ever owned this place but us," Ducot said.

"Exactly. We can't depend on anywhere owned by the Shadows." She scanned the street below, recognizing the rougher area of town she'd once used as her entry and exit to the Archives. This seemed to be somewhere opposite, but close enough to be useful. "I'm going to go and find us somewhere else to stay. I'm sure there's some back door left unlocked, or attic no one will look in."

"Isn't that more of a risk than staying in the attic here?" Alyss asked. "If we're somewhere else, people could be there."

"Any life a Pillar senses here they will automatically assume is a Shadow and weed us out. We need to hide among the masses."

Alyss nodded at that after a moment's consideration.

"I'll come with you," Cullen offered. "There's safety in numbers."

Eira briefly considered telling him no. But if they did run into trouble, it could allow one of them to escape and get word back to the rest. So she said, "All right."

A few minutes later, they emerged onto the street in new clothing and hooded cloaks. A benefit of emerging into a Shadow supply house was that there had been ample options to change their appearances. Despite this, she kept an illusion wound tightly over them as they left. To a casual observer, the door to the townhome hadn't even opened.

"You know it won't take much to goad him off the plan," Cullen said gravely. He didn't have to specify who he was talking about.

"I know." Eira sighed. "But what am I supposed to do? Let him run off?"

"Yes."

She looked at Cullen, aghast.

"I don't speak from jealousy," Cullen made sure to clarify, though surprisingly the thought hadn't crossed her mind. "But if it is his life or the rest of ours, it's not really a choice, is it?"

Eira gritted her teeth and looked toward the Archives looming over them. She imagined Ulvarth skulking in the highest, secret rooms where she'd met Taavin. Looking down across all of Risen as though it were a game of carcivi, and he was moving his pieces around.

He knew the corners he was pressing them into. Forcing them to take actions that'd lead to mistakes and play right into his hands.

"No, it's not," she said. A pirate wouldn't sacrifice the lives of an entire crew for one rebellious sailor. "Let's hope it doesn't come to that."

Those words lacked confidence. She tried to make up for it in her steps, charging forward. But a sense of doom had settled on her shoulders like winter's blanket. A deathlike chill.

You're not all going to make it out alive, it seemed to whisper.

I know, her better sense wanted to reply.

Watch me, every beat of her heart uttered.

After piecing together a few hours of rest, they moved at midnight for the Archives. They were running out of time before the coordinated attack would be launched. And, before then, she needed to get Yonlin and the pistol back and find Ulvarth to put herself in position.

The first part of their trek was relatively easy. The pathways unblocked and no one bothered them, save for the mildly curious glances of a few unsavory sorts that were cast their way. The inky shroud of night offered the perfect cover.

The three rings of walls that led up to the Archives were bigger than Eira had imagined. The first was a towering spectacle, larger than any of the surrounding buildings so there was no possibility of leaping over it. It was so thick that it made seeing the Archives—even high up on their hill in the distance—nearly impossible. If there was any noise on the other side at all, it was entirely muffled.

She'd expected the formidable sight of guards and hardened fortifications, regular patrols, or poised cannons on the ramparts, preloaded with flash beads. But, instead, they found a haunting stillness and an eerie emptiness. There was no one along the wall. No signs of Pillars or any other living soul at all. The gate itself was a mere archway. Equally unguarded and completely open. Within was nothing but swirling darkness, as black as pitch, that seemed to entirely absorb the light.

"I DON'T LIKE THIS," Alyss muttered what they all were thinking after Eira had filled in Ducot on what awaited them.

"Do we go in?" Cullen murmured.

"Of course we do, there's only forward." Olivin was as determined as ever.

Despite knowing it was rooted in all the wrong motivations, Eira was forced to agree. They couldn't go back now, even knowing it—

"It's a trap," Cullen literally finished her thought.

"What else are we going to do?" Olivin gave them all a pointed look.

Eira sighed. "He's right. But we're going to be careful about this."

"I can scout ahead," Ducot offered. "No one expects the mole."

"They might." Eira's mind was a whirlpool of thoughts, swirling deeper and deeper. She'd be pulled under, smothered by endless options and hypotheticals, if she wasn't careful about keeping her heading. "They've infiltrated the knowledge of the Shadows."

Olivin had good news for once. "Lorn said he destroyed the records before the Pillars could get to them."

But... "There are a lot of ways to acquire information on others beyond Lorn's written collection."

"We're wasting time debating." Olivin's patience was running thin. Really, it was a wonder he hadn't already charged in.

"Go, Ducot, but not too far and report right back." Eira

squeezed his forearm. "Noelle would never forgive me if I let something happen to you, so, please, be careful."

He nodded and, with a step, was in his mole form. Eira's heart was in her throat for every scamper of his tiny feet. She held her breath the entire time from when he disappeared into the perfect darkness of the archway to when he reemerged—blessedly in one piece.

Ducot slipped back into the alcove they had pressed themselves against before shifting back into his more human form.

"Good news and bad."

"Good news is rare, can we start there?" Alyss begged.

"There's no one inside the tunnel, so far as I can tell."

"Then what's the bad news?" Eira resisted the urge to celebrate too soon.

"It's a shifted world—just like the morphi demonstration during the tournament."

Eira remembered that night all too well, her eyes drifting to Olivin unbidden. He held her stare, his own gaze softening some. How simple things had been, then…if only there was a way back to that place.

"Can you unshift it?" Eira suspected she already knew what the answer would be.

"No…it's powerful magic. Ancient and secret, even—it's like the shift around the Twilight City itself, which is far beyond my abilities." He leaned against the wall, spine curling with an invisible weight. "How did they get a morphi to do it?"

That soft question stilled all of them.

Historically, Ulvarth had been unfriendly toward anyone that wasn't an elfin of Meru because they were not "chosen" by Yargen. It had been under his orders that Ducot's hamlet had been burned.

"He worked with the draconi; it's possible he cut a deal with the morphi, too," Eira suggested to Ducot with an encouraging hand on his shoulder.

"Or he gave someone no choice." Ducot's fist was clenched so hard it trembled. "I'll find out and someone will die for it…either the morphi that crossed our people and willingly worked for him, or Ulvarth, for whatever he threatened that got someone to do it."

"First we have to get through there." Eira released him and looked back toward the wall and its archway. So the darkness wasn't just the night playing tricks on the eyes and the mind.

"I could make a staircase to go over it?" Alyss offered.

"Impossible, the shift extends upward," Ducot said, dismissing the notion.

"We'll go through—there has to be a way for Ulvarth's own people to do it. We'll find the path." Eira held out her hand. "Form a chain. We'll keep ourselves illusioned until we're inside."

Hand in hand, they made their way to the wall, Eira's magic draped over them. She focused on her magic and movements, rather than anyone else who might be near. But the streets remained empty, the night silent, and with barely a whisper of clothing, they were plunged into a space completely void of light.

"I don't like this," Alyss said under her breath. "I'm blind."

"You get used to it," Ducot said.

"Oh my gosh, I'm sorry," Alyss apologized profusely. Ducot laughed, clearly unoffended, but the sound didn't carry. "What I meant was more than sight… I can't feel anything. There's nothing for my magic to sink into…it's…"

"Nothing," Cullen finished. "Even the air is still; it's almost like there's no air at all."

"How do we know we're going the right way?" Alyss asked, doing a poor job of scrubbing the panic from her voice.

"Let me shed some light on the situation," Olivin said.

"I doubt—" Ducot didn't have a chance to finish. There was a flash of Lightspinning that followed Olivin's command. Like a spark of flint. Bright. But only there for a second. Olivin tried again, to no avail. Ducot sighed. "This is a shifted space. It is not quite the world we all know any longer…the same rules cannot be expected to apply. The rules that govern this space were designed by the morphi who made it."

"Well I hate this even more," Alyss muttered.

"Don't let go of each other's hands," Cullen said firmly. "If you do…we might never find each other again."

"You're not helping," Alyss sighed.

"Can you give us any headway, Ducot?" Eira asked.

"My magic is as lost as yours."

She pursed her lips and carried on. There was nowhere to go but forward. Though it was impossible to tell if they were making headway at all. With no landmarks, no light, no sound or wind…they could be walking in circles for all she knew. But Eira remained confident in her abilities to keep a course and, soon enough, there was a whisper.

"What was that?" Ducot asked.

So it hadn't just been in her head… "Be on guard," she breathed, continuing.

Another voice. Another pause. But no one emerged from the darkness. There was no light or signs of any other living creature.

"What's happening?" Alyss asked. Though no one answered. None of them had an answer.

"Maybe we're close to the other side." Eira sounded more optimistic than she felt.

The whispers grew, more and more voices joined. It was a disorienting murmuring: every step there was a new voice, like a room of ghosts all having a conversation at once. Even though no one individual voice was loud on its own, the void had become deafening. There were prayers to Yargen and praises for Ulvarth. There were utterances disparaging those beyond Meru as forsaken and evil.

"What is happening?" Alyss shouted.

"There must be a way through it." Olivin's remark wasn't an answer to her question. But it was a good point and kept Eira focused.

"You're right." She couldn't see him behind her, but she knew he was somewhere in the darkness along the chain of hands held tightly. "There has to be some secret to it." If there were no guards on the outside then it must be because the Pillars presumed the contents within to be guard and protector well enough.

"Maybe they're telling us how to get through in code?" Ducot said.

"Great, if that's the case we're screwed." Olivin's muttering was almost entirely drowned out.

True to form, Alyss looked for a solution, undeterred by the disheartened remarks. "Perhaps there's some kind of riddle, or passcode, hidden in the remarks!"

"Or we're supposed to follow one voice?" Cullen suggested as the whispers faded in and out.

One voice. "Cullen, you might be on to something," Eira stated.

"What?"

"Really?" Alyss was just as shocked as he was.

"How will we know which one?" Olivin asked.

"We don't have to listen for any of the voices woven into the shift," Eira said confidently. "We're going to look for the ones that aren't. Keep your hands tight and stay with me. I suspect when we're on the other side, we'll need to run for cover quickly."

She took a deep breath and exhaled slowly through her nose, using it as an opportunity to steady herself. The world around her was carved magic. But there was a consistency in that. It wasn't the reality she was used to, but it was reality, of a sort. And that meant there should be echoes.

With her magic, she reached out and tried to ignore all the other whispers and murmurs, focusing only on what her magic said to her. The world fell away and the void consumed her. The only tether was her hand wrapped firmly around another, but even that felt far away.

Like a cloth across spilled ink, she swept away the chaos and looked only for what was *real*. There had been countless people who must have traversed through these passages. The original person to make it...one of them would've left an echo.

There.

We're following only the prayers, right? one disembodied voice asked another as an echo in the back of Eira's mind. *Yes. They changed what the voices said again.*

Eira didn't release her hold. Instead, she moved toward the point at which the voices originated. If the Pillars were changing the words within this labyrinth of whispers then she couldn't trust that prayers were still the right way. So, instead, she staked her hope on the path itself being set. The guideposts might change, but not the directions. That where those people stood had once been the right course.

Once she arrived at the source of the murmurs, Eira stopped, and repeated the process. Using her magic, she sifted through the churning whispers, working to find what was real and what was fabricated. Her free hand twitched, like she was plucking the strings of an invisible harp.

Time felt like fleeting moments and ages simultaneously. Every pause, turn, and slow march was uncertain progress. There was a time when being plunged into darkness of the Pillars' making would tug at the threads of her mind. But now she moved with confidence. With the knowledge that her friends and her magic were at her side and with them she was unstoppable.

At last, they beheld a dim point of light in the distance and the whispers began to abate.

"Is that…" Alyss didn't finish.

"An exit?" Cullen heaved a sigh of relief.

"We're not out until we're out," Eira cautioned them, her focus on the archway ahead. Now that they were a bit closer, it was easy to make out the roadway and houses beyond. "We'll go out under the cloak of illusion once more. Be ready for anything."

Heart hammering in her throat, Eira shifted the focus of her power to settle over their shoulders like winter's embrace. She readied herself for what awaited them on the other side of the wall. The moment they emerged, Eira found herself stopping short—face-to-face with a Pillar.

THIRTY-SIX

HERE HAD THE man come from? She hadn't seen anyone then, suddenly, he was there. But he looked right through her with vacant, dull eyes.

Eira's heart had gone from hammering, to thundering, to stopping entirely. No one made a move, no one breathed. If he took one step closer, they'd be caught.

But, with a sigh, the Pillar turned on his heel and went back the way he'd came, muttering about patrols and the wall acting up.

Breaths ragged from nerves, she pulled them down the street. The first faint lines of dawn were streaking against the bottoms of the clouds that dotted the sky and Eira knew they had to get to the Archives before the sun rose. The attack from the other nations would be launched at some point today. If she wasn't ready, she might miss her opportunity entirely.

Moreover, the houses between the first two walls were, as expected, much more occupied. And once all those occupants were awake and moving, it'd become significantly harder to maneuver unnoticed.

Everyone in the inner circles was no doubt a Pillar, or so loyal to Ulvarth they might as well be. Which meant they couldn't risk being seen at all. Eira kept her illusion as they wove through what side streets there were and squeezed through passages of buildings that Alyss managed to widen just enough for them to sidestep between by shaving off a layer of stone. But eventually they came to a point where their only option forward was the main road that led to the entry of the next wall.

None of them had said a word since they'd left the first wall. But now, as they caught their breath, it was clear they were all grappling with the same question: *What next?*

Unlike the first wall, this second wall was visibly patrolled both on the ground and by Pillars stationed at intervals along the wall's ramparts. Their robes *swished*, revealing ominous glints of steel plate in the lamplight. These weren't the same as the random Pillars they'd encountered so far. It was clear that these men and women were part of the Swords of Light—the illustrious force dedicated to the defense of the Faithful of Yargen.

"We could go up?" Cullen suggested, keeping his voice the barest of whispers. "Along the rooftops? Wait for an opening and use an illusion to get across?"

"Going up seems more overt than staying on the ground." Plus, while her illusionary skills were great, Eira wasn't sure if she could manage maintaining one across all of them, simultaneously, while jumping from rooftop to rooftop.

"Under, then?" Alyss chimed in. "I could make a tunnel."

Eira considered this. It was an elegant solution…but there was a reason they hadn't done it from the start. "Check for passages as subtly as possible." There was a reason Deneya hadn't used the tunnels to get Eira closer to the Archives all those months ago—there were none. So if Alyss sensed any passageways, it had to be assumed they were Pillar made and controlled.

Alyss pressed her palm to the ground. It only took a few pulses of magic for her to pull it away with a muttered curse. "There's many."

"As I thought." They were doubtlessly all trapped or patrolled, too. "Damn the Pillars for being such good moles."

"Indeed. Being a good mole is my responsibility," Ducot said under his breath. Eira didn't dare a laugh, but she did crack a smile.

"If we can't go over, or under, then…" Cullen let his train of thought trail off, as much at a loss as anyone else.

"We go through," Ducot said, a little louder but still mindful of the shuttered windows all around them and the sleeping people that were surely inside.

"What?" Cullen asked.

"There are too many patrols for us to just waltz through it." Olivin made it sound like Ducot was being ridiculous. "Moreover, the gate is closed."

"We go through," Ducot said to Eira, "just like we did to escape them before from the Champion's Village."

"*Ah*." The idea was brighter than the nearing dawn. "But then we had—"

"There's a building, not far, that is within a hand's width of the wall. We navigate through the buildings, out of sight of any patrols, to a place that's so narrow no one would even think to look." Ducot motioned toward Alyss. "Between her and me, we can button it all back up to look like no one was ever there."

"What about the people *inside* the buildings?" Cullen's question was hasty. They all knew they didn't have a lot of time to stand around and debate.

"We'll be careful. You're good at sensing people, Cullen, and Eira and Olivin's magic will be free to illusion while Alyss and I keep us moving." Ducot shrugged. It wasn't the most confidence-inspiring answer. But it was an honest one.

"We don't have time to scheme out a better plan," Eira murmured. Then, with more confidence, "All right, let's do this."

They all gave motions of affirmation.

"You lead," Alyss said to Ducot.

He took a step forward toward the side of the house and pressed his hand against it, walking toward the back. Finally he stopped and nodded, pointing to the stone. Alyss was there, unraveling the mortar and brick. It sounded like the whisper of sand on a beach underneath one's feet.

Ducot stepped inside, then gave a small wave. The rest of them followed into what was some kind of back entryway for another alley. With a wave of her hands, like spinning on an invisible loom, Alyss seamed the wall back up.

Eira moved for the door and unlocked it, glancing into the alleyway. There was a line of sight to the wall, but no patrols were there yet.

"Quickly."

They followed her lead out the back, Alyss closing the door whisper-soft. On light feet they raced toward the dead end of the alleyway as another patrol ventured into their line of sight. Cool stone at their backs and chests heaving, they all held their breath and waited, listening.

No alarms were raised.

Ducot and Alyss repeated the process and they found themselves in a stately parlor. Over the fireplace was a portrait of Ulvarth, face turned up toward a blindingly bright sun. Carved into its ostentatious frame were the words:

Trust in Her Champion.

"Gross." Eira nearly gagged.

Alyss wriggled her fingers and the carved wood shifted before Eira's eyes. Letters sank back into the frame. New ones rose. It now read:

Liar. Heretic. False Champion.

Alyss shrugged and caught Eira's eyes with a wry grin. "Maybe they'll think it's a sign from Yargen and listen?"

Eira opened her mouth to ask Alyss to change it back—it was too much of a risk—but Ducot tapped on the wall to the right of the fireplace. Perhaps it was a sign from Yargen that they didn't have a chance to return it to the way it was. The goddess worked in mysterious ways.

Alyss went to open another wall, and Eira followed.

"It is better that way," Cullen said.

"Wish we could burn it," Olivin mumbled.

Eira found herself agreeing with them both.

In the wee hours of the morning, they glided through the rooms and walls of the most loyal individuals to Ulvarth. Unseen. Their presence felt in little changes that Alyss seemed too eager to make while she waited for Ducot to point her in the next direction.

First it was the frame. After that it was a marble sculpture of Ulvarth standing upon the sun transformed into him being immolated by flames. Then it was a tapestry that unraveled around his outline, having his woven self slump to a puddle on the floor.

Eira knew better than to expect anything to come of it, but the little rebellions when they were otherwise being so cautious felt good. And a part of her that she'd never admit to secretly hoped that the citizens who owned these would genuinely take it as a sign from Yargen. That when Ulvarth fell, his name would be shamed and his memory would live only in slander.

They came to a stop in a sitting room, where Ducot ran his hand along the wall three times over before turning to Alyss. "I think this is it, the wall should be right on the other side."

Alyss went to the wall and placed her hand by the floorboards, her eyes fluttering closed. "I think so," she eventually agreed, looking to Eira.

"Keep the opening low and small. Even if we're only a hand's width away from the wall, I don't want to take any chances of a patrol seeking the opening and having a reason to linger, suspicious," Eira instructed.

Every decision she made and instruction she gave had the memory of Noelle living within it. Would Noelle still be alive if she had been more decisive when she'd had the chance? Eira forced the guilt back into its pen, allowing that monster to pace its cage. It'd be a forever occupant of her thoughts, escaping from time to time, but she couldn't let it run wild. That was how mistakes would be made. And more mistakes would lead to more of her friends dying.

Alyss opened the wall just as Eira instructed.

"Ducot, do you sense any patrols?" As he did, Eira kept her focus on Alyss. "Work on another hole in the opposite wall."

This was the deeply risky part. They didn't know how thick this wall was. Or if there were people within. But chances had to be taken.

"We'll have a window in another thirty seconds." Ducot opened his eyes. "About two minutes, I'd guess."

Plenty of time.

"We're through." Alyss leaned away from the opening. "But it looks like the wall is hollow. There's a passage within."

"Ducot, you first as a mole. See if there's anything inside we need to be worried about."

In a blink, he was in his other form, scampering across the narrow gap. But there was no time to wait for him to return. The floorboards overhead creaked loudly. The sound was followed by a few heavy footsteps and the rattling of pipes within the walls. Muffled talking.

"Go." Eira looked to Cullen and Olivin. They were on their stomachs in a second, wriggling through, arm over arm.

The footsteps crossed the room upstairs. Another pause, the creak of door hinges. Weight on stairs.

The sounds faded away as Eira raced past Alyss. There was only a breath of fresh air before she was inside the defensive wall opposite. It was so thick that Alyss's opening felt more like a tunnel. The second she was through, two sets of hands grabbed her arms on either side, pulling.

Eira's magic flared, but her eyes met Cullen and Olivin's. They stood on a sloping ramp that descended into the depths beneath the wall. They were keeping her from tumbling flat onto her face.

"Thanks." Eira accepted their help, her wriggling far from graceful, but still effective. She didn't summon her magic to soften her landing, not wanting to have too many different pulses of power that could alert the patrolling Pillars.

Alyss was behind, feet first. Eira took her delay as a sign of her closing up the house opposite. But the seconds ticked by in Eira's mind. The two minutes Ducot had warned them of had flown by. She'd be seen if she didn't—

With a push, Alyss practically threw herself off the upper ledge. Olivin and Cullen were still at the ready, helping ease her down. She must've known they were there, and assumed their help, as her focus remained on closing up where they had just entered from.

"Did anyone see you?" Eira was conscious about how her words might echo in the tunnel they now found themselves in.

"I don't think so." Alyss shook her head. "But it was close."

"No alarm is a good sign," Cullen said hopefully.

"Let's work on getting out the other side." Olivin remained ever focused on the task.

"What about Ducot?" Alyss scanned the tunnel.

At that moment, a frantically squeaking mole raced toward them. It leapt and landed as a man. Ducot was still running and wasn't slowing.

The rest of them took it as a clear sign and followed the untold instruction. They dashed down the tunnel.

"Pillars. Coming. Hide," Ducot panted. The effort of keeping his words soft was as strenuous as running.

"Where are we going?" Eira asked, trying to keep her voice as quiet as possible. Their footsteps were already too much of a risk.

"It's a dead end ahead." Alyss didn't even try to blot the worry from her voice.

The tunnel ended in a large, underground storeroom. Eira wondered if these were part of the network Alyss had sensed earlier. For a second, they were all dazed, staring at the flashfires.

"Look at all of them…"

"Carsovia still got out a shipment?" Ducot had hate in his voice. "What was the point of any of it?"

"They're flashfires, not flash beads." Eira's mind was moving faster than her feet had just been. "Carsovia is just like the Pillars—they wouldn't want to be seen as weak so they—"

There was no time to finish. Footsteps echoed down to them. Pillars were almost upon them.

"CULLEN, ALYSS WITH me. Ducot, Olivin together. Hide. Illusion," Eira instructed hastily.

Ducot and Olivin wedged themselves behind one of the racks of flashfires. Eira followed their lead, doing the same. Olivin's glyph winked out of existence and the world was plunged into darkness right as she wove her own illusion.

For a few breaths, there was nothing. Then, a new light bloomed.

Two armored Swords of Light marched into the storeroom. But their expressions were dull. Almost bored. The stockier one had flaming red hair; the other was of narrow frame with pale features.

"I'm not sure why he wants us to get these," Red Hair said.

"Because Hokoh fell and there's been sightings of movement in the bay. He says an attack is soon."

"I know Hokoh fell." A roll of his eyes. "What I'm saying is, I don't know what we're going to be able to do with these without flash beads, and there's not enough to go around."

"We will ignite them with the faith of Yargen. Those who walk in her glory have nothing to fear, and possess all the might they need." The one with the pale eyes had a reverent tone.

"You don't honestly buy all that 'his powers of Yargen' do you? You know it's just flash beads and theatrics…and putting anyone to death who would—"

Pale Eyes turned on his friend, pushing him into the rack Eira, Cullen, and Alyss had positioned themselves behind. The rack's supports dug into Alyss's shoulder and she physically bit back a scream. Eira squeezed her hand, meeting her friend's pained eyes.

Even though the agony of having the two men's weight, combined with all the flashfires, was apparent, Eira kept her gaze firm and determined. *Don't make a sound*, she communicated through sight alone. Alyss breathed slowly through her nose.

"He would put to death any heretics who speak against him," Pale Eyes finished Red Hair's remarks harshly. "That's why we are here to revere him, fight for him, and *keep our home safe*."

Even Eira could read between the lines. These young men weren't dedicated Pillars, even though the symbol was carved into the backs of their hands. They were trying to survive. Ulvarth had made his methods clear—follow him or die.

But Eira didn't assume their desperation would make them automatic allies. The opposite. Their fear would have them turning her and her friends in the second they laid eyes on them. They'd use their discovery as some kind of leverage.

Their presence made her revisit her choices in Hokoh. Alyss was right…there were probably people like these men in that temple. But she didn't feel guilty. Out of fear or love, they still would've fought to the death.

"So we'll get the flashfires to display his might and political prowess." Pale eyes leaned away and the stand rocked back into its normal position. Alyss did nothing. She didn't even summon her magic to mend her wound, no doubt afraid of it being sensed.

The men began to grab the flashfires from the rack right in front of them. Eira stared up through the slats of wood. Red Hair looked right through her. His brow furrowed, face twisted.

"Do you really think there's an attack coming?" His hand faltered, but only for a second before scooping up the weapon.

"First Hokoh, then Parth…" *Vi Solaris had been busy executing her plans to the letter.* Pale Hair paused, adjusting his grip as an excuse to try and hide the worry that flashed through his eyes. "It's no matter. Let them come. We will emerge triumphant."

"Let those who are truly good prevail." Red Hair's tone didn't sound like he was referring to the Pillars.

"Let the good prevail," Pale Hair agreed. "We should get the beads they wanted for the wharf cannons."

"Right…" The two said little more as they left, their footsteps disappearing with the glow of their light.

Eira relaxed her illusion as pulses of magic from Alyss preluded her rolling her previously injured shoulder as they emerged from behind the rack.

"Alyss, Ducot…" She trailed off. There was no time for hesitation. But could she ask them to execute the plan that was forming in her mind? Olivin's glyph flared back into existence and Eira saw all their faces in the golden glow, staring at her expectantly.

They expect you to lead, so lead. The words were a chorus. They were Adela's, Lavette's, Noelle's, even Fritz's and Marcus's. Tangled among the harmony was her own voice, strong and true. *You can do this.*

"Follow them, find out where the flash bead supply is. Take all they have left—or as much as you're able." They were going to solve one problem—the Pillars' ammunition—with another—the walls. "As soon as light breaks, take down the walls and all the barriers attached, to clear a path to the Archives. Then move to the wharf. Vi will be making her move and we can't let them load those cannons."

"Leave it to us." Alyss nodded, determination set in the clench of her jaw.

"*All* barriers?" Ducot clarified.

"Yes. Destroy the shift rift," Eira commanded.

"Did you somehow not hear me earlier? That is ancient and powerful magic. I don't even know the basics of how it's made."

"You don't have to know how to make it, only destroy it." Eira rested a hand on his shoulder. "You can do this. You are strong enough, I know it."

"Eira, a shift rift teases at the fabric of what is real. One wrong move and it could turn volatile."

"As long as you're safe, I don't care about the rest." She gave him a squeeze.

His throat bobbed nervously but he didn't object.

"The three of us will carry on to the Archives. If we can disable the third wall on our own, we will." Eira glanced to Olivin and Cullen. "Then, we'll find Yonlin and draw out Ulvarth. We'll end this as the attack begins, if we're able."

Her mind was racing, each thought louder than the fading footsteps of the two men. Alyss and Ducot had to leave. But was there something else she needed to plan? Something she'd overlooked?

"If things go sideways—"

"There's no time." Ducot stopped her worrying. "There's no need for contingencies. We succeed, or we die."

There wasn't an escape plan. There were no alternatives. It was all or nothing.

Eira nodded. "Don't you dare do the latter."

"We'll try our best." Ducot glanced to Alyss. "I'll go ahead. Keep up."

"You can count on me." Alyss hesitated as Ducot shifted into his mole form, her weight only half on the step she'd been about to take. Turning on her heel, she crossed the gap between her and Eira in almost a lunge.

Eira's arms wrapped around her friend's shoulders, clutching Alyss's tightly. They shared a shaky breath and exhaled all their fear. Eira's knuckles were white, nails digging arcs into her palms so she didn't leave bruises on Alyss's back from clinging to her so tightly.

"You can count on me," Alyss repeated, just for her. "No matter what happens—"

"I don't want your goodbyes," Eira cut her off and pulled away, holding Alyss at arm's length to look her in the eyes. "I'll see you on the other side. I have to get a copy of that book."

"You'll get the first one off the presses." One step backward, then another. Alyss turned. And followed Ducot back up the pathway.

Eira allowed herself one more second. In a blink, she was back in the Tower—Alyss running off ahead, always the one to get more jobs for the clinic. *Take me with you*, the girl that Eira had been whispered under her breath, begging for a chance to shine.

This was the opportunity she'd been asking for all those years ago. It wasn't a job. It was her destiny.

Eira returned her focus to the here and now, casting off the shadows of her past.

"All right, then. Let's go." Eira grabbed for Cullen's hand again, weaving an illusion over their shoulders. Olivin made his own concealment.

They navigated up, Cullen sensing for the presence of any individual. Fortunately, there weren't many Pillars and those that were around seemed more preoccupied with preparing for the impending attack. More than once she heard mentions of the flash beads, but saw no signs of Alyss or Ducot.

Eira tried to wring the worry from her heart. It'd do them no good and, if anything, the distraction would put her, Olivin, and Cullen at risk.

They glided through passageways that ringed the inside of the wall—not unlike the corridors within the coliseum. Finally, they reached a guardroom occupied by two Pillars.

"There's a battalion coming within the hour," one of them said shortly after the three of them arrived. "Sending them to the wharf. Our champion will lead the attack."

That meant Ulvarth would be moving from the Archives. She cursed her luck. Hopefully she was able to find him along the way to Yonlin.

Waiting was the longest hour of Eira's life. It might have only been ten or twenty minutes, in actuality. But it felt like an hour. Every second rolled on like the sweat down the back of her neck—her whole body tense with the exertion of not even breathing too loudly.

The gate opened for rows on rows of marching Swords of Light. It was their only chance. But it meant navigating around easily fifty men and women who were all armed and ready to kill them the heartbeat they were discovered.

The center of Eira's chest burned as she dredged forth even more power. The risk of someone sensing her was one she'd have to take. They side-stepped through the opening, where the two gatemen were watching the battalion march through. Backs sliding against the wall, they made their way down the corridor.

The last of the Swords of Light were near. The gate would be closed after. Eira stared up at the portcullis, willing it to stay open *just…*

…a little bit…

The last of the armored men and women passed them.

…longer.

Two steps and they were out of the tunnel that connected one side of the thick barricade with the other. Eira kept their backs against the wall as she started for one of the nearby buildings. The homes on this side of the wall were much the same as the last and, with any luck, they'd be able to be out of any potential sightline and slip into the obscurity of the tightly packed city.

The moment they crossed into an empty side street, a building between them and the wall, she stopped to catch her breath. It was a momentary reprieve and then they were off again. The sky was a glowing amber and there wasn't time to waste.

The distance between the second and third wall was less than between the first and second and they found themselves before an open but well-guarded gate. Knights formed a living barricade, shoulder to shoulder; there wasn't any way of slipping through. Even with her illusion, there'd be a brush of fabric, or a faint breeze that followed their movements.

Unless they couldn't feel that brush or breeze.

Keeping her grip on Cullen and Olivin, Eira shifted the focus of some of her power. Still maintaining the illusion over them for the benefit of the Pillars that patrolled the ramparts, Eira turned her attentions on the line of soldiers. They went deathly still. Underneath their helmets, their barely visible lips were blue.

She navigated around her frozen barricade of men, strolling to the other side of the final wall. Just as the sun was cresting the horizon, they stepped into the great courtyard that stretched before the Archives. It was illuminated by a roaring fire that encircled the entire compound—Ulvarth's new Flame of Yargen.

They'd only made it halfway across when an explosion threatened to tear apart half the city.

CHAPTER THIRTY-EIGHT

THE CITY WAS being sundered from the inside. Even from where they stood at the crest of the hill, the shockwaves from the flash beads threatened to knock them over. Far below them, the second wall crumbled in on itself.

The Archives came to life. Knights scrambled and began to form a barricade in front of the entry. The massive doors of the Archives—ones that took chains and wheels to open and at least ten people each to close—were beginning to shut.

"We can't let them barricade it." Olivin's eyes swung back to her and everything seemed to still.

"Then let's go."

He looked between her and the knights. "There's not going to be a way for us to get in, undetected…not without drawing their attention when they're already on high alert. Our illusions are good, but not that good, and you know it."

"With my rune, I can—"

He silenced her with a look. Kind. Gentle even. But knowing her emotions all too well, probably even better than she did. His hand rested on her cheek. "You are the most astounding woman I have ever met, but—though you might be loathe to admit it— even you have your limitations."

"Olivin…" Her heart was in her throat, threatening to choke her. She knew he had been planning to stay behind. That they would be forced to bear time apart. But she wasn't ready for it to happen *now*. She'd never be ready. And something about this moment felt so much more final than the goodbye she'd been bracing for.

"You wanted me to let you live your life as you were meant to do—extend me the same courtesy, what you always have done." He knew what he was going to do. His mind was made up. She saw it in his eyes before any words were said or actions were taken. The raw determination.

"Damn it, why do you have to be a hero?" she whispered.

"When this is over, we could have a beautiful little home. A place we return to after the toils of our adventure. A place of rest. Once Ulvarth is gone, there will be so much opportunity for us to make Meru—the place you always loved—just as we want it." His brows tilted up in the middle slightly, eyes alight with amusement at his own words. She choked on soft laughter. He was being ridiculous, and knew it. But there was something to the wild fantasy of them having a quaint little home to retreat to when it was all over that protected them for one last breath from the chaos rising around them. One last second in the eye of the storm. "This could be a home, *our home*."

"I have a home," she whispered, eyes stinging. "And it has a name: *Stormfrost*."

"I know. And I love you for it." Even with Cullen right next to her, Olivin grabbed her face and pulled her to him. Eira's eyes dipped closed and she kissed him. It even tasted of longing for a time that hadn't yet passed.

She didn't let him pull away when he tried. Eira grabbed his shirt with her fist and yanked, closing the gap between them once more. His lips crashed into hers and Olivin let out a startled yelp that she smothered with her mouth. She kissed him like it would be their last time. Like the stars that were her guides would burn out and the winds would never see her return to this port.

"I love you," she whispered across his mouth as he pulled away.

His eyes widened a fraction. Something akin to joy curled the corners of his lips. "I knew it," he finally breathed. "Now, get Yonlin for me. No matter what, keep him safe."

"You stay alive long enough to do it yourself." She ran her

hands over his face, mapping it. "Stay alive long enough to show me that stupid, quaint little house so I can tell you how foolish it is and kidnap you for good."

He laughed, eve the sound was tinged with pain. "I'll try."

She wanted to demand he say it again but, this time, convince her it wasn't a lie. The doors groaned as they began to open. Their time had run out.

He pulled away, her hands slipping from his person. With one final, roguish grin, Olivin dropped his illusion. She choked on shock. Even knowing what was coming, the world ground to a halt, every second slower than the last. Nothing escaped her mouth even when she wanted to call out to him. Cullen held her in place as she jerked forward—thrusting out a hand, as if she could grab him back.

"Wynry," Olivin roared, "Let's end this once and for all!"

A figure emerged from among the knights, slipping out from between the doors. Each one of her steps was slow and deliberate. Eira was reminded of a great feline, predatory and deadly. The familial resemblance was unmistakable. Knights encircled them, as if making an arena. Their focus was entirely on Olivin.

"About time, brother. I just knew you'd be dumb enough to come alone. You always loved Yonlin best." Wynry's remark had Eira realizing that the walls going down made the Pillars think that she was farther down the slope.

"It's easier to love the sibling that didn't kill your father," Olivin countered.

Magic blazed. Lightspinning words shouted magic into existence as Wynry and Olivin lunged for each other. Eira knew that only one of them was walking away from this and, just like she had to be the one to end Ulvarth, he had to be the one to kill his sister.

Eira forced herself to move. Every footstep felt like she was ripping off a part of her. The reverberation through her legs had her teeth rattling. Pain arced through her as they slipped into the doors of the Archives before they slammed shut.

What had she done? What had she done?

She navigated through the stairs of the Archives, releasing Cullen and relaxing her illusion only when it was absolutely essential—and no one else was around—to climb the ladders. He followed her without word or question, all the way to the secret door that she'd been instructed to go through by Deneya and Taavin nearly a year ago.

Her very first mission for the Court of Shadows had led to her last subterfuge in Risen.

She guided Cullen on the ascent through the pitch-black passages behind the great vault of knowledge. Though, they didn't make it far before he stopped all movement. Eira tugged. Cullen didn't move. Instead, he shifted his hand, gripping her wrist as much as she was his, and pulled her toward him.

They tumbled, landing awkwardly. They'd made more noise than they should, but realistically, the rising chaos masked any sounds that could be heard outside the secret passage.

Still, she pushed away, a stab of anger sharpening her words. "Cullen, there's no time."

"I'm sorry." He pulled her in again. Gently, he stroked the back of her head.

She opened her mouth to ask him what for, but then it dawned on her. The man was comforting her over Olivin. Her strength fractured and she buried her face in his neck by his shoulder. Selfishly taking a breath for herself. For every quivering beat of her heart.

"He's strong, he'll be all right," Cullen soothed.

"What if he's not?" Eira whispered, the words harrowed and thin. "*I left him.*"

"You trusted him," Cullen corrected. "To know what he was doing and have the strength to do it."

Just like she had asked of Olivin.

"What if he... Did I just create another situation like Noelle's?" she said, admitting to her greatest fear.

"He'll be all right," Cullen emphasized. She didn't entirely believe it. How could she with all those guards charging after him.

"I would've thought this would make you happy. Seeing Olivin left behind like this." Focusing on him, rather than herself, was a far easier task.

"I don't 'win' in a world where you are not happy." He kissed her temple, then her forehead, then her other temple. Cullen shifted to take both cheeks in his warm, rough hands and drew her face to his, claiming her mouth.

In the darkness, she eased into him. She kissed him like it might be the last kiss she'd ever have. Her hands stretched across his chest, kneaded his muscle, balled into his shirt.

"You're not wishing for his death?" she broke apart to whisper.

"I might want you all to myself, but I'm not a monster." The pad of his thumb dragged over her mouth. Without sight, she knew he was focused on her lips, wet with his affections.

"We shouldn't be wasting time. Come on, we're not far now." Even as she went to move, he held her hand fast.

"How are you going to do it?"

"What?"

"Kill Ulvarth."

"I've a dagger meant for him." Eira patted her thigh, where the one Ulvarth had left for her after she killed Ferro was strapped.

"Do you remember what I told you during the tournament?"

"You told me a lot during the tournament. You'll have to be more specific." She felt her words coming a bit faster, they needed to get moving. Olivin was offering a valuable distraction but would be subdued soon. If they wanted to have any chance of getting back to him and assisting, they needed to move.

"You cannot simply kill him." As soon as he said it, she remembered his cautioning against it. That, if Ulvarth were to die under mysterious causes, it would create a space for another to fill. Or he would be hailed as a martyr. His power would only grow.

"I have a plan," she assured him.

"Which is?"

"I'm going to use my echoes against him—I'll show all of Risen exactly the man he is."

"And if that doesn't work?" Cullen's tone sounded like he equally disliked the idea of doubting her. But Eira had begun to take it as a healthy skepticism—as him vetting her plans. And, to his knowledge, this was all new. She hadn't told any of them of her true plot out of fear that she wouldn't be able to accomplish her goals.

Eira's smile dropped, twisting into a grimace. "Then it doesn't work. I understand your caution, and there was a time where I would've agreed with you, Cullen. But even if I cannot undo him, I will still end him; that's all that matters. Whatever happens after, for good or ill, is Meru's concern. My fight—my loyalties— aren't to Meru. They're to myself. I'm not here as a liberator, I'm here because I have a personal score to settle."

"As long as you know what you're doing." He released her.

"I do." Eira started up once more, ascending through the last stretch of the Archives and her thoughts. She knew he was right. Ending Ulvarth might only be the beginning of problems for Meru. But those weren't her problems to try and solve. She would make it clear that any who threatened her, ever, would be met with brutality. Then, once free of this tiresome game, she'd sail off the edge of the map with her ever-expanding pirate family.

As they reached the top, another explosion rocked the earth. It was quickly followed by two more. The first wall collapsing? Cannons at the wharf? It was impossible to know, tucked in the walls of the Archives. But luckily, Eira knew where she could get a good vantage.

They emerged from the hatch that overlooked the Flame of Yargen, burning in its massive brazier at the apex of the Archives. Eira slowed for a moment, the heat of the fire battering her cheeks.

Eira led Cullen away from it, back toward the ladder that ascended to the final room of the Archives—the room Eira suspected Wynry and Ulvarth would've hid Yonlin within. And, if not Yonlin, then perhaps Ulvarth himself. This room was hidden and well protected, both things he'd desire if he didn't have his magic still. Especially with suspicion of an attack incoming. The coward would want to hide, ride out the storm, and then claim he'd managed to survive because of his own skill.

"Be ready to strike, just in case," Eira whispered. "There's a room just up that ladder. When we ascend, let me know if you can feel any movements in the air that would suggest a person inside."

Cullen nodded and they climbed. At the top, they paused on the tiny landing. Cullen crouched, resting his cheek against the floor. It looked almost as if he was trying to peer through the crack of the door, but Eira could sense every shift of his magic.

Without a sound, he eased away and gave her a slight nod. Eira bore a hole in the door with her stare, bracing herself. There was no sound coming from within, making it impossible to tell who was inside.

Unsheathing the dagger, Eira slowly pushed open the door. The room was empty. Cullen dipped his chin slightly toward the door diagonal from them in a gesture that read, *There*. Stalking through the room, Eira shifted her grip on the dagger as her palm splayed across the ajar door. There wasn't enough space for her to peer through.

She held her breath, listening. A faint *clanking* sound, almost like a glass being set on a table, or perhaps chains. Only one way to find out which.

In one swift movement, she threw open the door and lunged into the room. Wind was under her heels, propelling her. The dagger flashed in the first morning light streaming through the window.

She stopped short. It wasn't Ulvarth.

But it wasn't Yonlin, either.

"The goddess's red lines of fate are certainly tied in interesting knots to bring us together again in this forsaken place," Taavin, the Voice of Yargen, said almost nonchalantly.

A SMILE ARCED ACROSS his face, causing his eyes to crinkle ever so slightly in their corners. Dark circles hung beneath his sharp green eyes; they matched the bruising that covered his skin.

"Your…Majesty." Cullen struggled, either from not knowing the proper honorific for Taavin, or from shock.

"I didn't know you were here," Eira blurted, sheathing her dagger and kneeling to inspect the runic shackles that were clamped around Taavin's wrists. They were the same as what had been in Qwint, and the mines. "Another gift from Carsovia, I see," she muttered.

"He has many of those," Taavin agreed. "We knew he'd attempted courting the Empress's favor, but we doubted he was successful, given her nature."

"Her nature seems to be cruelty. I'd imagine they'd get along exceptionally." The chain the shackles were attached to was bolted to the floor, giving him an extraordinarily short leash. Eira continued to willfully ignore the squalor he'd been forced to exist within for her own benefit and his pride. "Do you know where the key is? On Ulvarth, I presume?"

"It'd be my guess."

Eira sighed heavily. "Of course." She was regretting sending Alyss off. But it wasn't as though she could've known she'd need the woman's skills. "Cullen, there was a torch in the main room. Get it, light it from the brazier, and bring it back."

He sprang into action without question. Eira's eyes drifted up to Taavin's.

"I can get this off," she continued, "but it will be painful. I cannot promise you won't have scarring, at the least."

"We all have our scars," he said easily. Did he fully comprehend what she was going to have to do to get the shackles off? Part of her hoped he didn't. It might be easier that way. But she suspected he did—Taavin was clever and knew what was coming next.

His wrists were only one link apart, but Eira brought them closer together anyway, holding metal and flesh with a single hand.

"I'm going to do my best to make this as painless as possible," she said.

"I'd rather it be as fast as possible." His brow was already set with determination.

Eira nodded and allowed her magic to pour over the shackles, drawing from the deep well the rune on her chest provided. It flowed through his veins and up to his elbows. Eira imagined it like waves lapping against the shore. His hands and wrists were fully submerged, slowly numbing. The sensation would be more mild up to his elbows before completely wearing off on the rest of his arms.

The transition was so fast and seamless that he didn't even wince as sensation left him. But tiny tremors did have his biceps twitching. Eira kept her grip fast. Frost was beginning to coat her flesh and his, collecting into crystals of ice.

Cold, cold, colder still. As cold as the bleak dawns in the high mountains where the air was so biting that it was impossible to feel your face the moment you emerged. Colder than snow or ice.

As cold as the hatred Eira felt for Carsovia and Ulvarth.

Cullen returning barely registered. He stood silently, torch in hand. She took him not immediately reporting any information to be a good sign that they still had time.

"Hold the torch to the lowest rung of the chain," Eira instructed, trying not to tear her focus away too much. "Keep the fire there."

He did as he was told.

When the chain below was red hot, she peeled her fingers

away. The thin layer of ice that had coated them cracked and fell to the floor. But she didn't release her magical hold; Taavin's cuffs continued to emit a frosty haze.

"We're going to do this on three." Even as Eira spoke, Taavin was shifting onto his knees, holding out his hand. He knew what was coming. "You'll press one side of the cuffs to the red-hot iron. Cullen, put the torch on the other side."

"But his skin…"

"Do it." Taavin was the one to speak. His mouth set in a hard line.

"On three, then." Eira glanced at them both. They returned a nod. "One…" She said a silent prayer that this worked. It was the same principle they had used the night they'd escaped Ofok to break the chain that had been holding the ship…but this time she didn't have Noelle to summon white-hot flames at a single point. "Two…"

They all sucked in a breath at the same time.

"Three," Eira exhaled.

Taavin moved swiftly, pressing the cuffs to the red-hot iron. Cullen didn't hesitate, holding the torch to the other side, the flames licking around the cuffs. Eira withdrew her magic from the metal, but kept it on Taavin's skin, trying to keep it protected as much as she was able from the fire.

It only took a second before cracking and popping filled the air.

Eira looked to Taavin. "Pull!"

He yanked. She fortified his wrists with a ring of ice underneath the shackles, hoping they didn't break. Cullen moved out of the way as Taavin reared back. The metal snapped into several pieces.

"Cullen, keep the torch at the ready." Eira moved to Taavin, placing her hands on the backs of his, running her fingers up his forearms. "I'm going to try and warm you back up slowly. That way your skin doesn't follow the metal's lead."

If she withdrew the cold at once, it'd be agony for him. Doing it slowly could potentially preserve the flesh. *Hopefully*. Eira couldn't imagine Vi's ire if she rendered her betrothed's hands utterly useless.

"You've improved," Taavin appraised thoughtfully. His voice was level, as if he weren't in what was certainly immense pain as sensation stabbed down his forearms and wrists.

"It's been a while since you last saw me. I've been busy." Eira kept her focus. His skin was an ashen blue color. But the blood flow was returning. If she could freeze a person but keep them alive, then she could manage this. It was a control and deftness not unlike managing an icy ship.

"So it'd seem… You met her, trained with her, didn't you?"

Eira's eyes drew up to his at the mention of "her." There wasn't a need to ask who "she" was. *Adela.* "I did."

"And? Is she everything you'd imagined?"

"More." Eira didn't bother lying. She'd thrown in her present, and her future, with the Pirate Queen. The world would know it soon enough. It might as well hear it in her words.

He chuckled, as if he already understood. "You're going to be a force to be reckoned with, aren't you?"

"I already am." Eira held his stare for another breath and then withdrew her touch. She looked to Cullen. "Bring the torch a bit closer."

Taavin could now move his fingers, and he curled and uncurled his hands into fists. The flesh was returning to an overall healthy color…minus angry, red rings around his wrists. Eira suspected that the skin there might be more damaged than she could heal at this point. But hopefully not beyond repair whenever he got into the care of a capable healer.

If only Alyss were here… The thought drew Eira to her feet and over to the window. She couldn't see the wharf from this direction. But she could see the chaos unfolding in the city below. The ribbons of smoke and echoes of shouting as clashes began to break out.

"Your bride is bringing the Solaris armada and aid from

Qwint. Adela is clearing a path to the wharf, helping take out other vessels."

"You managed to solicit Adela's help?" He sounded genuinely impressed.

"Temporarily." Eira wanted to make it clear that the nature of Adela, and her relationship with Meru, hadn't fundamentally changed. "The attack should begin soon in full force, if it hasn't happened already."

"Judging from the rumbling and explosions, I suspect it's happened." Taavin stood as well. He continued to rub his wrists, fingers trembling. Cullen stepped off into the main room to return the torch to its holder.

"Does Ulvarth have his magic?" Eira asked pointedly. She'd helped him and caught him up on what was happening. There was no more time to waste.

"I've heard rumors that he doesn't. But of course, no one wants to give them much credence or say so too loudly."

A wicked smile split her lips. It was so satisfying to know that she had regained her powers—and so much more—while he continued to languish. Without the armor to protect him, he'd be completely at her mercy.

A frown crossed Taavin's lips. "He does have a strange set of armor, however. One I've never seen him without. It's runic in nature but how it works is unknown to me."

"I'm aware and I have a way to thwart it." Eira stood and offered a hand to him.

He arched his brows and clasped his palm with hers. "You have been busy."

Eira shifted, focusing on Cullen. "We need to find Yonlin and get out of here as fast as possible." She still remembered that the Pillars had said Ulvarth would be leading the charge down to the wharf. She had to get there before he slipped through her fingers. What Taavin did from here on was his choice. Though she suspected he'd follow.

"Lead on," Cullen said.

"I'll show you a faster way out than the one you know." Taavin moved for the door. Despite the horrors he must have endured at the hands of the Pillars, he moved easily. Eira could only imagine the aches and pains of every bruise and wound across his body. The Voice of Yargen was stronger than she'd given him credit for.

Taavin led them out from behind an upper bookcase in the Archives. It placed them on the top rung, by the still-blazing Flame of Yargen. They all paused at the railing, looking down at the chaos below. The doors had been opened once more for Pillars to run in and out.

There was no sign of Olivin.

"Taavin, do you know where the Pillars would keep prisoners?" Eira asked.

"Beneath the halls of the Swords of Light," he answered.

Eira looked to Cullen, who already had a frown forming. He knew her far too well.

"Go and get Yonlin," she asked him. Eira readied herself for an objection, but the man surprised her when his only objection came in the form of an understandable concern.

"Do you think he's still alive?"

"Let's hope so. He's the best with the pistol." She knew Cullen wasn't only asking about Yonlin. "I won't step foot off Meru until I know what happened to my crew. *All* of them." Given everything she knew about Wynry, Eira bet that she'd take Olivin alive. She captured Yonlin when she could've killed him. A foolish hope, perhaps. But all they had was hope and wild plans.

"Stay safe," Cullen said by way of agreement.

"I will." She wasn't as confident as she sounded. But part of being a captain was not letting those she led see her fear. "Free them and then get to the front lines. I need Yonlin and that pistol."

He took her hand and pulled. His other palm rose to her cheek, cupping it. Cullen kissed her again, as deeply as he had in the passage.

"I will get to you soon," he vowed.

"I'd expect nothing less." She locked eyes with him. "When

you and Yonlin are in position, give me our sign." Cullen nodded and Eira shifted her attention to Taavin. "I know I can't ask a detour of you."

"Not when my future wife is down in the wharf fighting."

"We'll go together. But can you tell Cullen what he needs to know—where they might hold prisoners here?"

After Taavin gave him clear instructions, Cullen slipped back behind the bookcase, electing to take the slower but more secret passages down.

A dull ache bloomed in her chest with worry for him. Eira shook her head, trying to cast it off. He didn't need her worry. He needed her to stay mentally sharp and be ready for anything.

Eira looked to Taavin, surprised he had continued to linger. She'd been expecting him to run off. But his presence suggested a continued unlikely, and probably temporary, alliance.

"Let's go end this."

"Once and for all," he added.

They shared a hard stare, one that was full of determination. Then, Taavin moved, and Eira followed his lead.

"ARE WE TRYING to be subtle?" Eira asked as they neared the bottom of the Archives. The Pillars were too busy rushing about that none had noticed them yet.

"I think the time for subtlety has long passed," Taavin said over his shoulder, nearly drowned out by shouts and distant explosions.

"Good." With a dramatic sweep of her arm, ice coated the bottom of the Archives. It rose in jagged points, like a frozen wave crashing against the archways that led into the different halls of the complex. Before any of the Pillars had time to react, they were completely frozen solid.

"Improvement in your magic, indeed," he said under his breath.

"Careful, or you'll sound like you're impressed by the Pirate Queen's heir." Eira took the final steps two at a time, breezing past Taavin. When she landed on the floor below, the ice shivered away from her, carving a path so Taavin wouldn't slip.

"I am capable of both considering someone an enemy and being impressed by their abilities." He was a step behind as they crossed under the opening of the Archives.

"Am I your enemy?" Eira asked as the Pillars outside charged toward them, drawn by the magic.

"Not today." Taavin smirked and turned to the oncoming men and women. He lifted his hands and Eira mirrored the motion.

Magic exploded from them both. Taavin had been complimenting her skill, but his was just as stunning. He'd made an effort to keep his abilities somewhat under wraps, because Eira had consumed every rumor and word of the Voice of Yargen that she could in her younger years. But none of the stories had painted him as shining, golden death.

His movements were a blur, arms and utterances weaving an intricate tapestry of glyphs through the air. She gathered ambient moisture under her fingertips. With flicks of her wrists, she sent barrages of ice shards hurtling away from her. They whistled a deadly lullaby as they soared before sinking into the advancing zealots.

Risen unfurled before them, a bloody canvas already in the early hours. The walls that had protected the path to the Archives now had hollows carved from them, the farthest one a shadowy void swirling and snapping into place at its center. Apparently, flash beads and ancient shift magic that tore at reality didn't blend well.

They carved their path down the main road. Most of the Pillars were either focusing on running up to the Archives—that batch Eira and Taavin continued to deftly dispatch—or running down to the primary force that marched in the distance toward the wharf where vessels were moving cannons into position.

At the last wall, Eira caught sight of a familiar set of shoulders. Ducot stood at the edge of the living shadow, hands out, sweat dripping down his face.

"This is a mess!" he shouted as she approached. "Why did I let you talk me into trying to blow up a shift rift?"

"Because there was no other way."

As they spoke, Taavin pushed a man using a glowing glyph into the void that lingered beyond the edge of the cobblestones. The Pillar fell back with a cry that was cut short as the shadow consumed him. Eira wondered if he landed in the maze of whispers they'd traversed earlier...or if he had suffered a worse fate.

She hoped it was the latter.

"Do you have this under control?" Eira asked.

"It's only well beyond my expertise," Ducot forced through clenched teeth. "But don't worry, I'll just stay with this unwieldy, writhing, barely controllable ball of fragmented reality and fractured magic!"

"Is Risen at risk?"

"No. Shouldn't be. I don't know!" Ducot's exasperation was cut short by a series of deafening *booms* that rattled the foundation of the city. Eira's attention was instantly drawn in the direction of the sound, but she couldn't see past the living wall of shadow.

"She's here," Ducot whispered, voicing what they were simultaneously thinking. They both knew the sounds of those cannons in their bones.

"I'm going to get him." Eira clasped Ducot's shoulder.

He knew what she was asking. "I have this."

"I have faith in you." Eira chased after Taavin.

He continued to display impressive finesse as he traced luminescent glyphs into the air, carving a path forward. Eira worked to move in harmony with him, as much as she could. But, for the most part, they fought on their own, battling side by side.

"There!" Taavin pointed and Eira's focus followed his finger.

Slowly bumbling down the main road of Risen was a massive cannon. It was pulled by several horses and was followed by two metal carriages. Pillars packed tightly around it, guarding the weapon and ammunition…and the man who rode between the two.

Even from her vantage, Eira could make out Ulvarth perfectly from among them. He was atop a massive white steed, silver plate glinting in the daylight. The sun's rays seemed to bounce and swirl around it, giving him a protective, golden haze. A white cape with the symbol of the Pillars emblazoned in gold draped over the horse's haunches. He exuded calm confidence, as if he truly was ordained by the goddess herself.

A cannon shot whizzed toward them from one of the ships in the wharf and Ulvarth did nothing more than hold up his hand. The glow extended farther from him, enveloping the column. The shot exploded against the barrier and scattered harmlessly. The magic wavered, but held fast as Ulvarth drew it around himself again.

Eira's hand balled into a fist that was instantly coated in ice. It quivered. The whole world fell away into obscurity. There was nothing but him…and her. No fighting in the bay. No smoke and explosions in the city.

Stillness overtook her. All that filled Eira's ears were her ragged breaths and the thundering beat of her heart. It was time to end this.

But time had not stood still. The column was slowing to a stop. Pillars were bustling about Ulvarth, attending to the cannon.

Reality snapped back, and with it her full attention. She drew her eyes down the wide street and sloping hill, toward the open water—in the direction the Pillars' cannon was pointed. It was a clear shot to the full naval battle in the bay and wharf.

"They're trying to funnel them," Eira realized. The stolen ships from Meru's armada were pressing in on the Solaris and Qwint vessels. The only one free of it was the *Stormfrost*. But Adela had her hands full enough.

Taavin's attention swept over the city. He made a choked strangling noise and attempted to lunge to action. Eira caught his wrist but didn't explain. Her focus was on the river that split Risen.

Come to me, she instructed the water. And it did. A veil of water taller than the highest building drew up from the river. It loomed over Risen, casting a tall shadow that gave pause to the Pillars' efforts. With a curl of her fingers, she drew back her hand. *Come hither.* The towering wall of water roared forward, crashing against buildings, ripping through Risen.

"Eira!" Her name was a mix of shock and horror from Taavin.

But she didn't relent. The massive tidal wave crashed over the Pillars and their weapons, sweeping the frontlines and scattering the men. Bodies rolled and currents churned with wriggles of her fingers as she held them under. Yet, against her magic as well,

Ulvarth's barrier held fast. The water parted around him and his section of the column as though it were a boulder in a river.

"There were people in those buildings!" Taavin shouted.

"I tried to keep the water from inside of them," she snapped back, her focus wavering and the water falling limp. Eira glared up at Taavin. The frustrations she'd been harboring for weeks now burst loose. "We're not going to defeat an enemy who thrives on cruelty and inhumanity by *playing nicely*. I am going to try to avoid anyone else being lost in the fray but, damn it, it's going to take a monster to defeat him and I will be that monster."

Taavin held her stare, looking almost like he was going to object or reprimand her again. But he didn't. Instead, he turned back to the Pillars, working to recover as the water sloughed down drains and troughs on either side of the road like rainwater.

The moment she released him, Taavin was off like an arrow from a bowstring. Eira was close behind, drawing water up the hillside. It formed a smooth plane of ice underneath her feet that she slid down. Taavin summoned spears from sunlight, outlines glowing like threads of molten gold, breathtaking amid the death and destruction.

Eira sped past him, smoothing the ice, keeping it under the soles of her boots. At the bottom of the hill, her slope curved up and Eira ramped off, launching herself over the initial barricade of Pillars.

It was then that Ulvarth's attention slowly turned. Their eyes met as she landed. His barrier didn't extend outward to block her. Perhaps because he saw her too late. Probably because he wanted her there.

Once more, the world narrowed onto them alone. A tiny smile cracked the corners of his lips.

"Finally," he whispered for them both.

· CHAPTER ·

FORTY-ONE

S HE CRASHED INTO him, time speeding up once more. A spear of ice was in her hand that sheered against his armor. Magic sputtered and crumbled into a thousand glistening shards that skittered across the cobblestones.

Eira rolled, using the momentum to get herself away. Ulvarth was much slower in all his heavy plate—armor that was absolutely covered in Allun's runes. They crackled as if alive, connecting with arcing, protective magic. That was what was making the golden haze and she'd bet that, much like a trigger ring for a flashfire, the runes on his gauntlets were what gave him control of it.

"You didn't think it'd be that easy, did you?" Ulvarth reached for the saddle now beside him. The horse was of miraculous stock, still standing and calm among the chaos. Strapped across the saddle was a flashfire, runes emblazoned upon it.

"I certainly hoped not." Eira stood and placed her feet down heavily. Water cleared the ground around them, pushing out and rising up as ice—forming an arena before any of his men could rush in. "You and me, Ulvarth. No others, no tricks."

"I don't need a trick to defeat a pathetic child that has only been kept alive out of my own amusement." He made a show of loading the flashfire. Eira watched with keen interest, eyes flicking from the movements of his hands to his face as she began to slowly approach. She didn't want to seem too nonchalant. Otherwise, he might suspect something was amiss.

A whisper of familiar magic had the hairs on the back of her neck rising. Soaking the city hadn't just been for show, or defensive purposes. She now had a clear picture of every building as it dripped in the late morning sun. She could feel the people moving within and around them. Familiar magic scuttled up her spine on the edge of her awareness.

Not yet…

"But I will give you a chance to barter for your life," Ulvarth continued, none the wiser.

"You're so much more generous than me…" Eira unsheathed the dagger, holding it between them as she continued to circle, drawing closer and closer. "The best I could offer you would be a quick death. But even then…I'm not that charitable." The words grew cold.

He chuckled and lifted the flashfire, pointing its open end at her. "Return my magic to me, *now*, and I'll let you leave Meru so long as you swear to never return."

"Bartering with a heretic." Eira *tsked*. "What would your followers think?"

"They think nothing but what I tell them."

It wasn't succinct enough. She needed something more. *A little more goading…*

"You still don't have your power?"

"I have power enough."

"Your magic?" Eira paused, easing her stance. Surely she was close enough now.

"You know I do not." His voice shifted into a growl. "I wouldn't entertain you otherwise."

"What happened to being the Champion of Yargen?" Eira prodded. "Surely her handpicked Champion couldn't be undone by a mere heretic from Solaris?"

"You try my patience." Ulvarth lifted the flashfire once more. It quivered with his rage. "Restore my magic, now, or die."

He was always so confident…to a fault.

"Then admit it," Eira said calmly, but pointed the dagger in his face. "Admit that you have lost your magic because you are *not* the Champion of Yargen. That you have been lying to them all. Admit it to me now and I will restore your magic."

The ice around them was so thick that it muffled all other sounds. Her magic flowed through the air on unseen currents, strengthening it all. The pale blue walls cracked as they arched over Eira and Ulvarth—keeping this space for them, and them alone. At least…that was what she hoped he thought.

Ulvarth chuckled. "Such pathetically simple demands. Fine, I admit it—I am no more the Champion of Yargen than any other man." He stepped forward. Their weapons could nearly touch. "But you know what? It doesn't matter. Because I put on the cape, and I say the words, and all of a sudden I am touched by the divine. I am holy because *I* have ordained myself to be so. Men and women are ready to throw their lives away at my whim. With this power, I can bring down everyone who once tried to slay me."

Eira continued to glower up at him. Waiting. Silent. Sure enough, her patience paid off. Leave the silence standing for long enough and a man will hastily try to fill the space.

"So, you see, I don't *need* my magic. They've already given me enough strength to do everything I've ever dreamed of." Ulvarth took a slight step forward. The two weapons met, metal clanking softly on metal. Eira shifted her grip so her dagger wouldn't be in contact with the runes on his flashfire. The last thing she wanted was to tangle the magic she was weaving. "And that's why you'll give it back to me. Because all you want is to sail away and be someone. You don't care about me, or Meru, you care about yourself. So, give me back my magic, and we both get what we want."

The man was so arrogant. He really believed that he was a powerful enough force to command people to throw away their lives—to conquer an entire kingdom without magic. In a way… he was right. He'd always managed to command that loyalty in his twisted, enigmatic way for the most wayward of souls.

The world seemed to hold its breath as they continued to stare each other down. The battle raged on outside. But in the icy half globe she'd made for them…everything was still.

Yet, a current of air tingled her fingers, lacing between them. Barely more than a whisper. Hardly perceptible to even her. But Eira would know it from anywhere. It was a signal from Cullen. That tickle of magic she'd sensed earlier had been the pistol. Yonlin and Cullen were in position. For now, she could only hope Olivin was with them. But she wasn't going to let worry distract her.

Eira slowly, very, *very* slowly, eased away from Ulvarth. She was keenly aware of the flashfire that could take off her entire face. But Ulvarth still had the possibility of getting something he wanted from her…and that prevented him from firing.

Eyes locked on him, she slowly returned the dagger to her thigh. With a sigh, her magic began to relax. The currents shifted, but instead of pushing out from her, they spun inward. Eira began to withdraw her power.

"You're right," she said. "I don't care about Meru." Eira shrugged.

"Good to see you being honest with yourself at last." The words were more of a sneer.

"I know," Eira agreed easily. "It took long enough." The cracks in the ice around them grew deeper as it continued to thin. "But you're wrong about me not caring about you."

"Oh?" His eyes narrowed. Ulvarth was skeptical in an instant. She'd have to move quickly; the tide was shifting, and if she didn't move with it then she'd lose control of the situation. "And why would a girl from Solaris care about me?" The way he said it, he already knew the answer.

"Because as long as you're alive, I'll never be able to move on." She smiled in the face of his confusion and growing anger. The world was slowly beginning to return to them as the ice thinned. Shadows could be seen moving outside. But she didn't see any indication of her friends…all she could do was trust in the sign and her haphazard plan. "As long as you draw breath, I will know that the man who killed my brother walks free. I will be chained to my need for vengeance against the man who dared to lay his hands on me. Who hunted my friends—whose actions led to their death."

"Fine." The word was cruel and bitter. "If death is what you court then I will gladly give it to you."

Ulvarth tightened the muscles in his arm. The flashfire straightened. At the same time, Eira snapped her magic. The frozen walls around them shattered. It wasn't enough to fully distract Ulvarth…but it was enough to make him flinch.

A second was all it took.

Eira stepped back, farther away from him. As much as she wanted to scan the amassed people for her friends, she didn't. Eira didn't even know if they were winning or not. She kept her eyes only on Ulvarth. On the magic gathering around the gauntlet holding the flashfire.

"Die, heathen," Ulvarth snarled. As his thumb went to move, it caught on ice that held it in place. He bared his teeth at her, ready to levy verbal rage. But he didn't have a chance.

The echo of a shot rang out over Risen, louder than the bells from the Archives.

THE SHOT WAS blindingly bright, and the subsequent explosion threw Eira back with the rest of the Pillars and those who were battling against them. Ice clattered across the cobblestones. Eira twisted, her toes curled, muscles in her legs tensing as she got them under her. She blinked away the blue haze left behind from the shot, looking to where Ulvarth once stood.

The man had been thrown to the side, landing atop some poor, unsuspecting Pillars. They were bloody and crushed beneath him from the force of his heavy plate. The same plate that was now shattered and scattered across the ground.

It had worked.

Allun's magic had been strong enough to counter itself. A shot from the pistol was enough to shatter the armor. Not enough to kill the man, it'd seem—which made the armor even more impressive. A shame that it had to be destroyed.

Eira pushed herself up, ignoring the aches in her arms and legs. The day, and then some, was starting to hit her. But she'd turn herself into a frozen marionette and let the ice move her before she allowed him to get the best of her. A quick scan of the buildings to her left resulted in her being unable to locate Yonlin's vantage. But that was the least of her concerns. It was time to end it.

Just when she was about to take advantage of Ulvarth's prone state, a whisper from behind had her pivoting. A Pillar—Lightspinner—was there, the words for slumber half-formed. In a blink she had a dagger in the side of his face, sticking out the other side. She'd been going for his throat, but another Pillar had pummeled into her, sending her off-balance. If not for the thick ice around her boots, she would've lost her footing.

They descended on her like sharks on chum.

Magic crackled through the air. Blow after blow was dodged. Eira summoned walls of ice and left daggers and swords through appendages rather than taking the time to withdraw them—it was faster to summon another instead.

But there were so many. More than she remembered. Where was Taavin? The army? Her fellow pirates?

The sun was blotted out by smoke and frosty haze. The world was awash in gray. Somehow, her ragged breaths were louder than the clanking armor of the Swords of Light and swishing fabric. Hot blood splattered against her, contrasting with the cold numbness of the magic within her.

There was movement from Ulvarth, behind her now. She tried to twist and turn, to get to him, but only managed to capture glimpses of the Pillars assisting him. They frantically tried to strap his armor back together. To usher him away.

"Ulvarth!" Eira screamed. "Coward!" She placed her hand on the sheathed dagger, ready to draw it from her thigh. But would her desperate plan work? "Face me!" Eira shoved another icy blade into a different gut. She fought to get to Ulvarth. To carve her way through the writhing mass of bodies that had coagulated into a single monstrosity that was trying to hold her back and push her down. To strike and strike *and strike* her until she lay broken.

She would not break.

She would be the rock the waves broke around. She would be the current that would rip them out to sea and pull them under. She was Adela's heir—her legacy. And legacies were immortal.

Ice shot out from her with a scream that pierced the heavens. Eira froze the men and women around her in their places. She pushed past the frozen statues, only to be struck by a glyph that knocked her over.

They were on her before she could get up. Hands and feet. Blades.

She would submit. Or give in. Or give up.

Sweat and blood rolling off her cheeks, she fought to gain purchase. One knee bent, enough to push off with. Twisting and using momentum to bring someone else down and spring away. A blade plunged through her shoulder, ripping out flesh and another scream.

Eira grabbed the weapon jutting from her front. Ice shot through the blade, freezing the man behind her. Killing him. Gritting her teeth, she pushed the blade through.

Fire blazed overhead. It was fueled by currents of wind to the point that the flames were more white and blue than gold and red. Like tornadoes made of flames, the cloud descended onto Pillars.

She inhaled sharply. For a second, in the blaze, she could've sworn she saw the outline of a familiar woman. It was as if Noelle rose once more, blazing ever brighter, even when all seemed lost.

Eira righted herself and turned to the source.

There, down the slope of the main street, was the Solaris army. At their lead were Aldrik, Vi, Vhalla, and Cullen. The latter two were lending their wind to the former. Relief hit her like exhaustion, and Eira sagged. A smile curled her lips and her eyes met Cullen's.

They shared a breath. A moment of gratitude…and of understanding. She looked over her shoulder and then back to him. He gave a solemn nod.

I have to go, she said without words.

I know, he replied.

She could hear him in every beat of her heart. Feel his presence like the wind tangling in her hair—blazing and frozen. Eira gave him one more beat of her heart. One more second when she wasn't sure if she was saying *Thank you* or *I love you* or *Goodbye*.

The corner of his mouth quirked up. Somehow, she read even that: *I know; it's all right*. A chuckle escaped her. Brief. Little more than a sigh.

Then, she turned.

Fire and Lightspinning glyphs exploded around her. The Pillars who tried to move for her tore at their throats, faces turning purple as Cullen stole their air. Eira finally broke free of the writhing mass of death and escaped through the narrow alleyways of Risen.

She followed a trail of blood that went toward the river. It was roughly the direction Ulvarth had limped off in. But, more than that, she couldn't imagine where else a coward like him would go. He wouldn't return to the Archives—not with them compromised. There was nowhere else in Risen that would be safe. He could be planning on running down the river, perhaps all the way to Ofok, where he could regroup with help from Carsovia.

Unfortunate for him that his best chance gave her an advantage. He was running right to the arena that would be of Eira's choosing—somewhere with ample water. He'd know it, too, which meant he'd have to be fast about it.

Breaking free of endless buildings framing her sides, Eira burst into the afternoon sunlight. The sounds of the combat behind her were little more than a whisper now. Her pace slowed, an overwhelming sense of nostalgia hitting her.

With a turn of her head, she was faced with the building that had first housed the champions upon their arrival in Meru, while Risen was still in lockdown. It was strange to see the building still standing. Part of her had expected it to be destroyed alongside everything else that had once been a part of the tournament. But…this was different.

She shifted her weight and her attention. The line of blood droplets she'd been following continued off to the left. It wrapped around a building and out of sight, no doubt continuing to the water and a boat that Eira was certain would be there.

But something…*something* kept her from following it. Her focus returned to that stately manor house. The place where she'd first met the Court of Shadows. Where she'd found the dagger.

Yewin.

Eira hadn't thought of the woman in ages. She'd first met her as Mistress Harrot, the kindly, if a little bit strange, matron of the manor they were staying in. But then Eira had learned of Yewin's past. Her association with Ulvarth and that she had been Ferro's birth mother. The woman was loyal to a fault.

Eira started for the manor house.

If she was wrong…Ulvarth would get away. If he had fled on a waiting vessel, he could be anywhere along the river. He'd know she could use her magic to catch up, so he'd no doubt stop off at any point. Switch boats before she could see. Any number of possibilities.

Yet, none of them compelled her to follow that blood trail. It felt too…easy. Too predictable. And, more than anything, it wasn't flashy enough. Ulvarth was a showman. He loved a narrative, and what was a more poetic ending then their final showdown being in the place where his challenge had been laid months ago?

The door was ajar, like an invitation.

Eira let herself inside.

An invisible battalion of memories assaulted her. The manor was exactly as she remembered. Smudges clung to the banister from where everyone dragged their hands over as they went downstairs for meals. The still air was filled with the smells of the elfin's incense and oils, mingling with the perfumes of the Twilight Kingdom. Even a chest had been left behind in the entry. Forgotten in the haste of leaving for the Champion's Village.

Time had stopped here. If she closed her eyes, she could force herself back into those hours whittled away strolling the gardens and pacing the halls. Jumping at shadows, literal and metaphorical.

She still remembered every creak of the stairs. Every step she could confidently place her weight on, and which ones would groan if she put her foot in the center rather than one of the struts. The door to what had once been the Solaris quarters was open.

Had they closed it when they'd left? She couldn't remember.

She halted, straining her ears and her magic, listening across the echoes that lingered in the house. There were voices on voices… but none were Ulvarth. Not from these walls, at least.

Bracing herself and drawing her magic, Eira rounded the doorframe.

He stood at the far back of the room, arms folded behind his back. Armor was still strapped in pieces to his body. Eira didn't know if it was fully useless, broken as it was, or not. But, at the least, there were obvious faults for her to strike first.

Ulvarth turned slowly. His features were barely visible against the light streaming around him. Yet, she could feel the moment their eyes locked. Just as she had earlier.

"I've begun to think that you're right." The words startled her. Eira flinched, drawing an ice dagger into her palm, stance sinking. "You and I are bound by Yargen's red lines of fate."

"Then I will be glad of my destiny to kill you."

"No, Eira…you will be but another to fall. I will see they paint you as a coward when your body is never found. Meru will never know the truth. All they will have are my stories, and they will curse your name for centuries to come as the woman who tried to kill the Champion and failed." His words were little more than glancing blows, falling harmlessly around her feet. Eira kept her focus. He was stalling…but for what? Reinforcements, likely. She needed to strike. "Everyone you once held dear will—"

The second he began speaking again, Eira lunged toward him. At the same time, movement registered in the corner of her left eye.

Pivoting, she threw herself off-balance, avoiding the strike from the new assailant. A needle-point dagger whizzed by her shoulder—the strike having been intended for the middle of her back. There was a living shadow behind her. Plumes of smoke radiated off its shoulders as though it were a nightmarish figment of a shift user's creation.

No…not a living shadow.

Eira's eyes widened. *Harrot—Yewin.* The woman was covered

head to toe in soot from the hearth. She'd coated herself in it to blend in with the darkened stones. Small wonder Eira had missed her on entry.

Her boot scraped across the floor as Eira recovered her balance from the dodge. Shifting her grip on her dagger, Eira reached for Yewin's throat with her other hand. The wiry woman was easy to subdue. Eira positioned herself behind Yewin, her dagger point pressing into the woman's throat.

"Clever, I grant you," she snarled. "But did you honestly think that would be enough to kill me?"

Ulvarth's smile was a wicked crescent, gleaming brighter than his eyes. "Yes."

Eira tightened her hold on the woman. "Take off your armor, now. Or she dies."

"You're bleeding." Ulvarth still hadn't moved. His eyes were focused on Eira's arm. Just below her shoulder was a small cut.

She didn't care if she was or wasn't. Eira didn't ease her grip. "A mere drop of the blood spilled this day is nothing compared to what's about to happen to you. Your armor. *Now*."

His attention shifted from her cut to the woman Eira still held captive. "Well done, my love."

"All it takes is a drop." The words were an intentional mockery of Eira's phrasing. Rasped, as they were through Eira's grip.

"Fine. Then you both die." Eira shifted her stance and readied her ice dagger for a strike.

It clattered to the floor.

The left side of her body was suddenly ablaze. Invisible flames ran across her skin. They engulfed her throat. Choking her.

Her magic raged against it. The initial instinct was to cool the phantom heat to the point of numbness. But Eira tried to resist it, instead channeling her focus to try and stop the blood flow to the area. It was worthless.

Poison.

"Bastard." The word was as clumsy as her fall. Seizures wracked her and she unwillingly writhed on the floor.

Yewin loomed over her, once more a shadow in Eira's softening gaze. "I gave you a choice. I *begged* you not to. But you killed him, you butchered him for them all to see."

"He was…a monster," Eira forced through her tightening jaw. Her whole body felt like it was on a loom, stretching and tightening with every turn of the wheel. "Like mother…like father…like son." She didn't regret killing Ferro for a second and never would.

Ulvarth strolled over as she spoke. His hand rested lightly on Yewin's arm. The woman leaned to him, like a flower yearning for the sun.

"Let us end this, so we can return to building our glorious kingdom."

· CHAPTER ·

FORTY-THREE

EIRA FOUGHT TO push away from the ground. The invisible hands that set her ablaze continued to hold her. Ulvarth loomed over her as he leaned forward. His hand closed around the dagger on Eira's thigh, drawing it.

"I imagined killing you with this," he whispered.

"*That* will be your demise," Eira forced herself to say.

"Such bold words for a woman about to meet her maker." Ulvarth smirked. "Tell Yargen that her Champion will continue fighting for her glory."

He moved the blade toward her throat. The movement was slow and purposeful. Like one would approach carving a steak. It whispered, *I'm going to enjoy this*, without him having to say so much as a word.

Not like this. The words almost escaped. But she denied him the satisfaction of her desperation. She'd die on her feet, fighting. Not on her knees like an animal brought to slaughter.

Focus! The command was in Adela's voice. *Focus!* Once more, this time her own.

Ice coated her throat right before the blade could meet it. Ulvarth's brow knitted. Eira smirked up at him. Confusion turned to fury.

With a grunt of rage, he grabbed for the needle-dagger Yewin had been holding and stabbed it through Eira's left hand—nailing her to the floor. She let out a yelp, mostly from shock. Then from the pain of fresh waves of agony.

"I was going to grant you the honor of a soldier's death. But die like the cur you are." Ulvarth stood.

Glaring up at him, Eira ripped out the dagger. Ice coated the floor and walls. The room became a frozen coffin.

But it wasn't her magic.

"I was always told that you had a propensity for touching things that weren't yours." A voice as cold as winter slithered across the frost-covered room. "Seems some men never learn."

Adela.

Eira fell heavily when trying to turn. The poison was making her head spin. But it wasn't a hallucination. The Pirate Queen was there in all her snow-covered glory. She'd left the *Stormfrost* amid the battle and stepped foot on Meru…all to save her.

"I hadn't planned on being the one to kill you." Adela's eyes flicked to Eira and then back to Ulvarth. Cold swept up Eira's left arm. "But it seems you've left me with little choice."

Eira capitalized on the distraction. Dagger still in hand, she stabbed Ulvarth through the soft, worn leather of his boot—right by his ankle—plunging the weapon to the hilt. Yewin let out a bloodcurdling scream.

"My love!"

"I'm fine. There is nothing on it now. Focus!" Ulvarth barely had time to finish before Adela tapped her cane into the floor and a spear of ice jutted out from one wall. It crashed against his breastplate, shattering.

"*Oh-ho.*" The noise was part amused and part intrigued.

Yewin launched back, flinging Lightspinning in Adela's direction.

As the fight broke out around her, Eira was practically forgotten. One hand useless. A side of her body completely numb yet also in agonizing pain. She couldn't make it off the floor.

So she stopped trying.

As her breaths became labored, Eira rested her good hand on the ice. Her body was breaking, but her magic was still there—still strong. Closing her eyes, she extended her awareness through the magic coating the room. Just like every time she'd taken control of the *Stormfrost*, she could feel each footstep. The flows of the magic crashing against each other.

Adela… Her nails dug into the ice as Eira fought for a hold on Adela's channel. The *boom* of a flashfire was deafening in a small space. The magical surge was almost enough to break Eira's focus. But it didn't.

The Pirate Queen's magic deepened as Eira gave her increased access to her channel. The battle shifted. Keeping Adela's flow of magic as open as possible, Eira aided in other ways.

Spears of ice jutted from the walls and floors. She pursued Ulvarth with the jabs and stabs of a thousand formless soldiers. Warriors that were nothing more than ice and her will.

The tides of battle turned. Yewin fell and did not rise, blood pouring from a hollow in her chest. Ulvarth didn't so much as flinch. So much for mourning the mother of his only child.

Eira continued to stab, targeting what she had mentally recorded as each of the weak spots in his plate. Adela's assault was equally relentless. Together they found their mark at the same time.

Every bit of fleshy resistance was keenly felt as the spear she'd made jut from the wall plunged through his shoulder at an angle that could tear through his arms and reach his heart. Adela's cane skewered him through the gut. If he made a word, it was barely more than a whisper.

But what was said was lost to Eira. She was so far from her body that it was impossible to make out any sounds. Except…

Warmth returned to the back of her head. Through thin slits, a ghostly, ghastly visage came into view. A smile barely cracked Eira's lips. A similar expression folded the familiar lines on Adela's cheeks. Eira hoped she lived long enough that the mighty, horrible, and wonderful deeds of her life were written across her face like a map.

"Well done, girl."

"Everyone else?" Eira asked as she pulled herself into a seated position, with Adela's help. Shivers still wracked her body. Her left side was completely numb.

"They're fine."

"You?" Her usually white and gray ensemble was covered in blood.

"Theirs." Adela nodded toward Yewin and Ulvarth. Then her attention turned to Eira's thigh. Specifically, the empty scabbard.

Eira looked to where Ulvarth had dropped the dagger. "I got it. I think."

Adela retrieved it for her. "Then what are you waiting for? An invitation?"

Her knuckles were white around the hilt. "I…I'm not sure it'll work."

Adela clicked her tongue against her teeth. "I took you for more. Oh well then. It was a lovely experiment, Eira. Enjoy your mediocre life."

"You're such a demanding mentor." Eira didn't bother turning to look at her.

"You're such an aspiring pupil. Now, enough of this stalling. Do it, or not. I am done with this land."

It felt like the final test. The last opportunity for Eira to prove herself to Adela. It was also the only thing holding her back. With this, it'd be over. As finished as Ulvarth's cooling corpse.

Eira clutched the dagger and held it before her, bringing the pommel to the center of her chest—pressing into the rune. Ice encased her once more. Everything she'd learned. The mastery of her powers. The work she'd done to deepen her connection to her magic. It all came down to this.

She braced herself, and exhaled winter.

· CHAPTER ·

FORTY-FOUR

A FROZEN WIND SWEPT over Risen. It darted through narrow alleyways, tucked away into squares and broad plazas, giving the architecture frosted kisses from head to toe. Windows and doorways donned an intricate latticework of ice, the frosted patterns as unique as the city's residents themselves. Puddles that had collected in the drains and on the streets surrendered to frost, turning into glassy mirrors that reflected the vacant sky.

The frost ensnared the citizenry in Eira's icy grasp. It laced their hair with shimmering diamonds and collected on their eyelashes like an early winter's bluster. It invited itself into homes, sneaking under doorjambs and down chimneys to sink into bones old and young as an unshakable shiver.

Men and women stilled, turning their gaze to a bright blue late-afternoon sky from where snow inexplicably fell. The blood of the fallen in battle turned to little more than crimson mirrors, embedded into the grooves of the cobblestones where they lay. Risen was draped under a white veil of unexpected winter, of silence and stillness that placed it into the palm of her hand.

Hokoh had only been practice.

The cold brought with it an eerie and profound silence—the stillness of a deep winter's freeze. All of Risen was gripped within her spell, swept away by the tide of Eira's magic that had washed over it. Not one corner was immune from her spectral touch.

Her senses felt heightened to a nearly divine extent. She could feel all of them. The rhythmic thrums of their heartbeats, the sharp gasps of surprise, the wheezing exhales of the dying as they relaxed into the numbness her cloak of cold had brought with it. She stood beside all of them. Knew them as well as she knew herself.

Simultaneously, her own body was fading from her consciousness. Ice coated her feet, starting as frost on her toes and climbing up her boots to form a creeping shell that slowly embraced her body. It spread across her like creeping ivy, enveloping her in a crystalline cocoon. But, this time, she wasn't losing control of herself. Her powers weren't getting the better of her.

For the first time, Eira had thrown herself into her font of power and traversed it with the skill of a ship cutting effortlessly through the tides. She stood as the beating heart of the city. Her body was a monument to the power that flowed through her. She was both the vessel and the conduit.

It was time.

The ice creeping across her finally reached the dagger. It enveloped the blade and sank into the steel, drawing out the words she'd managed to lock within it. Every magic she'd ever learned and studied was brought forth—the echoes, vessels, manipulating a sorcerer's channels, a deft control over her magic, coating things in ice to extend her power and awareness, projecting echoes…all of it and more.

But never on this scale.

Ulvarth's words filled her mind as she drew out the echo she'd created.

Fine, I admit it—I am no more the Champion of Yargen than any other man.

Every sheet of ice cracked in time with the words. It was a symphony across the city. A whisper heard by every person connected to her.

But you know what? It doesn't matter. Because I put on the cape, and…

His earlier tirade continued. Every sinister intonation. The incriminating ruthlessness.

In the end, Ulvarth's arrogance was his ultimate undoing.

... So, you see, I don't need my magic. They've already given me enough strength to do everything I've ever dreamed of.

That was enough. It had to be. Her magic was beginning to waver.

Eira relaxed her hold and allowed her powers to dissipate on a much warmer breeze that broke through her chill. The frost retreated. Snow evaporated in the sun in a blink, not even leaving behind ghostly traces of moisture. Ice slowly faded from her body with a frosty gasp.

The whole thing, beginning to end, was over in minutes. But it'd felt like a lifetime. Like she had spent years in her frozen chrysalis and was just now reemerging into the world for the first time.

Eira blinked at the sunlight that still streamed through the windows in the back of the room. Somehow, everything felt completely normal…and yet like it all had changed.

Her gaze drifted back to Adela. The Pirate Queen was as unreadable as always. A stoic statue of gray and crimson.

"Did I do it?" Eira whispered.

"You did."

Two words and her strength gave out. Eira fell back, hit the floor, and succumbed to an exhausted, deep, and dreamless sleep.

FORTY-FIVE

S HE WOKE TO a steady and familiar rocking. A chorus of creaks and the faint whine of ropes straining filled her ears, followed by the scratch of a pen. Cracking open her eyes, she saw a familiar room surrounded her. An expansive bed, bookshelves dominating the opposite wall, a table that was used more often as a desk…and two wingback chairs positioned in front of the windows that overlooked the back of the *Stormfrost*. One of which was occupied.

Adela sat in the chair, somewhat angled toward the bed. She had her ankle propped on her frosty knee, a book perched on her lap. The pen Eira'd been listening to glided over the pages, the pirate queen's attention fully enraptured by whatever notes she was jotting down.

Or at least Eira thought her focus was wholly consumed.

"Took you long enough," Adela murmured without so much as glancing her way.

"Sorry," Eira mumbled. She went to sit and instantly found herself off-keel. Eira repeated the process to no more success. One of her arms wasn't working…

"Don't rush it." Adela was at her side.

Eira hadn't heard or seen her move. Her focus was entirely on her side. Eira reached out her right hand. Fingers trembling, they hovered where her left arm should be. Once was.

Her ears rang. She blinked several times, as if she could wake herself up from what was certainly a strange dream. The sleeve of her sleeping gown hung limply over a stump at her shoulder.

Bandages covered her skin, dulling the sensation of the fabric gliding over top.

Yet…somehow she felt it. More than the stump, phantom tingles and pains ran up from the hand Ulvarth had stabbed through with the dagger. She could still grip the fingers of the severed hand. Feel the muscles in her arm tense. As if it were still there. Except, it *wasn't*.

"The pain will go away, eventually." Adela's words were even and calm. But there was a touch of gentle understanding under her perpetual matter-of-fact demeanor.

"Why?" The word felt distant, like it came from someone else's lips.

"The poison." Adela sank to the edge of the bed, staring out the windows. Eira only saw through her periphery. Her focus was solely on the spot where her arm should be. "It's necrotic. It immediately starts rotting the flesh by the wound, but it spreads in the blood and will build up elsewhere, if you let it. With two points of injury, one as severe as it was, the only way we could stop it from completely claiming you was by removing the arm."

The pirate queen shifted. Eira didn't realize what she was doing until Adela's hip was exposed. She'd pulled her heavy coat to the side and adjusted her trousers just enough to expose her side above the leg that was missing. The leg she'd sought revenge for by sending Eira to the mines on Carsovia.

Adela's pale flesh was riddled with dark veins, gray, stony skin suspended between them. It was worse lower on the hip. Eira suspected that underneath her trousers, right by where the pirate queen's own leg had been amputated, was likely all black.

Eira lifted her eyes to meet Adela's. Shifting once more, Adela pulled back the collar of her shirt, exposing a portion of her upper chest. More of the dark veins were there. Less severe. But as prominent as they were undeniable.

"You…"

"That poison is as wicked as everything else that comes off Carsovia. I was too slow in cutting off the damn thing to stop its spread." Adela motioned to her leg made of ice. "I've been battling with it ever since." She turned to face Eira. "That's how I knew, with you, what had to be done. Stop it before it could go too far. Though, I admit, I wish I could've at least told you before it happened."

Eira's attention shifted back to her missing arm. She imagined herself moving it, as if studying a hand that was no longer there. Jolts of pain fired through her shoulder at the effort. Now, she wondered if the chill she'd felt on her left side had been the poison at all, but rather Adela beginning the amputation back in the fight with Ulvarth—trying to slow the poison.

"What now?" Eira whispered. She hadn't intended to vocalize the question.

Since she had, Adela answered, "Now you'll learn how to use a limb of ice."

Her Uncle Grahm had done as much. Adela had two limbs of ice. Eira had even managed with one, more or less, in Carsovia when she'd used ice to hold together her leg. It wasn't the end; logically she knew that. Emotionally…she was still caught on the spot where her arm should be.

Cool fingertips rested lightly on her cheek, guiding Eira's face back to Adela's. The pirate queen leveled her gaze. Eira swallowed thickly.

"This will not shake you."

Eira managed a nod. Adela was right; she'd been through so much…too much to have this be what stopped her in her tracks. The initial waves of shock and grief were already passing.

"Good." Adela's hand fell from her face and she stood. "Because the fates have shown their cards and I am more committed than ever."

"Where are we?" Eira tried to put her thoughts elsewhere.

"Not far from the Isle of Frost."

Eira blinked. *That far?* She knew she'd promised Adela that once she'd extracted her revenge against Ulvarth, she'd be her heir and sail across the lands. That she'd never look back.

But part of her had been expecting to be able to say goodbye. Were her friends even here?

Eira worked to hide her turmoil and disappointment. "Risen?"

"Fine, as ever. You didn't implement any lasting damage."

"Good." At the mention of "lasting damage," Eira took stock of the rest of her body. It didn't seem like there were too many other wounds. "So, Isle of Frost to restock, and then off to pirate some unsuspecting shores?"

"You know the general idea." Adela nodded. "Not much longer now." She retrieved a waterskin from the table by the chairs. She returned and uncorked the top. "You'll catch on to this quickly. And, while I'll admit there's nothing like your own flesh and bone, I daresay a part of you might enjoy having an arm that is part water, part ice, part weapon, and all magic."

Eira gave a slight nod. As Adela had said, the fates had shown their cards and this was what she was destined for.

"Summon the water," Adela instructed.

Eira did so, guiding it from the waterskin to the stump attached to her shoulder.

"First make it look like an arm."

Eira focused intently on the water. It was easy enough to forge into the shape. Both natural and unnatural. Natural in that it *felt* like an extension of her. The power was familiar and as second nature to control as her right arm was. But unnatural in sight. It was wrong to see that watery, nebulous arm taking shape where her body should be.

No, not wrong, different, she reminded herself firmly. Wishing for what had been would pass quickly, Eira vowed. This was a change. Albeit an unexpected one. But not one that would alter her course. She still had the power to forge her own path.

Mother above, she'd be all the more fearsome for it.

"Good." Adela's praise was genuine. "Next we will harden it to ice, and then work on its movements…"

Eira wiggled the fingers on her icy hand. It was still an odd phenomenon.

She'd been working on it with Adela for the better part of the day, but eventually the pirate queen had wandered off, declaring she had "better things to do" and that Eira would "simply have to figure the rest out on her own." With that, Eira had been left to dress herself as the setting sun streamed through the back windows.

The clothes were ones she'd never worn before. A pair of light gray, woolen trousers and a crisp white shirt with ruffles on the sleeves. Adela had set out two pairs of leather gloves—one black, one white. Eira selected the white ones.

At first, her frozen hand was too large and she nearly gave in to frustration with her struggles. Then she remembered that she could adjust the shape of the ice to fill it perfectly.

It was more natural with the sleeve and the glove. Staring at her arm now, she could almost tell herself that she hadn't lost the arm at all. Eira balled her hands into fists, and then rolled up her sleeves so the slightest bit of ice was showing.

She had nothing to hide from the world…or from herself. This was who she was now. Eira turned her gaze to the mirror, sweeping hair from her eyes.

The streak of white that had been left behind from her initial experimentation from the rune and echoes had migrated across all her hair, as if the color had been bleached from it. Her eyes were a pale blue, the color fainter than ever before. Yet, somehow, her gaze was sharper for it. Scars lined her cheeks.

She no longer recognized herself. Yet…had never felt more like the woman she was meant to be.

Eira started for the door, taking a breath before making her return to the world. Crow wasn't outside. Though it didn't take long for Eira to spot a friendly face.

"Ducot!" Eira sprinted up to the quarterdeck. He barely had time to react before she crashed into him. "You made it!"

"No thanks to you." Even as he huffed and muttered, his arms wrapped around her waist, returning the squeeze. "So dramatic, sleeping for days, losing an arm…"

"I know, I'm the worst." Eira released him with a slight smile. "You managed the shift rift all right?"

"Risen's still standing, as am I, so we'll call it good enough." His grin suggested there was lasting damage.

She almost hesitated before asking the next question but she had to know. "Everyone else?" Adela had told her nothing. Though, their focus had been elsewhere.

"Yonlin and Olivin are back in Risen."

"And Olivin?" Her heart skipped a beat.

Ducot nodded. "He was in rough shape. Would've offered to bring him aboard, but given his wounds and the chaos, it was better for him to stay and get patched up."

He's alive. The knowledge was bittersweet. Eira's attention drifted in the direction of Meru—opposite of where they were going. He was so very far from her now. But…even if Olivin hadn't been so wounded, he would've stayed behind. He'd said as much to her; he needed to ensure his brother was safe in the aftermath. There would be know way he could know peace if he wasn't sure of Yonlin's wellbeing. And Yonlin wasn't going anywhere without Alyss…

"Alyss is with them," Ducot said, almost in tandem with her thoughts.

A dull ache throbbed against her ribs. *Her friend, her* best *friend…* The goodbye she might never have a chance to say was ashen on her tongue. Eira continued to stare at the line of frosted sea that churned behind the *Stormfrost,* arcing in the direction of Meru. No land was in sight.

The pain was more muted than she'd otherwise expect because she wasn't surprised. Alyss had made it clear that this life wasn't for her. And then there was whatever was blooming between her and Yonlin… Not to mention, there hardly were printing presses at sea suitable to bind and distribute a book.

"Adela didn't give anyone much time." Ducot rested a hand on her shoulder, as if he could sense her turmoil. "Our pirate queen returned with you, wounded herself, and told us it was time to go. She didn't want to delay and be wrapped up in the aftermath."

"Yes. That's not her concern," Eira agreed. She could imagine it perfectly. Adela had no business to be on Meru and wouldn't want to outstay her welcome, lest hostilities turn toward her.

"We can go back," he encouraged. "Get another small vessel from the Isle of Frost, something that will be much less suspicious. Though, you're as recognizable as she is now."

"Luckily I'm good at illusions." Eira wasn't going to get her hopes up for returning to Meru. She was at Adela's whims now. Taking a small boat for a personal trip likely wouldn't be in the cards. "And Cullen?"

"Ask him yourself what possessed him to return to the jaws of the beast that is the *Stormfrost*. The man *ran* to the docks to make sure we didn't leave without him."

"What?" Eira whispered.

"He's down below now, I think. Took the night shift so he might be—"

Eira was gone before Ducot had a chance to finish.

Heart thundering louder than her feet down the stairs and into the first level of the vessel, Eira threw herself into the twilight of belowdecks. Her eyes were drawn immediately to the hammocks they'd last occupied. But they were empty. *Ducot wouldn't play such a cruel game…*

"Over there," Crow mumbled as she passed, eyes still red with sleep.

Eira followed the woman's finger, too speechless to even give her thanks. Sure enough, there Cullen was. Laid out and deep asleep.

The distance between them closed in a breath. Her arms were

around him. The hammock spun and they toppled to the floor, him flailing and shouting, her bursting with laughter.

He stilled as her laughter slowed. Cullen sat and she did the same. They simply stared at each other. Matching, bittersweet smiles.

"I thought you would've gone back to Solaris," Eira admitted.

"I told you that wasn't what I wanted." He reached out and cupped her cheek, his thumb grazing against her skin and sending shivers down her spine.

"I saw you with the Imperial family, it looked so right."

"Anywhere that isn't next to you couldn't be right for me." His other hand framed the opposite side of her face. His thumbs caressed over her eyebrows. He drank her in with his eyes and Eira eagerly awaited his verdict. "Your hair…"

"You like it?" Not that she would change it now if he didn't.

"There is nothing you could do that would make you less stunning in my eyes." He drew her forward. His lips met hers.

She still didn't know if she would want to kiss him for forever. If this was meant to be always. She couldn't promise him she'd never want to explore another lover on the side, perhaps even with him. But the uncharted territories of their future were as thrilling as the corners of the map yet unexplored.

It didn't have to be forever.

Right now, he made the day brighter, and the pain a little more numb. He made the nights less lonely and the hours pass a little faster.

So Eira leaned into the kiss. She grabbed him by the collar to half crawl into his lap. Damn whoever might see. Let them. She was Adela's heir, the frozen tyrant. She was free of the madman who'd hunted her and she'd never be made to feel guilt for anything ever again.

If she wanted, she would take. If she needed, she would have. And, for now, he was everything she needed and then some.

· CHAPTER ·

FORTY-SIX

THE ISLE OF FROST was lit up brighter than the Yule night celebrations hosted in the Solaris capital. Bonfires dotted the slopes of the hills and mountains that curved protectively around the far side of the island. There was dancing on the docks and gaming in the streets.

This pirate's paradise had truly come to life in a short time. Ships dotted the sheltered bay, all flying a top flag of black. But their smaller flags were a variety of different symbols that Eira had begun to learn. The White Kraken Crew was particularly warm to Adela. Gray Sharks were slightly less so, but if Crow was to be believed, they were aligned with anything that let them get their swords bloody and coffers full.

"And the Red Sparrow flags?" Cullen asked her. They sat on the edge of the festivities, perched on someone's cargo, offloaded as tithing to Adela or temporary holdover.

"They're friendly enough. Upstarts, so far as I'm able to tell by what Ducot has said. But eager to please, so they're worth keeping around."

He hummed in thought. "I know you were quite skeptical of how my upbringing would keep me from joining this world but, so far as I can tell, my knowledge is likely to be essential."

"And why is that?"

"Because in less than an hour I've captured the lay of the land of pirate politics."

"It's not *politics*." She scoffed. He only looked more smug.

"Isn't it though?"

Eira rolled her eyes and took a sip from her heavy flagon.

Nothing happened in moderation on the Isle of Frost, especially not the debauchery. The tankard was nearly as big as her head.

"How is it?" Cullen asked.

"Warm and mediocre at best."

"Firstly, I wasn't asking about the ale. But, secondly, couldn't you just make it cooler if you wanted?"

She laughed lightly and did just that, taking another sip before saying, "I knew what you were asking."

Cullen waited patiently as she set down her drink, curling and uncurling her frozen fingers. Some days, she wore gloves and long sleeves. On other days, like today, it was a sleeveless tunic, the mark of her survival and her power on display like a badge of honor.

"It's easier some days than others." Eira shrugged. "The magic is fine, that's no problem. Sometimes I find, though, that I like it there, and other times I find that I want to be me, as I am now. Without the magic."

He nodded. He'd seen as much in the nights and mornings they'd spent together. Sometimes she had the arm of ice, and sometimes she didn't. But he'd never questioned why or suggested one or the other. There was a lot Cullen had allowed her space for when it came to sharing…or not.

He'd not flinched at the sight of the scars that were the only remnants of where her arm once was. He'd kissed her all the same. Touched her with even more zeal than he'd ever had before.

The only challenging part was navigating touching him, seeing that he didn't have the same natural resistance to cold as she did. But there were times where a little bit of a chill touch wasn't bad. It could be fun, even. And for all the other times, there were thick gloves.

Before he could say anything else, Crow approached.

"Her Frostiness desires a word." Crow glanced between them, eyes settling on Eira. "Alone."

Eira squeezed Cullen's hand. "I'll be back in a few."

He nodded, unbothered. "Take your time."

Crow took his words to heart, setting a leisurely pace through the Isle of Frost. Adela's pirate stronghold was a stunning place—an island wrapped by a crescent of mountains on its outer edge, guarding the town in its valley and the bay the ships docked in. A river ran through the center of town, bridges of wood and stone crisscrossing it.

Adela's personal manor was up toward the very back edge of town, away from the bay, nestled in the shade of the tallest ridge. But that wasn't where Crow guided them. Instead, they turned right, into a section of town that Eira knew only in passing. While she couldn't be sure where they were going, she was sure that asking would get her nowhere. So Eira settled for admiring the icicles that clung to the eaves, the frost that gathered at the corners of doorsteps, and soon the unblemished snow that covered the path into the mountains where she and Crow trekked.

"Can you do something about that?" Crow gestured to their footsteps in the snow.

Eira didn't so much as move a finger. With a thought, the snow rose up to fill in where their boots had compressed it. But this did offer her the perfect opportunity to ask, "Where are we headed with such secrecy?"

"You'll see." Crow's tone was stiff, even for the usually closed-off woman.

"Is all well?"

Crow glanced over her shoulder, hesitating only for a second. She looked much like her namesake in the moonlight, striking a dark outline against the vivid snow. Her eyes flashed like a warning. Eira lowered her chin in acknowledgement.

They continued on silently.

Through a cave and out to the back side of the ridge, a narrow walkway was carved into the steep cliffs that switched back to a pebbled beach at the water's edge. There on the shore was a small skiff, tied up. A larger vessel—though nothing in comparison to the *Stormfrost*—was anchored just offshore.

Adela stood by the skiff, adjusting a few parcels inside. It struck Eira that the pirate queen was alone. The entire time Eira had known her, Adela had been surrounded by her crew. Right now she seemed…small. Adela had always been a legend, larger than life, surrounded by the mighty *Stormfrost* and a crew ready to kill and die for her. Now, she looked like a woman, as regular and as mortal as any other. Even her clothes were simpler: gone were her mighty coats with oversized cuffs and collars. In their place was a fitted pair of trousers and a sleeveless vest, not unlike what Eira wore.

"If you wanted to ship me off, you could've just asked," Eira said dryly as her boots met the smooth rock of the beach where Adela was making her preparations.

Adela snorted softly. "Girl, you have been a thorn stuck to my side since the first moment I heard of you. If I told you to go, I doubt you'd leave much farther than the quarterdeck of whatever vessel I'm on."

Eira chuckled softly. Crow held back as Eira continued crossing to Adela.

"Therefore, I'm the one who must leave." Adela finished securing one of the parcels to the skiff and straightened, meeting Eira's eyes. Eira came to an immediate halt.

For a breath, there was nothing but the brisk wind and waves. The sea foam churning around their boots. Surprise wasn't the first emotion that bubbled up within Eira. Rather…disappointment. She'd known what Adela had been planning for longer than the walk Crow had taken her on. If Eira were honest with herself, she'd known for months in the same way she knew a storm was in the distance.

But there was one question she didn't know…

"When will you be back?"

"Never, I suspect."

Every muscle in Eira's body tensed, making it hard to breathe for a moment. Making it hard to swallow down the brief wash of panic and grief that surrounded her.

"This poison that has wrought its decay throughout my body can no longer be ignored."

"We can find a cure."

"I fully intend to." Adela nodded. "But I will not wither away before their eyes as I make that attempt. And, should it come to pass, I will not die for them to see."

The notion of Adela dying was as foreign as a language Eira had never heard before. It glided right over her mind, not sticking. Not comprehensible.

"You can't die." The words slipped out. They twisted in her gut like a venomous snake. *She'd just found something like a family, a home…*

"I know." Adela wore a knowing smile. As if she could stare straight through Eira to all of those worries and fears that she kept concealed. The pain she barely knew. "That is why I must leave. And why you must carry on my legacy."

"But I—"

Adela's hand landed on her shoulder, as heavy as the weight of the responsibility she was bestowing. "Fate has brought you to me. Molded you for me—for yourself, for your own destiny. The time for doubt is well past. It no longer suits you."

Eira finally managed a breath. The tension left her, as if by Adela's command. She nodded.

"Don't weep for me, girl. I'm not dead yet, and there's much more out there for this old pirate." Adela smirked, looking as invincible as every myth that had ever been spoken about her. "And your legend is only just beginning."

"I won't let you down," Eira vowed with all she was. With all she would become.

"You'd better not. You've yet to disappoint me, so I'll let you live a few more days. But the moment I hear otherwise…"

Eira laughed softly and shook her head. Even though she knew Adela wasn't one for sentimentality, she couldn't stop herself. Her words were a whisper on the wind. "Thank you. For everything."

"You've only yourself to thank, and only yourself to let down." A pause. "Are you ready?"

Eira only suspected what Adela was truly asking. But even being unsure, she nodded. Whatever it was, she'd be ready.

Magic surged around the pirate queen. It swelled, overwhelming. Eira was drowning in the power such that she was left struggling to remember to breathe.

Adela's eyes shone with intensity and Eira maintained her focus. Endless currents were propelled out from the pirate queen. They swirled around the Isle of Frost, cradled the *Stormfrost*, and stretched farther and farther into lands unknown. Places Eira could now sense, but had no cognition of what they looked like or what the power was doing in these distant places.

From one hand to the next—one essence to the next—it was transferred. One by one, Adela relaxed her control with a sigh. Eira was right there to push her power through the currents and channels, strengthening the voids left behind. There was nary a drop of the permafrost thawing around them. Not a whisper of warmer winds blustering over the Isle of Frost.

Adela released her and stepped back. She exhaled softly and rolled her shoulders back, as if feeling relief for the first time in years. The drain on Eira's power was instant and immense. But she found it surprisingly manageable. Easier by the minute. Second nature, even.

The wind picked up, pushing the waves and sea foam between them.

"Good luck, Pirate Queen," Adela said.

"Good luck, no one," Eira replied.

A wicked smile, unbridled, crossed Adela's lips. As if the idea of being "no one" was both a liberation and a challenge. As much of an invitation into the vast unknown as what Adela had given her.

She stepped into the skiff and the water swelled, carrying it out to sea. Eira remained still. Watching as the mightiest woman she'd ever known went alone to a vessel that would otherwise require a crew of ten to twenty, at least, to man. But Adela would do it on her own.

Eira watched as the skiff rose to the side of the vessel. As the currents carried it farther out to sea. As the first pirate queen disappeared over the horizon.

There was an immediate vacancy left in the wake of that ship. One Eira knew she had to fill. For the crew that now counted on her, for the legacy of a woman who had put tremendous faith in her, and for herself.

Pebbles crunched under her boots as she ascended the beach back to where Crow remained perched at the foot of the path that led back up the cliffs.

"I'm surprised you didn't go with her," Eira said after a long stretch of silence.

Crow met her eyes and held them. "My place is with the *Stormfrost*, and the Pirate Queen Adela."

A smirk curled the corners of Eira's lips. The twinges of sorrow were giving way to excitement. To all the potential that now lay before her.

"Good. We have work to do."

"Cast off!"
"Dog hatches!"
"Sails, now!"

The crew was a chorus, preparing the *Stormfrost* for departure from the Isle of Frost. She'd stayed long enough to ensure the other pirate leaders had properly kissed her frosty knuckles. To ensure they knew of the new missives from their pirate queen.

A few had to die, unfortunately. But wasn't that always the way when it came to transitions of power? All things considered, she was pleased with the relative lack of bloodshed.

Behind her, Crow was perched. Eira stood at the bow, magic

swelling with the tide to help glide the *Stormfrost* away from its mooring in the bay of the Isle of Frost and out to sea. Despite the shouts of the crew, the creaking of ropes, and the snap of the sails as the wind filled them, Eira could hear the familiar footsteps approaching on the deck and knew who was approaching without needing to turn around.

"Where are we off to, Captain?" Ducot came to a stop at her left-hand side.

"I think that Solaris has been quiet for far too long."

"Are you sure it is wise to return there?" Crow chimed in, taking a small step forward. Her tone was informative rather than questioning. "There was a sort of fragile peace that was being honored."

"There *was*." She placed emphasis on the past tense. "But every peace eventually runs its course. And I think Solaris has felt a little too comfortable uttering the name Adela Lagmir of late."

"The Senate will have something to say about this." Cullen took his perch at her right hand, looking rather amused. The sun and sea loved him. They tousled his hair and tugged at the loose ties of his sleeveless shirt. He'd hammered muscles into his body that she'd never seen before from laboring on the deck. A physique she appreciated more by the day.

"Oh, I certainly hope so." She flashed him a wild smile. "I recently learned of a passage through the mountains of Solarin— one that goes straight into the castle proper. We'll give them something to talk about."

Perhaps Cullen would find his father again along the way. Perhaps he wouldn't bother. She'd give him the opportunity, and what he did with it would ultimately be up to him.

"Your heading, Captain?" Crow dutifully asked.

"Norin first. We've matters to attend to there." She glanced in Ducot's direction; in his hand was a worn pouch. Pirates weren't often known for returning jewels. But there was a debt to the dead to be paid before anything else. "Then, to Oparium." The closest port to the capital of Solaris, where her parents lived.

"And after that?" Cullen murmured. But what she heard was, *What awaits us when every matter is settled in the life we once knew?*

"After that…everything." She turned, walking to the back railing that overlooked the main deck. The Pirate Queen known as Adela Lagmir addressed her crew. "*Stormfrost*!" All eyes turned to her. "Let us catch the wind and the currents. Let us chase gold and glory. The world is ours for the taking!"

EPILOGUE

THE TUNNELS AND passageways underneath the city of Risen were mostly abandoned these days. There were a few cutpurses who had begun operating out of them. A few with murderous glints in their eyes who had taken to the safety of the grime and shadows.

But even Risen's most wanted skirted away like rats from a flame as Eira's boots echoed through the halls. They all knew better than to even so much as glance in her direction. That doing so would be akin to death…or worse.

Keeping up Adela's reputation was second-nature to her. In Oparium they continued to whisper in terror of the pirate queen, Adela's mere name spoken like a curse. Unknowing that the very same pirate came ashore, once, to visit with a man and woman in the home she'd once grown up in. Still a tenuous relationship, but as peaceful as a pirate could manage.

Solaris was going through its own rebuilding, much like Meru. The Emperor and Empress offered steady hands, as they always had to their Empire. A consistent enough leadership that Eira thought it wise for a good while to avoid the shores of Solaris. There were other shores of chaos that she could capitalize on.

Eira had sent Ducot ahead a few days ago to ensure the passages she now walked were still connected to where she intended to go. One slight diversion, but for the most part the integrity remained. It was all going smoothly. She should've encountered no one.

Yet, somehow, she wasn't surprised when a figure leaned against the wall by a staircase back to the surface. Not the staircase Eira had been intending. But one she'd been forced to pass.

A pair of dark eyes met hers. A tiny mote of flame illuminated the side of Vi Solaris's face. The two stared off. For the first time, Eira felt that, should it come to it, she could hold her own against the princess with mysterious and somewhat legendary powers.

"Vi Solaris." Eira slowed to a stop.

"Eira Landan. Or should I say Lagmir?" Vi continued to lean nonchalantly. Magic remained calm. So Eira didn't summon any of her own. "It's been some time."

"A few months," Eira agreed.

"Nearly a year."

"That much time already?" Eira said, even though she was well aware of how long it had been. Still, she hadn't dared come closer, sooner, to Meru. This was already risk enough, as evidenced by the woman before her and the uneasy haze of magic that hung in the air. "Why are you still hanging around these decrepit passageways? Don't you have a wedding to plan?"

It had been all the gossip across Solaris the one time Eira had visited. The crown princess, abdicating her throne to her younger brother so that she could remain on Meru with her beloved Taavin. A man who was now both Voice, and king. The Faithful of Yargen merged with the crown to form a new theocracy.

"I'll always make time for you." Somehow Vi made it sound like a promise and a threat.

"You flatter me."

"Indeed." Vi pushed away from the wall. "There was a deal that the *Stormfrost* would stay away from the seas around Meru and Solaris."

"I'm afraid I don't remember making any such deal." Eira shrugged.

Vi huffed softly, as if in disbelief. "So this is her play… Tell me, where has the real Adela run off to?"

Eira made it a point to hold the princess's gaze for an extended stretch of time before saying, "Real Adela? I'm not sure what you mean. I am the 'real' Adela."

In truth, Eira hadn't heard word or whisper about the woman

whose name and title she'd inherited. Wherever Adela had gone off to was far beyond the maps. Or, she had completely reinvented her identity. Either was possible. Adela was a woman who wouldn't ever be found, if she didn't want to be.

"Then you should know, as the real Adela, I cannot abide piracy on my shores."

"You're welcome to try to stop me." Eira gestured with her open palms in a sort of *go ahead* motion.

Vi let out an incredulous laugh and shook her head. "So you wish for war between us?"

"Pirates and princesses aren't often friends." Yet, neither of them moved to attack. Which said a lot more than their tense discourse.

"Perhaps not. But you did save the life of my beloved, Meru's king." Vi turned for the stairs. "And you have the favor of one of his councilors."

Eira's heart skipped a beat. She'd heard rumor Olivin had ended up as part of the king's council. As Olivin had expected, and feared, the deaths of most Meru's nobility had created a great deal of uncertainty. They sought for ways to benefit from consistency of leadership, much like Solaris had, and that meant leaning on familiar faces that were left.

And Olivin was a hero.

Eira had scoured for any word of him. Everything between them still felt unfinished. Even though the way he had kissed her felt like a goodbye, given all that had transpired, it now felt like a beginning. It all hinged on one thing—something none of the rumors could tell her and that all of her notions and fantasies relied on: Where his feelings toward her now stood.

"You're not stopping me? Putting me in irons? Dragging me through the streets to make an example of the great pirate queen?" Eira put a hand on her hip, shifting her weight and raising an eyebrow.

"Not tonight." Vi cast one more glance over her shoulder. "Something tells me that, tonight, you're not here for piracy. So consider it a kindness and a debt repaid. As long as you come to Meru for personal reasons, the crown might look the other way."

With that, the Princess Solaris, and future Queen of Meru, ascended. Eira continued on her way. She still wore an amused smile as she emerged out of a door and into an alleyway near a bustling market by the docks of the river that ran through Meru.

Cullen was waiting, leaning against the wall inconspicuously. "You're late."

"I had something hold me up." She adjusted her hood and he glanced her way. Eira shook her head. "Nothing important."

Cullen didn't ask further. Instead, he turned toward the shop he'd been sent to watch for the majority of the night. "Nothing to report. They're wrapping up. One couple left."

"Good." She caught his hand, fingers lacing for only a moment. Eira tugged him in for a quick but firm kiss, one he eagerly returned. "I'll only need a minute."

"I'll make sure the law doesn't get any ideas."

She hummed. "If you wanted to come with me, I think it'd be fine."

"But—"

"Something tells me the city guard isn't going to be stopping us tonight."

He didn't question her instinct. Instead, he squeezed her hand and said, "Then, together."

The bell on the shop door jingled as the last couple stepped out, and they slipped in.

"We're just about to close," the shopkeeper said with a note of warning.

"Ah, yes, we'll just be a minute…" Cullen said for both of them, starting for the counter.

But Eira didn't move.

Through the bookshelves she saw an achingly familiar profile. Her eyes prickled. Alyss wore her hair loose in corkscrew curls that ended now at her shoulders. She sat next to Yonlin. Leaning against a bookshelf at his brother's side was the same king's councilor that Vi had mentioned.

Olivin. Her throat went dry

"Here." Cullen was back at her side, handing Eira a linen-bound book. He wore a knowing smile.

Eira took it in both hands and started for the back of the store, Cullen hung back. Olivin saw her first and pushed off the bookshelf. Surprise and relief warred for his eyes, both lost to sheer adoration. She couldn't stop beaming, a thousand questions burning behind her war, expression.

How are you? How is the rebuilding going? Do you have the home you wanted, or do you still yearn for the seas? Did you miss me? Will you come with me now? Or, will you keep the pirate queen waiting, still?

He returned the expression, and she already couldn't wait until they had the time to recount every change and choice over the past few months.

Yonlin was on his feet next. But Eira nearly stopped in her tracks as Alyss turned her way. Time itself held its breath as Eira closed the distance, hands trembling.

She'd fought madmen. She'd ruled pirates. She'd become the bane of the seas.

But this had her shaking.

This had her ready to weep with something that was part relief, part joy, and part mourning for a life that had never been meant to be. A life she wouldn't have fit into. But a life that would've been closer to this woman. Her friend. Her family.

"Will you sign this for me?" Eira handed the book to its author.

Alyss's fingers closed around the opposite side, lips parting as she laid eyes on Eira. But no words immediately came. For a second, they held on to the book together as if they were holding on to each other.

"I will, but not this one." Alyss put the book aside and reached into her bag, pulling out an identical copy. "I'll sign this one, for you." Her eyes shone. "It was the first off the presses." *I knew you'd come, and I waited.*

"Th-Thank you." Eira managed to say through the lump in her throat. "I've heard the story is magnificent."

"I did a lot of research for it." A tiny smile quirked Alyss's lips even though her eyes were shining with unshed tears.

Taking a pen, Alyss dragged it across the page underneath the title, *Betrothed to the Winged Prince.* She closed the book and handed it to Eira, but her fingers didn't immediately unravel. Neither of them wanted to let go of the book—of this moment.

"I'm actually about to finish up… I don't usually ask this of random strangers, but something tells me you might be a woman who appreciates a sticky bun. It's on me, if you give this author a few good stories."

"Gladly." One word that was more of a sigh of relief. A reunion long past due.

For years, it remained a mystery why the *Stormfrost* would, on occasion, be seen in the great bay of Meru. Even more of a mystery when no towns were ever pillaged. No cities sacked.

The royal navy was never sent to investigate the purpose of the pirate queen's presence.

For years, on occasion, a bakery was paid to stay open late and keep their sticky buns fresh. The owner of the shop never knew where the money came from. But he would swear that, at his tables, late at night, on rare occasion was the oddest group of individuals that he'd ever seen:

The greatest author of a generation and her husband could be seen swapping stories over sticky buns with ever the odd mix of characters: a morphi man rumored to be a spy, a disgraced Senator's son from Solaris, two ministers from Qwint who happened to be in town on official business, a lord from King Taavin's inner circle, sometimes even the king and queen themselves…and none other than the dreaded Pirate Queen Adela.

But no one ever believed the baker, of course. Because who

would ever think such a thing would ever come to pass outside of one of Alyss Ivree's storybooks?

From the bottom of my heart...
Thank you for reading Eira's story! I hope you enjoyed it. If you are able, please take a moment to review on the retailer of your choice - reviews help authors and readers.

Turn the page to learn more about what to read next...

The World of Air Awakens

Now that Eira's epic tale has ended, read more from the world of Air Awakens!

Learn how Vhalla rose from commoner to Empress. Read her story in AIR AWAKENS. A library apprentice discovers she has a rare elemental magic and falls in love with a sorcerer prince.

Learn more:

https://elisekova.com/air-awakens-book-one/

How did the crown Princess Vi Solaris discover Meru, Lightspinning, and the elfin? Read her story of action, adventure, and love deeper than time itself in VORTEX VISIONS.

Learn more:

https://elisekova.com/vortex-visions-air-awakens-vortex-chronicles-1/

The Golden Guard is the most elite fighting force in all of Solaris. Learn about how they were formed in a series of three stand alone stories of action and deep friendship.

Learn more:

https://elisekova.com/the-crowns-dog-golden-guard-1/

MORE BOOKS BY ELISE...

DRAGON CURSED

"Pulse-pounding romance, vivid world-building, and badass dragon hunters make for a bloodthirsty and brutally fun read. The stakes couldn't be higher—I devoured every page. This is the YA fantasy I've been waiting for!"

~ Brigid Kemmerer, New York Times bestselling author of *Forging Silver Into Stars*

Learn More:
https://www.elisekova.com/dragon-cursed

ARCANA ACADEMY

A woman who has devoted herself to learning forbidden tarot magic to thwart the crown. A prince who claims her as his bride to use her skills to seize a legendary power. Enter the mysterious halls of ARCANA ACADEMY, where strength is survival and your future is your tuition.

An adult, epic fantasy by bestselling author Elise Kova. Ideal for readers looking for dark academia, intricate magics, slow burn romance, enemies to lovers, found family, and twists you never saw coming.

Learn More:
https://www.elisekova.com/arcana-academy-1/

Stand Alone. Fantasy Romance.

Perfect for fans of A Court of Thorns and Roses and Uprooted, this stand-alone, fantasy romance about a human girl and her marriage to the Elf King is impossible to put down!

Three-thousand years ago, humans were hunted by powerful races with wild magic until the treaty was formed. Now, for centuries, the elves have taken a young woman from Luella's village to be their Human Queen.

To be chosen is seen as a mark of death by the townsfolk. A mark nineteen-year-old Luella is grateful to have escaped as a girl. Instead, she's dedicated her life to studying herbology and becoming the town's only healer.

That is, until the Elf King unexpectedly arrives... for her.

Everything Luella had thought she'd known about her life, and herself, was a lie. Taken to a land filled with wild magic, Luella is forced to be the new queen to a cold yet blisteringly handsome Elf King. Once there, she learns about a dying world that only she can save.

The magical land of Midscape pulls on one corner of her heart, her home and people tug on another... but what will truly break her is a passion she never wanted.

https://elisekova.com/a-deal-with-the-elf-king/

Stand Alone. Fantasy Romance.

For readers who love romantasy novels with second-chance/long-lost love, life-changing female friendships, deep lore, forbidden romance, slow-burn, and a happily ever after.

To enter the woods as a human means death… But I am no mere human. They call me, "witch."

As one of the last surviving witches, Faelyn's sole duty is to keep the protective barriers on the forests where the lykin roam—creatures who can shed flesh for fur—sparing nearby humans from their violent, beastly natures. When she has an unlikely encounter with the rare, primordial spirit of the moon, Faelyn finds herself not only the object of the Wolf King's desire, but essential to his ability to keep his crown.

Taken to the magical land of Midscape, the Wolf King claims her as his bride to control the moon spirit's magic that now resides within Faelyn. But Faelyn refuses to resign herself and the spirit Aurora to a life of servitude underneath the king's cruel rule. Faelyn hatches a dangerous plan for them both to escape and help comes from an unlikely ally.

Evander is the king's blisteringly handsome, loyal knight, right hand, and Faelyn's sworn protector…on the outside. But appearances are not what they seem. He plots against the king's brutality at every turn and helping Faelyn escape will serve these ends. But altruism for Faelyn and the trapped moon spirit isn't his only motivation…

Evander is hiding secrets, and they might change Faelyn's life forever.

https://elisekova.com/a-duel-with-the-vampire-lord/

Stand Alone. Fantasy Romance.

For readers looking for a fantasy romance with deep lore, second-chance love, sacrifice, forbidden and slow-burn romance that sizzles on the page, and a happily ever after where love triumphs over all.

She sold her soul to a siren and now he's come to collect.

Victoria risks everything to leave a dangerous marriage and gain a second chance at life. But when her escape goes awry, she finds herself caught in the strong embrace of a mysterious siren, forced to choose: temporary salvation or immediate death.

And so, a cursed deal is struck.

Five years later, Victoria is alive—and the world's finest ship captain. But her debt to the siren looms while her conniving ex has demanded a king's ransom as the final price of her freedom. Victoria refuses to cause her family to suffer any more on her behalf, and is determined to make things right before her time is up. But that time is cut short.

The siren comes for her. Six months early.

Taken to the magical and deadly Eversea, home of the sirens, Victoria discovers she's the sacrifice upon which all sirens pin their hopes. If they want to appease an angry god and save a world on the brink of destruction, then they need her. Which gives her the perfect leverage...

https://elisekova.com/a-duel-with-the-vampire-lord/

About the Author

ELISE KOVA is a USA Today bestselling author. She enjoys telling stories of fantasy worlds filled with magic and deep emotions. She lives in Florida and, when not writing, can be found playing video games, drawing, chatting with readers on social media, or daydreaming about her next story.

She invites readers to get first looks, giveaways, and more by subscribing to her updates at:
http://elisekova.com/subscribe

Visit her on the web at:
http://elisekova.com/
https://www.tiktok.com/@elisekova
https://www.instagram.com/elise.kova/
https://www.facebook.com/AuthorEliseKova/

See all of Elise's titles on her Amazon page:
http://author.to/EliseKova

Acknowledgements

Rebecca, Melissa & Kate — This book was such a monster editorially, thank you all so much for your help in this, and every book in the series. It is truly a pleasure and an honor.

Robert — My love and appreciation for you is boundless.

Tarryn, Emi, Catarina, Angela, Dyani — I so immensely appreciated all the feedback you gave me on A Queen of Ice! It really helped me polish the manuscript into its final state.

The Tower Guard — I appreciate each and every one of you! Thank you for continuing to be a safe place in my digital world.

Emily — Without you I would be so much more scattered. Thank you for all your help!

My Global Publishing Teams — Thank you all for helping bring A Trial of Sorcerers to life in languages around the world!

My Patrons – Shaeli S., Zachary F., Michelle, Madalyn W., Francesca, Anika M., Kelci S., Jessica G., Emi C., Lauren B., Winter M., Courtney, Maryalyce B., Allie, Sharon B., Karin, Amanda H., Christine P., Ayragon, Pippa S., Tiffany H., Zoe B., Brooke R., Carolyn H., Courtney, Moa E., Aly N., Adrienne A., Kristýna, Elizabeth H., Dyani S., Pauline Stv, Chloe F., Jade, Amanda C., Imzadi, Vixie, Caitlyn P., MasterR50, Rebecca R., Steffi, Mary M., Anne, Laura R., Sarah T., Nancy S., Laura B., Mandi S., Melinda H., Taylour D., Stephanie H., Nichole M., Sarah M., Gemma, Rose G., Karolína N. B., Laura Henman, Dani W., C Sharp, M Knight, Jamie B., Jennifer G., Marissa C., Monique R., Ru-Doragon, Claribel V., Sarah L., Lisa, Sorcha A., Tea Cup, Caitlin P., Bridget W., Kristen M., Kelly M., Audrey C W., Allison S., Ashton Morgan, Mackenzie S., Kaitlin B., Amanda T., Kayleigh K., Alisha L., Esther R., Kaylie, Heather F., Andra P., Melisa K., Serenity87HUN, Chelsea S., Alli H., Catarina G., Stephanie T., Mani R., Elise G., Traci F., Samantha C., Lindsay B., Sara E., Karin B., Eri W., Ashley D., Stengelberry, Dana A., Michael P., Alexis P., Jennifer B., Kay Z., Lauren V., Sarah Ruth H., Sheryl K B., Lindsay Shurtliff, NaiculS, Justine B., Lindsay W., MotherofMagic, Charles B., Kira M., Charis, Kassie P., Angela G., Elly M., Amy B., Meagan

R., Axel R., Ambermoon86, Tarryn G., Cassidy T., Kathleen M., Alexa A., Rhianne, Cassondra A., Emmie S., Emily R., Tamashi T., Amy H., Michelle, Ashley J., Heather K., Anastasiya Z., Christina B., Amy & Trevor, Megan F., Darnell W., Michelle R., Meredith L., Javier Alejandro Matamoro L., Jenna L., Ekaterina O., Julie M., AJ T. – thank you for all your support!

To all the readers, reviewers, booktokers, bookstagrammers, book sellers, and everyone else who reads, shares, reviews, and talks about my books — I cannot do what I do without you. Everything you do makes a difference and authors like me truly wouldn't be able to survive without you. I'm sorry I don't always have the time to respond to each of you, but know that you are seen and appreciated. I cannot express the depths of my thanks enough.